LUCKY SCORE

KENNA KING

CONTENTS

The Hawkeyes Hockey Series

1. Cocky Score

2. Filthy Score

3. Brutal Score

4. Rough Score

5. Dirty Score

6. Lucky Score

7. Tough Score

8. Perfect Score

9. Wrong Score

Check out **www.kennakingbooks.com** for more books and information.

SCAN ME

CHAPTER ONE

Seven

Perched on a ladder beside my beach house in Mexico, I press a thick plywood sheet against a window with my forearm. While gripping an electric drill in my other hand to secure the sheet into place, I hear my phone ring in my front pocket.

I utter a few curse words as I pull the nail from the magnetic drill tip and place it between my teeth. I hook the electric drill into the holster of my tool belt while keeping my forearm against the plywood. This conversation better be important.

I fish out my cell phone from my cargo pants to see the name on my phone.

Reeve Aisa calling...

He's probably calling to check in. I have two more weeks left of my summer vacation before I board a plane and head back to Seattle for the start of the new Hawkeyes season.

There aren't many people I would take a call from in general, let alone while I'm suspended against a building, but my teammates and coaching staff make the shortlist.

I pull the nail from my teeth and then drop it into the pocket of my tool belt.

"Aisa," I say with my phone pressed to my ear.

"Wrenley... What's up, man? How are the fish biting today?" he asks, knowing that I spend my entire off-season at my house in Mexico.

He was already here for a week at the beginning of the summer.

My vision glides over the many windows still to be boarded up as a precaution for the offshore hurricane that's headed our way.

The weather channel predicts that the storm's trajectory will hit mostly out at sea and off the coastline, but I've lived here every summer for the last fifteen years, and I know well enough that a hurricane answers to no weatherman.

Hurricane "Josie"... or as I like to call her after my ex-fiancé, Josslin, will do whatever she damn well pleases, no matter whose family home is in her wake. Much like the woman I have re-named the incoming cyclone after.

"No bites today. I'm boarding up my windows and my neighbors this afternoon and gassing up both backup generators. We've got a storm coming in."

He's right to assume. I'd be out on my boat if there weren't a hurricane practically knocking on my front door. Even though half the time, I don't even fish.

In my case, fishing is more of an excuse to take my boat out of the marina with a cooler full of beer and no timeline to head back to shore. I mostly sit on the boat, enjoying the peace and quiet and the sun radiating against my skin.

The sun—something we don't get a lot of back in Seattle.

Being out at sea is as remote as a man can get here, which makes it my preferred activity. After all, that's why I spend my off-time at my beach house.

No one around here gives a shit about hockey, and even fewer people give a shit that I play for a professional team back in the States. Around here, I'm a nobody, which means I get left the fuck alone.

While spending my off-season in Mexico on a mostly secluded beach with Cancun over an hour away, my limited hobbies include fishing on my boat, whether the fish bite or not, whittling driftwood that washes up on shore, and reading whatever suspense thriller novel that I purchased in the airport concession shop on my flight over.

The occasional game of rummy and an authentic southern Louisiana-cooked meal at my neighbor Rita's beach house, is the only reason I bother to shave once a week.

A trip to Rita and Bart's local restaurant and bar for some fish and chips and a game of pool with my buddy Silas gives me just enough human contact to prevent me from completely transitioning into a recluse.

With Rita's husband Bart, passing away a couple of years ago, she keeps me busy with odd jobs here and there at either her house or at her restaurant, Scallywag's.

Except for the week or two a season when Reeve or Brent show up and want to do all the tourist shit that requires us to drive into town.

Windsurfing.

Scuba diving.

Deep sea fishing.

With every passing year, I feel more of a kinship with Bigfoot. That fucker got his priorities straight the first time. I commend him for his constant pursuit of dodging civilization and living in blissful solidarity.

It's a goal of mine, too. Once I retire from the NHL next year after my contract with the Hawkeyes expires, I'll consider retiring here full-time—or maybe even somewhere a little quieter.

Tourism continues to grow, and resorts are expanding further along the coastline. I still have two more seasons in Seattle to consider my options. There's no rush.

I've got one Stanley Cup win under my belt from years ago, but I'm aiming to win one more before retirement. Last year's loss in overtime was brutal. Especially with Slade getting carried off the ice and sent to the ER. Thankfully, everyone is healthy this year and ready for another shot at it.

"The storm is going to hit near you? I thought it wasn't supposed to hit the beach?" Reeve asks.

"It's supposed to miss us, but the weather is too unpredictable to assume it won't change direction before it does."

"Why not head back to Seattle early then and get out of there?"

It's a good question, and several of my neighbors who only live here part of the time, like me, have already left to head back to wherever they call home most of the year.

"I want to be here in case it does come any closer. If any damage is done, I'll have a couple of weeks to do repairs before I have to come back for practice."

I also don't like leaving Rita alone, and I couldn't convince her to head back to the States for a few days to weather the storm. She has two daughters in Louisiana and a handful of grandchildren she hasn't seen since Bart's funeral.

She spread his ashes out to sea and now refuses to leave until her ashes are spread the same way.

"Are you sure that's smart?" he asks.

"It'll be fine. Rita has a two-bedroom apartment above the bar. She's staying there until this blows over. She offered me the other room if I need it. I don't think the hurricane will be bad enough to require leaving, even if it does get closer to us."

"Rita is still running the bar?" Reeve asks of my seventy-five-year-old neighbor.

Rita and her husband Bart retired over twenty years ago and moved to Mexico after buying "Scallywag's. They had always dreamed of retiring down here, and they made it happen.

Two years ago, Bart suffered a heart attack and didn't recover. Rita wasn't ready to let go of their dream, so she's been running the bar with the small, established staff herself. I can't blame her for grieving the loss of her husband in her own way.

We all process loss and closure differently. God knows that I've been ridiculed for how I've managed my losses in life, which is why I think Rita should do whatever makes her happy.

"She's doing just fine. Let her do her thing," I tell him.

"Yeah, but she has kids and grandkids back in Louisiana. Who does she have there?"

"Me," I almost say, but then decide to keep my mouth shut.

Reeve isn't wrong for wanting to encourage her to move back home to be with her family, but it's also not his call.

"Did you really call me to chat about my bullheaded neighbor? Because if you did, I'm hanging up now. I have actual shit to do," I say, taking another step up on the ladder to give me better leverage once I hang up on my teammate and get back to work.

I still have Rita's beach house to board up next and a week's worth of backup canned goods to put away just in case things get bad.

The last thing on my to-do list today is to discuss the inner workings of my neighbor's future plans.

I still need to make sure to find the lanterns I have stored in the garage and fill both mine and Rita's backup generators with gasoline to keep our refrigerators and freezers running in case the power gets knocked out.

I have a few other neighbors that I said I would keep an eye out for their houses, but I won't be going as far as to board up their windows for them.

Depending on how bad the damage is, they'll get a call or maybe just a text. Rita, on the other hand, gets different treatment. I promised Bart that I would keep an eye out for her just like he looked out for me when I first bought this house sight unseen fifteen years ago.

The house was rougher in person than the pictures and the realtor led me to believe. It had been abandoned for some time before it went up on the market.

My beach house isn't the nicest one on the shoreline, but slowly, over the years, I've done a couple of things to spruce it up. This is mostly due to Bart griping that my house was the laughingstock of our beach community.

It's not the luxury beach house accommodations that my teammates are used to with their big bank accounts, but it suits my needs just fine.

Is it due for a fresh coat of paint?

Yeah, it's about twenty years past due and starting to flake off in some spots.

Could the windows be upgraded to windows of this century?

Sure, that would help with the draft on windy tropical days.

I upgraded the roof a few years ago to metal, which Bart hated but it's practical with the storms we get, and the kitchen appliances are all less than five years old.

Unlike mine, Rita and Bart's place is updated and in great shape. Bart took a lot of pride in ownership, and Rita has always kept the inside of the place immaculate.

"Alright, well... take care of yourself, and don't be a damn hero. The house can always be repaired. You're a little harder to replace, and we need you in one piece this season. We have a Stanley Cup to win."

"Yeah. I get it," I say.

I hear what sounds like a heavy metal door close. Reeve must have just walked into the Hawkeyes' gym. The familiar sound makes my muscles ache with the need to be pushed to their limits again.

When I'm away, the one thing I miss the most is the regular daily routine in the gym with the guys.

I run on the beach every morning while I'm here and meet Silas at a local gym twice weekly to lift weights, as long as his schedule allows. It's nothing like the strict regimen I follow during the hockey season in Seattle, but it keeps me in shape.

"Hey, Brent just showed up to lift weights. I'll let you get back to whatever apocalypse preparations you still have to do. We'll see you when you get home."

"See you in a couple of weeks," I say back.

I end the call quickly, knowing that the conversation is over. Reeve isn't one for long-out goodbyes, and neither am I. We both have things to do today.

He's a good teammate and an even better friend. I appreciate that he thought of checking in.

I start to push my phone into my pants pocket and return to work.

These windows won't board up themselves, and I still have a lot to do before nightfall when we're supposed to start getting some heavy rain.

Just as I'm about to put away my phone, I hear a text message come through.

I pull the phone up to quickly see who it is. Whoever it is, they'll get a response later when I have time, but I can at least check to make sure it isn't Rita.

Josslin

The name reads.

What the fuck does she want now?

I let out a groan at seeing her name on my phone.

I read the beginning of the text without opening the entire thing.

> Josslin: I'm worried about you and that storm.

That's all I can read for now, but I don't need to read anymore.

For the last six months, I've ignored Josslin's texts, phone calls, and emails unless they pertain to my niece Cammy.

Cammy moved to Seattle last year during her freshman year at Washington University, and we've become close as she's the only family member I tolerate. She comes to all of my home games and sits in my seats or joins the girls in the owner's box. We no longer need Josslin to play the middleman between us, and the loss of control over Cammy's relationship with me is probably killing her.

I always thought I'd be married with kids by now but at thirty-eight years old, being Cammy's uncle might be the closest I get.

Unlike Cammy's dad and my brother, who I haven't talked to in eighteen years.

But that's a memory lane I do not intend to travel down today.

I've got one pain-in-my-ass storm to deal with for now. Josslin can wait her turn.

And maybe if I keep ignoring my ex... she'll finally take the hint and go away.

One can only hope.

CHAPTER TWO

Brynn

Today is one of those golden days in Seattle. The kind that makes you forget why you have to book a tropical vacation every year in a futile attempt to regain the vitamin D you've lost from living in a city where it rains 152 days a year.

But on this last day of August... It's a rare sunny day and seventy-four degrees. I swear that when the weather is like this, there is nowhere else I'd rather live.

As an author, the weather isn't a massive determinant of where I live. I spend most of my working days inside my skyrise apartment, so the rain doesn't affect me much. And since I write primarily angsty historical romance books set in the Regency-era of England, the rain in Washington and the dreary weather help to put me in the writing mood.

On dreary days, I do most of my writing while paired with a hot Earl Grey tea London Fog, fuzzy slippers, and my desk perched in front of a large window that overlooks the city.

Now, as I transition my hand into a new sub-genre, contemporary billionaire romance, I find myself with some serious writer's block. Book one of this new six-part romance series was already supposed to be turned in a month ago to my publisher with a large advance already paid for the entire six-book installment.

"I think this trip is going to be good for you. When's the last time you even went on vacation?" Sheridan, my agent-turned-good friend, says, folding another pair of my shorts and dropping them into my suitcase as it sits atop my pale blue down comforter.

"It's been a while." I attempt to pull up a memory of the last time I was actually on vacation. "I guess the last time was about five years ago when Daniel graduated from law school. His parents paid for us to go to Hawaii as his graduation present."

After we got home, it was all hands-on deck for both of our careers.

Daniel started his internship at the law firm he still works for today, while I returned to my job as an HR representative at a large department store chain.

With Daniel's long eighty-hour work weeks, I spent a lot of time alone in our apartment. One night, I saw a social media ad for a writing competition with one of the biggest names in the romance publishing industry.

Since I spent most of our trip in Hawaii reading romance books on the beach lounge chairs, it's safe to say that I'm a bit of a bookworm. But I had never considered writing a book of my own before.

I wrote the short 10,000-word excerpt for a historical romance and entered my submission without allowing myself to think too much about it.

I practically squeezed my eyes shut when I hit send on my submission email. Then I suppressed the memory completely into the back of my skull, hoping that I wouldn't feel any sense of rejection when I inevitably wouldn't hear back from the publishing house. Or even worse—when I got the rejection letter.

To my absolute surprise, neither the ghosting from the publisher nor the rejection letter came. Instead, I received a letter stating that I had won the competition. They asked for the completed book and an outline for the entire rest of the series.

They wanted a series?

More than one book?

I hadn't even written a full first draft of the one I had sent them.

That's when I got an agent and a writing coach, all at my mother's advice.

My mother is easily my biggest fan. As an English major who teaches high school English in the town where I grew up, she instantly jumped on board when I told her about my new career change. My practical father, on the other hand, tries to be supportive, but that mostly comes out as "Well, at least Daniel is a lawyer and will be able to support you once you're married and your writing career fades out."

I'd love to remind him that I'm actually the breadwinner in my relationship, but since my father assumes my success could fizzle out at any moment, that wouldn't prove anything in his eyes.

He means well, I know deep down that he does—but he's old school, and I mean that quite literally. As a math teacher at the same high school my mother teaches at, my father believes in working a job, gaining tenure, and then working for thirty years until you can retire with a pension.

It's not that I don't understand his logic or that it's not a solid plan. It's just not the path I'm on right now.

Instead, I took my mother's advice and plunged headfirst into my agent search, which led me to Sheridan. In a matter of a year, my career went from a Human Resource desk job to a best-selling author. It's been five years since I published my first book, and now I'm ready for a genre change to mix things up. I need a new challenge in my life... something new to broaden my writing skills.

"See, you need a little sun. And maybe a little ocean breeze will drum back that creative spark that you need to start the new series. We need to get you away from this apartment. And a distraction from the constant reminder of Daniel wouldn't hurt either. You should have told him to move all his things to a storage unit while he's gone. He's not even on the lease and he left all his crap here. What happens if you come to your senses and meet someone else while he's gone?" she asks with a lifted brow.

I didn't ask Daniel to move out of the apartment when he left for Australia for eight months because he's still planning to come back. Wouldn't it have been weird to ask him to move out during our break, only for him to move back in less than a year later? Seeing his things still hanging in the walk-in closet reminds me that soon enough, this phase of our relationship will be over, and we'll be stronger for it.

"I'm not going to meet someone else—I love Daniel. I'm just keeping my head down to get this book finished. He'll be home in less than a month, and then everything is going to fit into place like it should."

"Do you really believe that?" she asks.

She's critical of Daniel, I know she is, but I have to believe that things are only going to get better for us once he gets home. After dating for eight years, the idea of starting a life with someone else is almost too difficult to imagine. Plus, starting over when I'm so close to getting the family I've always wanted, is too hard to let go of.

And how would I tell my parents?

As far as they know, Daniel and I are still elbow-deep in planning the wedding details, from the flower arrangements to the swan ice sculpture that my mother-in-law insists on paying for. If they found out that we're taking a sabbatical from our relationship, my mom would worry about my panic attacks recurring without Daniel nearby to protect me, and my father would worry about my long-term financial stability without Daniel's "secure" income to support me and our future family.

This trip couldn't have come at a worse time since we announced our engagement to our families right before he got the offer from the firm to go to Australia. It's also the longest that he and I have been apart since the day we were stuck in that dingy basement bunker of our college. The day when my entire life changed, and I became a more anxious person who has been co-dependent on Daniel for stability ever since.

It's the reason we moved to Seattle and away from those kinds of storms.

There aren't any tornados on the West Coast.

After that experience, the idea of ever coming face to face with a tornado again is more than I can take. Daniel was understanding and agreed to move to Seattle after we graduated.

He's made so many concessions for me.

Instead of taking an internship with his father's law firm in Oklahoma City, he agreed to move thousands of miles away from our home to a new state and had to settle for an internship at a large firm in the city instead of the fast track his father could have gotten him due to his father's connections.

If he had taken the job with his father's firm, he'd probably have made partner by now. Instead, he's only made it to an associate position after all these years of dedication. He's hoping that his commitment to going with the firm to Australia will get him a foot in the door for a junior partner position when he returns home.

So when he asked me for this one thing... "Use the next eight months apart as a break to discover ourselves and come back as better people for each other. Then I promise that we'll get married, and we can start having kids like you've always wanted," I felt like this was my turn to show my reciprocal devotion to our relationship.

It's not like he could turn down this opportunity to show his dedication to the firm. That would have been career suicide.

With the long distance, his eighty-hour work weeks, and the time difference between Australia and the US, I couldn't argue the points he made. The break made logical sense as long as it was temporary, a break that comes with the ability to see other people.

Our little arrangement does have me wondering what exactly I should call him now.

We're not technically engaged anymore, and since we're allowed to date other people, I wouldn't call him my boyfriend, either. Though we're still committed to a life together in the near future.

What would you call that?

A temporary uncoupling?

A relationship pause?

He is, after all, my future fiancé, or at least that's what we've agreed to.

Calling him an ex seems even less true than anything else.

"I'm not going there to forget Daniel," I remind her. "We're getting back together in a month when he gets home. And he's not the reason I'm having writer's block."

It feels like I'm always having to remind Sheridan that Daniel and I aren't permanently broken up. This is just a time of "self-reflection" and exploration before we spend the rest of our lives together.

"Are you sure about that?" she asks, folding more of the clothes I pulled from my closet to pack for my trip. "Because you've never had a problem writing a book in the timeline that we gave the publisher, and you were so excited about this series until Daniel dropped the bomb on you that he was offered a spot to go to Australia. Now you can barely even write the Table of Contents."

Ouch. Harsh, but not completely untrue.

I've written the first half of the book but now I'm stuck writing the first steamy scene between the two characters. Maybe I'm just not feeling inspired because Daniel and I aren't together right now. Not that I need Daniel to take care of my 'needs.' It's been over eight years since the last time I've had a man-made orgasm. My ability to climax is only achievable through the use of vibrating silicone toys.

I sought therapy after we miraculously all came out of that basement bunker with our lives after almost every building on campus but ours was flattened. But ever since that fateful day, nothing Daniel does gets me there. I have to use aids instead, and I know this has been really hard for him to accept. It's been a shot to his ego, understandably, and has caused issues between us that no amount of therapy seems to fix.

So now I've hit a wall and I'm struggling to get past this scene. I've been honest with my publisher about it. They've been kind enough to give me a two-week extension. At this point, it's do or die.

"Yes, I'm sure," I say, pulling a wad of underwear from my top drawer and counting out enough pairs, plus an extra for the two weeks I'll be in Mexico.

I can't help but feel that Sheridan is placing the blame on Daniel, but I'm the only person responsible for my writer's block.

She's been on this anti-Daniel kick ever since I broke down and confessed to her the new arrangement that Daniel and I agreed to before he left.

I can see from her perspective how it makes Daniel look. But she hasn't been around for the last eight years of my relationship with him. He's been my rock since my sophomore year at Oklahoma State when we first met, two months before the storm hit that changed everything. Is it really worth throwing it all away just because he asked for an eight-month sabbatical from our relationship for some self-discovery?

And it's not as if I'm denied the same liberties, though I haven't been on a single date since he left.

All I want to do is wait out the time and reunite after this break as a stronger, more confident woman who takes more chances and is open to new experiences. I want to prove to him that I'm not the same person who feels trapped in my past and unable to move forward.

I made a full list of all the things I want to work on personally during this off time. They're all jotted down on a well-organized spreadsheet on my laptop that I so creatively named the "Fix-Me List." The items are listed on a scale from easiest to overcome to most challenging.

Unfortunately, I spent most of the time focusing all my energy on eliminating my writer's block that I've ignored the spreadsheet. With only one month left, I want to get as many of these items checked off my list.

1. Go on a trip by yourself

2. Face your fear of sleeping alone through a storm

3. Try a new cuisine

4. Learn a new hobby

5. Make a new friend

6. Go on a first date again

7. Have a fling in Mexico

8. Go deep sea fishing

The list continues to grow, and item number seven was Sheridan's idea.

Her actual words were, "Find a guy to screw your brain out and make you forget all about Daniel."

I shortened it to "Have a fling..."

And even that was painful enough to write.

I know Daniel is out dating, too, but it's hard to imagine letting another man that close to me after spending most of my adult life with the same man.

I've seen the cropped photos of Daniel on social media, where he cuts out the women in the photos with him. He doesn't go as far as to photoshop out the well-manicured hand draped over his shoulder or the arm stretch around his waist.

And why should he?

He's free to date, and so am I.

But it doesn't make it hurt any less.

Once, I even spotted a photo he sent me, but he hadn't anticipated her reflection in the water fountain.

I couldn't see her face but her long blonde hair was enough to know what I was looking at.

Daniel had a type before me.

Blonde—tall—athletic... all of the things I'm not.

I'm five foot four, with brown hair to my shoulder blades and I didn't play sports in high school like Daniel did.

Sheridan continues to pack more items neatly into my large maroon-colored luggage, sitting on top of the queen-sized bed that Daniel and I have shared for nearly five years. It was one of the first big purchases we made when I got my advance from the publishing house that signed me.

The next big expense was the month's rent with the first, last, and deposit I have to pay to get into our gorgeous apartment in downtown Seattle.

Daniel loved that he was the only intern at the law firm with a skyrise apartment downtown, walking distance to his office and I was proud to be able to afford such an extravagant expenditure for our new future, especially since he moved here for me.

"You said there's a washer and dryer in the house you rented, right?" I ask.

Sheridan has been so adamant that I try booking a vacation as a writing retreat that she finally booked a beachside house for me when she got tired of waiting for me to do it myself.

Of course, she made sure the booking was non-refundable so that I couldn't back out.

"Yeah, that's what the booking said. And the picture makes the place look incredible. You're right on the beach, and it's not near any other resorts, so you won't have any distractions. This is going to be a perfect spot for writing."

The idea of going anywhere by myself is a little intimidating, but this is the exact type of thing that Daniel has been begging me for.

More spontaneity.

More adventure.

Pushing my limited boundaries.

I need to prove to him and myself that I can do this. I can stop overthinking about all the ways something could go wrong and just throw caution to the wind.

I didn't used to be this way and that's why he pushes so hard.

I used to be a more fearless individual. I never suffered from anxiety or panic attacks. I was a person who took chances and risks.

I guess seeing my life flash before my eyes gave me a new perspective on how fragile and short life can be. After we came out of that bunker, it took me weeks to venture back out of my dorm room.

Daniel was incredibly patient with me.

He understood that I needed time, so he brought me takeout every night for weeks to ensure that I was eating.

Those are the moments that Sheridan didn't see.

Those are the moments I want to give back to him and prove that I'm committed to this life. I want to show him the same patience and understanding.

Eight months is nothing in the grand scheme of a long life together anyway.

Sheridan is about fifteen years older than my twenty-seven years and has a husband, two kids, and a German shepherd named Spartacus.

Needless to say, we're both in different places in our lives and sometimes I feel a little envious of it. Mostly right now, while Daniel is a continent away from me.

She's a well-established agent with a booming business full of talented authors that she represents. She's married to her college sweetheart and lives in a gorgeous home just outside of Seattle. With her kids in high school, she's only a few years away from empty nesting and traveling the world with her husband, like they've always dreamed.

I, on the other hand, am still trying to carve out my spot in the author world while my love life is on a temporary hiatus. I have to remember that in a month's time, Daniel will be back and ready to settle down like we've planned.

Daniel proposed a few months before he received the invitation to go to Australia. His proposal wasn't conventional. He didn't get down on one knee and propose with an engagement ring. He just blurted it out one night while we were tucked up together in bed watching our favorite cooking show.

It took me by surprise.

In all honesty, I didn't think he was anywhere near proposing, even with the years of hinting I had been doing.

Then, when he came home with the news about the Australia trip, he said that this opportunity could fast-track him into being considered for a junior partner position. A few weeks later, he pitched me the idea of us taking a break over the time he would be gone and we could use the separation to work on ourselves.

"Long distance is hard enough as it is and marriage is a huge commitment. Plus, you have a huge deadline coming up with your book. You're going to be too busy to deal with my crazy schedule, and the time change will make it difficult for both of us. Besides, I've heard all the partners get a little crazy on these trips since most of the ones willing to travel to open new firms aren't in any serious relationships. There could be strip clubs and lap dances and I don't want to offend anyone by turning any of it down because I don't want to seem like I'm being unfaithful to you. I think we should take this time to put our relationship on hold and we can both date other people during this time. When I get back, I'll have proved myself to the partners, you'll have finished your first book, and we'll both be in a better place to start a life together. We can start wedding planning if you want, and we'll finally pick out that ring just like I promised. Eight months, Brynn, that's all I'm asking."

That's how he pitched it, and with how much he's backed my author dreams and moved across the country to make me feel safe, I wanted to show the same level of support for him.

I don't know much about the partners he works with, though I've met them from time to time during happy hour at the bar across the street from the law office.

The single male partners in his office do seem to act like a bunch of frat boys during office after-hours, and many of these men are on the board and have a vote on who gets promoted to junior partner.

So, I agreed to his terms.

"Thank you again for booking the beach house for me. I know this is going to be good for my writing, and hopefully, I will come back with a completed manuscript for you to read."

She drops the last folded summer dress into my luggage and then looks up at me.

"Don't forget to have a little fun too, okay? The best gift you could give me is to let loose a little and enjoy yourself. What happens in Mexico stays in Mexico. Daniel isn't the only one allowed to dip his toe into another ocean. You're free to have a fling too. And who knows, maybe you'll find a man out there to give you orgasms again," she winks.

"Sheridan, I told you... it's not his fault—it's me," I remind her.

"Are you totally sure about that? What better time to find out than right now? He's practically giving you permission to see if someone else can do it better in the bedroom. Why not give someone else a chance so that you know for sure?"

She's the only person, besides Daniel and the therapist that I had back in Oklahoma, who knows that my orgasms come by way of the energizer bunny.

Before the incident, Daniel and I had a great sex life, but we had only been together for two months before disaster hit. That's how I know that none of this is Daniel's fault. I know he feels emasculated sometimes but what can I do about it? I have no control over it.

"A fling sounds more like another distraction away from writing. I think I'm going to keep my attention on getting this book written and the manuscript to the editor," I tell her.

With my book due in two weeks, surely the book takes precedence over having a dirty one-night stand in Mexico with some random guy who's probably on vacation looking for drunk, sloppy sex that will only leave me unsatisfied anyway.

"Well, you look about packed to me? Are you sure you don't want a ride to the airport tomorrow afternoon? I'm happy to take you in," Sheridan says, surveying the three bags I have perched on my bed.

A large suitcase, a carry-on, and my laptop bag.

"Thanks, but there's no reason for you to leave your daughter's volleyball tournament just to take me to the airport. I already scheduled my rideshare to pick me up. Kate needs her mom cheering her on."

Sheridan gives a slight grimace. "Those bleachers are the worst and this is the biggest tournament of the year. Two days long and ten hours each day. The things we do for our kids."

My phone starts to ring and I grab it quickly, hoping to see Daniel's name on it since I haven't spoken to him in a week.

When I see my mom's name illuminated on my phone, I'm a little disappointed but she knows how nervous I am about this trip and she's probably calling in to check on me.

"Speaking of, it's my mom."

"You should get that. I need to get home and take a long bath in preparation for tomorrow," she says.

"I'll call you when I get to the rental house," I tell her and then swipe to answer the call, pulling my phone up to my ear.

Sheridan nods and then gives a little wave as she turns to exit my bedroom.

"Hey mom," I answer.

"Hi sweetie. How are you? Are you all packed for your trip?" she asks.

I told her about the trip that Sheridan booked for me and she thought that a little time out of Seattle might be just what I need.

"Yep, I just finished. Sheridan was here helping me pack. What are you up to?" I ask, imagining her sitting in the den back in my childhood home, curled up with a book while my father watches the news.

"Your dad and I are sitting in the den..." Just as I suspected. "And we're watching the storm on your dad's tablet. Did you know that there is a storm warning for off the coastline of where you're headed?"

The moment I hear the words "storm warning," my hands instantly clam up, and my heart begins to thump harder against my chest.

I know that this time of the year is hurricane season for that part of Mexico, but when I checked a few days ago, the storm was supposed to stay out to sea and wasn't projected to come anywhere close.

"Storm warning? I thought this one wasn't supposed to touch land," I ask, my voice just a little shakier than I want my mother to hear.

I made a promise to myself that I would use this time apart from Daniel to become a braver person. Going to Mexico by myself is one of the adventures and is listed as number one on my Excel spreadsheet.

I've been looking forward to checking this one off my first task the moment I get settled into the vacation house tomorrow evening.

"They haven't issued an official warning for the surrounding areas yet, but the storm does seem to have shifted, and now its trajectory is closer than they originally thought."

"So it might not hit land still, right? It's still out at sea?" I ask, gripping around the small silver chain necklace with a space needle pendant hanging at the end.

I bought it for myself in the Seattle airport gift shop the moment Daniel and I landed in Seattle, the day we moved here. I have rarely taken it off since then. It's like my good luck charm, but it's no longer as bright and shiny as it used to be. Its silver plating is starting to show its age from my fingers rubbing over it whenever I get nervous.

"As of now, the authorities have not issued an official warning, just an advisory," I hear my father's calming voice as if my mother has me on speaker.

"Are you sure you still want to go?" my mother asks.

No, of course I don't want to go.

But I need to go.

And my mom knows this better than anyone.

She's the one who ultimately convinced me to agree to this trip, though I didn't have much choice anyway since Sheridan booked it without telling me.

"I have to. The house is non-refundable and if I don't finish this book, I'll be in violation of my contract deadline. And anyway, I bet the storm will pass right on by," I tell her, trying to sound calm but gripping my pendant a little tighter to shield the worry in my voice.

"I just worry about you, that's all."

"I know. Thanks for the call, Mom. I'll text you when I land tomorrow. Okay?"

"I'm proud of you for facing your fears, Brynn," my dad says over the speaker.

"Thanks, Dad. I'll talk to you guys tomorrow."

I hear them both say their goodbyes, and I flop my phone on my side table, plugging it in so it's fully charged tomorrow.

Then I climb into bed to do a little light reading to get my mind off of what my dad just told me.

What if that storm continues to inch closer to where I'm staying?

I can't let the fear deter me.

I set my alarm, pull my tablet up, and slide into a comfort book that I've read at least a dozen times.

A comfort book is exactly what I need right now.

Tomorrow, I set out for an adventure.

CHAPTER THREE

Brynn

The next morning, my first flight from Seattle to LAX goes smoothly... right up until I walk past one of the airport bars to see a television screen with the weather channel on and a map of the coastline that I'm headed for.

With a hot coffee in one hand, my carry-on luggage rolling behind me, and my heavy laptop bag's nylon strap digging into my shoulder, I stop dead in my tracks as I watch the weatherman point at the menacing-looking white and gray swirls on the screen headed right for Cancun, the city near where my beach house is located and the airport I'll be flying into.

The sound isn't turned up loud enough for me to hear the TV from where I'm standing in the walkway of the airport terminal and with my connecting flight about ready to board, I don't have the time to stall any longer.

I can't understand exactly what the weatherman is saying, but based on his overzealous hand movements sweeping across the coastline, matched with the large print letters flashing above him, "Storm Warning," it's safe to conclude that the hurricane is now coming close enough to warrant concern.

I hear my flight number being called over the intercom. The flight isn't being delayed or canceled, which gives me some small amount of reassurance that the storm is still too far off-shore to stop flights in and out of the area.

My feet stay cemented in place, though I should be taking steps forward toward my flight's gate. Instead, my instinct is to turn right back and rebook my flight back home.

But I can't bring myself to do either of those two things.

I already told Daniel on our last call that I was going on this trip. He told me that he was proud of me so now the last thing I want to do is tell him that I chickened out and turned around in the LAX airport.

If I want to have any hope of Daniel returning to a better version of the woman he left, I need to prove that I won't let my fear dictate our lives anymore.

This is a test.

A test that I need to pass.

Not just to prove to Daniel that I can change, but to prove to myself that fear doesn't have to dictate my life if I don't want it to.

Besides, this isn't a tornado ripping through my college campus in Stillwater, Oklahoma... This is a hurricane that's still not expected to hit land.

I hate that a little Seattle lightning storm can shake me with fear. I hate that loud claps of thunder will have me squeezing my eyes shut so tight that I can see stars as I reach out for a sleeping Daniel in the middle of the night.

Daniel and about a hundred other students huddled down in that basement bunker all endured the same tornado that demolished several of the buildings on our college campus that day, and it hasn't caused him any of the same trauma that it has for me.

Daniel held me against his chest as we sat clinging to each other. The lights of the basement flickered wildly as the tornado came close to us until we lost power altogether, leaving us in the dark beside the small crawl space windows that let in barely any light.

Daniel's dorm building was spared, and luckily, no one on campus was hurt, though the local hospital ER was overrun with injuries from students of the college and residents of the city.

I can still remember how the screaming and crying of others trapped with us made me feel.

There's hopelessness in those moments. A feeling of dread and fear, knowing that there is nothing you can do about the inevitable outcome of your situation.

Your fate has already been decided and there is nothing you can do to change it.

Nothing I have ever experienced has made me feel so powerless and weak as hearing the wind howl and the brick building above us creak as it attempted to withstand one of Mother Nature's most destructive forces.

Even the sound of heavy winds against my skyrise apartment in Seattle brings me back to being held hostage in the dingy, musty-smelling basement with Daniel's arms wrapped firmly around me as he spoke against my temple, telling me that we would be ok.

I knew he couldn't hold to any of the promises he made. He was as helpless to keep the tornado from barreling through the building above us as I was.

But nonetheless, I held him back as if my life depended on it, and he's been my rock ever since.

My phone dings with a text.

It's from Daniel.

I changed his contact on my phone the day he proposed and I haven't had the heart to change it back. Here in another month, it won't matter anyway.

> Fiance: Where are you? Are you in Mexico yet? I just saw the storm warning.

My heart leaps seeing his contact come over my phone and knowing that he sees the risk I'm taking. I want this to mean something to him like it means something to me.

> Brynn: Not yet, but I'm boarding my flight right now. They haven't canceled the flight yet.

His reply is quick, and I can't help but smile that he's texting back quicker than he has in the last month. I've got his attention and that feels good after being apart for so long.

> Fiance : Are you sure you should go? I won't be there with you this time. Do you think you're ready for this?

This is exactly the moment I've been waiting for.

The moment when Daniel sees that I'm taking this break to heart and that I'm trying to become the best version of myself for our future.

> Brynn: This is what our break is for, isn't it? I need to prove to myself that I can do this. And I'll be spending most of my time inside writing anyway. What's a little wind?

I walk up to my gate and listen to the conversation of nervous travelers, but none of them seem concerned enough not to board the aircraft.

I take my place in line as the gate agent quickly moves us all through, scanning our tickets as we walk by.

Once I'm in my seat and my luggage is stowed, I pull out my phone from my laptop bag to see Daniel's text.

> Fiance: I'm proud of you. Just be safe and keep me in the loop about the weather.

Seeing his text resurges me with newfound courage to keep pushing through my fears.

> Brynn: I will. I just boarded. I'll talk to you soon.

I want to wait to put my phone on airplane mode until I get a last text from him but then the pilot comes over the speaker.

"Good afternoon, this is your pilot speaking. On behalf of our crew today, we want to thank you for flying with us. We have been advised that Cancun is shutting down its inbound and outbound flights due to the increased storm warning. We will likely be one of the last aircrafts making it in tonight. With that being said, please help the flight staff by stowing away all of your things and turning your cellphones to airplane mode so that we can get off the ground as quickly as possible. We don't want to miss our window to land in Cancun. We are expecting a little turbulence once we get closer to our final destination, so please always be aware of the fasten seatbelt sign at all times. Thank you and we hope to make your flying experience with us as comfortable as possible."

I do as the pilot says and turn my phone to airplane mode. Whatever Daniel's response is, it will have to wait until we touch down in Cancun.

Once I arrive, I'll still have to get my rental car and drive another hour to the house.

Four and a half hours later and with half of it white knuckle turbulence, our aircraft finally lands safely on the ground.

The airport is packed with people everywhere I look. Babies are crying and people are building makeshift beds with their luggage as if preparing to sleep here all night.

The pilot mentioned that we would be the last flight allowed to land tonight and based on the way our aircraft rattled through the sky like a tin can being kicked down the street, I can see why the airport is shutting down flights in or out.

The moment I get my luggage, I head for the car rental desk. My heart sinks the second I see signs in front of every kiosk that says, "No Rentals Available".

I look around only to find that not a single person is standing in at the customer's desk and all the lights are off behind the desks. All the employees must have left already.

"They gave away any car that was available because of the storm. If you had a reservation, you'd better call to get a refund."

I look to find an airport security woman speaking over her shoulder at me as she walks past.

"Wait, they can just give my reservation away like that?" I huff.

"Have you seen it outside? Or even all the stranded passengers around the airport. It's every man for himself tonight."

How am I going to get to my rental house now?

"My rental house is an hour's drive from here? How am I supposed to get there without a rental car?" I ask quickly before she gets too far away.

"If I were you, I'd hurry out front and see if there are any taxis left willing to take you out that far. But I'd go now. Most everyone who can is headed home to get out of this storm."

I don't wait another second as I jog towards the glass double doors with my luggage in tow and out into the windy curbside of the terminal.

Frantically, I look for a taxi or rideshare of some sort. I'm relieved the moment I see a taxi van with its light still illuminated, showing that it's vacant and taking fares.

I race up to the van as quickly as I can with my two bags wheeling behind me and my laptop bag, attempting to do everything in its power to trip me up, but I won't be stopped.

"Can you take me here?" I ask, pushing my phone through his open window.

"That far, senorita?" he asks.

"Si, si. My rental car company gave away my reservation. I'll pay whatever the fare is."

I watch as he bends forward, attempting to look further into the dark night sky through his front windshield. Between the overcast clouds and the pouring rain, I can't imagine he can see much, but it's obvious from the look on his face that he's concerned about taking me that far in this weather.

He nods reluctantly and then turns to open his car door quickly, racing around the van to help me put my things in the back of his van.

"We need to hurry. I need to get home to my family," he says.

I'm sure he did the quick math in his head and the amount of money for this fare isn't something he could pass up.

At this point I'd pay triple just to not end up stranded sleeping in the airports with the hundreds of other people waiting for the storm to pass so that they can catch a flight out of here.

He opens the back door of the van and loads my things into it as quickly as possible and then shuts it.

"Get in," he yells over the loud rain pouring down on the metal covered terminal above us.

Then he runs back to his side of the van and gets in.

I jump into the passenger side front seat, putting my laptop bag down by my feet.

"The address?" he asks quickly.

His fingers wait anxiously for me to read it off so that he can input it into his system.

I give him the address on the confirmation email that I got from Sheridan and within less than a minute, my taxi driver pulls off the curb of the airport and we're on our way.

A sigh of relief passes through my lips, watching the airport disappear in the car's side mirror.

Over the next hour, the driver fields phone call after phone call, but with my minimal high school level Spanish speaking knowledge, all that I can sequester is that his wife, mother, and daughter all called him within the span of our hour drive.

The conversations seem to make him even more anxious about getting me to my destination so that he could get back home to his family.

The pitch-black night sky and the downpour of rain make it hard to see. His windshield wipes are doing all they can to keep up, but I can't see much except for blobs that look like houses and palm trees. Luckily, my driver seems skilled and knows the roads well enough to keep up with the lines of the road, which seems harder to see with each passing moment.

I watch his navigation as the arrow on his screen creeps closer and closer to our destination.

Both relief and dread fill me at the thought of being alone in this storm.

I know I need peace and quiet with no distractions to write this book, but being in a hotel with other people could have potentially put my mind a little more at ease. As soon as my driver drops me off, I'll be all alone in these high winds.

The thought makes my hands turn clammy, though in honesty... it could just be the humidity.

Finally, the driver pulls down a short driveway. A house that looks a little like the house in the pictures, comes into view, though this is the back of the house and they didn't show much of those photos.

I read the house number and it matches up with the address on the email.

The rain seems as though it's actually picked up more, if that's even possible. I dread the idea of stepping out but the moment that my driver throws the van in park, he whips open his door and dashes out into the rain towards the back of the van.

This is it.

I need to make the most of it.

If I ever want to prove it to myself, Daniel, or my parents, this is the time.

I check the meter for the fare and am relieved to see that the rate is in both peso and dollar so that I can be sure I'm paying him the right amount. I pull out my wallet from my laptop bag and pull the cash I'll need to pay him.

Then I pick up my laptop bag off the floor of the van and pull the strap over my shoulder. I wish now that I had kept the greatest tool of my profession in a waterproof bag.

My biggest concern is now to attempt to get inside the house before my laptop bag becomes waterlogged in this monsoon.

Reluctantly, I push open my own door and then take a breath before I step out of the car. Of course, with my luck... I land into a huge puddle. Grungy, silty water fills my flip-flops, leaving rough sand between my toes as I wade through it ankle-deep and head for the back of the van.

It takes less than thirty seconds for me to become completely soaked through my jeans and t-shirt.

There isn't a dry spot on my body at this point.

I rush to the back of the van to find that the driver is already shutting the back door, and my two pieces of luggage are sitting in a couple of inches of water.

I roll my eyes at my situation, but I can't waste time on it. I need to get my laptop into the house as quickly as possible before the storm ruins my only source of finishing this story.

I'm smart enough to have at least everything backed up to the cloud should something ever happen to this particular laptop, which might not be far off. Regarding technology, she's probably considered a dinosaur at four years old and has been into the repair shop more times over the last two years than I've seen my gynecologist in the last five.

"Gracias," I tell him and hand him the amount of money plus a hefty tip for bringing me all the way out here.

He takes the cash, gives it a quick glance, and then nods at me, folding the cash in half and then stuffing it into the small pocket of his shirt.

"Gracias, senorita. Good luck," he says.

He then quickly turns back to his side of the van and hustles back to his door, wrenching it open and climbing in before slamming it shut again.

I barely have my hands on my luggage before he flips around in the wide driveway and heads back out to the main road.

I grab my things and run for the door, splashing up more water up my legs the quicker I run, but I don't care anymore. My laptop is the only thing I care about right now and it needs a dry place as quickly as possible.

The rainwater stings against my bare arms as I make a dash for the house.

None of the beach houses along the way seem to have any lights on inside, but at this point it's past one in the morning. Is everyone asleep? Or is everyone smarter than me and sought accommodations not this close to the beach and the storm raging out in that vast, deep, dark ocean?

Running around the side of the house to get to the front, which faces the ocean, I'm relieved when I notice that the front looks to have a covered porch. However, I noticed that the porch doesn't look nearly as nice as the photos.

Isn't that always how it is these days?

Nothing is ever quite as it seems online anymore.

At this point, I don't even care what the place looks like as long as it's dry inside and has a nice, comfy bed to sleep on.

Though if I'm making requests, a nice long shower wouldn't hurt. And if I can be hopeful for a moment, maybe the last vacationers left some chamomile tea to help calm the knots in my stomach from this entire nerve-racking day.

I should be completely consumed with the question of how I'm going to sleep tonight with the wind and rain raging on tonight, but the relief of finally making it to my rental where I have a place to rest my head tonight, unlike all the people I saw in the airport, is currently counteracting my fears.

A motion light on the front porch kicks on and nearly has me tripping over my feet. It took me by surprise, but only for a second, when I thought that someone the renters before me may be stranded too and decided to stay in the house. But when I don't hear the sound of the front door opening, I look over at the light and notice that it's just a standard solar-powered motion detector light. I'm grateful to no longer be in the dark.

I step up onto the porch from the side of the house and walk up to the brick-colored front door. The storms are even louder under this cover as the rain puddles on the metal roof of the house. A keypad sits on the top of the handle, just as the instructions in the email mentioned.

I had a chance to look over the check-in list that the rental company sent to Sheridan as I was waiting for my flight to board this morning.

With my luggage sitting right side up next to me, and the rain no longer trying to drown me, I pull up my phone and look for the house code to enter into the keypad attached to the door.

Door Code #7777

I looked at the email again and reviewed the four-digit code. It seems a little too easy, if you ask me, but I'm too tired and too wet to think any more about it. Maybe they do that on purpose to make it easier for people to remember the code.

That's certainly a logical explanation.

I could see myself forgetting a complex code, too, after spending a long day on the beach.

I step forward and input the four digits.

I give it a second but the code reader flashes red like I entered the wrong code.

It's hard to imagine how I could have entered that incorrectly, but I'm so tired that maybe I only hit three of the four digits.

I try a second time, but again, the code reader flashes red at me again.

Damn it.

I check my email again and read through the entire thing. Unfortunately, no other code is found in the email.

I question whether or not there was a door at the back of the house that this code could belong to, but the instructions clearly state that the code belongs to the front door, and all I remember about the back of the house was a garage door—no man door. I could walk back around and try to see if there is a code to the garage door, but I am not stepping out into that rain until I'm sure that I've exhausted all other avenues to get in from this entrance.

My arms are beet-red from the stinging of the rain and high winds, causing my wet clothes to freeze against my body.

I enter the number for a third time, but just like all the times before, the red light practically laughs in my face.

I make a growling noise and then input the number two more times in quick, rapid succession, only to be met with more failure.

I let out an annoyed scream, but it did little to lessen the tension headache that has been starting to form since I saw the weather report in the LAX terminal.

I take a deep breath and decide to very carefully enter the number one last time before I break down and call Sheridan while she is undoubtedly asleep.

I reach for the door, but as if by magic, it swings open as I twist the handle. Only, there's no fairy Godmother on the other side.

Instead, my eyes bulge out of their sockets, and my heart practically explodes in shock as a shirtless spartan in only a pair of boxer briefs whips open the door.

Skin... so much tanned bare skin.

And bulging muscles.

Finally, my eyes make it up to his face.

I don't follow hockey closely, but this man is easily recognizable.

Lucky Wrenley

Goalie for the Hawkeyes hockey team and the same face I've seen plastered over the jumbotron that hangs on the side of the Hockey Stadium only a couple blocks from my apartment. He's one of the oldest players on the team and at least ten years older than me.

"What the fuck are you doing here?" he growls.

I'm not completely sure if that's rainwater that just dripped down my leg or if I just peed myself a little.

CHAPTER FOUR

Seven

As if this day wasn't long enough with storm prep and more texts for Josslin, I woke to the sound of someone attempting to break into the house's front door.

I don't bother to put on a shirt or a pair of pants. Whoever this fucker is trying to gain access into my house at one in the morning is going to have to deal with the repercussions of their actions while getting their ass handed to them by a pissed off guy in his underwear.

The minute I swing the door open with one hand while clutching a baseball bat in the other, I'm ready to meet whatever unlucky bastard decided to try to rob this house. Only when I open the door, I'm taken back at first to see it's not some asshole robber hitting up all the houses that have been left abandoned by homeowners fleeing the area. Instead, it's a woman at my door.

A woman who, by the look of her dropped jaw and wide-eyed stare of dread, appears more shocked to see me on the other side of the door than I am to see her.

She looks more like a drowned cat than a red-blooded woman. Her brown hair is dripping wet and stringy from the rain and humidity, with some strands plastered against her face. Her black mascara has already started running, giving her tired, baggy eyes a raccoon-like effect.

"What do you mean, "What am I doing here?" This is my rental as of three p.m. check-in time yesterday afternoon. What are *you* doing here?" she asks.

I can't tell if the drowned cat has something against curse words or if she just wasn't listening closely enough.

I might have found the lack of her using the f-word as endearing if she wasn't copping up an attitude with the guy who owns the porch she's standing on and who she woke up in the middle of the night.

"I own it," I say simply.

She looks down at her phone and then back at me.

"That can't be right. I have a confirmation email saying that I rented this place for the next two weeks."

Two weeks?

Like hell, she's staying here for two weeks.

She has to have the wrong house. There's no other explanation.

I should just slam the door in her face and head back to bed, leaving her to figure it out on her own. I'm too fucking tired and too fucking irritated about being woken up in the middle of the night to pull together the very bare minimum of patience that I force myself to give.

It's dangerous for her to be out in the storm and though I'd like to know what a young woman, about half my size, traveling by herself, is doing entering codes on random people's house locks in the middle of the night, I know better than to get involved.

I've done a good job at staying uninvolved with anyone over the last eighteen years, and I'm not going to break my streak with a woman who looks like a creature who just walked out of the depths of the ocean behind her.

"I can promise you that you have the wrong house. And just a word of caution: you should double-check the address before attempting to break into someone's home. You never know who's going to be on the other side."

I begin to shut the door, but her hand slams against it to stop me from closing it.

She's no match for me in height or strength. Her efforts to push back on the door wouldn't stop me from closing it in her face if I wanted to. But I stop and look back at her through the small gap still left open between me and her through the door.

She's got guts; I'll give her that... but evidently, no brains, considering that she thinks taking on a pissed-off, half-naked man is a good idea.

What woman in her mid to late twenties knocks on some random house in the middle of the night and doesn't turn and run the second that they see me holding a bat on the other side of the door.

"This is house number 524, correct?" she asks.

She stares back at the house number to the left side of the house, screwed into the stucco.

I let out a frustrated breath. Obviously, she isn't going to leave me alone until I've convinced her that she's in the wrong place.

You'd think that telling someone that you own the place that you're currently standing in would be adequate enough, but not in this case.

I put the bat down by the side of the door where it usually lives and pull the door wider. Unless she's got a 45 caliber pistol hidden in that soaked laptop bag, she's no threat to me, except for putting me in an even worse mood.

"Obviously, that's the right number since you're reading it on the front of my house. But you still have the wrong house. I own this place, as I've already mentioned, and I don't rent it out."

Her eyebrows stitch together at my answer.

"Wait, you can't own this house," she says, pointing down at the porch.

"Why not?"

"Because it's a rental unit. My writing agent booked it for me," she says and then thinks for a second. "Oh wait, is this some kind of squatter situation? Although it seems that you of all people..."

Squatter situation?

Me, of all people?

What the fuck is she talking about?

Her eyebrows furrow even deeper at the idea of it.

"Hell no. I've owned it for over fifteen years, and I've never rented it for a single day in any of that time. I have no idea who told you that this house is a rental, but I certainly didn't."

It's the honest truth.

I have more money than I'll spend in a lifetime, even after I retire, which means I don't need this place to pay for itself in order for me to keep it.

Even if I did want to make a little extra money, I wouldn't do it by renting out my beach house. The entire reason I have this place is to get away and unwind from the life I live in Seattle.

How can I do that if every time I show up, I know that random people have been screwing like bunnies on my bed, the kitchen table, and every other inch of this house while they've been staying in it?

Half of the year, I spend sleeping in hotel rooms for out-of-town games, and the last thing I would ever do is take a black light to any of the nice hotels that the Hawkeyes put us up in. I wouldn't even trust the walls not to be smeared in bodily fluids.

Nope.

No, thank you.

I bought this place to have something that is only mine. Where the people don't give a shit about who I am, and where I don't have to worry about waking up to bed bug bites or getting chlamydia from the toilet seat.

"Well then, explain this," she says, holding up her phone so I can see a confirmation email.

I take a small step forward and bend forward to look at the email.

Why do I even give a shit?

I have no idea.

I should just close the door. She's intruding, and I don't have to explain anything more to her. But instead, something tells me that this woman wouldn't be standing on my front porch in a storm if she didn't think she was in the right place.

My vision roams over the confirmation email just long enough for me to see the name of the vacation rental "property management" company.

There it is.

Bingo.

It all makes sense now.

I lean back up again and look over to the woman still standing on my porch with her luggage at her sides.

"The luxury premier property management company that you thought you booked with, is a scam company. They're actually famous around here for that reason. They don't manage a single property, nor are they a real business. They just have a scam website where they take photos of houses on the beach of popular destinations and then wait for unsuspecting vacationers to "book" a house and take all their money."

Her face falls instantly. And though I didn't think she could look any worse for wear, I watch her complexion turn a sickly gray as the blood drains from her face when she realizes what this means.

She or her "agent" just got ripped off, and now she has nowhere to stay.

If she hadn't come in all hot and heavy, convinced that I'm the intruder in this situation, I might feel a little bad for the fact that she just got taken advantage of and paid a premium price for a beach house that she won't be staying in.

Does it give me some satisfaction that I'm vindicated?

Yep, it sure does.

Does that make me an asshole?

Probably.

Though I can't say that I'm happy she has nowhere to go. And unless she has friends or family around here, which I doubt she does, then she's in a really bad position.

"A scam website? How do you know," she asks.

She pulls her phone away from me and starts to scan the email with her own eyes trying to see where I figured it out.

"They're one of the prominent scam websites for this area. My neighbor's house has been "rented" out three times in the last few years, but my neighbor lives here full time, and she and her late husband have owned that place for almost twenty years."

"Oh my God..." she says, rubbing her palm against her forehead. "What am I going to do?"

She says to herself, staring back at her phone and then turning her head to look back over her shoulder towards the beach and the angry ocean that's thrashing against the shore.

Being out in this weather isn't an option.

"Do you know anyone around here?" I ask, though I feel I already know the answer.

"No, I don't know anyone," she sighs in defeat, looking back down at her phone as if it might come up with an answer for her. "And the airport is shut down. There are no flights going in or out. It's packed with passengers."

"All of the hotels are booked solid with stranded vacationers, too," I tell her.

"Do you know that for certain?" she asks, her frown increasing.

I'm guessing that was her next thought.

"I have a friend who manages one of the largest resorts in Cancun. He told me that everything is sold out right now since no flights are going out. People are stranded right now unless they were able to get one of the few rental cars and get the hell out of here."

"Yeah, I know. My rental car. They gave away my reservation before my flight landed."

It does sound like she's having the vacation from hell. Still, it has nothing to do with me.

"How did you get here if you didn't get a rental car?"

"A taxi driver was willing to bring me all the way out here. I figured I'd get a lift back into town tomorrow when the rental car company opens back up."

That won't be happening.

With every update I hear, the storm is inching closer, and I doubt there is a single car rental on this coastline for at least a couple hundred miles.

"I wouldn't plan on getting that rental car tomorrow. Nor is that taxi coming back for you. You know that there is a hurricane advisory right now, right? We're at least going to get the tail end of it, assuming it doesn't come any closer. And besides, where would you go? No one has vacancies anywhere close."

I can see the light in her eyes go dim, and she stares up at me.

I'd rather see the distrust in me that I saw earlier than the look of pure hopelessness that I see in them now.

I know I can't leave her out here to fend for herself, but something tells me that letting her in is going to cost me more than I can afford.

"Ummm... Can..." she starts hesitantly. "Can I stay on your porch tonight? I'll be gone in the morning. As soon as I can get a lift from someone back to the airport."

Just then, the wind whips hard enough down the beach that a beach chair that a neighbor further up must have left out, comes whirling out of nowhere and smashes against one of the large palm trees out front of my house.

The woman in front of me shrieks at the sound, wraps her arms around her shoulders, and cowers a little as the wind knocks over her luggage.

She jumps back out of the way so they don't knock her over.

I can't leave her out here.

It's too dangerous.

"Come on," I say, taking a step out into the wind and picking up both of the pieces of luggage that toppled to the ground.

"Come on, what?" she asks, her voice a little shaky.

"You can't stay outside."

I turn around and head back for the house.

"Why not?" she asks, following behind me as I take the steps inside the house with her bags.

"Because if I let you sit out there in this weather, you might not still be there by morning. Your luggage sure as hell won't be."

I look over my shoulder to find her still with her arms protectively crossed over one another.

"Close the door and lock the deadbolt," I instruct, and then start heading for the hall.

She hesitates for only a second but then does as I ask.

I hear the deadbolt engage behind me.

She's brave or stupid to be willing to stay with a strange man in a house alone, but that's not really my problem. She's desperate, and the only intention I have with her is to find her a different place to stay by the end of the day tomorrow.

"You're Lucky Wrenley, aren't you?" she asks behind me.

Now I get the "You of all people" comment. I guess she's making the assumption that a professional athlete wouldn't squat in a house. I have no idea if that is true, but in my case, it sure as hell is.

I'm surprised she knows my name. She doesn't exactly strike me as a hockey fan. Especially since she scowled at me the minute I opened the door.

"Seven. My name is Seven. And how do you know who I am?"

I've always hated the nickname.

The media coined the term after my first season when I was signed to a team that had never won a Stanley Cup in over twenty years.

They were thought to be a cursed team.

I ended up starting as the goalie when our starter got hurt the game before the last game of the championship, and I didn't let a single puck get past me that night. Maybe I had something to prove or maybe I just got "lucky" as most sports commentators suggested.

We won the Stanley Cup, and the name stuck, and I've resented it ever since.

You don't become one of the longest-player goalies in NHL history out of pure luck. My stats speak for themselves. It's not cocky. It's the facts.

I don't ask fans not to call me that, but she's not a fan, and thank God for that.

"I live in Seattle. Your billboard-sized head is hard to miss."

Does she realize how many dirty jokes she just set me up for? Too bad the last thing I'm in the mood for is a joke at one in the morning with a random stranger who just tried to break into my house.

She mentioned that she has an editor and that she's from Seattle. If she turns out to be a sports journalist and this is all a ploy to get an exclusive interview, her ass is going back out to the porch.

Maybe Silas, my buddy who manages one of the hotels, has a room opening up tomorrow. Or maybe he knows of a vacant rental house somewhere around here that I can call the owner to get her into.

If Rita still has that open room above her bar available, I might be able to put her there.

Either way, tomorrow, the girl is gone.

Chapter Five

Brynn

I follow behind the large hockey player dressed in only his boxer briefs as he carries my luggage into the house and down the hall.

I should have known that this trip would turn out like this. I should have listened to my gut and canceled. This is exactly why I don't put myself out there.

I keep myself safe by staying within my limits and within the boundaries of safety. Now I'm stuck in a country I don't know, with a storm that could possibly hit my exact location, and even worse than all of that, my accommodations are anything but certain.

Tonight, I have a roof over my head, and at the very least, I assume that the starting goalie for the Hawkeyes isn't an axe murderer.

I feel bad that I got his name wrong. I could have sworn that I've heard the sports broadcasters call him Lucky during the few games I've seen.

"But doesn't everyone call you Lucky?" I ask.

I hear him groan with annoyance, and now I wish I had just let it go.

Who cares what he wants me to call him? I won't be here long enough to use it much anyway.

"If you're staying here tonight, it's Seven."

"Got it," I say quickly. "I didn't mean any disrespect, I promise. I don't follow hockey that closely, and it's just what I've heard the sports announcers call you. I'm Brynn, by the way. Brynn Fischer."

He doesn't say anything back as we keep walking.

I follow behind him into the mostly dark house. All the lights are off except for the hall light he probably turned on when I woke him with my multiple failed key entries.

He leads me through a small entryway and then a large-sized living room.

A couch and a loveseat make an L shape set up with a flat-screen mounted against the far wall.

I look to my left to see an arched opening into a kitchen and dining room open concept.

Most everything in the house seems dated, besides the appliances in the kitchen and the large screen TV.

There's certainly no woman's touch in this house and based on the bland tile colors and late-nineties furniture, I'd say Seven bought this place and filled it with used furniture from a hotel getting rid of their old stuff.

The images from the website that Sheridan sent me don't match the insides of this house at all. The pictures of a modern vacation home listed on the website with updated furnishings and a completely different layout only further prove Seven's point that this house isn't the rental that Sheridan thought she rented me.

I need to call her as soon as possible and hope that she can turn this fraud in to her credit card company for theft and get her money back. The next thing I need to do is get a flight out of here as soon as the airport resumes operations.

I'll have to call tomorrow and see when they can rebook me. I don't care about the change fee, I'll pay whatever it takes.

I look down at my phone, hoping to see a text waiting from Daniel. With all the craziness, I almost forgot that he might have texted me back as I was flying. But then I realize that I don't have any cell reception. There's not a single bar to signal hope of getting correspondence out to Sheridan or my mother, either. I promised them both that I would call when I got situated in my rental house. The storm must be moving in and blocking the signal.

I quickly type up a text to Sheridan and send it as I follow behind the man who just so happens to be both my savior and my worst nightmare.

I know Sheridan won't get the text right away, but if reception hits at any point tonight while I'm asleep, it might just be long enough to send her the text.

> Brynn: Bad news. The house was a scam. Call your credit card company immediately. Good news. I'm not dead and the owner of the house is letting me stay tonight.

I think about it for a second and decide that just in case I'm wrong about Seven being an axe murderer, it wouldn't hurt for her to know whose name to give investigators when they start a manhunt for my killer.

> Brynn: If I go missing… Seven Wrenley from the Seattle Hawkeyes did it. Probably with a bat…

I fire off the last text and watch as my phone continues to attempt to send both texts with no luck.

"What do you write, Brynn?" he finally asks.

What do I write?

I don't remember telling him that I'm an author. It's not something I usually open up about, especially with strangers.

"How do you know I'm a writer?"

We pass by the first open door to our left in the hallway. The light is on, and from my limited visibility, it looks like a bathroom, with the door only cracked.

What I wouldn't give for a bubble bath to warm up in and decompress from this day.

"You said that your writing agent booked you this house. Are you a journalist?" he asks.

"God, no!" I say with more emphasis than I meant.

There's nothing wrong with being a journalist.

It's a respectable profession, but I'm not interested in the amount of research required for that job, and the real world is too boring. I like writing about make-believe characters.

I clear my throat and try again.

"I mean, no, I write fiction."

"You don't peg me as someone who writes thriller novels."

Seven is one of the last people I want to admit that I write steamy romance books to. Not because I'm ashamed but because guys like Seven just don't understand the world of romance books.

And that's fine. They aren't my intended target audience.

"No, my books are romantic in nature. Do you read?" I ask.

"Sometimes. But I'm not in the habit of reading romance."

"You should give it a try... who knows, you might learn a few things," I say, trying to lighten the mood, but he just makes a grunting sound of annoyance.

He doesn't ask any more follow-up questions. Which means he's probably judging me so hard right now, but whatever. He breaks people's noses and knocks out teeth for a living, and I suspect he makes a whole lot more than I make doing it.

I shouldn't feel inferior to this man, so I won't allow myself to.

I follow as Seven turns right into the first room down the hallway and flips on the bedroom light.

The room looks just like the rest of the house. Dated furnishings and no real personality, but beggars can't be choosers, and the queen-sized bed in the middle of the room is far better than sleeping on the hard porch out front.

I hear the creaking and wobbling of something against the window but it's too dark outside for me to know for sure.

I cringe at the thought of sleeping alone tonight.

I can't remember the last time I slept without Daniel in the middle of a storm.

Up until he left for Australia, he was the warm body lying next to me, reminding me that I wasn't alone.

We agreed that I would no longer wake him any more during a thunderstorm since his job is really important, and he needs a full night's rest to work on whatever deposition his team is pouring over.

Having him close does a lot to ease my mind and now I won't even have that.

I feel naïve for thinking I could set out on my own and face my fears in one night.

"This is the only spare bedroom in the house," he says, setting my bags down by the bed.

The bedspread is an older nineties tropical theme with palm trees and a coconut-print, with pillowcases to match.

"Thank you, this is more than enough. I appreciate you letting me stay here."

He nods and then abruptly leaves the room.

I just stand there in confusion for a moment.

That was weird, wasn't it?

I suppose I shouldn't be surprised that he's not a man of many words. I've heard a little bit about him from around town. He's the stoic, keeps-to-self player on the team. The rumor is that he hasn't been interviewed one-on-one with any media outlet in over ten years.

I start to take steps towards my luggage when he returns again.

"Here," he says, walking to the left side of the bed, setting a battery-powered lantern next to the lamp and alarm clock. "We might lose power tonight. If that happens, you might need this."

My heart begins to race at the possibility of losing electricity.

"Wait, we might lose power?" I ask. The anxiety I've been trying to push down is starting to bubble up again. "Do you think that will really happen?"

He turns after dropping the lantern off on the table and then faces me as he walks back.

"I wouldn't rule it out. And if it does and you need light, the lantern has enough battery life for a couple of days. I already charged it all day today. Just flip the power button on."

He keeps walking past me and towards the bedroom door as if this time he's leaving and he won't be coming back for the rest of the night.

A tiny moment of weakness has my brain begging me to ask if I can sleep in his bed tonight... or at least on his floor. The last thing I want to do is sleep in this storm alone, but sleeping with a strange man is out of the question, and I doubt he'd agree to it anyway.

No matter how bad my anxiety is, this is happening tonight, and the best thing to do is to remember my breathing exercises and prepare mentally as I've practiced with the therapist in Oklahoma that I used to see that helped with the anxiety after the tornado.

I had planned to find someone new when we moved to Seattle, but I just never got around to it, and I really felt like I had the tools I needed to combat my anxiety since my panic attacks were becoming less and less.

"My bedroom is at the end of the hall if something happens. Night Brynn."

I bet he'd be as interested in spending a night with me in his bed as he would if he were volunteering to sleep out on the porch tonight.

"Don't be such a scaredy cat, Brynn; you can do this. You can sleep alone in a storm. Your entire future happiness with Daniel depends on this." I coach myself.

I stare over at the bed and think about stripping out of these drenched and grimy clothes and pulling on some pajamas. But the idea of sleeping all night in the saltwater that I'm covered in has me squirming in my own skin.

I spin quickly towards the exit of the spare bedroom just in time to catch Seven before he leaves me here for the rest of the night.

I hate to ask for more favors, but I really need this one.

"Could I maybe take a shower before bed? I feel gross from traveling all day, and the rainwater feels sticky."

I doubt he cared about my reasoning, but I gave it anyway. I am inconveniencing him, after all.

He turns back to me and nods.

"Yeah, follow me."

Seven took a right out of the bedroom and then immediately left to go back the way we came.

He flips on the light to the bathroom before I enter behind him.

Unsurprisingly, the bathroom continues the house's general theme, but the walk-in shower looks like a new insert—something designed in the last decade.

Seven walks deeper into the bathroom, opening a floor-to-ceiling cabinet and pulls a crisp white fluffy towel out. Then he plops it down on the small countertop near the sink.

"If you need anything else, it should all be in the cabinet. There's nothing fancy in the shower, but you can use whatever is in there."

"Thanks," I say, still standing just inside the bathroom doorway as I watch him move from one area to the next to make sure I have everything I need.

He reaches into the shower and cranks the handle one way. A stream of water with good pressure comes out of the shower head, and as of this moment, there is nothing sweeter that my eyes have ever beheld.

I'm itching to get into that shower and wash off this day, especially since the sand has dried between my toes.

"The shower was plumbed in wrong when they remodeled it. Hot is cold, and cold is hot. I've been meaning to fix it. If you forget which is which, it won't take long before you figure it out."

I half expect him to give me a playful smirk, but he doesn't.

"Oh... okay. Got it," I say, making a mental note.

"Tomorrow, we'll find you somewhere else to stay."

He turns back from the shower and then heads for the bathroom door, not bothering to look back over his shoulder.

"I appreciate you letting me stay here."

I'm no more excited about the proposition of staying in this house with him than he is. The idea of finding a vacant room in one of the large, all-inclusive resorts in the city is far more appealing at this point.

"I'm headed to bed," he says.

"Night," I say, watching him walk out of the bathroom door frame and pull the door shut behind him.

I reach back and lock the door just for good measure, though I have a feeling that Seven has absolutely zero interest in me whatsoever.

He couldn't care less about the woman who's about to be naked in his bathroom, and the feeling is mutual.

I walk over to the mirror just to see the damage from this day, and I just about jump back the instant that I catch a glimpse of myself.

It's not as if I was expecting to look like a bombshell after trudging through a tsunami to get to the front door, but no wonder he couldn't wait to get away from me.

I look like a walk-on extra for a living dead movie.

My mascara is smeared under my eyes; my hair is matted against my head, and my fly-aways look like they've been dipped in hodgepodge and plastered against my cheeks.

My skin is an awful grayish color, while my nose is bright red.

Good God, I look as awful as I feel.

Actually, I might even look worse than how I feel.

Perfect.

I begin the exciting process of stripping out of every layer of wet clothing that clings to my body until I'm finally naked.

My skin is cold and a bright pink, even in this humidity.

The steam begins to billow from the top of the glass shower enclosure and my skin starts to warm.

I pull open the glass door and step inside. My freezing, sand-encrusted toes feel the healing powers of the shower water at first contact.

I let out a moan at how good it feels to be under the warm water. Even though a storm is brewing outside, and I could be homeless by tomorrow, or worse, depending on the hurricane, this shower is doing everything right to take away the tension in my shoulders.

I look around at the contents inside, which Seven said I was welcome to use.

It's no surprise that a single dark gray bottle of men's three-in-one shampoo, conditioner, and body wash sits in the shower nook, along with a lonely bar of soap.

Do people actually use bars of soap these days?

How old is this guy anyway?

I know he's one of the oldest players on the team but I don't think even my father uses soap bars anymore.

From the little information I've gathered, watching sports commentators talk about Seven during a Hawkeyes game, I believe he's thirty-seven or thirty-eight. There's a ten-year age gap between us, which means we probably don't fall into the same generation.

A loofa is slung over the shower handle, but I think he and I would both agree that sharing a loofa is where we draw the line.

I should have headed back to my room to get my overnight bag before I stepped into the shower, but it's late, and I'm exhausted.

I'll have to wait until tomorrow to pull out the contents of my overnight bag, and hopefully, by then, I'll be in the privacy of a hotel room with no grumpy hockey player in sight.

I bend closer to the single bottle of product he left in the shower. I guess tonight I'll be smelling like Blue Arctic Glacier. Whatever the heck that scent is. There is no way that I'm using the bar of soap that he probably rubs over his pubes.

I push the shower's glass door open again to quickly reach into the cabinet and grab a washcloth from the stack of items I saw when Seven pulled out a towel for me.

I close the door behind me and drench the hand towel under the shower and then squirt a decent amount of body wash onto it.

I begin to rub my body down with the blue gel that resembles toilet bowl cleaner, and I'm actually pleasantly surprised by its crisp, clean smell.

I won't be adding this product to my daily routine once I get home, but I'll admit that this isn't horrible.

I'll stick with the girlie stuff that Daniel swears he never uses, but I smell it on him from time to time, especially my leave-in conditioning hair detangler.

I can't blame him for sneaking a few sprays of it every once in a while. It leaves your hair silky and soft and protects it from heat damage. Plus, it smells freaking amazing. Nothing like this blue goop that Seven uses, that I know will leave my hair feeling dry and frizzy after it air dries tonight on my pillow.

I wince at the thought of how my hair is going to look in the morning.

I'm just beginning to wash off the suds that are covering me from head to toe when I hear a crack against the side of the house that makes me jump, and then the power goes out.

I scream bloody murder the moment I find myself in the dark with the water beginning to slow to a dribble.

"Help! Help!" I yell out, feeling instantly trapped in the shower enclosure.

I frantically push at the glass door a couple of times in different areas, trying to find the exit. The familiar feeling of an onset panic attack threatens to give way if I don't get out of here soon.

I hear Seven's heavy footsteps barreling down the hallway, and now I wish I hadn't screamed for help, even though knowing he's close is an unexpected relief.

Finally, I find the handle and lean my entire weight into it as if my whole life depends on my escape.

The glass door gives way in a rush the moment I find the opening, and I'm not prepared for how quickly the shower enclosure dumps me out into the bathroom.

I stumble out like an uncoordinated brand-new baby giraffe in the pitch dark of the bathroom.

I attempt to run for the door, but I forget one tiny detail. Tile floors and wet, soapy feet are a slippery combination.

The moment that my feet connect with the tile, I know I just made a grave mistake, and at that same moment, I hear Seven ram up against the bathroom door, and crash through it with ease as if that door never stood a chance against him.

I yip at his abrupt entry as my feet slide out from under me just as I ram right into Seven's bare chest. Seven swoops in, catching me around my waist with one arm, and hauls me up against his chest to keep me from falling flat on my ass.

The flashlight in his other hand illuminates the room well enough that I know he had to have just seen me completely naked.

I'm now wondering if I will ever forgive Sheridan for booking me on the writer's retreat from hell.

CHAPTER SIX

Seven

The minute I hear Brynn scream, my eyes fly open, and I realize that the fan in my room and my alarm clock are both off.

We lost power.

Shit.

"Help! Help!" I hear her scream from the bathroom down the hall.

That's all it takes for me to spring into action.

I'm up and out of bed as fast as I can be, flipping the blanket off of me and getting to my feet.

I reach out quickly, grab the flashlight off my nightstand, and race down the hall toward the bathroom, flicking on the flashlight right before I reach the door.

Did she fall?

Is she hurt?

Something had to have happened for her to call out to me like that.

I run straight for the bathroom door and slam against it when the handle doesn't turn.

She locked it, obviously.

I give it one more shove with my shoulder, and the door pops open with the splintering sound of wood cracking around the door casing.

I don't care about the door.

If she's hurt, I need to get to her.

It's the only thing going through my head.

The door is a shitty one anyway, and yet another thing I've been meaning to replace ever since I bought the house.

The bathroom is just as dark as the rest of the house since the windows are boarded up, covering any reflecting moonlight, though the storm clouds are probably too dark to let much light through tonight anyway.

My flashlight gives me enough light to see Brynn just before she barrels into me.

The minute we collide, she slips from her wet feet, and I catch her, wrapping an arm around her waist and pulling her against me.

Her soapy, wet, naked body slams against my bare chest, and I feel the wetness from her body soak through my boxers.

Fuck, did she have to be wet?

"Whoa, are you okay?" I ask, looking down at the woman clinging to me to regain her footing.

Now, with her hair washed, the dark mascara cleaned from her fresh face, and the pink back in her cheeks, I can see very clearly that Brynn is a beautiful woman.

Damn it.

This is the last thing I need right now.

"We lost power while I was in the shower," she says, clutching my arm to steady herself.

I pull her back up onto her feet quickly, and before I even know what I'm doing, I glance down at her bare tits against my chest. I can feel her nipples hardening against my pecs.

Goddamn it, that feels good.

I divert my eyes back up to hers but not fast enough. She just witnessed me checking her out after I bulldozed through the bathroom door that she locked to keep me out.

But what if she had been hurt?

What if I hadn't gotten to her in time?

Will she believe any of that?

Probably not after I checked out her breasts.

Not exactly my shining moment of chivalry.

But everything happened so fast, and she's a naked woman who fell into my arms and plastered her body against mine.

It was a reflex.

"Sorry. Shit, I thought you were in trouble."

She did scream for help, after all.

"The power went out. It startled me, that's all," she says, letting go of her grip on my arm now that she seems to have gotten back to her feet.

"Here, take this."

I release my hold on her just as quickly and push my flashlight against her collarbone.

The last thing I need is for her to feel my growing interest as my cock swells with her body up against mine.

Then I swipe the towel off the counter and hand it to her to cover up, looking in any direction other than at her. The moment her arm clutches both items, I spin around and head for the exit immediately.

"I'll fix the door tomorrow," I call out over my shoulder.

She doesn't call after me as I trudge past the broken door, and I don't blame her after what I just did.

I'm not interested in the crazy romance writer who tried to break into my house less than a couple of hours ago.

Besides my niece Cammy, no other woman has ever slept under this roof. And just up until a few hours ago when Brynn showed up, I had no plans to change that.

She might be beautiful with a body to match, but a bedroom wall is all I need to remind myself that Brynn Fischer, romance author and house crasher, is off-limits.

My hands ball up into fists as I march down the hallway, heading for the front door to turn on the generators.

There's only enough power to run the fridge and a few things during the night, but I can't have the food in both mine and Rita's refrigerators going bad.

Getting out of the house where Brynn is standing in my bathroom naked is probably not a bad idea either.

I knew letting her stay would be a problem, but I didn't have a choice when she showed up on my porch with nowhere else to go.

I flip the deadbolt and the lock on the front door and swing it open. I slam the door behind me to make sure it closes entirely in this wind, and to vent my frustration at my situation.

The wind is howling through the palm trees all around me. The rain hasn't let up since Brynn arrived, and the moment I step off my covered porch and onto the white sand heading towards Rita's, the rain continues to beat down on me, stinging as it pelts against my bare skin. I'll happily take any distraction that puts as much distance between me and Brynn as possible.

I don't like the way I instantly reacted to her when she called out for me, and I don't like the way I was willing to do anything to gain access to her.

Having her body up against mine lit something in me that I'd prefer to ignore.

My concern for having her in my space has now been validated, and she has to go.

As soon as physically possible.

Hurricane or no hurricane, I'll pay whatever it takes to get her into a different house or hotel. I don't care who I have to bribe to make it happen.

There's something about Brynn that tells me she's trouble for me and my future plans.

Keeping her here would be a mistake.

Tomorrow, Brynn leaves...

...or I do.

CHAPTER SEVEN

Seven

I got a few hours of sleep last night. Not as much as I'd like, but I have a lot to do today, and I know that Silas will be up early. I'd be surprised if he slept at all last night with the storm headed straight for the hotel he manages.

By five a.m., I'm up and out of bed, making a cup of coffee and checking to see if we've gotten any cell reception since Brynn showed up earlier this morning.

I'll have to order a new door for the bathroom, but I at least made it functional for now.

The minute that two bars pop up on my phone, I dial up my buddy.

"Seven, how did it go last night on your side of the beach?" Silas asks.

"The house is still standing," I say. "Any news on the storm? I lost power last night, and I just got back to cell reception. I might lose you again here soon."

"We lost power too. Luckily, we have generators to run everything, and the staff are following the emergency plan as well as expected," he says. "From the reports I'm getting, the storm won't make it to the beach but we're going to get the biggest hit tonight, and then it looks like it's going to boomerang back out to sea and head further down the coastline. We should be out of the woods by tomorrow late morning or afternoon."

"The winds are pushing it out then?"

"Seems as though the weather pattern is changing again but we're not getting out of this unscathed. We're anticipating property damage, and part of our beaches are probably going to get washed out. As long as the coastguard doesn't make us evacuate the hotel, I'll be happy," he says.

The good news is that after tomorrow, most of this should be over and Rita can come home as long as her house isn't too damaged.

But knowing that Cancun will get hit harder than here, the thought of sending Brynn closer to it doesn't sit all that well with me. And yet, keeping her with me isn't an option I'm interested in entertaining.

I have to at least ask Silas if he has a spot for her.

"Do you have any available vacancies for a woman who showed up at my house last night? She booked my house on a scam website, and I need to find a place to put her until the airport starts outbound flights again."

"Wish I did, but right now, I had to have maintenance set up our outdoor poolside cabanas inside the main lobby for stranded guests I don't have rooms for. I literally have people sleeping in lounge chairs around the hotel. People are using towels as blankets in the hallways," he sighs.

"Shit, man. That sucks."

"We're getting through it. And anyway, your unwanted guest is safer there with you. You're not going to get hit as hard as us. I'd keep her there."

"I can't," I say, though I know he's right. "I'll see if Rita can take her in at her apartment."

"You can't keep her for a couple of days? She's one person, right? Is she really all that bad that she can't stay while this storm blows over?"

I have a room for her and I stocked more than enough food to easily feed us both for at least two weeks, maybe longer, but that's not the point.

There's no reason she can't stay. None, except for the fact that her staying could be a problem for me. And if I try to explain that to Silas, he'll laugh his ass off.

"She can't stay," I say simply.

"Why not? Does she have some incurable disease you might catch?"

"No, not that I know of."

"Okay, well, what's the problem?"

The problem is that Brynn is the kind of temptation I've been avoiding for years. I barely know her but I'm smart enough to see that if I keep her around for long enough, I'll regret it.

I hear a woman's voice on the other side of the line.

It's an employee asking Silas what to do about the buffet line this morning and if they have enough food for the extra guests.

He has bigger things to worry about than my one house guest.

"Nothing. There's no problem. I'll figure it out. Thanks, Si. I'll let you get back to the hotel. Be careful out there and let me know if you need anything."

"You too. Beers and a game of pool at Scallywag's after this hell is over?" he asks.

"I'll be there."

We both hang up and I set my phone back down on the counter.

Rita is a night owl, so I don't want to wake her this early to see if she was able to get more sleep than I did last night.

It's still not even six in the morning yet.

I'll give her a little more time before I call her up and try to unload my unwelcome guest on her.

My phone starts to chime with text messages.

Probably ones that didn't come through last night after I lost reception.

The first one I see has me already pissed off.

Josslin: I'm worried about you.

Josslin: I just saw the weather report. Please tell me you're getting out of there.

Josslin: Are you at least safe?

Josslin: Are you just going to ignore me forever?

She must have sent these last night and I'm just now getting them.

I consider not responding, but ignoring her obviously doesn't get the point across.

Seven: The last eighteen years suggest that I might.

A text back comes in quickly.

Josslin: Finally. A response after the last two weeks of texting you.

Seven: You only get responses that have to do with Cammy. You know this.

Josslin: Your niece isn't the only family you have. The rest of us would like to talk to you, too. Your mom says you haven't returned her calls in over six years.

Of all people in my family, Josslin should know exactly why that is. She's half of the duo who drove that wedge into the middle of it, causing the fallout. And six years is exaggerating. I call my mom once a year—not more, not less.

> Seven: Cammy is the only one who hasn't stabbed me in the back. She's the only one I like. Deal with it.

I shouldn't even bother to engage with Josslin. We've had this same conversation over and over again.

Now that Cammy is going into her sophomore year of college at Washington University and she's lived in Seattle for the last year, our relationship has gotten stronger and I don't have to go through Josslin to have a relationship with my niece.

Half the reason Cammy picked WU was to get away from her mom and I don't blame her for it. Cammy still wanted family close wherever she decided to go to school, so when she told me she was thinking about attending WU her freshman year instead of the colleges near home, she asked if I would be okay with it. I told her that I would support her decision and help her move into her dorm.

She got a full-ride volleyball scholarship anyway, so it wasn't like she needed my permission to attend.

> Josslin: I don't think Cammy should come out to Mexico next week with this storm.

> Seven: It will be over by then, and she's an adult. She can make that decision on

her own. I'd never let her come out here if it wasn't safe.

Josslin: Maybe I should come out too. I'm worried about her.

Seven: Don't even think about it.

As of last year, Josslin's been making every excuse she can to come out to Seattle. There's not much I can do about her showing up to see her daughter, but I draw the line when it comes to her showing up here.

She won't be allowed to enter this house and since Cammy stays with me when she comes down for vacation, Josslin shouldn't waste her time.

Josslin: You can't cut me out forever.

Seven: Are you sure about that? At my age, I've only got another thirty-five to forty years before I leave this earth. I think I'm up for the challenge.

Josslin: We need to talk, and it would be better if we did it in person.

Seven: Then, was your plan to invite yourself on your daughter's vacation so you could spend time with her? Or was your real plan to ambush me?

Josslin: I'm not trying to ambush you. And why can't I want to spend time

> **with my daughter and get to talk to you in person?**

I back out of the text conversation.

Josslin is a world-class manipulator, but lucky for me, she opened my eyes to that years ago.

I have a long list of things to do today.

One of which is to ensure that both my house and Rita's are ready for the storm to hit tonight. The other is to keep busy and ignore the woman asleep in my guest room until she's safely tucked away at Scallywag's upstairs apartment with Rita.

Brynn

Last night could easily go down as the most humiliating night of my life.

Between showing up on some strange man's door, accusing him of squatting in a home he owns, and then screaming bloody murder loud enough that he breaks through his bathroom door in an attempt to rescue a woman who's afraid of the dark, I'm regretting not taking my chances out on the porch last night.

My eyes clamp down at the mortification of it all as I lay in bed this morning.

I'd just as soon march into the ocean until it swallows me whole, then head down the hall and face him today.

But what other option do I have?

All night long, I lay awake listening to the sounds of palm tree fronds thrashing around in the gale-force winds while loose pieces of debris smacked against the sides of the house. The memory of listening to the howling of the wind on that fateful day in Oklahoma while hunkered down in the belly of the three-story brick dorm building on campus came swirling back to torment me.

The sounds of the buildings around us getting ripped apart with no way for us to escape our apartment basement.

Toss in the crushing blow to my ego, watching Seven rush out of the bathroom as fast as he could to get away from me, and my first night in paradise could be considered an epic fail.

The one thing I was grateful for last night is that Seven is a loud sleeper. I may have slept alone last night without the comfort of Daniel lying next to me, but at least the sounds of Seven's heavy breathing reminded me that I wasn't alone.

I have no motivation to write today since I didn't get a wink of sleep last night, though I know that my deadline won't wait for the weather to clear up. Even now, I can still hear the storm winds raging outside my boarded-up window. Oddly enough, the thick sheet of plywood protecting anything from breaking through my window last night brought me more comfort than I would have imagined. I felt safer than I would have without it.

I glance over at the closed guest bedroom door and wonder if Seven is up yet. With the windows boarded up and the alarm clock in this room still not illuminated from the loss of power last night, the only thing I have to go on is my cell phone's time which says it's a little after seven am.

Is he dreading seeing me as much as I am to see him?

Probably not.

I doubt he's lost much sleep over the five-foot-four woman sleeping in his guest bedroom who's afraid of the dark.

He's a fearless NHL goalie who gets in fistfights with other large and angry players out on the ice as part of his occupation. And the man is definitely built for it.

I've never seen a human in that great of shape up close before. Let alone felt his hard chest against my bare body when he caught me from slipping on the wet floor.

All six-plus feet of muscle, brute strength, and sex appeal were hard to miss the moment he opened the front door in the dim lighting of the porch light. I'm starting to better understand women's fascination with professional athletes, though I won't be sporting a Wrenley jersey anytime soon.

The funny thing is, I've written about these types of men in my books.

My regency novels are chock-full of sturdy-built men with bodies to salivate over and my new contemporary books won't be any different.

I've written the intricate details of their imaginary six-pack abs and deep V cut of their pelvis. I create fantasies about the way they take the main female character passionately and protectively in the bedroom... and even outside of it.

I've written about the grumpy "misunderstood" demeanor of the hunky protagonist who shields his broken heart from the world, finally willing to shed his armor for the one woman he can't live without.

This is the first time I've actually been faced with the real-life situation of falling at the mercy of a grumpy adonis, and admittedly, it's not as sexy as the books portray these characters to be.

The idea that Seven is anything like the heartbroken male lead in my books is laughable. He's more likely breaking hearts than needing to mend his own with the number of women throwing themselves at him.

He's adored by the city of Seattle as the starting goalie for the beloved Seattle Hawkeyes Hockey team.

If this is really what my heroines are actually faced with in my books, I might need to rethink my meet-cutes going forward. How could they possibly fall for a guy like this?

Male athletes are well known for their promiscuity, and I can't imagine Seven is any different.

Tack on his permanent scowl, and I don't see how a single one of my female characters would ever fall for his nonsense.

I wish reality was as simple as rewriting a chapter in a book that you're not happy with. I'd love to delete the way my body reacted to him last night.

With the spike of pure adrenaline from being taken off guard by the loss of electricity, followed by the feeling of his warm skin against mine, my nipples reacted on their own accord—hardening against him with unconscious arousal.

Maybe the fact that it's been almost eight months since Daniel left, and it's been that long since I've been skin-to-skin with a man, had a small part to play. Not to mention the surprise of seeing Seven break through a door to get to me, and the feeling of his large bulge against my belly as he held me against him.

Is it possible that he unlocked new fantasies in me that I didn't even know existed? Or is this all stemming from the fact that I haven't had sex in months?

Am I just projecting my sexual frustration on Seven just because he's the closest man in my vicinity?

That has to be the reason for it because I'm still madly in love with Daniel.

How could I want to be with anyone else?

How could I consciously want to sleep with a grouchy hockey player who's known for being standoffish and rude to the media and hasn't shown me so much as a smirk since I got here?

In one month's time, Daniel will be back and all of this will be a distant nightmare.

My safe and steady, Daniel.

He might not be in as good of shape as Seven with his leaner body build, but he plays on a men's league basketball team a couple of days a week and is conscious about eating healthy. Seven, on the other hand, has well-defined muscle mass, and I wouldn't doubt for a second that he could bench-press me without even breaking a sweat if he wanted to.

The physical difference between Daniel and Seven is significant.

Neither Daniel nor I watch professional hockey, but I've caught plenty of Hawkeyes games in the local pubs and sports bars where I've met Daniel for happy-hour drinks before. You'd be hard-pressed to find any bar downtown that doesn't play a Hawkeyes game during the NHL season. It's on everywhere in the city and is almost impossible to miss.

I've seen Seven move across the ice on a flat-screen TV while I sip on a glass of Pinot Grigio and nibble on fried cheese curds and pita chips that Daniel likes to order when he wants to celebrate a courtroom victory at the bar across from his office.

I've just never wondered how much muscle was underneath all of those layers of padding before.

I, on the other hand, am still holding on to my freshman fifteen from college. And besides the occasional hot yoga sessions that Sheridan guilt trips me into attending with her, I don't do much physical fitness, unless the laps I do around our apartment building when I need to work out a scene I'm struggling with in the book I'm writing counts.

Let's just say that I'm a little softer than the man I clung to last night to keep myself upright. He must have noticed that I'm not in as great shape as his female fans that he's used to taking home.

As much as I'd like to hide out in here all day, Seven said that he would find me a new place to stay today, and really, the sooner I get moved over to a resort hotel room, the better for both of us.

I slide my sleep-deprived body out of bed, hoping for the sounds of Seven somewhere in the house so that we can discuss what arrangements he might have found for me, but I hear nothing.

I pull on a T-shirt and a pair of shorts and then grab a brush from my bag.

After Seven left the bathroom last night, I made it safely to my room and was able to towel dry off. Thankfully, I wasn't as soapy as I thought. The shower had rinsed away most of the suds before the power went out.

A nice thorough spray down of the leave-in conditioner from my overnight bag saved my hair from yet another terrible hair day.

I look in the mirror while I comb through my strands and decide against trying with makeup.

I just don't feel like putting in the effort. Not that Seven would have any interest in me with or without makeup. I think that was made pretty obvious based on the fact that he couldn't get away from me fast enough last night.

I set my hairbrush down and then took my toothbrush to the bathroom. I may skip my makeup routine but I won't gross either of us out with morning breath.

Once I have a clean, minty mouth, I open the bathroom door and listen for him. I hear the faint sound of pots and pans clinking together over the loud wind still pushing against the house. He's up, and it's time to face the music.

The sooner we're rid of each other, the sooner I can resume the reason for why I'm here.

To write.

"Morning," I say as I step out of the hallway and into the kitchen.

Seven is standing in front of a gas range stove, flipping over a pan full of over-easy eggs and slices of ham in a second skillet. He's dressed in thick canvas cargo pants and a t-shirt donning the logo of a bar called Scallywag's, with a cartoon Basset Hound stretched tight across his back.

I don't know why seeing Seven wearing a cartoon dog on his shirt makes me grin, but it's not what I expected to see on him. Maybe it's because I'm not used to seeing him in much clothing at all.

I bet it's hard for him to find clothes that fit his broad shoulders and trim waist.

I shake the thought.

The last thing I need is to be thinking about Seven's body and what he wears or doesn't wear.

I survey the scene in front of me as Seven continues to work diligently over the hot stove.

In a third pan, a massive mountain of hashbrowns that could feed a small village is crisping up and popping in the oil he's frying them in.

Seven's honey-brown eyes settle onto mine when he finally decides to acknowledge my existence. He watches me over his shoulder for a brief second while I lift myself onto the bar stool sitting at the kitchen countertop across from him.

"Do you want eggs and ham?" he asks.

My stomach starts to rumble at the smell of the delicious breakfast. I haven't eaten since LAX, after hearing about the storm getting closer. It unsettled my stomach, and then I couldn't eat the sandwich that I bought at the coffee shop in between my connecting flights.

"That would be great, thanks. The generator must be working?" I ask.

"It's enough to run a few things. I have solar panels on the roof that help, but there isn't much power coming in since it's overcast today from the storm rolling in."

From the storm rolling in.... I hate the sound of that.

I watch as he tentatively stirs the hashbrowns to get an even crisp on all sides, my mouth watering at the smell of everything he's making.

"Have you heard anything about the weather? Is the storm getting closer?" I ask.

"Tonight should be the worst of it. The hurricane is rolling in closer but it still won't touch land. We'll be okay as long as we stay here. It's going to hit Cancun harder."

My heart sinks at his update.

I had hoped to get a hotel room in one of the resorts but now I'm not so sure I want to be closer to the eye of the storm.

Do I have any choice anyway?

It's not as if he wants me to stay here with him for any longer than necessary.

"Have you heard if there is any availability at any of the hotels?"

"My phone got reception earlier this morning for a few minutes. Silas, one of the managers at the biggest hotel in Cancun, said that there are no openings in any of the hotels near there. People are sleeping in the hallways at this point. You're going to be safer around here. I have one more call to make after breakfast. My neighbor might have a spot for you above her bar."

My ears perk up at the idea of staying with his neighbor. I feel bad barging in on someone else but staying with her above her bar sounds promising.

A large bang makes me jump out of my seat and clutch my chest. Seven didn't even flinch.

Nothing seems to phase this man.

"The wind is picking up. It's going to get worse before it gets better, but it should be past us by tomorrow afternoon," he assures me.

He seems so calm about it all.

As if it's just wind and not a category-four hurricane about to hit nearby.

I release the grip on my shirt and settle back into my chair.

One more day... I can do this.

"Thanks for asking around," I say to him.

He doesn't have to do any of this. He could just as easily kick me out. And let me fend for myself. "Did you say that you got reception?"

A little hope sparks in me that maybe my texts got through last night.

"Yeah, a couple hours ago. It's hit and miss, but you might be able to make a call out if you keep an eye on it."

"I'll be right back," I say, slipping off the bar stool and heading for my room to retrieve my phone.

Sure enough, my heart leaps when I see that a text finally came through from Daniel this morning, as well as one from my mom, my dad, and a couple from Sheridan.

I open up Daniel's and read it as I head back towards the kitchen for breakfast.

> Fiance: Have a safe flight. Keep in touch.

Then nothing else after that.

Maybe I had hoped there would have been a follow-up text today, but he's probably asleep with the time difference.

I back out of his message and check the ones from my mom and dad.

> Mom: I haven't heard from you. Are you okay?

> Mom: Call as soon as you can. I'm worried.

> Mom: The Cancun airport is shut down. Did you make it there? Are you safe? CALL ME!

My dad's texts were a little less intense.

> Dad: I don't like the look of this storm. I think you should come home. Does Daniel know about the hurricane?

Of course, my dad would bring up Daniel. And since my parents still don't know that we're on a break, I'm sure my dad is wondering why Daniel didn't try to stop me from going. If it were up to my dad, Daniel and I would already be married.

I walk back through the kitchen after drafting up a text to all three of them and send them off, hoping that as soon as we get reception, they'll get it.

I sent the same text to each of them.

> Brynn: I'm safe and in the rental house, though it wasn't a rental. Luckily the owner is letting me stay with him. The storm should pass by tomorrow and I'll see about getting a flight home.

"Is this enough food for you? There's plenty more if you want," Seven says, placing a plate and fork in front of me.

I didn't see it right away as I read through Sheridan's texts that arrived early this morning.

> Sheridan: Oh my God! Are you serious? The reservation was fake? I can't believe this. I'll call my credit card company immediately.

> Sheridan: Wait... how would the smoking hot goalie for the Hawkeyes be responsible for your disappearance?

> Sheridan: Answer me back this instance! I need more information!

> Sheridan: Okay, your phone is off, so you must not have reception, but at least I know that you're safe in the house. Please send another text as soon as possible, preferably with a photo as proof of life. Be careful out there.

> Sheridan: I called the airline. I can't rebook you a flight until they resume operation out of Cancun. Call me!

When I look up, my eyes widen at the stack of food sitting in front of me. It's more than I'd eat in an entire day, let alone in one sitting.

"No, that won't be necessary. This is more than enough. Thank you."

I glance over to compare his portion size to find that Seven has two plates stacked with food for himself, along with a few pieces of toast.

I guess I never considered how much food an athlete eats. No wonder my gigantic plate of food doesn't seem like enough to him. My portion size would barely be a snack for his appetite.

He forks a piece of ham, egg, and then some hashbrowns and stuffs it into his mouth.

"I had a few texts come through this morning," I tell him, drafting up a quick text to Sheridan.

He just nods as he chews and then scoops up another bite.

> Brynn: Seven Wrenley owns the house. He let me stay here last night but he has a friend who has an apartment. I might be moving over there today. I'll keep you posted. I'm only getting reception occasionally so I'm not sure when you'll get this text.

I send off the text, grab my fork, and start on the eggs.

"I'll probably be out all day working on preparing the houses for the storm tonight. I'll call Rita as soon as I get reception and see if she has room for you."

He'll be out all day?

In this storm?

And what more can he do? He's boarded up all the windows and has the generators running.

I'm not going to question him, though. Having the house to myself without any distractions is something I could use to try to clear my mind and finish the rest of the outline for my book.

Though I want to curl up in a ball with the storm raging outside, I can't make any excuses anymore. Otherwise, I'll be returning my advance for this book along with any other losses that the publishing house endures due to PR and advertising losses. Not to mention that I'll let down my readers who are counting on this book to be released on time.

I can't let them down.

"I should write anyway. My book has a deadline in a couple of weeks. Hopefully, my laptop still has enough power to get me through today."

He takes another bite of his food, which he has practically inhaled up to this point, and then walks towards a closet in the kitchen. I watch as he opens the door and pulls out a small black square.

The second he walks back over and sets the item down next to me, I know what it is.

"I charged this battery bank a few days ago. It should have enough power for your cell phone and laptop today. Is there anything else you need before I leave?"

I shake my head and stare down at the item Seven brought me.

The man is prepared and thinks of everything.

He takes the last couple of bites and then puts his dirty dishes in the sink.

"Thanks for this," I say. "For everything, really."

He just looks over at me without a nod or smile.

"I'll see you later," he says.

I watch him head out of the kitchen and then see him turn towards the front door.

I listen as the door opens, and the wind whips through the house before he closes it behind him.

And just like that, he's gone and I'm in his house alone.

Chapter Eight

Seven

It's been a few hours since I left Brynn inside after breakfast.

Did I have a lot to do out here in this shit weather? No, not really.

But I didn't get a chance to make sure that my solar panels are screwed on tight and I wanted to make sure that none of the hits I heard against the roof last night caused any damage to them.

Any excuse to stay as far away from Brynn as possible is worth the risk.

The minute I saw her walking into my kitchen, my body tensed. Brynn is naturally beautiful, with bright blue eyes, dark lashes, full pink lips, and soft brown hair that I can't stop wondering how it would feel against my fingertips.

Not that I have any intention of finding out if her hair feels as silky smooth as it looks.

I have no intention of touching Brynn again.

Last night was a mistake, and I'll make sure it's not repeated.

What caught me off guard this morning was that Brynn didn't walk out with her hair perfectly styled, a full face of makeup, and her tits smashed together and hiked up to her chin.

It's not common for me to be in the proximity of women who aren't dressed to get my attention.

If I was going to date someone, I'd pick someone with Brynn's natural approach rather than the puck bunnies that show up at Oakley's after a home game slathered in makeup and doused heavily in perfume. Perfume that it turns out I'm usually allergic to because I can't stop sneezing as they walk past.

Not that it matters what kind of woman I'd date. It's been eighteen years since I've been in a long-term relationship, and I don't have any interest in breaking my impressive streak any time soon.

The second my phone picks up reception, I call Rita.

If I want to take Brynn to Rita's apartment, I need to do it before the storm gets worse.

Scallywag's is only fifteen minutes from here. As long as Rita has a spot for Brynn, I can get her packed up and moved over in the next hour.

"Rita, how's the bar holding up?" I ask when she picks up the phone.

"Thanks to you, hun, everything held up through the night. Silas called earlier and told me about the hotels around him. Sounds like they're in bad shape over there. How are you holding up?"

"That's actually one of the reasons I'm calling. I had a woman show up on my front door last night claiming to have rented my house for a writing retreat and booked it with that online scam property management company. I let her stay with me last night since there was nowhere else for her to go, but I was hoping that you still have that other room available above the bar."

"Oh, that's so terrible. That poor thing. Of course, I would be happy to take her in, but I'm afraid that I already offered up the room to one of our regulars and his family. She could sleep on the floor in the living room with the children, but that's less than ideal, I would think. Especially since you have a spare bedroom available," she says.

Damn, Rita's place was my last hope for getting Brynn out of my house but packing her into a small two-bedroom apartment with five other people doesn't feel right.

"What about your house next door?" I ask.

The house is boarded up so it would be safe enough in that sense, but Rita's generator is a lot smaller than mine and can only run the fridge. Rita has a full-size generator at Scallywag's, so they never felt the need for more than enough power at the beach house to run the fridge whenever they left due to a storm.

Brynn wouldn't have running water or toilets. And since the house has an electric stove, she wouldn't be able to cook either.

It's not a great situation for her to stay next door, but staying with me isn't any better.

The storm might pass us by tomorrow afternoon, but it could be days or weeks before we get full power back and Brynn would be without basically any for too long.

"Send her to my house? I can't imagine how she would be any safer there than with you. And if she's there to write, you probably won't even see her. She'll be busy writing in the guest bedroom," she says. "Is there a reason why you don't want her there?"

Rita's been trying to set me up with every single woman she comes across ever since she met me. If she knows that I'm trying to get rid of the beautiful author staying in my house, she might try to board up the front door while we're sleeping so that neither Brynn or I can escape.

"No reason. I just think she'd be better off with you. But, you have enough on your plate. I just figured if you had an extra room, I'd see if it's still available."

"It sounds to me like you already have the perfect spot for her. She'll certainly be more comfortable, and who wouldn't want a big hunk like you around when a storm is raging outside? I'd say she'll be getting plenty of inspiration."

The very last thing she says starts to cut out—I'm losing reception again.

"Rita, can you hear me?" I ask but the line gets muffled and I can barely hear anything she's saying.

"Rita... are you there?"

Then the line goes dead and my fate is now sealed.

It turns out that I'm stuck with Brynn until this storm passes.

What's another two to three days until Silas has a vacancy?

I can keep my distance and just like Rita said, Brynn will probably spend most of her time in her room writing.

I have six more days before Cammy gets here, and by then, Brynn should be in a hotel room or on a flight home.

I spend the next several hours making sure that I've done everything I can before tonight. With the wind starting to pick up to the point where the sand was blowing in my eyes, I headed for my garage to work on a few projects for my boat, which is currently anchored out in the bay with other boats to keep it from banging around in the marina.

It's dark out now and I'm starving.

I've done my best to stay out of the house and out of Brynn's way.

The first thing I notice when I walk in through the front door is the smell of something cooking.

I hear the sound of plates and utensils rattling around in the kitchen. Brynn must have made herself dinner.

I don't blame her for not waiting for me.

It's nearly nine o'clock at night and I'm surprised she waited this long.

I walk into the kitchen to find Brynn with tortillas, shredded cheese, and diced ham from the breakfast leftovers, all played out with a hot pan on the stove.

"Oh, hi," she says as she slices up a fresh mango and slides the fruit onto a plate. "I hope you don't mind that I helped myself to your fridge. I didn't know if you had eaten, but I'm just about to make some ham and cheese quesadillas. Do you want one?"

I look around the kitchen to find that there isn't a single dirty dish from this morning's breakfast in the sink.

She did the dishes.

Usually, I would have cleaned those up before going outside, but I was in a hurry to get out of the house.

"Sure, but I can make my own. You don't have to assemble it for me."

"You already made me breakfast and you let me stay here. I'd be happy to make you dinner."

I nod, giving in.

It's a nice gesture since I need to sit down. My body hurts from climbing ladders and squatting all day on the roof while I fixed the solar panels in the high winds.

"Take a seat and tell me what you want in your quesadilla," she says as I walk over to the barstool and take a seat.

Brynn pushes the plate of sliced mango between us as if to share it with me.

My mouth waters at the smell of fresh fruit, so I pick up a slice and plop it in my mouth before answering.

I must be starving because I swear, I've never had a mango taste this good.

"Cheese, ham, and some of that sour cream is fine. Just fill it up, and I'll take two, please. I usually eat a lot, and I missed lunch."

"Coming right up," she says, pulling out a large flour tortilla and tossing it on the pan to heat it up.

Next, she starts to layer on the cheese and ham.

"Is this enough?" She asks after only adding a handful of ham.

There's a large amount of ham sitting on the chopping block where she diced it all up so I know she's not trying to be stingy with the protein, she just doesn't understand how much I have to consume to keep up my energy at the performance level that my body is used to, I don't expect her to. She and I don't know each other at all.

I get off my chair and head towards her.

Showing her is going to be a lot easier for both of us.

Her eyes stay fixed on me as I walk around the counter to where she's standing and I walk up behind her.

"Did I do something wrong?" she asks.

"Not at all," I say.

I wash my hands in the sink quickly and then walk directly behind her, reaching over her shoulder and grabbing another large handful of ham and then another large handful of cheese.

The quesadilla is bursting with the contents I just loaded up, but I need to increase my calorie intake tonight since I missed a meal today.

"Like that. It takes a lot of food to feed me, and like I said, I didn't eat lunch."

"I bet it does," she says.

But the way she says it in a low voice makes me wonder if there is innuendo I missed.

I step back and away from her.

However, she meant it; the last thing I need to do is analyze it.

"You can make the next one?" I ask, backing away and heading back to my bar stool.

"I think I get the idea now," she says, starting to load up a second tortilla with a healthy helping like I showed her as she waits for the first quesadilla to heat up all the cheese. "So I'm guessing since I'm still here that means Rita didn't have space for me."

Brynn's eyes stay focused on her task and don't raise up to meet mine.

"She gave the available room she had away to a family who needed it. If I took you over there, it wouldn't be as comfortable for you as it is here."

She looks over at me finally.

"You don't have to worry about my comfort. I'm intruding on your space. As long as I have a safe place to lay my head, anywhere will be fine."

She grabs a spatula and slides it under the filled tortilla, and drops it onto a plate for me.

Reaching out, I grab the plate of hot food and set it in front of me. I'll probably consume this thing in less time than she'll have to make me a second one.

"Thanks for dinner," I say to her.

Being able to come in after a long day and not have to scrounge around for something quick to eat when I came in was a nice surprise.

"You're welcome. It's the least I could do."

"You have a book due, right? If you're going to spend most of your time writing in the guest room, we won't see much of each other. And in a couple of days, the airport should be back up and running. Then you can choose to either fly home or take up a vacant room in Silas's hotel once flights start taking vacationers out of here."

She puts the next tortilla on the frying pan and starts the same process again while I eat my dinner.

"That's very generous of you. If I can stay a couple more days, I'll stay out of your way. I promise."

"We'll make it work," I say, and then I get to work decimating the food in front of me.

I eat the first one in a matter of minutes, and just as I finish, she has the second one done and slides it onto my empty plate.

I watch her begin to assemble her own as I eat.

"Did you get any writing done today?"

"Actually, I did. I got the rest of my outline worked out. Now, I just need to start working through the chapters."

Ever since she told me that she writes romance books, I've been curious about what exactly that entails.

I've never met an author before and I would have never guessed if I passed her in the street that she writes fiction for a living. It caught me off guard when she told me last night.

"Good. I'm glad my beating on the solar panels on the roof didn't distract you."

"No, actually. I was relieved to hear you up there and know that you were close by if I needed something," she says and then pauses for a second like she's giving too much information. "I uh... I get a little uneasy in storms. I grew up in Oklahoma, and we had a bad tornado one year. It's not like I'm not used to the storm warnings or having to run for a shelter—I grew up doing that, but this one was different. Stuck in that damp cement shelter, we could feel the rumbling of the earth and the walls shake as it came close. Small pieces of the ceiling above us cracked and people screamed until they lost their voices. I didn't think we would make it out alive."

She doesn't look at me as she tells the story.

This isn't something she wants to talk about, but for some reason, she's telling me anyway.

"Did anyone get hurt?" I ask, hoping to God that she didn't lose a family member or a close friend.

"There were a lot of injuries. The ER was full for weeks but no fatalities—we got lucky. Storms like these bring back bad memories and flashbacks of being stuck in our building without knowing whether we would survive or not. It seemed like we were stuck down there for days, not hours."

She turns away to grab a plate for herself.

I decide to change the subject. What she just told me was personal, and I can see in her body language that she feels weird about what she just told me.

"You said you write romance. What kind of romance do you write?" I ask.

"Most of my currently published books are of historical type romance, but after five years, I want a little change, and my publisher is giving me some freedom. Now I'm writing a new series in contemporary romance about a billionaire family who all have to marry to receive their inheritances."

"How the hell do you write a billionaire romance series?" I say, forgetting not to be a dick.

I didn't mean anything by my comment, but I really have no clue what any of that means.

She laughs like she already knew I was going to have a reaction to it.

"You write it just like any other romance book. It's not that different from what I wrote about before. My Regency-era heroes are earls, dukes, and counts. In the modern day of my new series, my male leads will be billionaires. It's kind of similar in that way. The biggest changes are the societal rules between that time period and now."

"And let me guess. All the men you write about are jacked and good-looking, too?"

She lets out a little giggle and covers her full lips as she flips her quesadilla.

"Well, of course. I'm building the ultimate fantasy with spicy scenes. These men have to be gorgeous. Haven't you had a girlfriend that reads romance books?"

"What, girlfriend?" I say out loud, though I didn't mean to.

She looks over at me with an inquisitive brow.

"You're a professional athlete... I'm sure you've had plenty of girlfriends. Or are you the typical player type," she says, a subtle annoyance in her voice to the latter of the two.

Does she have something against me being a hockey player?

That's rarely been an issue with women I meet.

It's usually the reason most of them want to talk to me in the first place.

"I don't date, and I wouldn't consider myself a player by any stretch."

"That's exactly what a player would say."

I think for a second that she's serious but then I see a glint in her eye.

Her quesadilla is finished, and she scoops it up with her spatula and flops it onto the plate.

"Okay, so you write billionaire romance with spicy scenes. What are spicy scenes?" I ask, taking my next bite.

"Spicy scenes are basically open-door romance scenes."

She says with hesitation in her voice.

"What is an open-door romance scene?"

She grabs a knife and fork and starts to cut up her tortilla filled with cheese and ham.

"It's basically a sex scene that I write out in graphic detail."

Suddenly, everything I thought about this woman changed completely.

"How much detail are we talking about?"

"Very specific and explicit content," she says and then takes a bite of food.

"I see. So what's this book about then?"

"It's the first book in a six-book series about these brothers that inherit a billionaire dollar empire when their father passes away, but in order to keep the businesses from being sold off, they each have to find a bride."

"I see. So each brother gets his own book, and they all find a wife and live happily ever after?"

I get up, take my plate with me, and head for the sink, waiting for her to finish her bite.

I wash my plate and put it on the rack to dry.

"Of course they do. Otherwise, it wouldn't be following the rules of a true romance."

"That doesn't seem realistic. What family of six brothers all end up happy? Statistically, that isn't probable."

She turns and stares over at me with a raised eyebrow.

"That's why my books are found in the fiction side of the bookstore. And that's also why it's a damn good thing that you're a hockey player and not a romance author. Your books would tank."

I let out a chuckle, and her lips pull up into a smile at my reaction.

I can't help but stare for a second.

I realize this is the first time I've seen a real smile from her, and that's my fault.

"And then they fuck?" I say.

She laughs this time.

"Yeah. Something like that."

She finishes up her food and then walks it over to the sink.

"Here, I'll do the dishes. You made dinner," I tell her, reaching my hand out for her plate.

"Are you sure?" she asks and then breaks out into a yawn that she attempts to cover with her hand.

"Yeah. You'd better get some rest. It might be hard to sleep through the storm tonight. I'd get as much shut-eye as you can now."

She hands me her plate and then stares up at the roof as if she'll be able to see the storm clouds above us.

"Ok, thanks again for letting me stay here."

"You're welcome. Night Brynn."

She walks out of the kitchen, and that's the last time I see her for the night.

CHAPTER NINE

Seven

It's been hours since I fell asleep and even longer since Brynn went to her room, but a loud bang against the roof wakes me.

The wind is blowing hard enough that I can feel a slight draft through the boarded-up windows.

I have no doubt that by the time we wake, broken palm tree fronds and scattered debris will be everywhere along the beaches and up against every one of my neighbor's houses.

I listen for a few seconds longer to determine if I need to go outside and check things out, but I don't hear anything on the roof anymore. Whatever possible damage that is done will have to wait until tomorrow when it's safer to go back outside.

I close my eyes again, when my ears perk up to a completely different noise.

It's almost a whining sound.

Or maybe it's more of a sob.

I pull the sheets off of me and swing my legs over the bed. I head for my door when I finally pinpoint that the sound is coming from Brynn's room.

I knock on the door softly at first.

"Brynn, are you okay?" I ask, but she doesn't respond.

Now that I'm standing at her door, I'm sure that the sound is coming from her room.

Maybe she's having nightmares, and she's not really awake.

I debate, turning back and heading to my room, but the sounds continue.

I can't knowingly leave her like this—I won't get any sleep.

I knock again.

"Hey, Brynn... are you okay in there?"

Still, I get no response, but the distressing sounds continue.

I check for the door to find that she didn't lock it.

Twisting the doorknob, I carefully push through the door slowly.

"Brynn, I'm coming in," I warn and then open the door the rest of the way.

I find Brynn sitting on the floor at the foot of the bed, in the fetal position.

She's holding her legs against her chest with her face buried against her knees, and she's shaking like a leaf.

A panic attack.

I've seen a few in my life, and this one is unmistakable.

"Hey, you're okay," I say, walking quickly up to her and bending down to touch her arm.

She feels clammy, sweaty, and cold all at the same time.

"Come on, you're coming with me," I tell her.

She doesn't move or nod in agreement but I can't knowingly leave her like this.

I scoop her up under her legs and around her back and pull her up against my chest.

The second that she's pulled against me, her arms wrap around the back of my neck and she buries her face against my shoulder.

She told me that she'd been in a bad storm before, but I wasn't expecting her to react like this.

I carry her out of her room and bring her into mine.

"You're going to stay with me tonight until the storm passes, Okay?" I ask.

I feel the subtle nod of her head against me.

It's a good thing that I didn't push her to stay next door by herself, though maybe the option to stay in the cramped apartment further inland would have been better than keeping her on the beach where we're going to get the biggest brunt of the storm.

There's nothing I can do about it now except to keep her close and try to soothe her out of her panic attack.

I lay her down in the middle of the bed, and then climb in behind her.

I wrap my arms around her and pull her flat against my chest.

"You're going to be okay, Brynn," I whisper against her ear, and rub my right hand up and down her arm in an attempt to stop her from shaking. "I swear that I won't let anything bad happen to you."

I need some kind of answer, even if we don't know each other long enough for her to give me that kind of trust. But I need to know she's listening.

"Do you believe me?" I ask.

She nods, but she's still shaking uncontrollably.

My hands continue to rub up and down her arm until her shaking starts to subside a little. After what feels like an hour of listening to the storm carry on outside while applying firm strokes against Brynn's arm, I finally hear her breathing deepen and slow.

She fell asleep.

Thank God.

She wiggles against me, though it's unintentional, and soon enough, her perfect ass is pressed against my crotch.

I can't stop my cock from hardening against her with every movement she makes against me.

Each time I attempt to pull back, she follows me in her sleep and it doesn't take long before she's plastered against me again.

"Being this close and wanting you this bad is dangerous for me. Can't you understand that?" I whisper to myself, knowing that she's fast asleep and won't hear me.

I knew sharing a roof over our heads could become a distraction that I didn't need. But I hadn't anticipated that by the second night of her being here, we'd be sharing a bed.

I'm now playing in dangerous territory, and I need a way out immediately.

Brynn

In my dream, I hear Seven's voice call out to me.

"I've got you Brynn... I won't let go."

"Go back to sleep. You're safe with me."

I feel his warm arms wrap around me, and a feeling of instant relief and safety comes over me.

I can't tell where my dreams and reality meld, but even without opening my eyes, I know that I'm in Seven's bed. The room and the pillow I'm lying on all smell like him.

Like his body wash but also that masculine smell of salt, sweat and deodorant mixed with a light smell of peppermint mouthwash

Smelling him all around me in the safety of his arms lulls me back to sleep each time I wake to the sound of something loud outside.

I've never felt safer in a storm than I do with Seven.

Not even with Daniel.

The realization sends a small sense of panic through me but it was only one night. There's no way I can tell that from only one night.

When Daniel told me that I was going to be okay in the deep darkness of that basement in Oklahoma, I wanted to believe him, but I knew he was just as vulnerable and helpless as I

was. But when Seven said it last night... I almost immediately
believed that Seven could hold back a storm with his bare hands.
That he would stop the winds from tearing the house apart and
that he'd shield me if the roof came down around us.

How could a stranger who wants me out of his life make me
feel safer than the man who loves me?

I groan awake, wishing to stay asleep a little longer but the
storm winds aren't near as loud as they used to be and my
curiosity to find out if the worst of the storm is over has my eyes
fluttering awake.

The moment my eyes open, I notice where I am.

In my room.

There's no more masculine smell of the man who stayed up
all night, keeping my panic attack at bay, besides the lingering
smell of him on my skin and clothes.

Disappointment sets in first, and then a sense of embarrassment when I realize that not only did Seven probably not sleep
a wink in order to coddle a grown woman out of her fear of
storms, but he moved her back into her own bed the moment
he got the chance.

When will I ever stop humiliating myself in front of this man?

The answer is unclear.

I rub my hand over my face and brush away the sleep crusties
from the corners of my eyes.

I hear the phone that's lying next to me on the nightstand
begin to ding wildly. I must have gotten reception just now, and
texts are flooding in.

I reach for my phone when I realize that it's no longer plugged
in to the battery bank that was here last night. I open Sheridan's

text first, though the excitement of seeing Daniel's text is almost too tempting not to check first.

Sheridan: You're staying with Seven Wrenley? Please tell me he's as gorgeous in real life as he is on the television screen.

Sheridan: I'm glad to hear that the storm will pass soon. I'm sorry you're having such a crappy time, but maybe you can use this inspiration for the book.

I tap to reply and start typing out a text to her.

Brynn: Well, I'll tell you this… he's just as grumpy in person as he seems to be on the television screen. He's not faking that "give-no-fucks" attitude. It's 100% authentic.

Sheridan: Tell me more. As a completely uninterested married party who can only live vicariously through you, I need to know the details.

Sheridan: How did you hold up last night? I was worried about you. Did you get any sleep?

Brynn: I ended up having a panic attack. Which is really disappointing since I haven't had one in years. Seven heard me in the other room and carried me

> into bed with him. I think he thought I
> was going into shock. I'm mortified!

I still can't believe that happened last night.

He probably thinks I'm a total nut job, and I can't exactly blame him.

> Sheridan: You slept with Seven last
> night?! Are you kidding? You need to use
> this in your story. This is gold!!!

It doesn't feel like gold.

It feels like a mistake.

This whole plan to come out here and face my fears feels like a mistake.

For just a moment last night, making dinner in the kitchen together, it felt like we found common ground, but then I went and made things even more awkward than ever.

I don't blame him for disposing of me back to my room as soon as he got the chance. He probably thinks I'm a train wreck.

> Brynn: It's not the kind of "sleeping" you
> have in mind. I made a complete fool out
> of myself, and now I don't know how I'm
> going to face him this morning.

I see a call coming through.

It's the first time that I've had reception long enough to answer a call.

Sheridan calling...

"Hi—" I start but Sheridan cuts me off immediately.

"Brynn! He's totally into you. What else has happened while you've been there?" she asks.

She wouldn't be saying that if she saw the way he scowls at me.

"Nothing. Except that he saw me naked in the shower when I screamed bloody murder when the lights went out and he rushed in thinking I was in trouble."

"Oh, poor you. A big, manly hockey player keeps coming to your rescue. You're right, that must be so unbearable for you."

Maybe... just maybe, I can see how this might sound to someone on the outside. That Seven keeps finding ways of saving me. But she's not here to see how he never smiles at me or how he risked his life out in high winds just to avoid being inside the house with me.

He's tried to place me with two different friends without any success and I could tell by the look on his face how disappointed he was to be stuck with me still.

"I'm telling you, this guy can barely stand me being here."

"At the very least, he's giving you great material for your book. Your writer's block should be cured by now. The way you described the first brother, Colston, in this new series, he's got that Seven Wrenley energy written all over him. He seems cold and needs a warm woman to thaw him. You can work with this."

She isn't wrong.

Colston, my male character in the first book, has that smoldering personality. He's the tattooed brother who rides back into town on his motorcycle after getting a letter from a lawyer stating that he has five half-brothers whom he never knew about.

"Maybe if I squint really hard, I can find some kind of inspiration," I say sarcastically.

"That's the attitude," she teases. "Go get him, tiger."

"Wish me luck. I'm going to find Seven, apologize for last night and then get back to writing. If you haven't heard from me in twenty-four hours, I probably died from embarrassment. Don't bother sending out a recovery team."

"So we've decided on the dramatic route... good. I'm glad to see we're taking the mature course of action."

If she were in my shoes, she would understand how bad this whole thing is.

She isn't staying with a man who has seen her completely naked and held her all night because of a panic attack.

"You know me so well."

"Keep me posted on your writing whenever you get reception. I'd love daily updates on your word count. And if you get lucky enough to have internet access, send me any new chapters you can."

Sheridan is my agent and not the editor that my publisher uses, but she's highly invested in my success, and I love the notes she gives me during my first round of drafts.

"I will, I promise."

"You got this girl. I believe in you. Never forget that. This story is going to flow out of you. You just need to find what inspires you to write about love again. I know that's hard right now."

She's right.

I love Daniel so much, and it seems like it's far easier to write about love when you're in it—when you feel it.

"You're right."

"Love ya, sweetie," she says.

"Love you too."

Then I hear her click off of the phone.

I know she's right, but that doesn't mean it's easy.

I pull up my texts and see Daniel's text.

> Fiance: You're staying with some guy? I don't like the sound of this. Who is he? Has he tried anything with you?

> Fiance: Call me as soon as you can.

> Fiance: I don't care what time of the night it is.

This is the first time I've seen this many texts in a row from Daniel since he left town.

My heart flutters seeing his concern for me.

I understand that we decided to take a break, but it feels like he's been more distant and distracted during our phone conversations ever since he left. I know that they have him working long hours to get everything ready before they leave and head back to the States.

I just hope that when he gets back home and we start again from where we left off, everything will be back to normal.

I know he said to call, but it has to be at least one a.m. I don't want to wake him, though it's tempting to hear his voice. Instead, I draft up a text.

> Brynn: I'm safe. The storm blew through last night. It should be passing at this point. And don't worry, the house owner is the goalie for the Seattle Hawkeyes,

> and he's been very accommodating. The guy is practically a doomsday prepper. We have everything we need.

I see my parent's text and shoot out a quick text to both of them as well.

I should call, I know, but I want to get this apology out of the way first and get something to eat. I'm starving, and I know my mom will keep me on the phone for as long as she can.

I walk out of my room and head for the kitchen, not bothering to change out for the t-shirt and pajama shorts that he's already seen me in. I need a cup of hot tea at least before I can function today.

I don't hear Seven moving around in the kitchen as I walk down the hallway.

Could he still be asleep?

He was up most of the night attending to me, but I heard him snoring at one point when I stirred awake in the middle of the night.

The moment I walk into the kitchen, I see a plate covered in foil sitting on an open notebook at the end of the countertop next to the black battery bank that he gave me to use.

I pull a corner of the foil back and steam billows out from under it. The food is still hot.

Scrambled eggs and french toast this time.

My stomach growls with hunger.

I pull the plate off the notebook to read the note that Seven left for me.

Brynn-

I went out to assess the damages on both houses and start repairs. I'll be out all day, so you'll have the house to yourself to write.

We still don't have power besides the generator, but I charged the battery bank for you. You should have power on your laptop all day, and there's enough power for you to take a shower if you want.

I saved you some breakfast.

He lists his phone number at the bottom of the note for emergencies. I save his contact information in my phone... just in case.

A shower, a fully charged battery, and french toast.

Yep, this man thinks of everything.

He must have taken the battery when he carried me back to my bed this morning and charged it while I was sleeping.

I realize that he didn't say anything about last night in the note, and I appreciate that he didn't call me out, but does this mean that we're just going to pretend that it didn't happen?

And did he sneak out early this morning just to avoid me again?

I can't worry about that now since there's no discussing it right now with him anyway, and I need to get back to writing. I wouldn't doubt that there's probably a lot to do outside after last night. He probably has his work cut out for him.

I need to eat, shower, and then get back to work.

CHAPTER TEN

Brynn

After eating the breakfast Seven made for me and taking a much-needed shower, I head back to my room to work.

I thought a lot about what Sheridan said this morning as I enjoyed every moment of my shower routine. She thinks I should use Seven as my inspiration for the book, and now, against my better judgment, I can't *stop* imagining him as Colston.

Each time I try to picture a dialogue scene between my female character, Leanne, and Colston, I can't stop seeing Seven's scowl, his full brown eyes, and the sound of his deep, raspy voice against my ear as he wrapped me protectively in his arms last night.

I take a seat at a small desk inside the guest bedroom and set my laptop and Bluetooth mouse on the lacquered surface.

The scene that has me stuck and unable to move forward is a steamy scene.

I stare at the book file in front of me and click to open it.

A white screen with black lettering of text I wrote months ago stares back at me, taunting me to put my fingers on the keyboard.

I close my eyes for a moment and take a deep breath, and all at once, inspiration hits when I least expect it.

My imagination takes me back to Seven's bed last night.

I keep my eyes closed as I try to remember the smallest details, and lift my hands to the keyboard, preparing to write whatever comes to mind. Then the moment hits and my eyes open as I write the words.

I feel Colston's body as he slides behind me on the cool sheets of his bed.

His strong arms wrap around me as he pulls me against his firm chest to comfort me.

"Go back to sleep, Leanne. You're safe with me," Colston whispers against my ear.

Goosebumps cascade down my spine at the sounds of his deep, raspy voice. The heat of his mouth radiates against the pulse point of my throat.

I'd give anything to feel his lips against my bare skin, but we both know this attraction is off-limits.

His hands trail down my body, and every inch he touches sends shivers of need through me, as if every touch is a tease, showing me what it feels like to be stroked by him but never giving me what I truly need... his fingers pressing into my center.

"Colston, touch me," I beg.

He doesn't respond, but I know he hears me.

I press my ass against his hardening cock in an attempt to coax him on. His erection pressed against my lower back and between the crack of my cheeks.

"Being this close and wanting you this bad is dangerous for me. Can't you understand that?" he says.

I know that we shouldn't continue but my body is desperate, and I need to know, once and for all, what it would feel like to be filled with Seven's cock—

I stop as soon as type those last two words.

A shiver of panic shoots through me.

That was an accident.

Immediately, I go back and change out the name. It was an honest mistake and no one knows what I accidentally wrote but me.

I shake the jarring moment out of my mind and then continue.

For once in months, I'm finally writing, and I won't stop now just because I accidentally wrote Seven's name instead of Colston's. I'll have to be mindful of that, but luckily, there's the find and replace all button in my editing software.

Before sending it to Sheridan to read, I'll ensure that there is no trace of Seven in this book—anywhere.

She'll never let me live it down if she finds out that she's right, and using Seven as my muse is the thing that finally broke my writing slump.

My mind begins to wander, and a flash of an alternative version of what could have happened in the bathroom when Seven stormed in, starts to play in my mind.

My imagination takes over as I watch Seven bust through the bathroom door and wrap an arm around me to keep me from slipping.

Then he lifts me into his arms and carries me to his bedroom, laying me out, and then steps back to take a slow sweep of every inch of me.

I watch as Seven strips out of his wet boxer briefs and stands at the edge of the bed, pumping his long hard cock in front of me as he lets me watch—

My phone begins to ring, startling me from my fantasy.

I look down to find the name "fiance" on my phone.

I know he's seeing other people, and fantasizing about Seven isn't wrong since we're on a break, but a flash of guilt rises in me.

"Hi! I'm so glad you called. I didn't want to wake you, but I just got cell service again. Did you get my text?"

"It's just after five-thirty in the morning here, but when I woke up and saw your text, I got concerned. I wanted to hear your voice."

My heart warms at his admission.

We might not be together right now, but we still care about each other, and soon, we'll be living the life we planned, and this time apart will feel like a chapter in someone else's story.

"I'm okay. The storm is mostly behind us, though it's still windy, and it's been raining all day."

"I don't understand... What happened with the house? And how did you end up with Lucky Wrenley? Is he being respectful? Do you feel uncomfortable with him? Are you sleeping in separate rooms? I'll call around later in the morning and try to find you accommodations somewhere else."

Are we sleeping in separate rooms?

What an odd question. Of course, we're sleeping in separate rooms. Seven can't stand me.

But I'm glad he's concerned, though technically, it's not really his business if I'm sleeping with Seven.

I don't remind him of this fact because I don't want to argue over our situation. It's not as if he's told me about anyone he's seeing. I've just heard from mutual friends that he's dating around, and since that was part of our arrangement, I can't be mad that he is.

If I wanted to sleep in the same bed as Seven, I could. And I guess I did last night.

I decide to skip past the question altogether and move to the last one he asked.

"Accommodations aren't exactly available right now, which is why he let me stay. He tried to get me into a couple of different places, but it didn't work out. I think he felt bad for me and didn't want me sleeping on the beach in the middle of a category four hurricane."

"Sure he did. I bet he tried really hard to get an attractive woman out of his house," he says sarcastically. But then he moves on quickly before I get the chance to assure him that Seven has no interest in me. "Jesus, Brynn. How did you do without me being there with you? You must have been a wreck with that storm."

I take a second to consider whether telling him that I ended up having a panic attack and slept with Seven is a good idea. I'm just worried that it will sound so much worse than it was, and he knows that I haven't had a panic attack in the years since my therapist and I came up with a way for me to combat them with visuals and breathing exercises.

I don't want him to think my anxiety is getting worse and reconsider getting back together.

At the same time, I view honesty as the best policy, especially since we're getting back together soon. He needs to know what's going on with me, and it's not like anything happened while I was in bed with Seven.

"Seven was really helpful, actually. He stayed with me while I worked through a small panic attack. And I did get through it with a little time. I think not having you here was good for me."

I say, hoping to spin my panic attack into a positive.

"See? My whole world won't crumble without you. I'm getting stronger so that I can become the equal partner that you deserve."

Maybe I didn't tell him that Seven held me all night and that I woke up several times to Seven's erection poking me in the back, but he never made a move on me when he could have tried. And erections are a natural thing that sometimes can't be helped.

It's not as if it changes anything between me and Seven. He still ensured he was out of the house this morning to avoid me. And what he said last night when he thought I was asleep could have meant anything.

Seven isn't interested. That's the takeaway at the end of the day. He's just a man with normal working equipment, and Daniel doesn't need every single detail.

The good news is that I survived my first storm without him after all these years together.

"I'm proud of you. I just wish I would have been there with you last night instead of him."

Wait, is Daniel jealous?

Of Seven?

If he saw the way that Seven acts around me, he wouldn't have a single worry.

"I know, me too."

"Just a few more weeks left, and then we can look forward to starting the family you've always wanted."

"I can't wait until you're home," I say.

"Yeah, me either."

I hear a door open and then close in the background.

"Hello? Anyone here?" I hear a female voice.

"Shit, hey, I have to go. I'll talk to you later, okay?" Daniel says quickly.

"Who's there?" I ask.

Part of me thinks it's a dangerous idea to ask. Knowing might not make things easy for me.

"It's just Courtney. You remember Courtney, don't you? She's one of the senior partners that they sent with the rest of us. We have to work on a case. The rest of the team is on their way over," he says. "I'll be right out." I hear him call out to her. "I'd better get going. Everyone's about to show up, and I need to finish getting dressed."

"Ok," I say.

"I'll call you again tomorrow, ok? And just..." he stalls for a second. "Don't let the player talk you into anything that you're uncomfortable with. You don't owe him anything just because he let you stay there. And professional athletes have a reputation of using women for..."

He stalls for a second.

"For sex?" I ask, finishing his thought.

He clears his throat.

"Yeah. I just don't want you to feel taken advantage of after. And the guy is ten years older than you and is still a bachelor. He's not looking for what you and I have. He'd never marry you and give you kids. You know?"

I'm sure he's right.

If Seven wanted to settle down, he has plenty of available women at his disposal willing to be Mrs. Wrenley.

"I know. I miss you."

"We'll talk tomorrow," he says quickly and then hands up.

I try not to read too much into it.

He's obviously on a time crunch and has people knocking on his door.

I stand up, needing a second to decompress from that conversation and to get my mind back into writing.

I head into the kitchen to make myself a cup of tea when I hear the sound of a drill coming from the living room.

All of a sudden, the room gets a lot brighter.

I see Seven on a ladder, pulling down a large piece of plywood from the window it was covering up.

I can now see the palm trees still whipping in the wind, but nothing like the night I arrived. Seven's eyes make contact with mine, and water is dripping off the bill of his hat.

It's still raining pretty steadily, but Seven doesn't look the least bit concerned. He's just out doing what needs to be done.

There's something attractive about a man who seems capable of taking care of a lot of different things. Not that Daniel is any less of a man just because he's never owned a pair of work pants and has to call the superintendent of our building for a clogged toilet.

Daniel works long hours, so why not call? That's what they're there for.

I bet Seven wouldn't call for anything. He'd just fix it himself.

They're the polar opposite, that's all.

He looks away as he climbs down the ladder with the first sheet of wood, and then he moves his ladder down to the next window.

I wait in the kitchen for him, thinking that he'll come in for lunch at any moment, but once he takes down all of the living room and kitchen plywood, he vanishes again.

After waiting an hour, I head back to my room to write.

I can't stall forever.

I need to work.... That's the whole reason I came.

And to screw a stranger, if you ask Sheridan.

I shoot off a text to Sheridan as I walk down the hall with my cup of hot tea.

Brynn: I started writing. It's coming together.

Sheridan: I have a really good feeling about this. Let's shoot for you to send me your word count at the end of the day so that we can celebrate together.

It's late by the time I hear the front door open.

I sent Sheridan my word count for the day and then made dinner, but when Seven never showed up, I left a plate in the fridge for him and a note in the infamous notebook, and I got ready for bed.

Looking over at my phone, I see that I've been asleep for over an hour before Seven finally comes in.

This feels like a confirmation that he tried to avoid me all day because the man ate like a sumo wrestler and didn't stop for lunch or even a snack.

I lay awake listening to him struggle to take off his boots in the front entry, which are probably water-logged from all the rain today, and then I hear him enter the kitchen.

He stalls for a moment, and I wonder if he's reading my note. Then I hear his footsteps and the sound of him opening the fridge door and taking out his plate.

I listen for a little while to hear what he does next, and then I doze off again before I hear him leave the kitchen.

Tomorrow is another day, and I plan to be up early before he leaves in the morning.

I still owe him an apology for the night of the storm. I'd also like to know if he's heard when the airport will open back up again so I can go home.

I think that's the best solution for both parties.

CHAPTER ELEVEN

Seven

It's the next day after spending yesterday outside in the rain and wind, trying to assess the damage on both houses.

Rita and I got lucky.

I took a morning run on the beach, running a couple of miles down both sides. Some homes didn't fare as well as ours.

Broken windows.

Clay roof shingles shattered on the ground.

Downed palm trees that didn't hold up in the gale-force winds.

Most of the homes that were left in bad shape were abandoned days before the storm hit, and no preparations were made.

On the other hand, Rita and I were prepared, and both of our homes will only need minor repairs.

Some of the stucco on both homes has areas where large items hit the siding and will need some patchwork. Since most of these are purely cosmetic, I'll hire a good contractor before I leave for Seattle to fix them while I'm gone.

The number of broken branches, palm fronds, and random debris scattered around the beaches and against our homes was significant, and cleaning up those took most of the day.

I made a large pile of organic material and another one of garbage.

I did have to take down two of my solar panels, which must have taken the big hit that I heard right before I heard Brynn in distress that night and brought her into bed with me.

That was yet another mistake.

I knew she'd be a distraction for me if I let her get too close, and her ass against my cock was definitely too close.

I moved her back to her bed as soon as I knew she was through the worst of it and the storm was starting to pass us.

Then, the moment I walked in and saw that she had made me dinner, I knew that she had a kindness about her that I haven't seen in another person in a long time.

She's beautiful and a smart, accomplished author. She's also about ten years younger than me, with her entire life in front of her. No doubt she probably wants a family. Something I've also thought I'd have by now. But then my ex happened.

Letting Brynn sleep in my bed and waking up to her in the morning would be too easy a temptation. Which is why I moved her as soon as the storm settled down last night and she was fast asleep.

I need to keep boundaries between us, and my cock pushing up against her ass cheeks all night was the reminder that we need to keep a large gap, both physically and otherwise, between us.

I meant what I whispered to myself in that bed.

Brynn is trouble, a danger to my current plans to not let another woman into my life who can set fire to everything I care about.

It's been eighteen years since anyone's been capable of doing that and I don't plan on handing anyone else the matches and gasoline again.

I head into the house after my run to take a shower and then get back to work,

I still have a lot to do to clean up the beach and a few more things to do on both houses, but I'm not in as big of a rush this morning since most of the time-sensitive repairs that could cause water damage were fixed yesterday.

The power is still out but at least the generator I bought seems to be holding up and keeping most of the important things powered.

I walk into the bathroom and open the glass shower door. Reaching inside, I turn on the shower to let the hot water start up, when I get a call.

Rita calling...

I close the shower door and let it heat up as I slide the bar on my phone over to answer.

"Morning Rita," I say.

"Good morning my hero. I heard about the other houses on the beach and that ours are in good shape because of you."

"Who did you hear that from?" I ask.

Did she drive down to take a look this morning?

"I opened up this morning to start taking breakfast customers since our generator at the restaurant is big enough to handle our daily operation needs."

She's already opening up to take customers?

It shouldn't shock me. Rita is one of those stubborn-headed individuals who probably would have kept the place open all through the storm if she didn't think it would encourage people to put themself in harm's way just to come in for dinner at Scallywag's.

"Are you sure you're ready to start back up so soon?"

It's been less than forty-eight hours since the storm came through here.

"Yes, I'm sure. People need to eat, and many didn't have a capable young man to fend off a hurricane for them. They could use a little pick-me-up today, and we're going to provide it. I'm only offering a small menu, and everything is discounted to cover the cost of ingredients."

Rita and Bart have always done stuff like this for their customers since I've known them.

They're good people who have a solid community of individuals who love them. She praises me for taking care of her home, but if it hadn't been me, one of her many regulars would have taken care of it for her.

"Well, that's very generous of you. I'm sure everyone is grateful to have a hot meal with the power still being out."

"Speaking of which..." she starts.

"Yeah? What is it?"

"Could I convince you to come down and look at the generator for me? It's acting a little fussy this morning and I just want to make sure everything runs smoothly today. I'll bribe you with whatever you want to eat."

She knows that she doesn't have to ask for a favor. Anything she needs, I'll show up for her, just like she and Bart have always showed up for me.

"You don't have to bribe me. But I also won't turn down breakfast. Is Miguel cooking this morning?" I ask of her long-time chef, who should probably be cooking at a Michelin-star restaurant in some large city but instead he likes the freedom and low pressure of Scallywag's. He and his wife Marie have lived here almost as long as Rita, and he's been the chef since Scallywag's opened.

His cooking has a lot to do with why Scallywag's is as popular as it is.

Between the company and atmosphere that Rita and Bart created, along with the food, there's never a slow time for them.

I miss the long days on my fishing boat with Bart, discussing current events, human nature, the thriller book I borrowed from his bookshelf, and, occasionally, Greek mythology.

The man knew a lot about a lot, and I could have listened to him talk about how concrete dries, in real-time, and he'd still keep me engaged and interested until the very end.

Since I lost touch with my parents after Josslin and I broke up, Bart and Rita filled in a gaping hole that I didn't know needed to be filled until I showed up on this beach with a house that needed more work than I was told and a lack of stability in my life.

They are the place I call "home" when people ask where I go after the hockey season is over for the year.

"I'm jumping in the shower now, and then I'll load up some tools and head over," I say.

"You're a doll. Bring your house guest with you. I'll feed her, too. See you soon, hun."

Bringing Brynn along is the opposite of what I'm trying to accomplish by keeping my distance until I get her on a plane and head back home.

With Brynn's tight deadline coming up, I doubt she'll agree anyway, and since she's not awake yet, I'll be gone before she gets up.

After our conversation, I take off my boxers and step under the shower spray letting the hot stream of water run over my aching muscles from all the hours I spent outside yesterday.

The smell of my body wash pulls me back to two nights ago when I inhaled the same fragrance in Brynn's hair all night long.

For a second, I'm taken back to the feeling of her against me, but I know better than to let myself go back to that night. Rubbing one out to the memory of a terrified Brynn is too fucked up, even for me.

After she leaves, I'll have to pick up a different bottle of the men's three-in-one shampoo because this one no longer smells like an ordinary body wash. Now this fragrance is attached to a memory, a memory I need to forget.

I dry off, get dressed, and then head for the kitchen to leave Brynn a note.

Right as I finish telling Brynn that I'll be gone for the day, I hear her door open.

I guess telling her in person works too.

"Good morning," she says, turning into the kitchen.

"Did you sleep well?" I ask.

"I did. And I got a lot of work done yesterday," her eyes connect with the pen in my hand and the notebook that I'm hovering over. "Did you see the note I left you about dinner?"

She made me a plate of food and left it in the fridge. It wasn't necessary for her to go out of her way. I appreciate the effort anyway and I inhaled the food.

"I did. The food was good. Thanks for doing that."

She nods.

"What are you writing?"

"I was leaving you a note to tell you that Rita needs a hand at Scallywag's. I'm going to round up my tools and head over there. I'm not sure how long I'll be gone, but you'll have the house to write alone again today."

Her eyes go wide with excitement.

"You're going out? Can I come too? I'm feeling a little claustrophobic after being stuck in this house for almost four days. I could use some fresh air."

She's right; she hasn't been out since the night she showed up at my front door days ago.

I don't blame her for wanting to get out and Rita will keep her entertained. It's not as if I won't be busy the entire time anyway.

"Sure, but I need to leave soon—"

"I'll be fast, I promise. Just let me change and brush my teeth. I'll be two minutes, tops."

The second I nod in agreement, Brynn turns around and races down the hallway as if I'm timing her.

"Bring your laptop. We might be there awhile," I yell after her.

I head out to my garage to load up my black four-door Jeep with all of the tools I might need to work on the generator and any other surprises that might come up while I'm there.

At the very least, I should check on the roof since it's also made of clay roof tiles and a few have looked a little loose to me this summer.

I don't want any of those to come loose after the storm and whack someone in the head when they're coming in or out of the restaurant.

"I'm ready!" I hear Brynn say.

I'm standing at the back of the jeep with the back gate open, loading up my toolboxes, when I look up to see Brynn.

She's in a short, yellow, flowy summer dress with brown leather strappy sandals, her short brown hair in a ponytail, and her black laptop bag over her shoulder.

She smiles at me, and my vision narrows in on the hem of her dress, swaying back and forth over her tan thighs as she walks through the garage and towards the back of the jeep.

She slips on a pair of shades as she steps up to me.

"Are you all set?" she asks, but I barely hear the words she's saying when my eyes lock onto her pink glossy lips, begging me to dip down and taste them.

I look away quickly and clear my throat.

Kissing Brynn is out of the question, because once I start, I'm not sure I'll be able to stop.

"Yeah, let's go."

I close the back of the jeep and move away from her, heading for the driver's side door.

Should I have helped her put her laptop bag in the jeep?

Sure, that would have been nice.

Could I have walked over and opened the door for her?

My dad would have expected me to do so.

But avoidance is still vital in this situation, and the longer I stay close enough to touch her, the higher the probability it is that I'll do something stupid, like run my hands up the back of her thigh to see how short that dress really is.

She lifts her laptop bag and passes it through the open window of the jeep, setting the bag on the back seat. Then she walks up to the front passenger door and opens it.

I watch as she thinks through how to navigate getting herself into my lifted jeep.

It shouldn't be cute watching Brynn's five-foot-something put effort into climbing into my Jeep, but fuck me, it is.

"Grab the "oh-shit" strap up there," I say, pointing to the nylon handle strap built into the roof of the jeep's frame. " And then step up on the running boards."

She follows my instructions quickly as if she's worried that if she doesn't hurry, I'll back out of the garage and leave her here.

The second that her ass slides into the seat, she beams proudly over at me as if this is one of her greatest accomplishments.

"Got it!" she smiles.

"I see that. Nice work," I say, trying to hold back a smirk that threatens to surface.

"I've never been in a lifted jeep before. And topless too? This is fun," she says, reaching behind her to grab the seatbelt.

The image of her more than topless in my bathroom the first night she stayed with me, flashes through my memory.

"It's nothing special. Hopefully, the weather holds up, or else it won't be much fun on the drive home in the rain."

She stretches her seatbelt across her chest while the nylon nestles between her full breasts and then secures it into the clip at her hip.

I've never been envious of nylon before.

"I don't know, as long as it's not a hurricane, that could be fun. You're popping every single one of my jeep cherries in one day, aren't you?" she snickers.

I whip a look over at her.

That comment caught me off guard.

The moment Brynn sees the look of surprise on my face at her last comment, her smile fades quickly, and her sunglass-covered face shifts forward.

I've been told that I have a resting asshole face from plenty of the guys on the team, whatever the hell that means. I can seem uninterested and put off without realizing it. Assuming I show any interest or notice of their existence at all.

But this time, she took me off guard, and for the first time in a while, I got tongue-tied, and my mind went blank.

Pop her cherry?

She has no idea how many firsts, or seconds, or thirds of hers I'd like to take. Though as a romance author, I'm curious to know how many she has left.

She must have to do "market research" with someone, right?

I've never asked her if she has a boyfriend back home. Though I think she would have brought it up by now if she had.

But considering I've been avoiding her for the last couple of days, we haven't had a lot of time to have a heart-to-heart.

And it's better this way.

I don't need to know if she has someone waiting for her to return to Seattle because nothing is going to happen between us.

Still, I don't want her thinking, I have a stick up my ass and can't take a joke, so I say the first thing that comes to mind to smooth things over.

"You should have told me. I would have been more gentle with you for your first time."

I look down, reach for the stick shift, and put the jeep in reverse to back out of the driveway.

I can feel Bryan's eyes on me now; her jaw dropped. She wasn't expecting that after my first reaction.

And then I hear the sweet sound of her laughing.

I pull out of the driveway and head down the road towards the bar.

"Radio?" I ask, reaching for the nob.

"Definitely." She grins and leans back into the passenger seat.

I turn on the radio, and of course, Rupert Holmes – Escape starts blasting through the speakers.

Brynn knows every word and belts the song out as we drive down the road, her hand hanging out the window, letting the breeze whip through her fingers like she doesn't have a care in the world.

I wish it did nothing for me.

But that would be a lie.

Being with Brynn is becoming uncomfortably... too comfortable.

CHAPTER TWELVE

Brynn

Surprisingly, the drive over to Scallywag's was enjoyable.

Whatever radio station Seven turned on played all the right tunes that spoke to my soul.

The Eagles- Hotel California

The Beach Boys – Kokomo

The Beatles – Here Comes The Sun

Being in the passenger side of a topless jeep blasting old sixties hits while we drive along the beach is the first time since I got here that I feel like I'm on vacation.

And Seven even made a joke... a dirty one.

Seven pulls up to a two-story building, and we're lucky to find a parking spot right up front since the place looks like it is booming with customers.

I look up at the stucco façade painted a lively yellow and see the large lettering spelling out Scallywag's on the side of the building with the same cartoon dog logo that was on the back of Seven's shirt days ago.

A balcony on the second story has gorgeous pink and purple potted plants with flowery vines that cascade down the balcony and the sides of the building, bringing it all to life.

It feels bright and lively.

Whoever owns this place has obviously put a lot of love and care into it. There's so much pride of ownership.

"We're here," he says, then puts the jeep in park and kills the engine.

I can already smell whatever they're cooking in the kitchen, and it smells delicious.

"It smells good already."

"The chef is impressive. You can't go wrong with anything on the menu."

Seven and I both exit the jeep, though I do it carefully so that I don't twist an ankle when I jump down.

I reach into the back, grab my laptop bag from the back seat, and then walk around to the front of the jeep.

Seven stands there with his keys in one hand and his other tucked in his pocket. He waited for me.

He didn't technically have to wait, but it was a nice gesture, considering I can never tell if he wishes I'd just vanish one day and never return.

"You said that your neighbor owns this place, right?"

"Yeah, Rita. She and her husband have owned it for nearly twenty years. He passed away a couple of years ago, but she still runs it."

My heart breaks immediately for her.

How awful.

I follow behind him on the narrow walkway that leads along the front of the building.

When we get a little closer, I see a sandwich board parked in front of the door.

WE'RE OPEN!!!
Neighborhood Breakfast
Everyone is welcome!
Kids eat for free.
If you can't pay, come in anyway.
If you have extra to spare,
consider sponsoring a meal ticket!

Just by looking at the sign, I know I'm going to like Rita.

Seven looks at me as we pass by the sign.

"Rita is sort of like everyone's favorite aunt around here. She does a lot for the community. She's offering free and discounted meals for everyone while people try to get back on their feet after the storm. We got lucky, but not everyone did."

"And you're here to make sure that any repairs Rita needs are done so that this place can run smoothly and take care of the community that you live in," I say.

It's not a question.

"Something like that," he says.

Then he reaches for the front door and opens it for me, letting me walk in first.

I'm already starting to see that Seven is a fixer.

It's how he shows he cares since verbal communication seems to be limited with him.

In a matter of seconds, I'm starting to understand him more than I have over the last few days.

Walking into the restaurant, I should have been prepared for how packed it would be since the parking lot was full.

The lobby is standing room only while people wait to be seated.

"Sev! Honey, you're here! Thank God," I hear a woman's booming southern drawl before I see her.

A small older woman in her mid-to-late seventies weaves through the crowd as they all part for her to come through.

She's no bigger than five-foot-one, but I can already tell that her personality makes up for the whole foot-and-a-quarter-size difference between these two.

I watch as Seven crouches down a little, and the woman wraps her arms around Seven's waist.

"You call, and I come running," he says with a smile, and I think my heart just erupted in my chest.

I've never seen that smile before, and I doubt very many people have, which is a shame because it's really beautiful.

"I have someone for you to meet," Seven continues.

Seven turns to me, but before he can introduce me to the woman I assume is his neighbor, Rita, she releases Seven and quickly pulls me into an embrace.

"Sev, you didn't tell me your roommate is a knockout. No wonder you wanted to keep her all to yourself."

I can feel my cheek warm into a blush and Seven stutters something as if he's going to object to what she just said. Then she cackles and puts one hand in each of ours, pulling us forward.

"Come on. Let's get you two kids fed."

I look over at Seven, and I see him bite down on his lower lip for a second. He shakes his head at the woman we're following but he keeps his attention forward and doesn't meet my eyes.

Walking Rita pull Seven through the restaurant is like watching a toddler pull the lead rope on a Budweiser Clydesdale.

And the fact that he goes along with it without complaint makes me like him all the more.

Rita leads us to a small booth that's perfectly built for a party of two but not much more.

"How about this?" she asks. "It's the only thing I have available at the moment."

Seven looks to me instead of her.

"Is this enough room for you to write?"

I nod enthusiastically.

Rita just let us cut at least forty people. Even if there wasn't enough room, I'd make it work.

"We're a little short-staffed for the crowd. I underestimated how many people need a warm meal today. I'm going to take your order now if you know what you would like so that you're not waiting for over an hour," she says.

"How about whatever Miguel wants to make us? Tell him to make whatever is easy and that takes the least amount of effort," Seven tells her.

Then his eyes shift to mine. "Is that okay?"

"I trust you," I tell him.

He looks back at Rita. "I'll get us bottled water from the back. You don't need to."

"You're a lifesaver; thanks for coming. I'll get you chips and dip," she says, about to rush off.

"Don't worry about that either. I'll take care of it. We'll be fine, just take care of your customers," Seven says, pushing out of the booth to retrieve the items he just mentioned.

She pats him on the shoulder and then scurries off to the next thing.

"Do you want chips and salsa? It might be a while before we get our food."

"Sure, if it isn't any trouble."

"No trouble. I'll be right back."

Seven walks off, weaving through the crowds of people, and I take the time to start pulling out my laptop. I glance under the table, and I'm in luck that there's a plug-in outlet under the table, and it takes my kind of plug-in.

I ordered an adapter online before I left the States just in case I'd need one but I've been lucky so far.

A few minutes later, Seven comes back with bottles of water and a basket of chips and dip.

He sets it all down on the table, but he doesn't sit down.

I grab a chip from the basket and dip it into the salsa.

"Whoa. I think that's the best salsa I've ever had. Is that Mango I taste too?"

Seven grabs a chip, dips it into the salsa, and tosses the entire chip in his mouth. He chews for a second, like he's trying to taste the mango.

"Probably. Miguel is an incredible chef. He makes everything from scratch, and he likes to change it up."

"You're not kidding," I say, going in for another chip.

"I'm going to check on the generator while we wait for our food. It might be a while before Miguel gets to our ticket, and I don't want him to lose power while he's trying to get everyone fed. Will you be ok by yourself?"

"Yep, I'm all set. I can write while I wait."

Even if I had nothing to do, I would understand. I invited myself on this excursion, and everyone but me is pitching in to help the people who still have no power... or worse.

"I'll be back in a little while. Hopefully, it's an easy fix."

Then he turns to leave, and I watch him head for the front door.

I reach down, plug in my laptop, and then set it on the table to start working.

In the last few days, I've completed several chapters, and Sheridan is really happy with my progress. However, I need to keep up my momentum if I want to finish this book by the deadline.

I push the power button on my laptop and wait for it to load. While I wait, something catches my eye. I look over to find Seven talking with one of the hostesses.

He hands her what looks like a credit card, and she nods and walks over to the cash register.

A minute later, she walks back over to him and hands him his card. He puts it back in his wallet and then walks back out of the front door.

I watch as ticket after ticket starts to print from her computer. I keep my attention on her as the printer finally finishes, and she takes a large wad of tickets and starts pinning them to the corkboard, where people who don't have money can take a ticket to pay for their meal.

The hostess probably pins up fifty tickets, and the stack doesn't seem to dwindle in the least. Since everyone inside the restaurant is busy eating or visiting, I think I'm the only one who saw it.

Seven just bought all of those meals and acted like it was no big deal.

I have to admit, with everything Seven is doing to help out, I'm feeling like his worthless counterpart.

A family of five stands up and vacates a table near me. With only four waiting staff, a single busboy, and one hostess in this restaurant, I see my opening to jump in and help.

Seven

My phone dings with an incoming text just as I finish fixing the generator and get it back up and running. It had some old gasoline and needed a new spark plug, and now it's humming along.

> **Cammy: My flight is showing online that it's still departing tomorrow. Is it still ok if I come?**

> **Seven: We don't have power right now but the generator is running and the house is still standing.**

> **Cammy: Who needs electricity any-way? Hugely overrated.**

> **Cammy: Please tell me that the boat survived.**

It figures that Cammy cares more about the boat than electricity or running water. When she comes to visit, I can barely keep her off the damn thing. She'd go out fishing on the boat everyday if I let her.

She likes the peace and quiet of being out on the ocean as much as I do. It's something that we have in common.

> Seven: The boat survived out in the bay. I'll ask them to pull the anchor and bring it back to the marina tomorrow. The water is still a little rough right now. We should give it another day before we go out.

> Cammy: Your sense of adventure is astoundingly underwhelming. Are you sure we're related?

Sarcasm... yet another thing we have in common.

> **Seven:** Looking forward to it kiddo. Let me know if your flight is delayed; otherwise, I'll be at the airport at three to pick you up.

> **Cammy:** Can't wait. See you soon!

I check the time on my phone before pushing it back into my pocket.

It's been a little over an hour since I left Brynn in the restaurant to come out and see what I could do.

I'm not a mechanic, but I learned how to do a few things growing up with a dad who owns a farm equipment sales and mechanic shop in Minnesota.

My dad is one of the handiest people I've ever met. He can fix anything, and my mom is one of the hardest working. He handled the mechanic shop while my mom managed the office and the equipment salesman on the other side of the shop.

I heard they finally sold the business to retire last year, but that's just the information I got from Cammy since I haven't talked to my dad since I came home one Christmas during my rookie year to find out that Josslin still wanted to marry a Wrenley brother... just not me.

My older brother Eli came home on an honorary discharge from the Marines after suffering from an incident overseas that caused him to almost lose a leg. His battalion lost two men that day, one of whom had been my brother's best friend since elementary school.

When my fiancé decided to make a brother swap, Eli was facing a long road of recovery and crippling PTSD, so naturally, my family rallied around him, and that was my plan, too. Right up until he decided that Josslin was part of his recovery plan.

My parents begged me to let it go.

"He needs Josslin more than you do right now," my mother pleaded.

"I'm not happy about how they handled this son, but the most important thing we can do is focus on Eli's recovery. He's lost so much already, and your life is just getting started. You'll find someone else," my dad tried to reason.

I guess I'm the asshole for not understanding how sleeping with my fiancé behind my back, in the house I bought her for our future together, was his only solution for recovery.

I left on Christmas morning, and I've never been back.

My mom calls every couple of months, though I don't take her calls except on her birthday once a year. Some habits are hard to break, and as much as I resent my family for taking my brother's side, my dad raised me with a strong sense of honoring the woman who gave me life, so she gets her token call on her birthday.

My dad, on the other hand, stopped trying after a few years of attempting to reconnect with no luck.

He texted me last year on the night that we lost the Stanley Cup game and told me that I still played a good game and that he was proud of me. It was the first correspondence in over fifteen years, and it told me something I didn't know—my dad still watches my games.

I didn't respond.

Eighteen years might seem long enough to let go of a grudge, but I believe loyalty should be matched.

I only have as much for you as you have for me.

It's part of the reason I've stayed in the NHL for so long. I could have retired years ago, but the locker room is a place that shares my outlook on loyalty. We look out for one another. And if you ever find yourself on a team where the players believe that it's every man for himself, they're usually upfront about it, or you find out quickly who you can trust and who you can't.

Walking back into the restaurant, I glance over at the table in the corner, where I expect to find Brynn typing away on her book.

I see our food has been delivered, and her laptop is up, but nothing on her plate looks touched.

Searching the restaurant and bar, I see no sign of her.

I walk over to Marie, the hostess.

"Have you seen the woman I walked in with?"

She looks up from the receipts she's adding together from the morning rush, which has died down a little.

"Oh, Brynn?" she asks with a bright smile, as if I just brought up her favorite subject.

"Yeah. She's not at our table," I say, pointing to the empty booth in the far back corner.

Marie looks around the restaurant quickly and then turns back to me.

"I bet she just took a tray of dirty dishes to the kitchen for the busboy to wash. I'm sure she'll be right back out. She moves quickly."

"What? Why would she be taking dirty dishes back?"

Marie turns back to her calculator and receipts.

"Because she's been bussing tables ever since you left so that the busboy could focus on keeping the dishwasher going. She's been a Godsend. I don't know what we would have done without her," she says, her fingers typing up receipt after receipt.

"Rita asked her to help out?"

"Oh no... you know Rita would never do that. Brynn just jumped up and started busing tables. Rita told her that she didn't need to but Brynn said that she'd rather be helpful and that she wanted to wait to eat with you anyway," Marie glances up at me quickly and then looks over her shoulder just in time to see Brynn walking briskly out of the kitchen with an empty black busing bin and a wet tablecloth in her hand. "She's a real sweetheart. I'm glad you finally found a great girl to settle down with. I was beginning to worry."

A great girl to settle down with.

Where did she come up with that?

"We're not together. She's just staying with me for a few days until Silas can get her a room."

"Really?" she asks with a lifted brow as if she doesn't believe me.

"I swear. I wouldn't lie to you."

"Well, that's disappointing, to say the least."

"Why do you care if I'm dating Brynn or not?"

"Because she's the kind of person that helps out a group of total strangers without being asked and has no motivation to do it except that she's a good person. She matches your energy perfectly. And now I can tell you're going to let her walk away, aren't you?"

"Marie... I barely know her—"

Marie cuts me off with a tsking sound.

"Figures. You big dumb man. Buy a clue with all that money you have sitting in the bank, will you?"

She turns back to her work, and I can see that the conversation is over.

Marie and I have never shared anything besides kind words with one another since the day I walked into Scallywag's years ago. She usually lets Rita, Bart, or Silas read me the riot act within the walls of this establishment.

She and Miguel usually stay neutral, so I'm surprised to see that Marie's facial expression shows that she's genuinely disappointed that Brynn and I aren't dating.

I take a second to think over everything Marie just told me. About how Brynn wanted to wait to eat with me and how she jumped in without being asked to help out since the staff wasn't expecting this kind of turnout.

I stare out towards the woman in the yellow sundress, watching her weave in and out of tables, wiping a couple down with her dish rag as she goes.

She smiles and waves at a family that just finished eating and is getting up from their table to leave.

I still don't know very much about Brynn, but the more time I spend around her, the more I'm beginning to think that she's different from anyone I've ever met.

I make a beeline for the romance author, who's pilling up dishes from the table that just left.

"I'm done. Are you ready to eat?" I ask.

She glances over her shoulder at me for a second and then back at the table.

"I still need to—"

"Yep, she's ready and all yours," Rita says, coming up from the right side of me, cutting off Brynn's words.

"Just as soon as I finish this last table," Brynn says, kneeling on the wooden bench of the booth to reach further in to grab plates.

"I've got it from here. You've done plenty, and we're finally caught up with guests. Go sit down and eat your food."

Rita isn't asking at this point.

It's now a demand.

I see Rita wave over to the busboy to help. Then she elbows her way to push Brynn to the side as the busboy and Rita start taking over.

"Go sit. That's an order," she tells Brynn. "Do you want me to ask Miguel to remake your food? It's probably cold by now."

"Oh no... he just finally got caught up in the back and needs to take his break," Brynn says quickly. "We're fine, right?" she asks, looking up at me.

I stare down at Brynn's beautiful blue eyes, practically pleading with me not to send the food back so that Miguel can have a break. I hadn't considered sending the food back anyway, but Brynn's concern for Miguel doesn't go unnoticed by me.

"We'll be fine. Thanks, though," I confirm to Rita.

Brynn smiles up at me and then turns around and heads for our table. I follow, trying not to watch the way the hem of her mini-dress swishes high against her thighs.

She scoots in on her side, and then I do on the other side.

"Are we going to stay for the lunch rush?" she asks.

"There's a lot of repairs I can do if you want to stay."

"Can we? I think they could really use me."

And that's the moment that confirms it.

Brynn isn't like anyone I've ever met before.

Now the question is... what am I going to do with that information?

CHAPTER THIRTEEN

Brynn

"How did the generator repair go? I've noticed that the lights are flickering a lot less since you came in," I say.

"It didn't need too much. Just had some old gas that I had to change out and it needed a new spark plug. It seems to be running smoother now. I should have checked on it before the storm, but we didn't know that the storm was going to come this close until a couple of days before."

Of course, he'd blame himself for not going the extra mile. That seems to be on brand for him the more I get to know him.

"You said that you have more to do while we're here?"

"There are not enough hours in the day to get to everything I'd like to work on, but I want to check the clay roof shingles before they fall off and hurt someone, and I want to check out the balcony in the upstairs apartment. I don't know when the last time that someone checked to see if any of the wood was rotting. Bart and Rita haven't used that apartment in years, and since Rita is staying up there right now, I should take a look."

The way that Seven thinks about Rita's safety and the way that she makes sure that he's fed and smiling warms my heart. He mentioned that they have a special bond, and now I'm seeing the true evidence of it from both sides.

"Take your time. I'm in no rush. I can always write if I have downtime."

"I have a question..." Seven asks.

"Go for it," I say, skewering a piece of avocado and egg from my plate and then take a bite.

It looks like Miguel made us an elevated version of Huevos Rancheros. Not exactly a fast and easy dish that Seven requested to make our meal easier on the kitchen staff.

Each egg is served on crostini-like bread with fresh avocado, beans, the same mango salsa, and other veggies. The second the ingredients touched my tongue; I knew that Seven wasn't exaggerating Miguel's talents. His food is delicious.

"How does someone become an author who writes regency and billionaire romance books and does it full time?"

Seven takes a bite of his own food as he waits for my answer.

I smirk at the question.

When people find out what I do, it's a common curiosity.

Not only because becoming a full-time author doesn't seem like an occupation that you just fall into. Most people think that most authors go to college and get a literary degree before setting out to write their first novel, but since my degree is in Administration Management, it confuses a lot of people.

"I entered into a competition on a whim, actually. Applicants could submit a short story for any sub-genre within romance and I picked historical romance. The editor at the publishing house loved mine over the others that she had read. The winning submission came with a publishing deal for the book, but then they asked me to create a full series, and the rest is history."

"Really? You just sent in a submission that you wrote for that specific contest? Had you already been shopping it around to publishing houses before?" he asks.

"No. I just wrote ten thousand words over a short few days and then sent it in. It was surprisingly easier than I thought to write. It just flowed through me. Still, I didn't think I even had the slightest shot."

I take another bite of food in between the questions.

"I'm impressed," he says, his eyebrows lifting up to his hairline.

This is the most engaged that Seven has ever been in a conversation with me, and I'm enjoying his undivided attention.

Not to mention that he just told me that he's impressed by my author's origin story. For someone like Seven, who doesn't seem to be impressed by much, I'm honored to have him bestow any praise my way.

"So you're smart," he says.

It's not exactly a question but I don't see myself like that.

"I wouldn't say that."

"Okay, then you're creative and imaginative, and smart."

I try to keep the blush at bay. Compliments aren't easy for me to accept and especially not for being an author. Imposter syndrome is real... even five years after being a successful author.

When I don't say anything, he speaks again.

"It's a compliment. You're allowed to accept those."

I give a little chuckle. "I know. Thank you. It's just that my dad isn't exactly on board with it."

I quickly realize how that sounds, and I try to back down my comment. "I mean, he supports me. He sends me flowers whenever my new release comes out. It's just that he thinks this is all a phase."

And that I'm lucky to have Daniel for so that he can support me when it inevitably fizzles out. I can't even imagine how my father would panic if I came clean and told my parents that Daniel and I are on a break right now.

"A phase?" he asks. "I'm not trying to pry, but I'm going to assume that if your agent bank-rolled your beach house vacation for two weeks, she must make a good amount of money off your books. I make my agent millions, and I don't get so much as a Christmas card from the guy. You got a whole vacation."

I snicker at the thought of the big, bad hockey goalie getting bent out of shape for not receiving a Christmas card.

Could it be that Seven Wrenley has a soft side?

"You'd think that the fact that I can afford a skyrise apartment in downtown Seattle, only a couple blocks from the Hockey stadium, that he sees I'm not exactly slumming it," I say

Seven stops chewing for a second.

"You don't live in The Commons, do you?" he asks.

I've heard that most of the Hawkeyes players live in The Commons but I wasn't sure if he did.

"No, I live in the apartment next door. Seventh floor."

He takes another bite and mulls over the information I just dropped.

"Does your window face the commons?" he asks.

"Yes, actually, it does."

"Then I bet you can see directly into my apartment from yours."

"Are you serious? Are you on the seventh floor, too?"

He nods.

A little zip of excitement at the idea of getting home and testing it out comes out of nowhere.

What will it matter?

He'll just be looking in on me writing in the window, and if he's up late enough, he'll see Daniel coming home.

Daniel.

Right, of course.

In three weeks, Daniel will be back and living together in our shared apartment.

"Sev," I hear Rita's voice break through my moment of reality. "Miguel says that the fridge is acting up. Any chance you can take a look at it before you go back outside?"

Seven can fix fridges, too?

"Sure, I'll look at it now," he says, putting his fork down on his empty plate.

He looks back at me.

"I'll see you later?"

I nod with a bite of food still in my mouth.

"Have a good lunch rush," he says with a grin and then scoots out of the booth.

I start to dig back into my food when a call comes through.

Fiancé calling...

I pick it up and slide to answer.

It has to be getting late there.

Maybe midnight?

"Hi," I say.

"Hey, I called around during every break I had today to get you out of Wrenley's house with no luck. There's nothing available right now. I called the airline, and they resumed operations starting this afternoon, but I couldn't get you a flight out any earlier than your original departure. They said everything is booked solid for the stranded passengers."

His voice seems to echo like he's in a bathroom and... is he whispering?

"Are you okay? Are you in a tunnel or something?"

"No, I'm just sitting in the bathroom."

In the eight years that Daniel and I have been together, I've never received a phone call from him while he's in the bathroom.

He's always told me that it's an odd place to start a conversation.

He used to say that if the conversation isn't important enough to warrant a certain amount of decorum, then it's not important enough to make.

"Why are you sitting in the bathroom, and why are you whispering?" I ask.

There's a short pause for a second on his end.

"I'm... I'm not whispering. It's just late. I don't want to wake the neighbors. The walls are thin in this apartment."

I don't know why but something just isn't sitting right.

"Is someone else there?"

I swore to myself that I would never ask this question, because God knows I don't really want to hear the answer, but there's a nagging feeling in me that says I should know before he and I get back together.

"What do you mean by "someone else"?"

He doesn't want me to clarify the question; he's just trying not to answer it.

I know he's been seeing other people, and he's allowed, but with how badly he wants me out of Seven's house, I need to know if he's currently sleeping with anyone.

"Daniel, do you have a woman in your bed right now?"

Even hearing the words come out of my mouth makes my stomach a little queasy.

Again, there's another small pause.

"Would it matter if I did? It's not against the rules."

I know we agreed to date other people, but his refusal to admit it makes this feel more like infidelity than it should.

If he didn't feel guilty about it, then he wouldn't feel the need to hide it.

He's allowed to sleep with other people and so am I.

"No, it's not against the rules. I agreed to sleep with other people. Thank you for calling around but I think I'll stay where I am for now. Seven and I are just starting to get along, and I feel safe with him since the power is still out all around the area."

"Are you sleeping with him?"

There's almost an accusatory sound in his voice as if me sleeping with Seven would be wrong.

"Would it matter if I did?" I ask, throwing the same question back at him.

"He's just going to use you, Brynn. You're beautiful and vulnerable. Assholes like him prey on women like you."

"Women like me? Maybe I'm using him too? Have you considered that?"

"Brynn, I'm just worried about you. I don't want you thinking that something more is going to happen with him and you give up what's real between us."

"I have to write. I'll talk to you later."

I hang up before he can respond.

I can't believe he thinks he can demand an answer from me when he won't be honest about whether or not he has a woman staying over right now. Even so, I don't like the feeling of hanging up on Daniel. With so little communication between us over the last seven months, I hate that this is how the conversation ends. But whatever jealousy he's dealing with right now isn't fair.

No matter what squabbles we've gotten in over the years, I've never hung up on him once. We usually are good about talking through our issues even if we don't see eye to eye. But this... this is too much.

Maybe Sheridan is right.

Maybe I need to dip my toe in a new ocean, just like Daniel.

Here we are, three weeks from getting back together, and he's still actively sleeping around.

Though it sounds so juvenile, maybe I need to even the score so that Daniel and I can move on from this and start fresh when we get home.

Can I live the rest of my life with Daniel, knowing that he took full advantage of the break and I didn't?

I'm just not sure anymore. Especially since he just acted as if there is a double standard to the "sleeping with other people" rule.

Daniel tries to call me back, but I send it to voicemail, and then a text pops through.

> Fiancé: I can't believe you just hung up on me. You never hang up on me.

I don't like the way that things are changing between Daniel and me, but until we're both back in the same city, what can be done to salvage this right now?

I pull my laptop over and start writing to distract myself. I can't fix things between us right now, but I can finish this book so that I can focus on us when I get home.

After taking a look at the fridge in the kitchen, Seven went back outside.

The restaurant stayed busy the entire time and I tried to get up and help but Rita told me that if I really wanted to be helpful that I would save my energy for the lunch rush.

Luckily, between the time Seven left and when the lunch rush started, I was able to get in almost two hours of writing, and

I'm glad I did because Rita wasn't kidding. The lunch rush was almost double the number of people as the breakfast rush.

Word was starting to spread that Scallywag's is open for business, and since many people are still complaining about not having power, they know they can get a hot meal here at Rita's place.

Marie kept putting up the receipts from the pile that Seven had purchased, along with receipts from other contributors, and it still felt like Seven's stack wasn't decreasing in the least. How many meals did he sponsor?

Another break between lunch and dinner came, and I was able to get even more writing done.

I contribute the increased word count to the adrenaline, and running around during the rushes helps me think clearer between breaks.

It makes sense since taking walks out around the apartment building when I've had writer's block in the past usually works.

Well, up until this book when it seemed that no amount of walks around the block would help. I'll admit that being here is inspiring me to write again.

Sheridan was right.

I just needed a few days and some new perspective to get my groove back.

We were a couple of hours into the dinner rush, with the sun setting outside of the large windows of the bar when I saw Seven finally walk back into the restaurant. I didn't realize that I'd been checking regularly for the door, waiting for the moment when he'd eventually walk back in.

Marie took him lunch outside, so I hadn't seen him in hours, and I couldn't help but feel giddy when I saw him walk in just now.

Eating breakfast together was quick. Not only does Seven eat three times the amount that I do, but he also does it in half the time it takes me to eat mine.

Our conversation, although short, was eye-opening to a different side of Seven that I hadn't seen before.

"Excuse me?" I hear a voice behind me ask.

It breaks my attention on Seven just as his eyes meet mine.

I turn to look behind me at the large U-shaped booth and the five top full of guys, probably around my age, sitting there. They look like the quintessential group of guys coming to Cancun for a bachelor party, though they're a distance from the resorts.

Who knows? Maybe they got stranded like I did and had to find somewhere else to book a spot when they got here.

"Yes? Can I get you something?" I ask, stepping up to their table with a smile and setting my hand on the table.

Since my Spanish is limited, I haven't been able to communicate as effectively as I would have liked with other patrons today, so I'm excited when I see my opportunity to grab these guys' chips or guacamole without having to ask one of the servers to do it.

"I sure hope you can," says the guy sitting at the booth to the left.

All five of them smile at me while one snickers uncontrollably like he's been overserved somewhere else.

Actually, they all look a little glassy-eyed, as if they've been indulging all day.

"What can I get you?" I ask.

The guy who got my attention lays his hand over mine. I don't want to pull away immediately and cause a scene.

Some people get overly affectionate when they drink, and as long as this is as bad as it gets, I'll be on my way soon enough with their order.

"My buddy over there is getting married next week, and he thinks you're cute."

Oh no.

"Excuse me?" I ask.

I hope he's not insinuating what I think he is.

I look over at the supposed groom, who's laughing.

"He's kidding... he's drunk. Marcus, let her go," the groom says with a chuckle.

"Come on, baby, it's his last week of freedom, and I swear he'll give you a good time. Just come back to our rental house with us," Marcus says.

I don't want to make a scene in Rita's restaurant, so I try to be as professional as possible about the situation, though I'm cringing on the inside and want to get away from them as soon as possible.

"I'm not interested. I'll go find your server for you," I say, attempting to pull my hand back, but Marcus grips a little tighter and doesn't let go.

"Are you really going to let this guy get married to the troll of a girlfriend he's got without letting him have one last pretty girl?"

Umm ick.

I can't tell if his attempt was to flatter me into agreeing by calling me a pretty girl or if he was going the guilt trip route, but either way, neither landed successfully.

The groom is definitely drunk as well and smiles at me, "Ignore Marcus. He's had too much to drink. And my fiancé isn't a troll," he tells me and then stares over at Marcus. "...she's your sister, remember that? Let her go, Marcus."

"Yeah, Marcus. Let her go."

I hear Seven's deep voice behind me, and then I feel his chest press against my left shoulder like he's about to take one step forward and put a six-foot-five wall between me and Marcus.

"Whoa, whoa, he didn't mean anything by it. He's just drunk and having a little fun," one of the other friends finally pipes up.

"Yeah, he's just being an idiot. We don't want any trouble," the groom pleads.

I look around at the other four guys, who are all looking at Seven like they're all about to get their asses kicked. There's a little tinge of fear in each of their eyes... all of them except Marcus's.

"She's a grown woman who can make her own decisions," Marcus says.

I pull my hand back again, and Marcus releases it this time, but he doesn't take his glare off of Seven.

He squares his chest towards Seven like he isn't scared, but there's still uncertainty in his eyes about whether he can take Seven on and win.

...he couldn't.

I've seen Seven in a fight on the ice once or twice on TV. If Marcus would like to skip a visit to the ER tonight, he'd better back off.

"She said she wasn't interested, but you wouldn't let her go. So now I'm going to let you and your friends off with a warning since there are kids currently in this restaurant, and I don't want them to witness your blood splattered all over the floor," Seven says. "You and your friends are going to stand up and leave right now and swear that you'll never come back here again. Do you understand?"

"We understand, thank you. We're leaving now," the groom says as he pushes the guy sitting in front of him, blocking his exit out of the booth.

Marcus doesn't move an inch. He just stares Seven down.

"Do you have some kind of claim on her?" Marcus asks.

Seven takes a step closer, blocking Marcus's view of me.

"I'll tell you this. If I see you in here again laying a hand on any one of the female wait staff here, I'll make sure you no longer have hands to jack off alone in your mom's basement. Do I make myself clear?"

I swallow hard, hoping this time Marcus takes him seriously and leaves before he gets hurt.

I don't really care about Marcus's well-being, but I don't want to see Seven get in a fight over me, even if he would level the idiot with one blow.

"We got it. We won't come back," one of them says.

Marcus's friends swoop in front of Seven, risking life and limb to get their friend out of there. I watch as two of them manhandle Marcus off the booth seat and pull him toward the front of the entry.

Clapping erupts as soon as the five drunk idiots pass Marie's hostess desk.

Seven turns around and looks at me as if we're the only two in the restaurant. As if he doesn't care that a packed restaurant of people just witnessed him threaten bodily harm to anyone who brings any unwelcome attention to the women who work here.

He reaches out, gripping my hand, which is down by my side. My belly flutters the moment our fingers touch. His grip is gentle but firm as he guides me to follow behind him. I could let go, and I know he wouldn't force me to follow him, but I don't want to let go, and I don't want him to let go, either.

He makes a beeline for the booth, where I already have my laptop bag packed since I figured we would leave after the dinner rush.

"Seven, where are we going?" I ask.

I'm not interested in protesting whatever he has planned; I just wish he would share his plans with me.

He reaches into the booth and grabs my laptop bag, slinging it over his shoulder.

"I finished everything. Now it's time to go."

"It's time to go? It's the dinner rush, and there's a line out the door," I say.

Rita comes running out of the kitchen with Marie on her heels.

Marie must have just informed her of what transpired out here in the restaurant while she was waiting for an order to finish.

"Seven, what happened?" she asks him, following behind us.

Seven turns from the booth and heads for the restaurant's entry.

"It was nothing, I swear. Just some drunk guys. They left," I say over my shoulder to Rita before Seven can make a big deal out of it.

"But not before one of the guys grabbed Brynn," Marie chimes in, following behind Rita.

"Oh my God! What?" Rita says.

I hear Seven growl something to himself in response to Marie's event breakdown.

"It wasn't that bad. I promise," I try to tell Rita. "Tell her it was fine, Seven."

"I'm taking her home," he says back.

He weaves us through the long line of guests standing inside and outside of the door, waiting for their turn to get seated for dinner.

"I'm sorry I can't help with the rush. I guess we're leaving," I say before we take a sharp turn out of the door, and we lose them in the crowd.

Now it's just Seven and I walking down the narrow walkway the same way we came in.

We parked at the end, and in the darkness, as Seven leads us further away from the entry, it's beginning to feel like we're the only two out here.

"I don't understand why we're leaving. Nothing happened. He didn't hurt me, and Rita needs the help."

"I shouldn't have brought you out here," he mumbles.

He regrets bringing me now?

"Why? What did I do?"

"Nothing. You didn't do anything. That asshole did."

"Then why does it feel like I'm the one you're upset with?"

"I'm not upset," he says.

But his long, heated steps that I'm trying to keep up with say something different.

"Really? Because you just passed the jeep about five cars back," I tell him.

He stops immediately without warning and I just about run into the back of him.

He turns around and looks down at the row of cars and then back at me when he sees that I'm right.

"Seven," I say again. "What if I want to stay and help? What if I don't want to go home yet?"

"Is that what you want? Do you want to stay here? I won't force you to come with me, Brynn. Miguel and Marie have to drive by my house on their way home," he says, releasing my hand. "They'll give you a ride whenever you want if you'd rather stay."

Is he really going to agree to leave me here?

What just happened in there?

It was one drunk idiot and his stupid friends, and it's not like it's the first time a group of guys have said inappropriate things. However, I will say that asking me to help his future brother-in-law cheat on his sister is a new low.

Still, how is he so worked up over this? He stepped in before anything got out of hand and I haven't even thanked him for that yet.

"No, I want to go wherever you're going," I say. "I just don't understand what happened in there that made you want to leave so quickly."

He takes a step closer, and his hands lift to my face and then his thumb soothes over my jaw.

I look up into his eyes, searching for some kind of explanation. He's never touched me like this before.

"Because I'm losing my ability to keep away from you. Something I've never had a problem doing before with other women."

I swallow hard at his admission. When did he start feeling this way? I thought he could barely put up with me.

"I can't tell which is worse. Walking into the restaurant to find someone else touching you and feeling jealous for the first time in over a decade. Or seeing him grip you tighter when you tried to pull away, feeling the last thread of my sanity start to unravel as I fought the urge to knock his head clean off.

"You held back because of the kids in the restaurant." I remind him.

It's the reason he gave Marcus.

I reach up and grip around his wrist, willing him to stay right where he is. I want him this close, and if I'm being honest with myself for once, I want him even closer.

His fingers slide behind the back of my neck as he takes another step closer and then he pulls my laptop bag off his shoulder and sets it on the ground.

"No, I didn't hold back because of the kids, even though it's a good excuse. I held back because if I had sent him to the ER, I'd be in the back of a police car right now and I wouldn't be able to do this."

"Do what?" I ask.

Seven dips down and pulls me forward, planting his lips against mine.

A shock wave zings through my belly at the feeling of Seven's warm lips against mine.

His other hand wraps around my waist and pulls me even closer against him.

I slide my arms around the back of his neck, moaning into his mouth as I open for him, letting his tongue enter and glide against mine.

He releases the back of my neck as his hands drift down the sides of my body, just as he did that night when he held me in the storm. Only this time, his hands have a different purpose.

He grips my ass with both hands, pulling a whimper from my lips as he pulls me tight to his body.

"I could have killed the guy for touching you," he says.

"You're the only one touching me now."

He starts to move us, backing me up against the wall of the restaurant. The moment my back hits the stucco, Seven squeezes my ass and lifts me up. My legs wrap around his waist while the hem of my dress rides up so that when Seven presses against me, it's only my thin pair of panties between me and his canvas-covered zipper.

The large bulge in his pants presses his zipper flap perfectly against my clit as he grinds into me into the wall.

The little scrapes from the Stucco against my back should be uncomfortable, but they only add to Seven's aggressive thrusting against me.

I hear him groan against my mouth. He wants this as badly as I do, and I don't think that anyone, including Daniel, has ever wanted me as badly as Seven is showing me right now.

I need to know what it feels like to be with Seven.

I need to know what being taken so possessively against a building out in the open feels like.

I've never done anything this risky before. Daniel would never have agreed to do something like this, but with Seven, it feels so natural, and I've never felt so safe in this moment before, even though anyone could walk by and see us.

The way Seven shields my body with his, I know he'd protect me if we got that far. And by the way he's rocking into me and his hard erection, I don't see how this doesn't end without him inside of me.

The anxiety of not getting off and Seven thinking I'm broken scare me. Or worse, that because I don't get off from penetration, his ego will be hurt like Daniel's and then things between Seven and I will become awkward after tonight.

"Fuck, Brynn, I could reach down right now and get you off. Those thin little panties don't stand a chance," he says. "What am I allowed to do to you?"

I told myself that I wouldn't let fear stand in my way anymore. And maybe Sheridan is right and this is the chance I'm given to try with someone else.

"Yes," I say.

Seven reaches between us, his thick knuckles gliding over my inner thigh as he reaches down between my legs.

I feel the moment he pushes my cotton thong out of the way and then gently coats his fingers in the arousal he created.

The moment I feel the pads of his fingers push against my center; I sigh into our kiss.

"Jesus Christ, you're dripping wet," he says. "How long have you wanted this?"

I'm too embarrassed to admit that I've noticed Seven's perfect body since the moment he opened the front door.

"Since you broke into the shower to save me," I tell him, thinking about the scene I wrote between the lunch rush. It's the alternate version of how I would have seen that moment going if things between him and I had been different. I never thought this moment would happen, so I gave that fantasy to Colston and Leanne instead.

"Me too," he says. "I was hard all fucking night for you. That's why I left. But I'm not leaving this time," he says.

His admission has more hot heat coating his fingers as he works two fingers in and out of me.

I hold on tighter around his neck as my body begins to tingle in a way I haven't without a vibrator.

Oh God, is he doing what I think he's doing?

If I come on Seven's fingers, what will that mean for Daniel and me?

I'm scared to find out but more scared not to chase this orgasm and know if this is real.

"Keep going," I beg.

My thighs begin to squeeze against his wrist as I can feel my body getting closer and closer.

Everything Seven does is right. Every movement, every touch he gives me only increases the pleasure.

"Seven," I whimper.

He adjusts his hand, and his thumb presses against my clit. Now my body is starting to pulsate, and there's no hope of stopping it now.

Seven takes my bottom lips and bites down and then I come on his hand.

Whimpering out in ecstasy at the first man-made orgasm I've had in over eight years. It's better than any of the silicone, vibrating ones I've had.

Seven eases his fingers out of me slowly and then pulls his hand up to his mouth and sucks me off my fingers.

"You taste as good as I thought you would."

I bite down on my lip to keep from squeaking out a response.

Daniel isn't a selfish lover, but he's never reveled in the way I taste, and since I don't get off from oral either, he stopped offering.

But just because I don't orgasm from it doesn't mean it doesn't feel good.

Seven wraps his arms around me to hold me against him, giving me time to come down from euphoria.

"Are you okay?" he asks.

"Yes," I tell him.

But the truth is, I'm not sure if I'm ok.

What I do know is that I'm not done exploring my lost and found orgasms.

Are they because I finally faced my fears and am now, I'm cured? Or is it because Seven is the only man capable of giving them to me?

Seven leans in and kisses me tenderly one last time, and then I hear someone shout, "Get a room."

I jump and look around, hoping that whoever just said that only saw our kiss. But if they saw more, it was worth it.

"What do you say?" Seven asks. "Should we get a room?"

I need more than one time to see if Seven has skills or if this all was a fluke.

"Yeah, let's go," I say.

He sets me back on the ground, leans down, grabs the laptop bag lying by our feet, and then leads me by the hand back to the Jeep.

This time, he opens my door and grips my hips, lifting me into the passenger side as if I weigh nothing.

I turn to him, expecting him to close the door, but instead, he leans in and kisses me again.

Who is this version of Seven, and where has he been?

CHAPTER FOURTEEN

Seven

Watching Brynn fall apart in my arms has me fucking addicted.

I called it.

I knew the moment that I let her into my house that she'd be trouble for me. Now I just need to see how badly I'm fucked.

Will this last for the rest of the time she's here?

Do we go our separate ways once we both head back to Seattle?

Jesus, I have no idea.

For right now, I'm only planning on tonight until morning light when I can figure out what the hell is happening to me.

I pull out of the parking spot and get back on the road, headed for my house.

I don't know what possesses me to do it, but I reach for her hand and slide my fingers between hers, pulling the back of her hand up to my lips to kiss her skin again.

She smiles over at me, and it dawns on me that I might be willing to do a hell of a lot to keep that smile on her face.

I rest our hands on the middle console, but I wish now that it was a bench seat so that she could be closer.

"Did you like Rita?" I ask in order to keep from asking the question I really want to know.

Like, how many positions am I allowed to fuck her in tonight?

"Everyone was so nice. I really enjoyed helping out today. Thank you for letting me tag along," she says and then reaches into her bag and pulls out her cell phone to check the time.

Tag along?

I just finger fucked her against the restaurant wall and got my first taste of the woman I haven't stopped thinking about since she showed up four days ago. I should be the one thanking her. Not to mention the fact that she helped out my friends in a big way today.

"You're welcome to come with me any time, though you probably should finish that book."

I glance over to find Brynn staring at me.

"What?" I ask.

"There's only one thing I want to finish," she says, setting her phone in one of the cup holders.

I look back and forth between the road and Brynn as she unbuckles her seat belt and lifts her knees onto her seat, and bends over the console. Seeing Brynn bent over in my jeep facing me with the top of her dress gaping open wide enough that I can see down her dress at the thin bra hugging her perfect breasts has my cock painfully hard.

"And what's that?" I ask.

She licks her lips, and I'm fucking gone.

"You."

She releases my hand and then reaches over, her hand slowly gliding over my right thigh as she watches my facial expression.

Is she trying to gauge how far I'll let her go? Because she's welcome to touch any part of me that she wants.

Her eyes lock onto the bulge that I can't hide and then her fingers glide over the top.

I groan as my head hits the back of the headrest.

I keep my eyes on the road to keep us from wrecking, but I can feel everything she's doing.

Her hands begin to rub up and down my shaft through my pants, and I debate, pulling over because if she keeps this up, I'm going to come in my pants before we even make it the last ten minutes we have of this drive.

That would be unacceptable.

I can't let her get the wrong impression that I can't last because I have no plans of stopping with her tonight until I'm sure that she'll be too tired to walk tomorrow.

"You should stop," I tell her. And it might be the most painful words I've ever uttered. "Unless you want me to pull this car over and fuck you in the back seat of this Jeep."

"Oh... that would be another popped cherry, wouldn't it?" she teases.

My eyes flutter closed and a groan rumbles through my throat. I take a second to regain my self-control from yanking this vehicle off onto the shoulder.

"I'm serious Brynn. If you don't stop, you'll leave me no choice, and I'd rather make it home so that I don't have to be separated from you all night."

Her hand comes off my canvas-covered cock slowly.

I look over to see her reaction, hoping she didn't misunderstand what I mean.

I don't want her to stop, I *need* her to stop if I want any chance of making it back to the house with our clothes still intact.

I can see a sparkle in her eyes when I glance her way. She took it how I meant it.

"All night? That's quite a while. Can you even last that long?" she asks, sitting back down in the passenger seat and reaching for her seat belt to secure it back in place.

I whip a look over at her with an eyebrow lifted.

Did she just put my capabilities into question?

When she sees the look of surprise on my face, she throws her head back against the headrests and laughs.

The sound of her laugh clears away the expression on my face and replaces it with a smirk because this side of Brynn has to be my favorite so far.

Brynn is smart, beautiful, and giving. But this flirtatious, teasing side of her is the one I want to see every day that we're together until the trip ends.

She's comfortable with me for once, and unguarded. The tension between us seems to have dethawed since we got back into the jeep, heading back to my house to take care of something that has been building between us for days.

Something we both want.

"I'm sorry..." she says, squeezing my hand with a genuine smile. "I didn't mean to call your manhood into question. It's just that... all night...?"

"Have you ever watched me play an entire hockey game, Brynn?" I ask.

"No," she says, biting her plump lower lip softly.

I pull down my driveway, heading for the garage.

"Then coaxing me on without seeing my stamina on the ice was your first mistake. My endurance carries over from the ice into everything I do. If you were hoping for a quickie, you'll be sorely disappointed."

I glance over at her to see a glint in her eye.

"How *sorely* are we talking?" she asks.

"Sore enough that the ice packs in the freezer are finally going to be put to good use in the morning."

I pull into the garage and notice that the overhead lights are on.

We finally have power back, not that we'll need it tonight. Nothing could keep me from finding her, even in the pitch dark.

I'd follow her scent.

Honeysuckle and citrus... and a little bit of me.

Despite the ten other products she has in the shower, she's still been using my body wash, and I hope she doesn't stop. Every time she walks past me and I catch the scent of Blue Arctic Glacier, she smells like mine.

I kill the engine and then quickly open my door.

"Hold on," I tell her. "You've been on your feet all day. I'll help you down."

I walk around the front of the jeep and head straight for her door.

"Are you always this chivalrous before sex?" she asks.

I open her side of the jeep and reach down by her feet to grab her laptop bag, tossing it over my shoulder.

And then I take her hand in mine to pull her out of the jeep and over my shoulder to carry her in like a caveman.

"Is this what you had in mind?"

She giggles behind me as I make my way quickly into the house.

Little does she know, I don't have a shred left of decency or chivalry in my body for her. I have no more self-control when it comes to Brynn.

I hope she likes it hard and rough because I don't plan on being gentle.

Brynn

It only takes us a few minutes of rushed hands and Seven's long strides to get us from the jeep to his bedroom.

As soon as we enter his room, his mouth is on mine. Every kiss he presses to my lips is tender but anxious, and I know the feeling.

Even the first time with Daniel wasn't this exciting. I don't remember being with anyone and feeling this much rush and excitement like I do with Seven. Something about the way he's looking at me now and how easy it was to drive him crazy in the car with my touch makes my heart pound rapidly. Having this effect on a man like Seven, stoic and strong. Who's practically stormproof and dauntless, like a lighthouse out at sea with its beckoning light and safe harbor.

To be the woman to claim his attention and have him fighting with himself to keep the jeep on the road makes me feel empowered and beautiful. Something I haven't felt in a long time, if ever.

How does he make me feel more irresistible and wanted than anyone has ever made me feel in my life with only one look?

He backs us up with his lips on my mouth and my arms around his neck.

When my legs hit the bed, he pulls his lips off of mine and I reach up for the spaghetti straps of my dress, pulling them down, one at a time. He watches as I drop my yellow dress down to the floor; my dress pooling around my feet with only a small bralette and thong covering the rest of me.

Then I watch as he pulls off his shirt and pushes down his pants. His cocks strains against his boxer briefs and within seconds, Seven discards those too until he's completely naked in front of me.

Everything about Seven is perfectly to scale with his six-foot five stature. He's big everywhere and the thought of taking him is a little daunting but also thrilling. After what he did to me in the parking lot of the restaurant, I need to know what else he's capable of doing to me.

I reach for my bralette and then my panties, pulling them both off for him.

He takes one long look and then I hear a deep growl humble through his chest right before he wraps his arms around me and tosses us onto the bed.

I giggle as Seven pulls me up on top of him until I'm sitting bare on his stomach.

"Come here," he says, gripping my hips and pulling me up his body. "I want to taste you."

My hands immediately flatten against his chest to stop my progression up his body.

"Wait, you want me to..."

"Sit on my face."

"Hold on... are you sure that's safe?"

He chuckles. "What do you mean safe?"

"I mean, what if I'm too heavy? What if you suffocate under me."

His grin widens, and not only am I turned on by how special Seven makes me feel when he smiles at me, but I feel a little silly for asking the question.

I've had oral sex with boyfriends in the past. I'm not a prude. I'm just used to being on my back for this or at least a sixty-nine situation. And even that's been so long ago now that Daniel no longer sees the point in giving me oral since I don't get off from it anyway.

"Good thing that's exactly the way I want to go out," he says and then attempts to pull me up higher once more.

I push against his chest as his hands tug on my hips.

"But..."

"Brynn, you're not going to suffocate me. I could bench press you in my sleep. If you want me to, I'll prove it."

I yip as his fingers grip tighter around my hips as if he's about to lift me right off his body, and I know he could.

The feeling of being in Seven's capable hands has more of my arousal pooling against his chest.

"You want this as much as I do. And you're doing a terrible job of trying to hide it. And I give you my word that you're not going to hurt me."

"You promise?"

He pulls my hands off his chest and then brings them up to his lips and kisses both of my palms.

"I promise. But if I were given an option of ways to die, suffocating under your pussy would be my number one choice."

I let out a chuckle as he smiles back at me.

"Just swear to me that if I do, you'll make sure that they put the cause of death on my tombstone. And as my last dying wish, make sure that you tell anyone who will listen... that you came first."

I shake my head at him but I can't stop the blush from warming my cheeks.

"You have my word, though I'm not so sure I'm worth dying for."

His eyes lock on mine and then he releases my hands as he grips my hips again.

"That's where you're wrong. You're the only one worth suffocating under."

It's so oddly sweet that I bend down and press my lips to his.

He releases one hand from my hips and wraps his fingers around the back of my neck, pulling me closer.

The moment I pull back from our kiss, Seven pulls me up the rest of the way until I'm straddling his face.

His hands grip around my ass cheeks as he pulls my pelvis against his mouth.

His tongue flattens against my pussy lips and parts them as he devours me, lapping up every drop of arousal as if it's feeding him. His tongue, nose, and face burrow into me, lighting up every nerve ending and making my clit pulsate and my body shutter.

I've never been eaten like this. Not as if both of our lives depend on it. He's not holding back as if he's only doing this as a sexual favor. He's devouring every inch of me like he does his breakfast.

He groans against me in approval as I roll my hips forward, his lips suctioning tighter around my clit.

"Seven..." I moan out.

I reach down, sliding my fingers through his hair. Not that I need to hold on to stay in place. Even if I had a pry bar, I couldn't wiggle out of Seven's hold.

He has no intentions of letting me go until he's had his fill, and I've never wanted to be held at someone's mercy more than his.

The tip of his tongue starts to swirl around my clit in a circular motion, and then Seven releases one of my cheeks and snakes his hand up the front of my torso, sliding his hand gently along my belly until he reaches my breast. At first, his hand rubs over each breast as he watches me coming apart for him, and then his thumb and pointer finger secure around my nipple and pinch down.

"Oh God..." I whimper.

The pain and pleasure from his fingers shoot down straight to my clit, sparking more nerve endings until I don't think I can hold back any longer.

I thought that the orgasm from the restaurant was a fluke... a one-off, but my body is spiraling towards its second climax at the hands of this man, and there is nothing else I want more than to be finished off by him again.

He releases my nipple, his long arm reaches up even higher and his hand gently wraps around my neck. I look down to see him watching me as he sucks down hard on my sensitive nub, and his hand gives a quick squeeze against my throat.

I've never had a man's hand around my throat, and the surprise sensation has my body bursting with tingles as my center squeezes so tight I think I might pass out. All together, my body free falls into the most brutal yet incredible orgasm of my life.

I try to catch my breath when Seven pulls me down his body, laying my head against his chest and wraps me up in his arms, pulling me under the blankets with him. I can hear his heart beating almost as fast as mine, and the feeling of his hard-on between us.

"Are you okay?" he asks, a true look of concern on his face.

I nod, I have no words for what he just did to me. I didn't even know orgasms could tear you apart and put you back together all in the same instant.

"Yes, I'm more than okay. I just can't feel my legs," I tease.

My thighs are still tingling and shaking with the aftershock of my release.

"Good thing you won't need them for what we're doing next," he says. "Are you ready for a third?"

"A third orgasm?" I ask, as if the idea is unheard of.

"Have you ever had three before?"

"Have you ever given three?" I say quickly, avoiding the question of my lack of orgasms.

He stalls for a second, searching my eyes. I know my reaction probably seems odd to him. What woman wouldn't want to come multiple times in a night wrapped in the arms of a man who looks like him?

"You asked me if I could go all night, and I told you I could," he says. "So why does that feel like a trick question? Am I going to get in trouble if I answer it?"

By that reaction, he obviously has.

And should it surprise me?

He's already proven he can give me two in the same night.

Does three mean I'm cured? Or does it mean that Seven is the only man who can unlock this hidden part of my body that even I barely understand? And is the possibility of ever having a normal sex life with Daniel still doomed?

I shake my head.

"You won't get in trouble, but you don't have to answer it either. I know now."

My hesitation isn't because of the women before me like he thinks, though I'm curious about that, too. It's just that three orgasms for me doesn't seem possible. Even when I had orgasms before the accident, two in one night was rare enough as it is. So, the idea that Seven can pull as many as he wants from me is both thrilling and terrifying.

"I don't care about my number. The only number I want to top is yours," he says, brushing a few strands of my hair out of my face.

"Why my number?" I ask.

"Maybe because I want to impress you."

He doesn't say it with a cocky grin. Instead, there's an honesty in his eyes.

"Then consider me impressed," I say, smoothing my fingers over the light hairs of his chest.

"Not just yet. Make me work for it."

He leans in and kisses me, the taste of me still on his lips.

It's not the first time I've tasted myself when a man's gone down on me, but it's the first time I've enjoyed it. Everything Seven does is more erotic than anyone before him. I never thought I'd like having a hand around my throat during sex, but the way Seven does it has me wanting him to try it again.

He rotates his body over mine and pulls me under him, deepening our kiss and settling his hips in between the warmth of my thighs as his hard cock nestles against my stomach, demanding not to be forgotten. Not that I could ever forget. He's too big to miss.

He reaches over to his bedside table and pulls out a condom.

He rips it open with his teeth, and in a quick motion, he's sheathed and ready.

My hands cup his jaw, keeping him anchored to me as he pushes to align us together.

I feel his tip at my entrance, but he doesn't push in right away.

"Tell me if I'm hurting you. I'll slow down," he says against our kiss.

I moan into his mouth as he pushes against me, his head gaining entrance inside of me as he coats himself in my slick heat.

My tight walls squeeze around him, and I hear the moment he lets out a sigh of relief as if he's been needing me all this time.

His lips pull off of mine as they travel down my throat, his thrusts becoming heavier and deeper as my body gives way to him, stretching around him to accommodate his size and strength.

The more he advances back and forth into me, the more slippery his cock becomes until he slides in and out of me at a more rapid rate, pinning me under his body. I'm at his mercy as his body drives into me harder with every thrust of his hips.

His grunts and my moans fill the space between his bedroom walls with the sounds of pleasure as he kisses his way down my chest until his hot mouth finds my pebbled nipples.

The moment his lips latch onto my breasts and suck down against me, I arch up into him, moaning out as I wrap my fingers around the back of his neck.

I feel the small amount of sweat at the bottom of his hairline. He's working me with everything he has and I can feel the tension in his shoulders and the need in his groans.

He wants to come, and so do I... for the third time tonight.

"Every inch of you tastes good," he says, his mouth against my breast.

"Are you going to come?" I ask.

"Only after you," he says but I hear the strain in his voice.

"I'm almost there..." I barely manage to get out.

Then I feel Seven's teeth scrape along the base of my nipple and I cry out, the climax hitting and sending my center into spasms that pulsate around his cock.

"Jesus Christ..." he curses as my body squeezes down on him. "Where Brynn... tell me where I can come."

I'm still on birth control, and he's wearing a condom, and I don't have to think about the answer. I'm not ready for him to pull out just yet.

"In me," I plead.

His lips descend down on mine, muffling the growl he makes as he thrusts his own release into the condom that's buried inside of me.

We stay like that for a while longer, my arms wrapped around his neck, keeping his lips to mine. His elbow presses against the mattress to prevent him from putting all his weight on me, and we pant through the aftermath.

Finally, he pulls his lips off of mine on rolls off.

"Give me a second to get rid of this condom."

I watch as he steps out of bed, his cock still as hard as when he started.

"Will you bring me something to clean up with?"

He stops his path around the bed and glances over at me, lifting a brow.

"What makes you think we're done? I'm just reloading the condom," he says and then gives a delish grin. "Don't go anywhere, I'll be right back."

I watch as Seven turns around and heads for the door, giving me a perfect view of his bare ass.

He's coming back for more?

Oh God, I'm in trouble... and there's nowhere else I want to be.

CHAPTER FIFTEEN

Seven

I wake to the sound of one of our phones pinging with messages and Brynn peacefully asleep in the crook of my arm with only a pair of panties on. She convinced me that she can't sleep completely naked, though that would be my preference. If I can keep her naked for the rest of the time she's in Mexico, I have every intention of making it happen.

At a quick glance, the clock on the bedside table reads that it's five in the morning. We've been asleep for about an hour, but fully sated and feeling a little raw after our night last night.

I never could get her to tell me her top number but the look on her face after we hit five this morning, told me that I was somewhere in the ballpark.

Her phone dings, and though I'm not one to look at other people's phones, it's bright and captures my attention.

Fiancé... reads as the incoming text.

> Fiancé: I'm sorry for how I reacted to-
> day...

And then another one hits.

> Fiancé: I miss you. Maybe I should fly
> out...

What the fuck?

She has a fiancé?

Brynn's sleepy eyes open as she looks behind her at her phone sitting on the bedside table where she put it before we fell asleep last night.

I can see the moment her eyes widen and then her eyes flash back over at me.

She knows I just read her text.

I watch as the blood drains from her face. She's now the ghostly gray color she was when I opened the door to find her trying to access my house four days ago, instead of the flush cheeks she just had after the orgasms I just gave her.

"You have a fiancé?" I ask, demanding the answer.

"It's not what it looks like," she says in a panic.

She sits up quickly to grab at her phone. I take the opportunity to pull my arm back from her and step out of bed in my boxers. Turns out that putting on underwear wasn't as bad of an idea as I thought.

Now I'm hovering over the king-sized bed, wondering how the hell I didn't see this coming.

"Who the hell is that? When were you planning on telling me? Over pancakes and eggs the morning after I fucked you all night?"

My hands pinch at my hips, trying to keep myself calm.

"Seven, I'm sorry..." she says.

Jesus, that's not a good start.

"It's sort of complicated," she continues.

Is that the best excuse she's got?

"It's complicated? Your "fiancé" is texting you while you're naked in bed with me. What's so complicated about that?"

Not that any excuse right now would make a difference. I've heard them all from Josslin and my family. They thought they could reason with me about why I should have been okay with Josslin and Eli's betrayal.

"I'm not cheating on him. We're allowed to see other people," she says, naked and scrambling to get closer to me.

I take another step back away from the bed. She reads the situation perfectly now.

Don't come near me.

"Maybe I was wrong to step in between you and that asshole groom and his friends? Maybe that's closer to your type. I'm sorry if I got in the way."

I usually go silent when bad shit happens.

I'd rather internalize it all until I suffocate it to death, so it has no air to survive, and then I move on. If you tell people about your problems, they can live somewhere else and come back whenever they choose to bite you in the ass again, but I can't stay silent this time.

"We're not engaged anymore. I swear I'm not a cheater. He's sleeping with someone in an apartment in Australia right now. Please believe me."

It would be easier if he wasn't in her phone– listed as fiancé.

"I'd believe you if you were telling me the truth, but that explanation doesn't sound complicated at all. And by the looks of your contact information, you're still engaged. So what part of the story are you leaving out?"

She lets out a sigh and slumps back into the bed, pulling the blanket up to her chest to cover herself.

"Daniel and I agreed to take a break while he went to Australia to help open a new law firm. He thinks that going on this trip will help him make partner, and we thought that doing long distance would be too stressful on our relationship. The agreement is that we get back together when he gets home after eight months apart, which is three weeks from now," she turns to look at me again. "But we're not together right now, and he's been dating this entire time."

She's right; this shit is complicated and sounds like the kind of unnecessary drama I try to stay miles away from. Unfortunately, a little over an hour ago, I had my cock buried deep inside of her and my tongue down her throat. I'm a little more invested in this situation than I'd like to be.

"And what about you? Have you been with anyone else since your break?" I ask, not sure what I want her answer to be.

Does it matter?

Either way we're done before we ever started.

"No, you're the first and I swear I didn't think anything was going to happen between us but then you kissed me in the parking lot and things just escalated. You've been avoiding me ever since I got here. It's not like you've put in an effort to get to know me over breakfast. I never thought we'd end up here," she says, motioning to the bed.

She's right—we don't know anything about each other. I can't blame her for not telling me before the kiss. My intentions from the moment she showed up on my porch were to not get to know her. She didn't owe me her life story. But she had time between the kiss outside of Scallywag's and the drive back to my place, where we spent the night together.

"You could have said something when I pinned you against the building and asked you how far I could go."

She nods slowly.

"I'm sorry. You took me off guard. I thought I was nothing more than a nuisance to you until you kissed me out front. Then everything happened so fast and being in your arms felt so good. I should have found a way to tell you before we took it any further tonight. But it's been over eight years since I've had an orgasm—"

She stops immediately when she realizes what she just admitted. She and I both look at each other with equal looks of shock on our faces.

"Did you just say that you haven't had an orgasm in eight years? How is that physically possible?"

She looks down at her hands and folds them together nervously in her lap.

"I shouldn't have told you that. It's not relevant to our situation, but my agent booked me on this trip to finish my manuscript and to find someone to have a fling with during my breakup to see if maybe..."

"If maybe your incompetent ex-fiancé is the reason why you're not getting off," I say, finishing her sentence.

Or at least finish it the way it should have ended.

How in the hell does a man you've been with for eight years not know how to give you an orgasm?

The better question is, why would she have agreed to marry someone like that in the first place?

"It's not his fault. I had a traumatic experience years ago during a tornado that ripped through our college campus, and ever since then, I haven't been able to get off without sex aids," she covers her face after she blurts it out. "I didn't mean to tell you that either."

What the hell is happening to me? I've never given any other woman this much time to explain her situation to me but the more she tells me, the more complicated her situation is becoming.

She pulls her phone up and opens it.

I look to find her almost in tears.

"See. I swear I'm not lying to you."

She turns her phone around for me to see the illuminated screen.

> Fiancé: The woman here means nothing to me but it's too late to kick her out of the apartment and she's already asleep. It would be an asshole thing to do.

> Fiance: And you can't be mad at me; we agreed to sleep with other people. And you know that I need this. I need reassurance that it's not my fault that you can't orgasm during sex. And now that I know I'm not the one to blame, and I can commit to a lifetime with you.

I just about grab her phone and huck it out my bedroom window, but this isn't my relationship; it's hers. I've already had a manipulative ex who dumped me. Thankfully she did it before it was too late and I was locked in for life. Josslin did me a favor in the end. However, it cost me my entire family in the process.

Brynn's ex has a firm enough pull on her to convince her to let him fuck his way through Australia and keep her on the hook until he gets home. And that the asshole is blaming her for something that should be a team effort. I'm not sure how to feel about this situation anymore.

Then, my stomach turns uncomfortably when a question comes to mind.

"I need you to be honest," I ask her.

"I'll tell you anything you want to know as long as you keep talking to me."

I can't promise that I'll keep talking. It's not my strong suit, but I haven't walked away yet.

"Did you fake it?"

"With him?" she asks, her eyebrows drawn together.

"No," I say. I don't give a shit about her worthless ex-fiancé. "Just now. With me."

All five times...

She rolls her eyes.

"Oh God... not you too."

If she thinks that my ego is that delicate, then we have a problem.

"I just want to know if you were faking all those orgasms to appease me. Because if you didn't fake it, then maybe your agent is right. Maybe the guy isn't right for you," I say, bending over to pick up a t-shirt off the floor.

She watches me pull my shirt over my head and pull it down my torso.

"Let's say, for argument's sake, that I didn't fake it with you. Then what? Daniel and I break up after being together for eight years just because I don't get off from sex with him? How do you throw all those years away? Sex isn't everything, right? What if there's still love there?"

Even after everything that she just told me, hearing her say that she still loves him makes my stomach turn. Maybe because his texts prove that he doesn't care about her like she thinks he does, or maybe because there's a flicker of jealousy in me that I wish wasn't there.

If I had a choice, I'd feel nothing at all.

What did I actually think was going to happen between us after tonight?

"I don't know. I guess this is something you two will have to work out," I turn and head for my bedroom door. "I'm going to take a shower and wash off. It would be better if you weren't in my room when I get out," I say, making sure that she knows this is where our conversation ends.

I'm not interested in helping her work out her sex life with another man. That's something she needs to figure out herself.

I keep walking towards the bathroom, and then I hear her jump off the bed and run to the door frame.

"I didn't fake it," she blurts out right before I enter the bathroom.

I turn to look over my shoulder.

She's standing there, wrapped in my sheet, her hair is a tangled mess from our night together and as painfully beautiful as ever.

"What?" I ask.

"I didn't fake it tonight... with you. I just thought you should know."

I should be relieved that I gave her more than her fiancé has in eight years, but instead, I feel like an idiot. I gave into something I knew I shouldn't and it turned out the way that I knew it would.

I've spent the last nineteen years trying to avoid complications like this, and until Brynn, I was doing a damn good job.

"Then maybe you should find someone else to explore that further with before your fiancé gets back," I say.

"Someone other than me."

Then I walk into the bathroom and shut the door.

CHAPTER SIXTEEN

Seven

I wake up before my alarm this morning, planning to get an early start to the day and get out of the house before Brynn gets up.

I let out an annoyed groan as I take a deep inhale, and my lungs fill with the smell of Brynn still on my bed sheets.

But when I walk out to the kitchen, Brynn and Rita are already sitting at the table with a cup of tea, and breakfast is already made.

"You're here early. Is everything okay?" I ask, a little surprised to see Rita in my kitchen.

"Well, good morning to you too," Rita says, pretending to be offended. She's been around long enough to know what she gets with me. "And yes, everything is fine. Marie called this morning and said that their power is back on. I figured I should drive down to check on my house, too. Then I saw Brynn in the kitchen window and decided to stop in first to invite you both over for dinner tonight. Just a little thank you for yesterday."

Dinner with Brynn?

Spending any more time together than absolutely necessary has proven not to be a smart idea.

"Tonight isn't exactly a good night. Cammy's flying in to-morrow, and there are still a lot of repairs I need to get done before she gets here," I say.

Brynn looks over at me when I mention my niece's name, but I don't feel the need to explain that Cammy is my eigh-teen-year-old niece.

With Cammy coming to visit, I'll need the guest bedroom back. Otherwise, Cammy will be sleeping on the pull-out couch in the living room, and that's not my favorite scenario. I want Cammy to always feel like she has her own space and that I prioritize her.

Back in Seattle, during the season, Cammy and I don't see each other as much as I'd like. Between my out-of-town games and her taking on extra classes in order to fast-track her sports management degree, I typically can only count on seeing her during my home games. But I'm happy to see her sitting in my seats every time I play on home ice.

She's family, and since I'm not speaking to anyone else, I'm glad to have her living close, though I don't like how some of the rookies look at her when she meets me down at the locker rooms at the end of the game.

As soon as Silas calls me back this morning to let me know if they have any availability, I'll know if I can move Brynn into a hotel room by tomorrow morning.

After last night, I think it's time to put some distance between us.

I walk over to the coffee maker, load a single pod into it, and then push the start button.

"Don't be a buzzkill. I'll make your favorite," Rita entices.

"What's his favorite?" Brynn asks, pulling her cup up to her pink lips.

I wish I didn't know how good her mouth tastes... or every other inch of her. And if I'd been able to control myself with her last night, I wouldn't have her sweet taste still lingering on my tongue.

"He loves my signature jambalaya, fried Cajun shrimp, hush puppies, and dirty rice. But I make it with a flare. It's a family secret recipe," she tells Brynn. "If you want to win Seven over, the quickest way is to his stomach. Which I can already see that you figured out."

I follow Rita's attention over to the piles of food that Brynn made this morning. I hope that she didn't slave away on Rita's advice because what happened between us last night is beyond what a tall stack of pancakes can fix.

"Actually, breakfast is more of a thank you and a sorry for last night," Brynn says.

I glance over to find Brynn sending a quick look my way. I don't know if the thank you is for the multiple orgasms last night or for scaring off the asshole who grabbed ahold of her, but I have a damn good idea of where the sorry is coming from.

"Those boys sitting at that table? I can't believe what Marie told me had happened. It was a good thing that Seven was there to kick them out. I'm so sorry that you experienced that situation last night. I always want people to feel safe in our establishment. "

"It's okay, really," Brynn says. "And dinner sounds delicious; thank you for the offer. I can't speak for Seven, but I'm free. Can I bring anything?"

"Just yourself," Rita says and then looks over to me. "And can you put something in the firepit for tonight? I think a celebratory bonfire that our houses are still standing is in order. Brynn over here told me that you haven't had one while she's been here yet."

When exactly did she think we would have had time?

The night Brynn showed up at my house attempting to break in? Or the night after that when a hurricane was threatening to blow down both of our houses?

"We haven't had a bonfire yet because we were a little busy trying to stay alive, Rita," I tease her.

"Oh, you and your excuses," she says, waving me off. "Tonight is the night then. And I have the perfect bottle of wine to pair with it. I'd better get back to the house and get to cooking. See you two later."

I watch from the kitchen island, sipping on my just-brewed coffee, as Rita gets up, leaves her mug of tea on the table, and then walks out.

The door opens and then closes behind her, and I watch out the window as Rita strolls back over to her house.

"I made breakfast," Brynn says.

"Rita's wrong about what she said. Food isn't the way to my heart."

I feel stupid for even repeating it.

I walk over to the cabinet and take out two plates. It doesn't look like she's eaten either.

"I have no motive except to apologize for what happened last night. I figured that making you breakfast would be a good start."

I look over at her sitting at the table, not getting up to make her own plate of food.

"You don't need to apologize. It happened, now it's over. In a week's time, we'll both be back in Seattle, and we can forget this ever happened."

She withheld some vital information that I would have liked to have known before I fucked her until sunrise, but she didn't cheat on the guy. And it's not as if she and I were starting a relationship—it was just sex.

She doesn't owe me anything, but this situation is too close to mirroring my past, and I'm not interested in repeating it.

Brynn is about to say something when my phone starts ringing.

It's Silas.

"I have to take this," I tell her.

I slide the unlock button and answer the call.

"Hey, thanks for calling me back," I say.

"I wouldn't thank me just yet. I wish I were calling you back with better news, but after discussing the vacancies with my assistant manager and taking into account all the people still sleeping on our lobby floor and needing a room, I don't have any availability. I should have some vacancies as soon as the airlines start catching up with rescheduling everyone today or tomorrow."

It was worth a shot, though I knew the odds weren't good.

"I appreciate you for trying. We'll figure out another arrangement. Let me know if a room opens up, will you?" I ask.

"You'll be my first call."

I could always ask Rita about Brynn staying in one of her two other guest rooms. Now that the power is back on and no storm is in view, it's safe for Rita and Brynn to stay in the house.

"I'll let you get back to work. Drinks this week at the bar?" I ask.

"As soon as things slow down over here."

We say our goodbyes, and then I set my phone on the countertop and start dishing up my food.

"Was that Silas?" Brynn asks.

"Yeah. There aren't any rooms right now, but he thinks maybe tomorrow. My niece is supposed to be flying in tomorrow morning, and I could use the guest bedroom for her."

Brynn's eyes drop to her mug, and she wipes at the rim as if trying to wipe off a lipstick smudge.

"Right, I understand. This was always supposed to be temporary until I found somewhere else to go or got a flight back home. I'll find somewhere; don't worry about me."

I don't know where she thinks she's going to find a place to stay. Rita's is the best option that I can think of for the next couple of days, at least.

"I'll check in with Rita tonight about a spot for you. Are you going to eat?" I ask.

"Eventually. I think I'm going to take a shower first and then I'll take a plate of food to my room. I have a lot of writing to do today."

"I'll be outside most of the day doing repairs."

Brynn stands up out of her seat.

"I'll see you before dinner at Rita's then?"

"Yeah, I'll see you tonight."

I continue to dish up, watching in my peripheral as Brynn walks out of the kitchen with her mug still in hand.

Ten hours later, I walk back into the house feeling spent from completing all the repairs and moving brush off the beaches.

I head for the bathroom first for a shower. I still have thirty minutes before dinner and I can make it fast.

As I enter the hallway, Brynn's bedroom door opens, and I watch her step out of the guest bedroom.

"You're back," she says, jumping a little in surprise.

She looks beautiful, her hair down in loose waves cascading over her shoulders. It's the first time I've seen her in makeup, and whatever she did to her eyes made the blue shine even brighter.

She's wearing a tight-fitting white dress with a blue flower pattern that fits like it was made for her. If I thought she looked good last night, then I should call off dinner because staring at Brynn all night is going to be hard to resist.

"I didn't mean to startle you. I'm just headed to the shower and then I'll be ready for us to head over to dinner."

"Oh, did you want me to wait for you? I just figured you'd come over whenever you're ready, but I can stay—"

Shit, that was stupid of me to think that we would walk over together. She doesn't need to wait for me. We're not one unit. And Rita's place is less than a hundred feet away.

"No, that's fine. You don't need to stick around. I'll see you both when I'm done."

Her eyebrows downturn a little like she's torn.

"Are you sure because I can—"

I cut her off again. The last thing I need is for her to think that I have any attachment to the idea of us walking over together.

"No, you should head over now. She's probably popped that bottle of wine already and is looking for someone to pour a glass for. I won't be long."

"Okay, see you over there."

I nod and then turn into the bathroom, closing the door behind me.

I took a longer shower than I originally planned and used the time to gather my thoughts. Tonight, I'll ask Rita if she can take Brynn for a night or two until I get her a hotel room or a flight back to Seattle.

Once we both get back home and forget that the other person exists, life can return to normal, and I won't think about the woman who showed up on my porch one night in Mexico and narrowly had me debating whether I was ready to date again after all these years.

CHAPTER SEVENTEEN

Brynn

I knock on Rita's door, after leaving Seven to take his shower and get ready in peace.

She must have seen me walking over because she opens the door within seconds of my knuckles touching the bright yellow painted entry.

I smile at the thought that Rita has a front door that's as loud and inviting as she is.

"You're here! Good," she beams, pulling the door open wider to let me in. My mouth waters at the smell of dinner wafting towards me from her kitchen.

I step through the door of Rita's house and the place looks almost identical to Seven's, except that everything is updated with new furnishings and decorated beautifully.

"Wine?" she asks.

"Yes, please. I'd love some."

I'm tempted to tell her not to bother with the glass. I'll just take the entire bottle in order to get through tonight with Seven, but I don't need anyone else asking questions about how he and I are getting along. Sheridan is more than enough people to have to retell the harrowing tale of how I made a complete idiot of myself last night.

You'd think I'd be used to embarrassing myself in front of Seven, but then I find a whole new low.

Seeing him this morning was awkward after what happened between us last night. But worse than that, my belly flipped with excitement the second he walked through the kitchen archway to find Rita and me chatting.

"Follow me," she instructs, taking a sip of her own long-stem glass.

I follow her through the living room and into the kitchen. "I got so caught up in wanting to make sure that you're ok after everything that happened at Scallywag's and to thank you for everything you did to help us out, that I forgot to ask how Seven is as a host. Do you have everything you need next door? Is he being a gentleman?"

Is Seven being a gentleman?

Nothing about what that man can do in the bedroom would be considered gentlemanly, and my cheeks still warm at the thought of it.

She pulls another long-stem glass from the cabinet and then grabs the bottle of wine she has already opened.

"He's been more than fair and accommodating, especially considering the circumstances. I'd like to get out of his hair as soon as possible, but the hotels don't seem to have any vacancies at the moment and I can't seem to get a flight out any earlier than my original itinerary for next week since they need to book other passengers whose flights were canceled before mine."

I watch her as she uses a heavy hand to pour me a full glass.

God bless her.

"Why leave now anyway? You're here and the storm is long gone. Why not just finish out your trip? Seven said that you're here to write, so stay and write."

She sets the full glass in front of me and I pick it up to take a sip.

The wine is good, really good.

The full-body fragrance and the slight fruity undertones of this wine have my tongue begging for another taste.

"The living situation is less than ideal at the moment. I can't ask Seven to stay another week. I feel like I've outstayed my welcome as it is. The best option is a hotel room in Cancun, but I don't see that happening."

"Cancun? That's way too far from here. We'd never see you," she says. "Stay here with me. I have plenty of room."

"That's very kind of you, but I think Seven and I could use a little more space."

"Then take the apartment. The family who was staying with me just moved back to their house this morning. You are welcome to use that space if you'd like. You'll be a lot closer to us if you need anything."

It's no surprise to me that Rita would offer up her apartment. She has such a giving heart. But I can't ask her to let me stay in it for free for an entire week.

"I couldn't ask you to do that. Someone else who needs it more than me should use it."

"Oh, nonsense. If it keeps you close, it's the best option for everyone."

The best option for who?

I'm sure Seven would be more than happy for me to be as far away from him as possible.

"I can pay you for the rental at least. Just tell me what I owe for the week."

It's not as if I can't afford it. My author business is booming, and I still have most of my advance from this new series. Plus, I can write it off as a business expense.

Rita shakes her head.

"No need to pay. You're my guest and I don't need a dime."

I think for a second about what I could do to make the exchange feel more equal.

I really enjoyed bussing tables and being a part of a team again. It's been years since I worked as a server in college. It also kept my brain sharp and active while I worked through my storyline. I wouldn't mind having that creative flow moving again.

"I have to give you something. How about if I take a few shifts to help clear tables in exchange for rent?"

Rita beams back at me.

"That's a great idea. Do you think you can manage that along with your writing? We'd love to have you downstairs with us and you'll get a chance to work with Cammy."

Seven mentioned his niece Cammy already.

"Cammy's working there? I thought she was coming for vacation?" I ask.

"She is here for vacation, but she usually takes a shift or two. She says that being a server helps her practice her conversational Spanish whenever she comes to visit. It's gotten quite good over the years that she's been coming. And you'll love her, she's the best."

"She's supposed to be here tomorrow. Would it be alright if I moved over tomorrow?"

The sooner that I'm out of Seven's house the better.

"I see no problem with that. I just need to change the sheets on the bed."

"Thank you. I really appreciate this. Can I help you with dinner?" I ask, looking around at the food that looks like it's already been prepared.

"No, everything's done. We're just waiting on the man of the hour," she says.

I take another sip of the wine to see if the first sip was deceiving but the second sip is even better.

"Mmm, that's really good."

Rita swirls her wine in her glass and then takes a sip as well.

"This is one of my favorites. My husband took me to Italy a few years back for our anniversary, and we traveled around, wine-tasting our way through Europe. It was the last vacation we took before he passed, and it's one that I'll never forget."

She smiles bittersweetly. I can tell that her memories of her husband are ones she holds dear instead of seeing the tragedy.

"He knew that I loved our trip so much that he wanted to make the memories last even longer, so he ordered several cases of the wine we had at this tiny villa in Tuscany and had them shipped here for me. I'll never forget that long weekend we spent there. We felt like newlyweds even after nearly fifty years together."

"He sounds like he was very special. I'm not so sure they make them like that anymore," I say.

I hear the front door open and close, and then, before I can prepare myself, Seven is in the archway of the kitchen.

I hold my breath the moment he steps into the kitchen, and our eyes lock.

I divert my attention back to Rita and see her smirking at me like she caught me red-handed.

"No, honey... They still make them like that. They're just limited edition now and come standard with a scowl to ward off predators."

Seven walks over to the fridge and opens the door looking inside for something.

"Who's warding off predators?" he asks.

He must have gotten only the very end of our conversation and has no idea that Rita is hinting that Seven is one of the last good men left. She might be right, but that's not for me to investigate. As soon as I get back to Seattle, Daniel and I will have a lot to discuss to determine what the future looks like for us, and Colston's character in my book will be written and I won't need Seven as my muse any longer.

He reaches into the fridge and pulls out a long-neck beer and then pops the top off and takes a long pull as he walks over towards us standing by the stove as Rita starts to dish three plates.

"The local jellyfish. Haven't you heard? They're getting picked off left and right. Researchers don't know why."

Rita hands him a plate full of food, and when Seven isn't looking, she gives me a wink.

I chuckle at her quick-witted thinking, though I'm pretty sure the jellyfish story isn't true. I watch as Rita starts to plate me up a typical helping of food. Not like the portions that Seven is always trying to feed me.

"Fine with me if jellyfish go extinct. I've stepped on enough of those assholes on the beaches here. I wouldn't shed a tear if I never saw another one for the rest of my life," Seven says.

Rita hands me my plate and then I follow a good distance behind Seven towards the kitchen eating nook where a round table with four chairs sits.

I take the seat the furthest away from him. It puts us directly across the table from one another so that we have to face each other but at least we're not close.

Rita finishes filling her plate and then joins us.

We all dig into the food that Rita must have slaved over all day. Every single bite I take is even more delicious than the bite before. I've never had Creole food, which means I can barely wait until we head back to Seven's and I get to check off "Try a new dish" off my "Fix-me" List.

"And what about your family? Where did you grow up? Do you have siblings?"

"I grew up in Oklahoma City. My parents were high school sweethearts and they now both teach at the high school where they met. I have one older brother, but he's nine years older than me and lives in Boston with his wife and twin girls. He got my dad's brains and works as a software engineer for a big tech company. He and I don't stay in touch as much as we should. Sometimes it feels like we weren't even raised together with our big age gap."

Not that I'd ever say this out loud but I know my dad understands my brother so much better than he understands me and my passion for being an author. At least my mom gets it. But I wish so much that marrying Daniel wasn't his highest achievement for me.

"Seven has an older brother too. What is the age gap between you two?" Rita asks.

Seven looks down at his plate as he flicks a piece of shrimp over with his fork. His jaw clenches just slightly for a second. Does he not get along with his brother?

"Eli and I are four years apart," he says and then scoops up a bite of dirty rice and jambalaya.

"Seven grew up in the Midwest. His family owns a farm equipment repair shop, right?" Rita says.

"Something like that," he says between his next bite of food, scrounging down his food like he usually does.

Only this time, I have a feeling he's eating as fast as he can so that he can end this night as quickly as possible.

"That's why he's so good at fixing things. I probably rely on him more than I should. I probably ask for too much help."

He finally looks up from his plate.

"I never mind when you call me to fix something. You know I'm here for anything you need."

Rita reaches over and squeezes his wrist.

"I know, I was kidding. You're a godsend," she pats his forearm and then grabs her glass of wine and takes another sip. "Have you gotten the boat back for mooring it out at sea?"

"I called earlier this morning and they'll have it docked for me by tomorrow. Cammy already asked if we can take it when she gets here. We'll probably go fishing the day after tomorrow once she's settled in. Unless you have her on the schedule already?"

"I have her on for breakfast that day, but I can move her. It's not a big deal," Rita offers.

"No, that's fine. It's her first day out since last year. I'll just pick her up after the breakfast rush, and we'll take it out for a half day."

Hearing Seven talk about his boat and fishing with Cammy, reminds me that I only have a small amount of time to complete my "Fix-Me" list before I head back home. Now is the time to get serious.

For the rest of dinner, Rita regales us with stories of all the adventures she and Bart have experienced since they married fifty years ago. She spoke about the letters he wrote to her as a young nineteen-year-old medic in the army before they got married and how he proposed by mailing home a simple silver ring that he had purchased in a small village in France. He couldn't wait another minute to get home and ask her. He needed to know that they would be together forever once he got back home... if he got back home.

Their story should be told on a Hollywood movie screen.

I hung onto every word, and so did Seven. I was grateful to have a distraction from the tension between me and the man sitting across from me.

Rita and Bart's love story made me think about my own.

Bart couldn't wait even a couple more months to ask Rita to marry him, so much so that he took the last little bit of money that he had to buy her a ring and risked it getting lost or stolen in the mail, all to ensure that Rita knew of his intentions and affection for her.

As the saying goes, the grass is always greener on the other side. But when I think about Daniel's proposal... and then his reversal, it has me wondering what kind of story I'll get to tell fifty years down the road.

Bart knew that Rita was the one. He had no idea when he would return from the war or even if he would return, but he refused to allow distance to dictate their future. Rita and Bart sent letters back and forth, sometimes not getting a letter from the other person for months, whereas Daniel and I can text and call at any time of day or night, and yet we don't.

Everyone has their own love story, and before I heard Rita and Bart's, I believed that Daniel and I had one of the strongest. But have I based our entire love story on one commonly shared moment in time? Does surviving a tornado and moving across the country together make for a box-office smash love story?

Would I even write that as the premise for any of my romance novels?

Is our love story enough to hold us together?

Seven clears our plates as Rita finishes her story about the beautiful vineyard that she and Bart stayed at in Tuscany.

"That place sounds amazing. I'll have to add it to my bucket list one of these days and see it for myself," I tell her.

"Oh, I hope you do. You would love it there. And I hope you get to experience it with someone you love."

I watch her eyes flicker over to Seven, who rinses off our dishes in the sink, and then her eyes settle back on mine.

Seven doesn't hear her, nor is he paying any attention to us as he finishes up any leftover pots and pans still sitting in the sink.

"It's getting late, and I have a strict bedtime, so we should get this firepit underway," Rita says.

"Sounds good to me. I've never been to a bonfire on the beach."

"Never?" Rita asks.

I shake my head.

"Good thing that we're going to rectify that tonight."

She stands from her chair, and I do the same.

"I'm going to go grab another bottle of wine from the cellar and then we'll head out. Is the firepit prepped?" Rita asks Seven.

"All set. I just need to light it," Seven says, drying his hands on a dishcloth after finishing all the dishes.

"Good boy. I'll be right back."

I walk over to the kitchen island to wait for Rita to return when my phone dings.

I pull it out to find Daniel has sent a text.

> Fiance: I didn't hear from you yesterday.
> I'm going crazy over here.

And then a second one follows.

> Fiance: I'm going into a meet and greet
> early this morning but we need to dis-
> cuss this. We need to have a discussion
> about us. I'll be home in a few more
> weeks and then we can go back to nor-
> mal.

Then, a third one.

> Fiance: Are you staying with Wrenley as
> a way to punish me or something?

I'm surprised that he's reacting like this. I've never seen Daniel seem so anxious before. He's a lawyer and he's usually so cool and calm about everything.

> Brynn: First, I'm not using anyone for
> anything. Second, I'd never do some-
> thing just to be vindictive.

Wanting to even the scale before we get back together so that I don't constantly wonder about all the women he was with while we were apart and *getting* even to make Daniel jealous are entirely different things. Ending up in Seven's beach house with him wasn't something I planned or looked for. It was merely for survival at the time.

> Fiance: I know, I'm sorry. I just don't want him to take advantage of you. Please answer when I call later, okay?

> Brynn: It's been a really long day. If I'm still awake by the time you call, I'll answer. Otherwise we'll have to talk tomorrow. I have a long day of writing ahead and I have a shift at the Scallywag's for the lunch rush.

> Fiance: The Scallywag's? I thought you were there to write? You have a job now? You make more than enough money.

> Brynn: It's a long story. I'll tell you about it later.

> Fiance: Ok. I'll call soon. I love you Brynn.

I push my phone back in my pocket and when I look up, Seven is watching me quietly.

I clear my throat, trying to think of something to say but nothing helpful or funny comes to mind. I just feel tongue-tied.

The sound of Rita's footsteps down the hallway breaks our locked eye contact.

"Here it is," she says as she enters the kitchen. "The last bottle of Pinot from the crate."

I spin around to face Rita and break off the tension between Seven and I, plastering on a smile as Rita makes a beeline around the kitchen island for me.

She's beaming from ear to ear as she holds out the bottle of wine.

"The last bottle from your anniversary trip? Are you sure you want to open it tonight? Don't you want to hold onto it?" Seven asks.

I see his concern for her plastered on his face.

"Hold onto it for what? Bart isn't here to drink it with me, and I have a guest in my home who will appreciate it for once. Wine was made to drink with wonderful company, good conversation, and delicious food. Bart wouldn't be happy that this bottle has been collecting dust," she says.

Rita hands the bottle to me, and I take it, though I don't know if I should. It's not as if I don't agree with Rita's sentiments that wine should be enjoyed, but it's the last bottle of wine that she and her husband purchased together while touring the vineyards of Italy on the last vacation they ever took together before his passing.

I can see why Seven is concerned about her decision to open the bottle.

"Are you sure?" I ask, just as a precaution.

She nods.

"You're the perfect company and Bart would be happy to see you enjoying it."

"If this is what you want," Seven says and then turns back to grab two new glasses off the countertop, linking the glass stems between his fingers.

"Are you ready?" he asks, looking over to Rita.

"All set," she beams. "Let me just grab a blanket, and I'll meet you two out there."

I turn without needing any more incentive.

I want out of this kitchen with this weirdness between us. I have a better chance of escaping this awkward moment in the cloaked darkness of the September night and the warm glow of the firepit.

If Rita's lively storytelling can't distract us from everything going on between us, then nothing can.

I just need to make it through tonight, and then tomorrow, I'll be moved into Rita's apartment.

I head for the door with the bottle of wine securely in one hand and my phone in the other.

I can feel the heat of Seven's eyes on my back with every step I take.

The moment I reach the front door of Rita's house, I realize my hands are full.

I nestle the wine bottle against my arm in order to free up one hand but then Seven's bicep brushes past my arm as he reaches out in front of me, his chest gently pressing against my back ever so slightly as he opens the door for me to exit.

The second the door opens, I step out onto the porch, not letting him see how every little touch from him has me waiting for the next.

I set my eyes on the firepit in front of us, steadily moving forward though my ears are perked up, listening for how close he follows behind me.

"This is a great spot you have out here, Rita," I say, looking over at the four teal Adirondack chairs with their feet dug deep into the sand and a circular stone fireplace constructed directly in the middle.

I keep my pace moving forward, but when she doesn't answer and I only hear the footsteps of mine and Seven's feet moving down her porch and into the soft, warm sand, I glance back over my shoulder.

It couldn't take her that long to grab a blanket, could it? After all, the living room was on our way out.

The moment I look back, I see Rita standing in her front door.

"Oh, look at the time. It's way past my bedtime. I'd better let you kids enjoy it without me. I'll take a rain check," she says, keeping her front door barely cracked enough for her tiny body to stand in between.

"Rita, we have the last bottle of wine for you to open. We can't do that without you," he says, trying to encourage her.

"Don't be silly. Just drink a glass for me in honor of Bart," she smirks. "Night, you two."

Rita closes the door before Seven or I can protest.

Then we both hear the deadbolt lock engage on her front door.

She just locked us out and now I'm beginning to see that this was a setup for the beginning.

The only question is, was the entire dinner a ruse to get us here? To plant the firepit idea? To get a romantic bottle of wine in my hands and guilt trip us into making sure it doesn't go to waste?

"Did she just pull one over on us?" I ask Seven as we both stare back at Rita's front porch, dumbfounded.

"That woman is on a different level than the rest. She's a grand master schemer but I never imagined she'd go this far."

My eyes shift from the door to him as he stares back at her house.

"What is she up to?" I ask though I have my own ideas.

He turns and looks at me, his warm brown eyes settling on mine.

"Whatever it is, she's wrong," he says and then stares over at the firepit for a second. "Maybe we should head back to the house. I'm tired. I was up all night."

Yeah, up all night with me, but he doesn't look back at me. It's as if he's already blocked out that we spent the night together. It was a night I'll never forget for so many reasons, but mainly for the way Seven made me feel things that I haven't felt in so long... or maybe ever.

I look down at the wine in my hand and he follows my line of sight.

"What about the wine?" I ask.

Should I drop it back off on her front porch?

But what if an animal comes by or the wind knocks it over, and the bottle breaks, losing the last bottle that she so graciously gave us, even if it had been part of her plan?

I hear the deep sigh of a man knowing when his seventy-year-old neighbor outwitted him.

Really, she outwitted us both.

"How about one glass to appease the senile neighbor and to honor Bart? Then tomorrow, I'll set her straight that nothing is going to happen between us."

And there it is.

I needed confirmation that whatever interest he had in me last night was quickly squashed when he saw Daniel's texts. And I don't blame him, not really.

Now that I know it for sure, I can focus back on where I should have been all along... waiting for Daniel to come back so that we can start our life together as we planned.

But I'm not in a rush to go home. Rita convinced me that I should stay. I'm writing better than I have in a long time and now that I have her apartment to stay in, I have accommodations for as long as I want them. Besides, I can't move my flight up any earlier at this point.

I turn from Seven and start towards one of the Adirondack chairs, the heat of the flames starting to heat my skin the closer I get with each step.

"Here," I hear Seven say behind me. "I'll open that for you."

I turn and hand him the bottle of wine.

I watch as he uses the wine opener corkscrew to pull out the plug from the bottle, and then he pours the glass for me and hands it over.

"Thanks," I say. "Are you going to have any?"

He shakes his head.

"It's all yours. A wine glass looks better in your hand than in mine anyway and wine has a weird way of making me say stupid shit. It's a different kind of buzz that won't be helpful tonight."

A different kind of buzz?

What does that even mean?

"What kind of stupid shit could you possibly say to make this night any more awkward?" I ask, leading the glass up to my lips to take a sip and take a seat in the wooden chair.

"Trust me, Brynn. You don't want me to go off-script. It's better I stick to beer and keep my thoughts to myself."

He hands me the bottle and picks his beer back off the wide armrest of my chair.

I watch him as he walks to the furthest chair across from me in the circle and takes a seat.

Silence falls over us for a minute. Then a minute turns into two, and two turns into five, and five turns into ten. My second glass of wine for the night is starting to dwindle, and I know better than to indulge in a third glass. The last thing I need tomorrow is a hangover.

I alternate between staring at the flames between us and the moon reflecting against the ocean.

I listen as the relaxing sounds of the ocean waves crash along the shore not far from where we're sitting. It does a little to drown out the unspoken words between us.

"Rita is letting me move into her apartment tomorrow so that Cammy can move into your guest bedroom. If you have any spare, clean sheets, I'll make the bed before I leave tomorrow."

"I have a full set of sheets in the hall closet. I'll get them for you tomorrow. Do you need a lift over to Scallywag's in the morning?"

It's a kind offer, but I've already asked him for enough.

"It's no trouble. I'll just call a taxi."

"I can take you. I have to leave to get Cammy to the airport and pick up some things at the hardware store while I'm in Cancun. I'll drop you off before heading out."

"But it's the opposite direction."

My gaze meets his from across the firepit as he reclines in the wooden chair.

"By thirty minutes round trip. I don't mind taking you."

"Are you sure that's not an imposition?" I ask.

"Can you be ready in the morning so I can drop you before I have to leave?"

"Yes."

"Then it's not an imposition."

I take another sip of my wine.

"Okay, thank you. I appreciate you taking me in."

"Don't mention it," he says and then he finishes off the last of his beer and his eyes break from mine, staring back at the flames between us.

"So Cammy is your niece? Is she your brother's daughter?"

I can't help but try to pull out any tidbits of information about Seven. He keeps a tight lid on most things, not giving much away.

"My brother Eli's. The one and only grandkid in the family."

"Do you plan on keeping it that way?" I ask, realizing that was one step too far, especially when it comes to Seven.

His eyes abandoned the fire and glanced up to mine.

I can practically see the flames reflecting off his eyes. I could take back the question but at this point, he'll answer or not. No point in backing down now. He had already heard the question.

"I wanted kids... once." he says, and then his eyes shoot back down to watch the fire again, cutting off my ability to read anything in those brim and firestone eyes.

"But not anymore? Why not? Because of hockey?"

"I can see you're not going to give this one up."

"If I can help it. So tell me, why doesn't a guy like you want to settle down and have a family?"

I take a sip of my wine, exuding as much confidence as possible, though the intensity of Seven's stare makes me want to hide behind this Adirondack chair.

"Are you sure you want a story? This isn't going to be the kind you write in your books with a happily ever after at the end."

The look on his face suggests that whatever story he has, he's numb to. But he knows that I won't like this one. Still, I can't let this opportunity go. He likely won't give me another.

"I was engaged to Cammy's mom first," I hold my breath the second he says it. "One Christmas Eve, I made it home after our weekend games. The flights were all canceled, and the bus system was down, so I bribed the last guy to get into his rental vehicle, and I paid him triple to let me take it. I drove a two-wheel drive car the size of a toast, about twenty miles per hour for five hours on the highway just to get home to see her.

"I don't like the way this is going."

"You're right not to," he says and then clears his throat. "Long story short, the rest of it is as cliche and unoriginal as they usually are. She and my brother were already asleep in our bed. In the house, I bought her with my rookie signing bonus. And an ultrasound sonogram on the kitchen island of a baby that wasn't mine."

"Oh God, Seven, I'm sorry."

"She begged me to let her stay in our hometown while I traveled. She said she wanted to build us a home for the off-season and that it would be easier to start a family if she was close to family. The truth is, I was always the backup plan, and she was the girl next door who had always had a crush on my older brother. If I hadn't been cocky enough to think a professional contract with millions and her dream house could buy her love, I might have been smart enough to have seen that I was never the one she wanted. I was the backup plan. And when my brother came back injured from overseas, she saw her opening."

"It's hard to imagine you as anyone's backup plan," I say.

I have a feeling that a large number of female hockey fans would agree.

"Really? Aren't I your second choice?" he says.

"Wait what did you just say?"

Second choice?

He's a hockey god with washboard abs and the ability to make me orgasm practically on demand. He's not my second choice because I'd never be so bold as to add him to the list. As of less than twenty-four hours ago, I thought the man couldn't stand me and was putting up with me out of decency.

"Forget it," he says quickly, standing out of his chair. "Are you ready to go back to the house?"

Before I can answer, he walks over to dump two large buckets of water over the fire. Smoke and steam billow between us, making it hard for me to see him now in the dark and then he turns and heads for the house, leaving me behind.

"Seven, please stop and talk to me," I say, trying to catch up with his long strides in the sand.

"I'd rather we didn't," he says, trudging ahead of me.

He moves so much easier through the sand than I do.

He gets to the door before I do and opens it, leaving it open for me and I jump up on the porch, now finally able to gain a little speed on flat ground. My hurried steps follow after him down the hall and just as he reaches for the handle of his bedroom door, I grip around his wrist to get his attention.

He looks down at me, our eyes connecting but I can see the blankness in his stare— the indifference he's always trying to broadcast.

"You're not my second choice," I say, a little out of breath.

"I never should have touched you, Brynn."

I'm shocked into silence.

I guess I didn't know what he would say, but I didn't think he would tell me that he regrets what we did—he regrets me.

A little part of me shatters and before I can say anything back, he pushes open his bedroom door and I release him.

He walks into his room and closes the door behind him as I stand there like an idiot.

Tomorrow, I move out to Rita's, and maybe, if I'm lucky, I'll finally stop making a complete fool of myself.

CHAPTER EIGHTEEN

Seven

The drive to drop Brynn off was done in complete silence.

Well, not complete silence. I had the radio on to drown out the lack of conversation between us.

It was a stark difference from the last time we drove this route together to Scallywag's a couple of days ago, with Brynn singing every note to the songs playing on the radio.

This time, she didn't sing a single note.

She kept her arm out in the breeze of the side window, watching the palm trees and ocean pass us by.

I saw the look on her face when I told her that I never should have touched her, and I meant it. I never should have touched Brynn because now it's physically painful not to reach out and do something as simple as take her hand into mine or glide my hand down her thigh as we drive down the road.

If I didn't know how incredibly smooth her skin is or the soft approving sounds she makes when I touch her, I wouldn't know how much I lost... though none of it was ever mine. Just like Josslin never really belonged to me. I think I always knew that deep down.

There was politeness in Josslin's eyes for me, not romantic affection. But I was a stupid kid back then, with my sights on making a name for myself in the NHL, and I didn't look close enough.

If I'm honest with myself, I saw it when I got down on one knee in front of that fountain with ten dozen roses all set up by the florist. Instead, I convinced myself not to notice the hesitation in her body language when I popped the question.

At the time, my brother was off serving his country, and Josslin was never on his radar. Josslin wasn't the only one with a childhood crush. I had one too, her.

I couldn't believe how lucky I was. I had an NHL contract and the girl I had loved since I was a kid was wearing my ring. Little did I know that my brother was jealous of my hockey career, which never materialized for him. So when he returned home from overseas without his best friend, he became broken and bitter, and he thought that taking the one thing I wanted most would help him feel better or vindicate him in some way.

It's too bad that stealing someone else's happiness doesn't convert the way he hoped it would.

Brynn already made her choice well before we met. I won't be Brynn's alternate choice. I've been there before, and in the end, no one wins.

I pull up to Scallywag's, and Rita comes out when she hears my jeep.

I don't shut it off since I have to leave as soon as Brynn gets her things out of the back so that I can be at the airport on time.

"Good morning, you two!" Rita beams.

She sees Brynn and I both jump out of the jeep and I move to get the luggage out of the back so that Brynn doesn't have to. I loaded it all for her, and with the lift on the jeep, it's too high for her to have to pull it all down.

"You don't need to do that," Brynn whispers to me as Rita approaches the side we're standing on.

"I can help you with your luggage. I loaded it."

"You didn't have to do that either," she says just as Rita walks up to us.

I pull all three pieces of luggage out of my jeep, and Rita grabs one of the bags.

"Off to get our girl?" Rita asks me.

"Right after I stop at the hardware store first. I need to pick up some supplies in town for a few of the repairs."

"Then off you go. I'll help Brynn get settled."

I'd insist on not letting Rita take the luggage upstairs and do it myself but I have to leave or I'll be late if there's any traffic, and Miguel is inside if they need help.

"I'll see you later," I tell Rita.

"Thanks for the ride," Brynn says, grabbing for her bags to read inside. "I can't find my necklace. The clasp is old and I think it fell off somewhere in the house. If you find it, will you let me know?"

"Sure, I'll look for it."

I can't stay any longer if I want to make sure that I pick up everything and get to Cammy before she deboards the aircraft,

I jump in my jeep and pull out of the parking lot and head towards the airport.

I stand outside of the jeep, leaning against it when my phone buzzes in my hand.

> Cammy: On my way out, but brace yourself. I didn't tell her she could come. She was waiting for me in the airport outside of security when I arrived.

The second I saw Cammy's text, I had a good idea of what was coming.

I watch the glass double doors, anticipating my niece and my ex to walk through the airport exit.

And then I see Cammy come through first. Her bright smile and brown hair were up in a ponytail with her backpack slung over one shoulder.

Next, Josslin pushes through the door, trying to shove a tube of lip gloss or lipstick back in her bag as if she just reapplied it before coming out here. I watch through my sunglasses as she pulls a designer bag behind her as her full-length beach dress swirls around her wedge heels. It's low cut in the front, which doesn't shock me, and her hair is perfectly styled with a thick mask of makeup on in typical Josslin fashion.

I head straight for my niece, wrapping my arm around her shoulders and bringing her in for a squeeze. I'm grateful she looks more like a Wrenley every day and nothing like Josslin, except for those deep green eyes and that tall, slender ballerina figure.

I take her bags and turn back from the Jeep before Josslin has a chance to catch up.

"How was your flight kiddo?" I ask.

"Long but good. I'm starving, though. My connecting flights were too close together so all I ate today were some crackers and a couple of fruit juices. Can we go to Scallywag's for dinner?"

"Yeah, sure, whatever you want—"

"Hello," I hear Josslin's voice behind us. "Are you two just going to ignore me?"

"That was the plan, yes," I say, turning around to face the woman I had already warned not to come.

"Well, I'm here now. So we might as well make the best of it," she says, glancing from Cammy to me with a smile as if she didn't just intentionally force her way into Cammy's vacation.

I sneeze twice in a row the moment Josslin's heavy perfume wafts past my nostrils.

"Are you getting sick?" Josslin asks.

"No, I'm just allergic to you."

I hear Cammy try to stop the giggle that bubbles out from my response.

Though I agree that was funny... sometimes I wonder what happened between Cammy and Josslin to make Cammy despise her mom and move all the way to Seattle to get some space from her.

"I hope you secured a rental car and a hotel for yourself. You're not staying with us," I tell Josslin.

"Can I at least have dinner with you two? My car rental won't be ready until tomorrow."

I know better than to give in to Josslin, and if Cammy weren't here, I'd happily leave her stranded in the terminal.

Cammy leans in closer to me. "We could just leave her here," she whispers.

"She's your mom, Cammy."

"So...? You don't talk to your mom either."

She has a point, but how would that look in front of my niece if I abandoned her mom right in front of her?

I'm trying to be the best example of what a man should be since Cammy's dad is an alcoholic who plays video games all day to hide away and avoid getting the help he needs. I don't want Cammy ending up like Josslin. Married to a guy who isn't present in Cammy's life. Not that Josslin doesn't deserve some of the Karma she's getting. I just don't want that for my niece.

"You can come to dinner, and then I'll drop you off at your hotel after. After that, you're on your own," I tell her.

"See? We're getting along so well already," Josslin says, handing me her bag as if I'm her chauffeur.

I'm going to fucking regret this. I already know it.

I take the bag anyway. It's obviously heavy, and if I leave it for Josslin to attempt to lift in the back of my Jeep, we'll be here all day, and my goal is to get dinner over with and drop Josslin back off at whatever hotel she booked.

Cammy gets in the front seat before Josslin can and then soon, I'm back in the driver's seat,

Cammy bends closer to me again.

"You'd better not let her talk you into going fishing with us tomorrow like you caved on dinner."

I lean in closer to Cammy. The jeep is loud but whether Josslin hears me or not is none of my concern.

"I'll throw myself overboard if that happens."

Cammy starts laughing, and then I pull off the curb, and we're off to Scallywag's.

Brynn

It's been a few hours since I got settled upstairs in the apartment.

The space is your basic run-of-the-mill, two-bedroom apartment but Rita has every wall painted in a bright color.

There are two small rooms with a shared bathroom, a small living space with a couch and TV, and a small L-shaped kitchen with everything I'll need. It's perfect for one more week while I pound out the last of my book.

Downstairs, the lunch rush is over and there are a few tables coming in for early dinner.

"Cammy!" I hear Rita's voice from across the restaurant.

I quickly glance up to find three people standing at the entrance of the restaurant.

Rita throws her arms around the young woman standing next to Seven. That must be Cammy.

The moment Rita pulls back, I'm struck by the resemblance of Seven and Cammy standing next to one another. The Wrenley family must have strong genetics or Eli and Seven must look a lot alike.

Then, my attention is taken up by the striking, beautiful woman standing behind them.

She's gorgeous, with long blonde hair and a body that looks like it has never missed a Pilates class.

Seven mentioned that his niece was coming but he didn't mention another woman would be accompanying them. I could understand why he would want the spare bedroom for Cammy, but is there more reason for why he wanted me out of his house so desperately before Cammy arrived? Is it possible that Seven also has a confession about his relationship status?

I watch as Seven introduces the blonde woman to Rita, and then his eyes flash to mine as Rita and the blonde exchange pleasantries.

I quickly divert eye contact, not wanting him to know that I was staring at them.

Pulling the bin full of dishes off the table that I just cleared, I glance up, pulling the bin into my arms, and find Rita leading the other three straight toward me.

"Brynn, I want you to meet Cammy, Seven's niece and my favorite human on earth."

Cammy smiles over at me and reaches out a hand.

The box is too heavy for me to shake her hand, but Seven grips the bin and pulls it effortlessly out of my hand before I can decline.

"I'll take this to the kitchen for you," he says and heads for the back door, where the busboy is already loading and unloading the dishwasher before the dinner rush.

"Oh... uh, thank you," I tell him, but he's already halfway across the restaurant in seconds.

It's almost as if he was looking for an excuse to leave.

"Hi, I'm Brynn," I say.

"It's nice to meet you finally. I'm Cammy. I've heard a lot about you. You're the woman who's been sleeping at my uncle's place, right?" Cammy smiles at Rita, and now I know where the informant came from.

"What?" I hear the blonde woman beside Cammy say, her face scrunching up a little.

Certainly, if the woman is here to see Seven, Cammy's comment could seem a little jarring.

"That was a misunderstanding. I got scammed out of renting his house, and then he generously let me stay until Rita found a spot for me here."

"Hi, we haven't met yet. I'm Josslin, Cammy's mom and Seven's fiancé—"

"Ex-fiancé," I hear Seven say as he takes steps toward us on his way back from the kitchen. "And I think sister-in-law is the title you settled on almost twenty years ago, if I'm not mistaken."

This is the woman he told me about last night?

"You still proposed marriage to me once, or have you forgotten."

Cammy and Rita both send Josslin sideways looks.

"No Josslin. I haven't forgotten any of the things you did in our past," he says.

There's almost a threat in his eyes, and she crosses her arms over her busty chest as if she's upset that he called her out.

Well, that confirms it. This is the woman who broke Seven's heart.

Why didn't he mention last night that Josslin was coming, too? I guess it's none of my business.

There's a pang of jealousy that shoots through me at the thought that the woman before me used to hold that much power over him, especially when I'm merely the woman he regrets spending the night with.

Josslin is the polar opposite of me. She has long blonde hair, is tall, and has a perfect body. She's Daniel's usual type as well, and she's nothing like my short five-foot-four stature and brown hair.

"You three came for food, so let's get you seated, shall we?" Rita says.

The three of them follow Rita to another table, and I watch as Josslin attempts to sit next to Seven on one side of the booth, but he narrowly escapes and decides to sit with Cammy on the other bench, leaving Josslin on her own.

I'm grateful when I notice that my shift is almost over, and I won't have to find busy work around the restaurant while we wait for the dinner rush to start.

I head back to the kitchen to see if I can help with the dishes, but everything is about caught up.

"You can take off a little early if you want. Everything is looking good in the back. You can head upstairs and get some writing done if you want," Marie says, walking into the back with the receipts from the lunch rush that ended a couple of hours ago.

"I think I'll take you up on that."

With only a week left, it's crunch time to finish this book. And avoiding the possibility of running into Seven again tonight is appealing all on its own.

I clock out and head back up to the apartment, sending a quick text to Sheridan.

> Brynn: Wrote 6,000 words last night.

> Sheridan: How's it going with Seven?

> Brynn: It's a long story. Talk later?

> Sheridan: Sure thing. Are you staying the rest of the week?

> Brynn: The writing is coming together and I have a place to stay now.

> Sheridan: Call me when you can.

> Brynn: I will.

CHAPTER NINETEEN

Seven

As soon as we order dinner, I excuse myself and head for the kitchen to check on the refrigerator for Miguel... the one that I already fixed.

I push through the doors of the kitchen, partly expecting to see Brynn on her break, but she's nowhere to be seen.

Just as well. I don't exactly want Brynn anywhere near Josslin and if I could have prevented them from ever meeting, I would have.

"Hey," I hear Miguel say as I move to the server side of the pickup window.

The smell of freshly fried chips fills the kitchen air as a server starts to fill dozens of clean baskets to the brim with golden-fried tortilla triangles in preparation for the dinner rush to start.

Miguel's kitchen staff are all prepping for dinner while I watch him start our plates of food.

"How's the fridge running for you?" I ask, since it's the excuse I used to get away.

"No problem today. Thanks for your help."

"No problem. Let me know if it acts up again," I say, grabbing one of the chips that dropped off the basket and onto the serving table.

I crunch down on it as I watch Miguel squirt oil onto the frying pan.

"I heard you have your hands full out there," Miguel says, with his back to me.

"Cammy's mom showed up uninvited."

Marie walks through the office that's located against the back wall of the kitchen. She probably just made the afternoon deposit into the safe.

When she sees me, she heads straight for me.

"Where's she staying? With you?" Miguel asks.

Josslin should know better than to test that boundary, but she's been pushing a few too many for my liking lately.

"Are we talking about Cammy's mom?" Marie asks, grabbing a basket of chips and a bowl of salsa and pushing it towards me.

After all these years, she never has to ask if I'm hungry.

"Thanks," I say, dipping a chip in the red sauce.

Miguel usually has a strict "no eating in the kitchen" rule, but he's always bending it for me when I'm back here working on something and between Rita and Marie, I always have something to eat.

He scrapes the onions and bell peppers that he chopped up on a cutting board into the hot skillet and steam billows up the large kitchen exhaust fan.

"If she tries to stay with me, she'll end up sleeping outside on the beach. She's not stepping foot in my house. I made that clear before she came."

"And how does Brynn feel about this?" Marie asks, snagging a chip out of the basket she gave me and plops it into her mouth.

"Brynn?"

"Don't play dumb with me. I saw how your eyes flashed to Brynn when Josslin called herself your fiancé. I was only a table away, picking up a check from the customer. I swear you almost turned completely purple for lack of oxygen."

Miguel looks over his shoulder and smirks at me as his wife calls me out.

Before I can answer, we hear the double doors to the kitchen push open.

Marie and I both look over our shoulders to find Cammy sauntering in.

"I figured you were hiding out in here," she says, as she walks up beside me, grabbing a chip out of my basket.

"Get your own chips," I tease.

"They taste better when I steal them from you."

Marie snickers at my usual back-and-forth banter with my niece.

"Are you sure she's not yours?" Marie jokes.

Cammy just smiles up at me with a smart-ass grin.

Unfortunately, she inherited the Wrenley personality. I can't take full credit for it. My dad is pretty similar. My brother on the other hand, can't take a joke.

"I'm headed back to work. You two behave," Marie says and then heads out of the kitchen.

"You left your mom out there?" I ask.

"No, Rita is entertaining Josslin."

"Mom. You call her mom," I remind Cammy.

"Why do you care what I call her?"

"We've been through this. She birthed you, and though I can't stand the woman, you turned out okay. I have to give her some credit for that."

"Then you call her mom."

"Cammy..." I warn.

"Grandpa sure brainwashed you into a die-hard momma's boy, didn't he?"

"Cam—" I warn again.

"Speaking of which," she cuts me off. "Grandma begged me to attempt to call her while you're on speaker so she can tell you how proud she is of you since you won't take her call until June 2nd of next year."

I let out a frustrated sigh. Of course, my mom is trying to use Cammy's time here to get to me. If my mom weren't a nervous flier, she'd probably have already visited Seattle a handful of times to see Cammy in hopes of running into me, too.

"She gets a call on her birthday. She knows the rules."

"Has anyone told you that you're a massive hypocrite?"

I look down at her as I crunch on another chip.

"Eat your chips, little girl."

Miguel turns around and pushes a plate of freshly cut mango, papaya, and pineapple toward Cammy.

"Yum, thanks!" she beams over at Miguel, who has already turned back and is working quickly on our food.

"So what are they talking about out there?" I ask.

"Rita offered to let *mom* stay in one of her guest bedrooms at the house."

I drop the chip I just picked up and shoot a look at Cammy.

"She did what?" I ask, the shock evident on my face. "Why would she do that?"

"You know, Rita. She probably wants to keep her enemies closer. I bet you Rita is planning to gather all the intel she can on mom's weaknesses so that she can hatch a plan to use them against her in the near future."

It figures that Rita would see some kind of challenge in this, but now I'm stuck with Josslin staying next door.

"How long is your mom staying?" I ask.

"She has a shift at the hospital in two days, so she can't stay long."

Two days is manageable. I can survive that. I think. As long as she stays with Rita and leaves me the hell alone.

Miguel turns around with our plates of food.

"All set. Need anything else?" he asks.

It's more than enough food. He gave us bigger portions than normal, and I'll probably still end up finishing up whatever Cammy doesn't eat.

"You ready?" I ask Cammy.

"Let's go."

She and I grab the plates of food and head out of the kitchen.

The sooner we get through dinner, the sooner I can drop Josslin off at Rita's and be done with her.

Tomorrow, after Cammy's shift, she and I will be miles out to sea with no Josslin in sight.

CHAPTER TWENTY

Brynn

With Cammy in today, Rita said that she won't need me on shift.

I spent all morning and afternoon trying to write but this apartment isn't drawing out the inspiration in me. I hear my stomach groan and check my phone to see that it's after two in the afternoon, which means that the lunch rush downstairs is probably over.

I haven't eaten all day and maybe it's time for some new scenery. Grabbing some lunch while I work through my next chapter might help to get things rolling again.

I'm nearing the end of the book, and all the chapters that I've been sending Sheridan have been met with a solid two thumbs-up. The book is coming together, and relief is starting a soothe the anxiety that I've been carrying around for months over this manuscript.

I head downstairs to order some food and while sitting in the small booth that Seven and I sat in the first time he brought me here, I think about my "Fix Me" list. It's been a while since I opened it back up and with only a handful more days left in Mexico, I should consider getting a few things marked off my list.

For a moment I feel like I'm being watched. I look up to find Josslin staring back at me from another booth. I give a small smile and wave though it feels forced, but I can't very well ignore her. She's staring at me and now I'm looking back at her.

She doesn't return the wave or the smile.

Awesome.

The spreadsheet pulls up, and my attention is pulled away quickly. I glance through the list to see if there is anything I should add or anything I might be able to check off.

One specific line item has a grip hold on me.

#7 – Have a fling in Mexico.

I don't know if one night with Seven constitutes a full-fledged fling. And since it ended the way it did—quickly and with Seven storming out of the room—I feel a little guilty about checking it off my list. But not bad enough not to get that satisfaction of seeing one less item on my list.

I mark it complete and feel an instant endorphin boost from my accomplishment.

"Good afternoon," I hear a voice say at the end of the booth.

I glance over to find Cammy standing there with a smile. She's dressed in a pair of board shorts and a Scallywag's t-shirt and white apron with an order notepad and pen in the pocket. Her brown hair is pulled up in a messy bun with tendrils of hair framing her face.

I study her face for a moment, noticing all the ways in which she looks so much like her uncle. I suppose they share DNA which makes sense.

"Hi, good afternoon," I say back.

"We didn't get to talk much yesterday. You left before dinner came," she glances at my open laptop. "Rita tells me you're a writer?"

"I am. That's actually why I left early. I have a book due next week that I'm trying to finish. The publisher is waiting on it and I'm way past my due date."

"What are you working on now?" she asks, glancing at my screen. "It doesn't look like a book. It looks like a list."

I snap back to my screen, almost forgetting that my "Fix Me" list is pulled up instead of my book.

"Oh, right. I guess you could call it a self-improvement bucket list. I want to accomplish a few things before my boyfriend—" I stop the second I say it.

This is the first time that calling Daniel my boyfriend has felt weird and awkward.

"You have a boyfriend? I thought you're dating my uncle."

I whip a look up at her in surprise by her comment.

She thought that Seven and I are dating?

I can only guess that Rita made her think that because I can't imagine she would have gotten that idea from Seven.

"No, he and I aren't dating. I just ended up at his house due to a misunderstanding with a scam website. He was generous enough not to leave me to sleep out on the beach during a hurricane."

She snickers. "My uncle can come off crabby, but despite his best efforts to hide it, he's a really good guy."

I can't argue with her there. He is crabby, and yet, I see the other sides of him too. When he shows up for Rita whenever she needs him and how protective he is of Cammy.

"Yeah, I'm starting to see that."

"So, you have a boyfriend?" she asks.

"We're not technically together right now. We're on the break... thus the list. It's a list of things I want to do before we get back together to improve on myself."

Her eyebrows furrow at my explanation. "Is this a list of things he's making you change before you get back together with him?"

I can hear it in her tone. It's the same one I get from Sheridan.

"Oh no!" I say quickly. The last thing I need is yet another person getting a bad opinion of Daniel, even if it is someone I may never see again. "We broke up while he left the country for work and there are a few things I want to accomplish for myself before he gets home and we get back together."

I can see in her eyes that she doesn't seem convinced, but she drops it and lowers herself to the booth, taking a seat next to me.

"Mind if I take a look?"

She doesn't wait for an answer as she reaches for the laptop and turns it towards herself.

I've never shown anyone the list before, but it's not as if it's anything crazy. There's no reason why she can't see it.

"Go on a first date—Sleep through a storm alone—Go deep sea fishing," she stops listing them out loud as she continues to read down the list.

"It's nothing crazy, but I want to try to check off as many items as possible before leaving."

"It looks like you've made some progress. Number seven, "Have a fling in Mexico," is checked off," she smirks over at me, and all I want to do is slink under the table and hide by burning red cheeks. "Does the number have any correlation with the man?"

Damn it, I didn't think about how she might draw a conclusion that her uncle is the one responsible for completing that task. And in my defense, I listed the activity as number seven before I even left Seattle. That's a pure and unfortunate coincidence.

I divert my attention away from her to hide the obvious tell across my face. The last thing I want to do is discuss what happened between me and Seven to his eighteen-year-old niece, nor do I think Seven would appreciate me divulging the details to a member of his family.

"Sorry, that's none of my business," she says and then glances back at the list. "This guy... the boyfriend that you're not currently dating, is he bettering himself for you during this break, too?"

I think about it for a second, but the only thing he's mentioned working on before we get back together is his career.

"Not exactly. I'm sort of the one with the neurosis that needs to be fixed, not him."

I heard what I said the second I said it. It's a little hard to take back now.

Cammy shoots me a look with a lifted eyebrow. The kind of look people give you when they think you're exaggerating. If only she knew that I wasn't. If she asked her uncle, I'm sure he could tell her about the time he had to break into his own bathroom when we lost power and I screamed like I was trapped inside with an ax murderer. Or the time I had a panic attack the night of the storm and he brought me into his bed to monitor me all night.

I'm a mess, and Seven can vouch for that. I do have things to work on, and I have every intention of doing them.

Cammy looks back over at the list.

"Ok, well, you're in luck. We can check another one of those items off today."

"We can?" I ask, unable to hide my intrigue.

"My lunch shift is almost over and I'm taking Rita's car over to the marina to meet my uncle to go fishing. Come with us."

My instant reaction is to jump on the opportunity. Cross off another item would feel like a huge accomplishment today, especially since my time here is running low. The thing is, I can't imagine that Seven will be thrilled with being stuck on a boat for hours at a time with me.

"As much as I'd like to say yes, I don't think your uncle would love that idea."

Her eyebrows scrunch together. "Why not? He won't even know you're there. The boat is huge and he's only taking me out because I begged him. If you haven't noticed, my uncle can kind of be a stick in the mud. I'll have more fun with another girl around and he'll leave us alone to fish by ourselves. Please come?" she asks, practically batting her eyelashes.

The offer was already too good to pass up, and now, with her begging, I can't turn her down.

"Ok, I'll come. But if he's pissed off when we show up, I'm leaving. Can you give me a minute to change and take my laptop upstairs?"

Cammy beams back at me and claps her hands together.

"Absolutely! I'll meet you out front in ten minutes."

I watch as she pushes herself out of the booth and then makes large slides towards the kitchen doors.

Before Cammy disappears into the kitchen, I see Josslin get up for her booth from the corner of my eye and head straight for Cammy. Josslin doesn't look happy when she approaches, and Cammy seems almost annoyed. I'm too far away to hear them but it doesn't take long before Cammy turns and walks away leaving Josslin standing outside of the kitchen doors alone and fuming.

Josslin turns towards me, her eyes narrowed, but she doesn't head towards my direction. She turns and leaves and I have to wonder why she's so upset with Cammy.

I close my laptop and slide out of the booth, wondering what people wear on fishing excursions.

Eleven minutes later, I speed walk out of the restaurant and out to the parking lot looking for Cammy. I lost track of time texting my mom about how my book is coming along and updating her on my new living arrangements.

I hear a car horn honk and then the same newer truck that I've seen in Rita driveway pulls up with Cammy at the wheel. I start walking towards her when she yells out to me.

"You look cute! Let's go," she yells.

"Thanks," I yell back.

I glance down at my outfit as I walk. I chose a pair of distressed denim shorts that Daniel always says makes my butt look good, and a racerback tank top and sports bra, that admittedly shows off more of my cleavage than is necessary for a fish trip, but it's hot today and I'd rather avoid pit stains in a t-shirt since we'll be out in the sun. Paired with a set of leather flip flops and a Scallywag's baseball cap with my ponytail pulled through it, I'm ready to knock off this next item on my list. And hopefully Seven isn't too pissed off that I'm joining in.

I open the passenger door and then hop inside, closing the truck door next to me and clipping in my seatbelt.

"I wasn't sure what to wear," I say.

Cammy gives me a once-over as she puts the truck back in drive and heads to exit the parking lot.

"No, this is perfect. If this doesn't do the trick, then nothing will.'

"Doesn't do the trick for what?" I ask.

"Getting you entry on my uncle's boat. One look at you and he won't be able to resist our request."

A zip of excitement races through my spine at the thought of Seven not being able to resist me, but then I remember the look on his face when he found out about Daniel.

"I don't know what you think is going on between us, Cammy, but I assure you that it's nothing. Your uncle has no interest in me and I have plans to get back together with someone when I get back home," I tell her.

"Just so you know, neither you or my uncle hide the looks you give each other when you think the other one isn't watching. I might not know you all that well, but I know Seven and I've never seen him show interest in a woman before. I've certainly not seen him follow a woman's every movement around an entire restaurant before yesterday."

I just about laughed out loud at the absurdity of her comment.

"Show interest? You think your uncle is showing interest in me? He couldn't wait to get me out of his house. I promise you, he isn't interested in me. And if he was following my movements it was probably to keep tabs on me to make sure I don't come anywhere near him."

If I told her about how Seven found Daniel's texts on my phone right after we had sex and now thinks the worst of me, she'd have a better understanding.

"My uncle can seem complicated when you don't know him. I can relate to not understanding how put off he always seems. With Seven, you have to see the things he does for you... his acts of service. I know he can seem like he couldn't care less about your existence at first, but once you're in his keeping, he's a different person, ask any of the guys on the Hawkeyes team. Ask Rita, Marie, Silas, or Miguel. They'll all tell you the same thing."

We pull into the marina parking lot. A building for boat rentals and an attached restaurant sit along the water. Beyond that are rows and rows of docks that are mostly empty. Out in the distance, several boats seem to be making their way back. Seven said something about the boats being anchored out at sea during the storm and now they must be bringing them back in now that it's safe.

I search each of the boats currently docked to see if I can spot Seven. It doesn't take long before I see Seven standing on one of the larger sport fishing boats with a large, covered cockpit and a tall flybridge above it. I know Seven has one of the largest paying contracts in the NHL but this is the first time I've seen him show any of that off. His beach house could use a renovation, his Jeep is at least ten years old and he mostly wears Scallywag's merchandise that Rita probably gave him along with canvas work pants or the occasional board shorts.

He stares back at us from a distance, neatly coiling up a long rope, probably to stow it away. He continues to coil up the rope as he stares back at me, his eyes narrowing. He doesn't look happy to see me sitting in the passenger side of Rita's truck. I knew this was a mistake.

His intense stare makes me want to slink down in the passenger leather seats and hide from sight.

I'm tempted to pull up the rideshare app now and get the heck out of here. I don't need to guess that I won't be welcomed if I stroll up to that boat.

Besides, I need to write anyway.

"Wait here a second, Ok?" Cammy says, opening up the driver's door and then hops out of the truck.

I should have known that she was selling our fishing excursion too easily. Seven's already mentioned that he wants time with his niece without distraction, and here I am, showing up on their fishing trip.

"Cammy, I should go—" I try to argue before she closes the door.

"Don't move a muscle. I'll be right back."

Before I can offer a rebuttal, she's gone, practically skipping down the boat launch and headed for Seven's boat slip.

He sees her wave to him, but he has a look on his face like he's already preparing for what Cammy is about to drop on him.

I see Cammy's animated hands as she starts to explain something to him the closer she gets to the boat. He stands there, listening to her, his expression softening to whatever she tells him. Then, quickly out of nowhere, his eyes darken again and they flash over to the truck I'm still sitting in. He stares back at me for a moment and then nods down to her.

They exchange a few words, and then Cammy spins around and heads back toward me, a skip in her step and a bright smile across her lips. I watch as Seven turns his back on us and moves inside the boat's covered interior.

He must have agreed but he doesn't look happy about it.

The last thing I want to do is cause more issues between us. After all, Seven has done a lot for me when he didn't have to. I should probably let him off the hook and say I'm feeling under the weather but giving up this opportunity to check off one more box is hard to pass up.

Cammy trots up to my open passenger window, beaming from ear to ear.

"Told you that he'd agree. He'll stay out of our way and let us do our thing."

"Are you sure? Because he didn't look very happy when you were talking to him just now." I say, glancing back at the boat with no Seven left in sight.

He hasn't reemerged after ducking into the enclosed cockpit of the large fishing boat.

"Oh that? That was about something else. Don't worry about it," she says, swatting at the air as if their conversation was no big deal. "I told him that you've never gone ocean fishing before and it's on your bucket list. He's cool with you coming along, I promise."

My bucket list?

My pulse jumps at the mention of her telling him about my "Fix Me" list.

"Wait, you told him about the list? What exactly did you tell him?"

Oh God!

I hope she didn't tell him that I checked off the "Have a fling in Mexico".

That one night together is why he avoids me when he can. How would he react if it seemed like I used him to fulfill a checklist of things I wanted to do before Daniel and I got back together?

Cammy grabs for the handle of the passenger side of the truck and opens my door for me. Now I'm not so sure I want to get out.

"Nothing. Just that you have a list of things you want to check off before you go home. That's all. I told him that I want to help you mark another item since you're leaving in a few days."

Something tells me that there is more to what she told him, but she and I don't know each other well enough for me to drill her without making this awkward. Whatever she said to him, I'll just have to face the possibility of him trusting me even less than he already does.

I unbuckle my seatbelt and then slide out of the truck.

"Has he ever told you no?" I ask, already witnessing that Seven seems to be much softer regarding his niece.

Cammy shuts the passenger door behind me as I step out of the way.

"Are you kidding? He tells me no all the time. I'm convinced that the word makes up fifty percent of his vocabulary," she teases as we start towards the docks. "People think he lets me get away with everything, but that's not even close to the truth. He's just a lot harsher with most everyone else."

That's not as comforting as she probably thought it would be.

"I just don't want to make things worse between us. I only have three more days and I don't want to make enemies."

"It's going to be fine, trust me," Cammy starts to feel around her pockets as we walk.

Seven's boat comes closer and closer with every step we take. "Shoot, I left the keys in the truck. I should grab those really quick before we leave on the boat for the rest of the day."

I do as she suggests. Maybe there are a few words that Seven would like to have with me before Cammy returns. I'd rather she doesn't hear all the gory details of why he doesn't like me.

"Ok, I'll meet you at the boat," I say.

Cammy turns and heads back speed walking towards the truck.

The moment I reach the boat, I prepare myself for whatever Seven might say.

As I approach, I hear the loud humming of the boat's six engines running, all lined up agains the back of the boat. The water swirling from the propellers underneath. Seven finally walks back out of the cockpit.

"So, you're coming out with us?" he says.

"Cammy said she would teach me to fish. I've never been deep sea fishing, and there's no better time to experience it than right now before I go home."

"Speaking of Cammy, where is she?" he asks.

"She forgot the keys in the truck and ran back to get them. She'll be right back."

We both over at the parking lot to see Cammy jumping into the truck, starting the ignition, and then speeding off out of the parking lot.

My jaw drops.

I have no clue what just happened.

"Where is she going?" I ask, hoping he knows something I don't and not that I've just been stranded here with him.

"Looks like Rita is rubbing off on my niece. I would say this is a firepit repeat."

I turn back to him quickly. "Why are they doing this?"

"You're going to have to go straight to the source with that question. I have an idea of why Rita is doing it, but I don't know how my niece got roped into it now too. Just tell Rita that you're getting back together with your ex. That should clear a few things up."

There's almost a sharpness to his voice at that last sentence.

"You don't have to take me fishing; I'll just call a rideshare to come get me. I warned Cammy before we left the restaurant that you wouldn't want me to tag along anyway."

I turn back towards the direction I came but I only take one step and then I hear his voice.

"She said you have a list."

Damn it, of course, he's going to bring that up.

"It's just a bucket list, and not something that you have any responsibility to help me accomplish. I can hire a guide to take me out. It's really not a big deal," I say, trying to let him off the hook.

Seven sighs loudly and then steps closer to the side of the boat and offers up his hand.

"Come on, let's get this over with. Rita and Cammy won't rest until they think they've done everything they can do to force us to spend time together. We'll give them what they want and prove they have it wrong."

There it is again.

He said it at the firepit, and now he's repeating it here. It's exactly what I expect him to say, and with Daniel coming home in a couple more weeks, the outcome makes the most sense. However, it doesn't stop my stomach from feeling a little queasy with disappointment every time he says it.

"Right, we'll prove them wrong," I say, sliding my hand into his.

His warm fingers wrap completely around mine, and then he pulls me in and guides me carefully into the boat.

As soon as I'm standing on the back deck Seven releases me immediately. Something catches my eye on the dock. I turn to see someone from the marina walk toward us.

"Are you ready, sir?" he asks.

"Yeah, we're ready."

Seven walks to the cockpit as the attendant unhooks the ropes and tosses them onboard. I take the couple steps up towards the cockpit and then walk along the side of the boat until I make it to the front where it looks like some kind of sundeck in the front of the boat. This boat couldn't have been cheap.

"Have a good day at sea," the man yells to Seven and then smiles at me.

Seven gives the man a quick wave and then starts to pull the boat out of the boat slip we're parked in.

I take a seat on the large, padded bench in the front of the boat while Seven moves us out into the open water.

"The spot we're headed to is over an hour from here," he yells over the wind and the engines.

I just nod instead of attempting to compete with the overbearing sounds all around us.

I turn towards the ocean, feeling the wind whip through my ponytail and watch under the visor of my hat as the vast ocean surrounds us the further away from land that we get.

The beauty and the serenity of it might be just what I need today.

I already feel more inspired to write than I did all morning and afternoon.

I don't dare look back at the cockpit behind me. Instead, I try to forget that I'm alone on a boat with a man who probably wishes he were anywhere else other than here with me.

Chapter Twenty-One

Seven

Driving out to my favorite fishing spot, I can't stop myself from glancing over at Brynn every few minutes since we left the marina.

She looks relaxed, sitting on the bench that runs along the boat's side, watching the ocean go by as we cut through the deep blue water.

Her long tan legs stretch out in front of her on the cushion, and cross at her ankles. I follow them up her thighs until they disappear under her tight denim shorts. I know what that soft skin feels like under my fingertips.

When Cammy first walked up to the boat to ask if Brynn could come, my first reaction was to deny her request. I've spent the last couple of days keeping my distance from Brynn so that I don't do something stupid again, like push her up against the side of a building and put my hand up her dress.

But then Cammy told me about the list.

A fucking list of things she needs to do to better herself for her asshole ex-fiancé.

It's hard enough not to demand an answer for why the hell she puts up with her ex but what Brynn does after she leaves in a few days and heads back to Seattle, is none of my business. I doubt we'll ever cross paths again. We've lived across the street from each other for years and neither of us have noticed the other person from the windows of our apartments before, there's no reason for that to change.

The difference is, now I know that her apartment is directly across the street and on the same level as mine.

I guess I'll be living in my apartment for the next couple of years with the window shades pulled down until I retire and move to Mexico more permanently. I don't need to witness Brynn living an unsatisfied sex life with the prick who doesn't deserve her.

We finally make it to our destination almost an hour later. Now that it's just after five o'clock, we won't have much time to fish, if we want to get back before dark.

I kill the engine and walk out of the cockpit and onto the main deck.

"Are we here?" she asks, swinging her legs off the cushions and planting her pair feet on the boat's decking.

"This is where I've had the most luck catching fish this year, so we'll try here first. If we don't get anything, we'll move on. The goal is to get you a fish today."

"Aren't you going to fish, too? I assume you didn't bring the boat all the way out here just for me."

I don't look back over at her as I head down the steps toward the fishing deck at the back of the boat. I pull out a fishing rod from the cabinet I keep them in and start setting up a spot for her in the right corner of the boat.

"Don't worry about why I'm out here. You wanted to fish, right? So, let's get fishing."

"Ok…" she says softly, standing behind me as I prep her fishing rod and bait the hook for her.

"You've never fished before?" I ask.

"I went lake fishing a handful of times with my dad and brother when I was a kid. We stood on the shore to fish, but I never caught anything. This is my first-time fishing in the ocean… or in a boat. It seemed like a good opportunity to try while I was here," she says, stepping around me to get a closer look at what I'm doing.

She watches every movement I make as if jotting down notes for future use.

"It's not all that different from fishing on the shore. You just need to cast the line out, slowly reel it in, and wait."

I demonstrate the movement, sending the line out into the water with a smooth flick of my wrist and then show her how to reel it all the way back in. Once I complete the action from start to finish, I hand her the rod to try.

She takes the fishing rod from me and then mimics my movements. Her cast isn't perfect, but with a little practice, she'll improve. The bait at the end of the line makes a small splash when it hits the water. "Like this?"

"Here, let me show you what it should feel like." I move closer, wrapping my arms around either side of her. The swaying of the ocean causes her back to glide across my chest occasionally as I reel the line back in. Once the line comes out of the water, I adjust her grip slightly, trying to ignore how her ass rubs against my cock every time the waves in the ocean have her losing her footing and swaying back into me. She doesn't have her sea legs yet. "Hold it like this. It gives you better control," I say and then move her hands into a better position on the rod.

A bigger wave hits against the boat, swaying us harder than the waves before. Her breath hitches when I grip her hips and pull her back against my chest to steady her and keep her from losing her balance.

"You ok?" I ask over her shoulder before I release my hold on her.

"Yeah," she says, clearing her throat. "I'm fine. How are you so good at keeping your balance?"

"Exceptional balance is part of the job description for a hockey player and I spend a lot of time on my boat during the off-season. Are you ready to try again?"

"I'm ready," she says, glancing down at her hands on the fishing rod.

I place my hands over hers and pull her hands back as she clutches the fishing rod. I guide her wrists over her shoulder, and then, with a flick of both of our wrists, we send the fishing line reeling out toward the ocean.

"Was that better?" she asks.

Her cast could still improve, but it's good enough for today, and since she's leaving in three days, I won't likely get another chance to work on it with her.

I release her hands and let her take it from here.

"It was a lot better. Did you feel the difference?" I ask.

She swallows hard and then nods. "Yeah... I feel the difference."

I can't see her expression, but something in the tone of her voice has me wondering if we're still talking about fishing.

The tricky thing about questions is that they most often lead to answers. Sometimes, those answers are ones we're not ready for.

"Will you fish with me?" she asks, looking over her shoulder. "I feel a little self-conscious with you just standing there watching."

"You shouldn't feel self-conscious; you're doing great."

However, using fishing as a distraction to keep my mind off of Brynn, isn't a bad idea.

I grab one of the other fishing rods that I keep on board and do the same thing to prep my line. Then, I take up the opposite corner of the fishing deck and cast out my own line.

"What are we fishing for?" she asks.

"There's a lot of options out here but in this spot, I've caught a lot of kingfish, mackerel, and snapper, among other things."

"Have you ever caught anything really big out here?"

"Not in this spot. If you wanted to fish for bigger game, we'd use fishing rods and reels with a higher weight rating and different bail. Plus, you'd need to be strapped in."

"Strapped in?" she asks, looking over at me, her eyebrows stitching together.

"I'm guessing you've never seen anyone reel in a monster. It would rip your tiny little body right out of this boat."

"Oh..." she says, looking back out to the ocean.

I chuckle to myself at the look of her disappointment. Did she think we were going to come out here and she was going to hook a trophy Marlin on her first try?

"Let's start with trying to catch your first fish, then we'll take it from there, huh?"

She nods slowly but doesn't look back at me as she slowly reels her line back in just like I instructed.

Her list didn't specify which kind of fish she wanted to catch, only that she wanted to go deep sea fishing.

We stand there, on opposite sides of the boat, our lines in the water and silence swallowing all the words I want to say to her about the list and the dick she's doing them all for. The only sound is the gentle lapping of the ocean water against the side of the boat.

It's going to start getting dark in the next couple of hours and we'll need to head back. If I want to say something about Daniel and this list, now is the time.

"Cammy told me about your list," I say, breaking the silence.

Brynn stiffened slightly. "Did she now?"

"She said that you have a list of things to check off before you get back together with Daniel." I glance over at her, finding her turned halfway towards me and a guarded look in her eyes. "That's what this is all about, right?"

She clears her throat, still slowly reeling in her line.

"It's not all about him. I know that there are things about me that I can improve on. And there's nothing wrong with wanting to try new things and become a more open person who is adventurous and wants to experience new things."

"You're right. There isn't anything wrong with wanting to try something new, but be honest with me. Did you make this list strictly because it was your idea, or did you start it because Daniel made you think you need to improve something about yourself before you get back together?"

She doesn't respond immediately, and the silence is the answer I hoped isn't true.

"It's a bucket list. That's all it is," she says but we both know that it's more than that.

"You named it the "Fix-Me" list, Brynn," I say, my voice sterner with her than before.

"I know what I named it. And that was private. You were never supposed to know about that." she argues.

"Why? Because if other people knew that your future husband manipulated you into giving him a hall pass, convinced you that your lack of orgasms isn't his incompetence in the bedroom, and made you believe that there's something wrong with you that you need to fix, that you'd have to finally face the truth?"

I can see the fire burn in her eyes. She doesn't like that I'm calling out her relationship, and maybe I shouldn't have.

"The truth?" she asks. "What's the truth then, Seven? You seem to know everything about Daniel... about me... about our relationship. For a guy who hasn't had a long-term, meaningful relationship for most of his adult life, please enlighten me with your holy hockey wisdom, and whatever you do, don't leave anything out."

Every word she speaks drips with sarcasm.

I don't answer. There's nothing I can say in response that will defuse this situation and get her to see where I'm coming from. I want her to see that there's nothing wrong with her. He's the one with the issues.

If those daggers in her eyes weren't pointed at me, I'd probably applaud her for standing her ground, but instead, all I want to do is shake her until she wakes up and sees that Daniel is using her. But this is her life and her relationship—I should have left it alone.

Besides, what difference does it make to me if she ends up with Daniel?

She's staying with him because he's promised to marry her. Based on that information alone, I can assume that Brynn wants the one thing I've been avoiding giving any woman for the last two decades, —a relationship.

There was a time when I wanted that more than anything... more than hockey. Then I learned how painful it can be when you give someone access to one of the most vital organs of the human body—your heart—and they decide to take a chainsaw to it.

I reel in my line and set my fishing rod in the plastic holster attached to the inside edge of the boat. Somehow, I'm no longer in the mood to fish.

She shakes her head with irritation and then turns back towards the ocean, continuing to reel in her line.

I head up the stairs towards the cockpit to grab my phone and check the time. But mostly, it's just an excuse to get a little space between us. We both need to cool off.

"I got something!" I hear Brynn yell behind me as I take my first step up the stairs.

I turn quickly to see Brynn fighting against the line and digging her feet in as whatever fish she has on the line is pulling her closer and closer to the edge of the boat. Whatever fish it is, it's large enough to have the fishing rod practically bent in half.

Before I can react, the fish forces Brynn to take two large steps forward in a game of tug-of-war that Brynn has no chance of winning.

"Brynn! Let go of the rod," I yell.

"I can get it. Just give me a chance!" she argues.

"It's going to pull you in. Let go!" I yell once more.

When she doesn't listen, I jump off the stairs and head straight for her. She's determined to reel in this fish, and though I would appreciate her determination at any other time... this fish is about to take her overboard, and if it does, I'll have no choice but to jump in after her.

If Brynn doesn't come back up for air, neither will I.

I won't go home without her.

"No, it won't, I almost have it," she yells back, her eyes locked on the fishing rod, trying without success to move the reel forward.

The fish jerks her again, this time pulling hard enough to smash Brynn's hip right into the solid white fiberglass of the boat.

"Let go, Brynn!" I say, running toward her.

The fish thrashes again, as I thought it would, and pulls Brynn up onto the side of the boat.

She lets out a shriek just before I get to her and wrap one arm around her while my other hand yanks out the small knife I have in my pocket and slice the line to the fishing rod, letting the fish get away.

We stumble back into the boat with my arm protectively around her until I'm sure she has her footing.

I let out a sigh of relief—Brynn's safe in the boat and not at the bottom of the ocean.

"Why did you do that? I told you that I almost had it," she says.

"Because you didn't have it. That fish was about to drown you. You're welcome for me saving your life, by the way."

She turns back to look out at the ocean.

There's no evidence of the fish that got away, but when she turns back to look at me, she's beaming—the polar opposite facial expression she had a moment ago.

"I can't believe I just caught a fish!" she says, her smile so bright; it's almost painful to see that after over a week together, this is the first time I've seen her really smile. "Oh my God... feel my heartbeat."

She lifts my right hand and brings it up to her chest, laying it flat against her body.

My hand covers her heart and most of her left breasts.

I don't need to be reminded of how her bare breasts feel in my hands. I remember it vividly from days ago. My cock twitches the moment I feel her hard nipple under her tank top.

Does she know I can feel it?

"It's racing from catching that fish." Her entire face is lit up with excitement. "Can you feel that?"

I nod, feeling the pounding heartbeat. "Yeah, I can feel it. It matches mine," I admit, though my heart races for different reasons.

Without warning, she reaches toward me. The heat of her fingertips glides up my ribcage until her palm rests over my left pec.

"It's beating almost as fast as mine," she says, her hand covering the organ she's infiltrated so easily despite my best efforts to keep her out.

I drop my hand from her body. If I keep it there any longer, she'll end up laid out on the bed below the deck cabin with my head between her thighs and my handprint on her ass.

"It's racing from watching you almost get pulled overboard," I admit.

Her eyes reach up to mine—her eyebrows softening.

Her eyes meet mine, her eyebrows softening. "That's one way to get me out of your life for good. You'd never have to worry about me sneaking onto your boat again uninvited," she smirks, but nothing about the idea is funny to me.

Losing Brynn to Daniel is bad enough; losing her to the ocean is something I'd never get over and something I'll never let happen. If the ocean requires one of us, it can take me. As long as I'm of sound mind and body, I won't ever allow a single strand of hair on her head to be harmed.

"Where did you get that from? I don't want you out of my life for good," I say, but Brynn rolls her eyes in response. "And what part of the last week and a half leads you to believe that I'd let you get hurt? If you would have gotten pulled in, I would have dove in after you."

Her eyebrows pull together, and her pink lips turn down into a frown. A look of confusion covers her beautiful features.

"You would have gone in after me? Why would you do that?" she asks, her eyes frantically searching mine.

"Because there's no limit to what I'd do to keep you safe. And I wouldn't have bothered to come back up for air unless you were coming up with me."

She gives a slight shake of her head.

"That's ridiculous. You're saying that you'd risk drowning to protect a girl you don't even like. That makes no sense."

"You think I don't like you? Nothing could be further from the truth."

She clucks her tongue to the roof of her mouth, rolling her eyes and then turns to walk away from me.

I gently grip her wrist and spin her back to face me.

She's ready with her rebuttal the second our eyes connect again. "Of course, it's the truth. You couldn't get me out of your house soon enough; you avoid me at any cost, you—"

I interrupt her from listing any other infractions she's ready to hold against me. I've fucked up over and over again; it's not as if I'm not well aware of all the things I wish I could do over with her. But the more I let her in, the harder it will be to let her go.

"None of it has anything to do with not liking you. It's the opposite. It's because it's getting harder and harder to keep my hands to myself whenever you're close by. I've kept distance between us so I don't slip up and we end up repeating what happened outside of Scallywag's"

She rolls her eyes again like she doesn't believe me.

"You could have fooled me. You're making it look pretty easy to keep your distance from where I stand."

She has no idea how difficult it's been for me to stay away.

How I hear her voice singing at the top of her lungs to the music on the radio whenever I drive my Jeep.

How I take a deep, inhale every time I walk into my bathroom because it still smells like her shampoo, though she took the bottles when she left.

How much I hate seeing the mug she used for her daily tea sitting vacant and idle on my kitchen counter.

Something in me snaps and my feral craving for her is too strong to ignore anymore. I hate that she believes I don't want her. I'll never be her worthless ex who wants her when it's convenient. Is that how she sees me?

I have to touch her. I have to know what it feels like to hold her in my arms again. And I need her to know that she's wanted... she's wanted by me.

Soon, we'll both be back in Seattle, living separate lives, and this could be my last chance to prove that to her. If she's about to spend her life with a man who can't satisfy her and gave her up once to stick his cock in anything that moved while on work vacation in Australia, I want her to remember that there was once a man who worshiped every inch of her.

"You think this has been easy for me?" I say, taking a step closer. She holds her ground and straightens her spine defiantly. "If you want the truth, Brynn... it's that I can't stop thinking about you—day and night—whether we're together or we're apart."

Her eyes widen as my hand wraps around her back and pull her to me.

I bend down, pressing my lips to hers and inhale her gasp.

She wasn't expecting me to kiss her... and neither was I until I could no longer hold myself back.

I should be keeping my distance—I should be resisting this pull towards her at every turn.

It only takes seconds for her rigid body to soften, melting into me. Her hands come up, gripping my shirt just below my collarbone as she pulls me closer to her.

I pull her back with me as I back up, taking a seat on the back bench by the stairs.

Our lips don't break from each other, not even for a moment as my hands travel down further to grip around her hips, pulling her into my lap. She releases my shirt, and then her arms reach up, securing around the back of my neck for stability.

She comes willing, not an inkling of hesitation in her body language or her kiss.

I pull her further up my lap until her shapely ass is nestled atop my growing erection.

A little gasp of surprise and excitement flows through her lips against mine when she feels how hard I am between her thighs. Pride fills my chest that I'm able to garner that reaction for her again.

She's no stranger to what's behind my board shorts and if this continues, she'll have a repeat performance of what I can do with it.

"He's wrong about the list Brynn. You're perfect the way you are and if it were up to me, you wouldn't change anything."

She pulls me tighter, her mouth opening for me, and I take her offering, sliding my tongue over her bottom lip first and then swiping gently into her mouth to taste her tongue.

She tastes sweet, just like she always does. Her hum of approval when I slip my tongue in and take her mouth, has me ready to lay her on the teak wood of the deck, completely naked and let the sea air listen to the way I fuck her. I should take her to the bed in the downstairs cabin to shield her from the rare potential of another boat coming close by but the twenty steps to get us there is too damn long to wait when it's felt like months... no, years, since the last time I've had her.

I need her naked now so that I can consume every inch of the woman I can't stop thinking about.

I want to hear her whimper out my name every time I drive into her, bottoming out in her tight pussy until she comes and her body pulsates over me, gripping me and bringing me to my own release.

"One last time... before you leave and head back to Seattle," I say, staring down at her swollen lips that I caused with my own.

"One last time," she agrees.

Having her one more time isn't enough—it will never be enough, but I have to stop this addiction at some point before it shatters my world like it will the day she leaves.

I slide my fingers over the hem of her shirt, asking silently for consent. Brynn nods against my mouth.

I want to strip her naked of everything so that I can see what she's thinking and feeling, but I'll have to settle for her clothes only. She's going back to Daniel, and she hasn't given me any inkling to think she's open to an alternate ending, not that I could give her what she wants even if she told me that I have a chance.

I discard her shirt and then sports bra and once she's bare for me from the waist band up, I slide my hands up her sides, my thumbs glazing over her rib cage until my hands come forward, cupping her supple breasts carefully. I'm in no rush with her this time. Instead, I want to savor and memorize every touch, every taste, and every sound she makes.

Just before I begin to ease her into my touch, she slides off my lap.

I make a disappointed groan and she chuckles in response.

"Don't worry, I'm coming back. I thought you might like these off," she says, gesturing to her shorts.

"Am I that transparent?" I ask.

"Maybe a little."

I take her lead and pull off my shirt and slide down my boardshorts quickly until every article of clothing I was wearing is now on the floor below me.

My cock stands at attention as I sit there, fully naked, waiting for Brynn to do the same.

She glances down at the erection she caused, her tongue slipping out quickly to lick her bottom lip.

Jesus Christ, this woman is going to end me.

I watch her stand in front of me, topless as if she wants to tease me, standing just out of my reach. Not that one quick move on my part wouldn't have her back on my lap in half a second or less if I wanted to. Years of hockey drills make me faster than most. But I like this part of Brynn. I like it when she feels so confident and sexy that she can stand in front of me, hinting at a possible strip tease.

My gaze roams over every inch and curve of her body, from her full breasts and peach-colored nipples all the way down to her tiny belly button that has a small scar where I presume a belly button piercing used to be. From the look of it, it healed up years ago. But something about that piercing tells a story of the girl Brynn used to be... or the girl she thinks she used to be.

Confident.

Adventurous.

Sexy as hell.

The girl that she thinks the list is supposed to turn her back into, I presume.

Why can't she see that she's still that person? I know that she is because she lets me see that side of her ever so often.

But the woman she is now, is all the best parts of who she used to be, and who she's becoming. I'd tell her, but I know she won't believe me.

Brynn makes a show of it—unbuttoning her shorts slowly, her eyes locked on mine. She wants me to watch and I don't plan on looking at anything but her. She unzips them next and bites down on her lower lip. Finally, she wiggles them off her ass, her tits bouncing with the movement and then pushes them down to her ankles, along with her panties.

"Fuck," I mutter to myself.

I can't tell if her cheeks turn pink at my reaction or if they're a little sun-kissed from our time out at sea.

The two other times I've seen her naked, it's been in the dark. She's gorgeous in any lighting, but seeing Brynn completely naked in the light of day with the ocean and the horizon at her back is by far my favorite.

How does a man walk away from this? How could Daniel think that there's anything out there better than her?

In my long career, I've met more than my fair share of women, and not a single one of them could measure up to Brynn—not even close.

Daniel's a fucking greedy-ass-bastard.

"Come here," I say.

She takes a step closer, just close enough that I lean forward and reach for her hand, taking it into mine.

I pull her closer and then she's back on my lap, skin to skin.

She lifts up on her knees, scooting herself closer on the bench down my legs. I adjust myself to fit under her, the tip of my cock sliding through her slit in order to fit. All of the sudden her eyes widen.

"Condom," she says, wide-eyed.

"Shit. I forgot."

I never forget.

Not since Josslin.

This is the first time I didn't think about using a condom with a woman in two decades. There is no better evidence of how bad I want Brynn than this, I almost slip up right here. I would have gone bare inside of her and not cared about the consequences—I've always wanted a family. But watching Brynn still choose Daniel while pregnant with my baby isn't something I could stand aside for, and I won't hold her back from being with her first choice, which isn't me.

I'll blame the fact that I almost forgot the condom on the fact that I wasn't expecting Brynn to be on the fishing trip to begin with, but once she boarded the boat, I still foolishly thought I could resist her for long enough to get us back to land without pulling her under me.

It turns out that I underestimated my addiction to her and overestimated my level of self-control.

"Do you have any on the boat?" she asks.

"No, I don't."

"What? Why not? Did you run out?" she asks, as if I'm having large orgies out at sea and forgot to restock.

Who the hell does Brynn think I am?

Sometimes I get the feeling that Brynn thinks I'm a player who uses his professional hockey status to smash through women on a daily basis back at home. She hasn't come out and directly accused me of it but I can feel it sometimes. It's as if she doesn't think that being with her is special to me.

I think though the possibilities of where I might have a condom and then it dawns on me. I have one in my wallet. One that I put there every recently due to the woman sitting on my lap.

"Hold on, I have one," I tell her.

I pull her closer to hold her into place as I reach down for my boardshorts and then pull out my wallet. I grab the single condom out of it and then drop my wallet back on my shorts.

Ripping open the condom, I slide the latex down the full length of my shaft and then run my hand down the condom again to make sure it's secure. Brynn watches each movement I made and as soon as I finish, she scoots her way closer.

Her legs are too short for my cock to fit under her while she's straddling me. In one fluid motion I cup her ass with both hands and lift her up. She squeals and grips my shoulders. I took her by surprise but then she giggles when she realizes that she's not tall enough to ride this ride without a boost.

"You're so controlling during sex, aren't you?" she asks.

"You must like it because you kept coming on my cock all night long. What was the number again? Five?"

I can see the glint in her eye. She likes me demanding and a little rough. Would she admit it though... I don't know.

She's a romance writer but something tells me that she doesn't get her inspiration from Daniel.

"Maybe I shouldn't tell you when I come anymore. You're starting to get too cocky about it," she teases.

"You don't have to tell me... just promise you won't ever fake it. Let me work for it until I get it right."

"I won't fake it."

"Swear to me."

"I swear."

Brynn reaches between us, lining up my tip with her center and then I let her down slowly until my tip presses into her warm tight body. Her wet heat coats my cock and a deep groan rumbles out of me at how fucking good it feels to be back inside her—like entering nirvana... or my own personal heaven. Nothing will ever top this.

I look down to watch myself slide into her with each movement.

"Fuck, your pussy looks good with me inside."

I keep her suspended in my hands as I thrust into her a little bit at a time, until I'm deep enough that her knees touch the bench. She whimpers as she rolls her hips against me, her movements forcing me to quicken my pace to match hers.

"Slow Brynn, I don't want to hurt you," I instruct.

But she doesn't heed my warning and she keeps up her rhythm. Her pussy stretches further to accommodate my size.

"Jesus Christ, I said slow," I tell her, halfhearted.

In truth, the last thing I want for her to do is slow down. I've never had anything better than Brynn and I want to take her in every way physically possible. But if this is the last time I get to be inside her, I need her to know that she's not broken, and she doesn't need to change. She's perfect... just like this.

"All of it... please," I hear her beg.

She wants me deeper and I'm more than happy to oblige her with every inch I have but I refuse to hurt her in the process.

She'll get all of me just like she wants but I'm determined to make it good for her while I'm doing it.

"Anything you want, you can have. Just tell me if I'm hurting you," I tell her.

I pick up the pace, fucking her harder from the bottom, advancing into her inch by inch. The little sounds she makes every time I push inside of her eggs me on further. Our bodies slapping together and the smell of sex mixing with the smell of the salty ocean creates a fragrance that I wish I could bottle up.

Her arms wrap around my neck tighter, and her eyes flutter closed the deeper I bury inside of her. Her head drops against my shoulder as she focuses on her orgasm. After bringing her to five orgasms in one night, I've started to pick up on the signs. I know when she's about to come.

"More..." she whimpers in a plea.

I can't say no to her, mostly because I don't want to. I want everything she's asking for.

I want "all of it," too.

I want "more" just like she does.

I feel more of her arousal coat my cock until it starts to drip down my balls and pool on the bench.

"Seven... please... harder," she begs again.

"You sound desperate Brynn. How bad do you need it?" I ask.

I may never hear her beg again. This is my last shot to hear that she needs what only my cock can deliver for her.

"I need it now or I might explode. I'm so close..."

I can sympathize with her. I'm nearing the end of my ability to hold back any further, but I need her to come first.

I grip her hips and pull her down the last couple of inches until I'm fully seated in her. Brynn screams out my name and grips my neck tighter, her body clenching around me tighter. And then I feel her body pulsate as she comes on my cock. I follow right after; my ability to hold back my own release is futile.

After giving ourselves a moment to catch our breaths, I took Brynn down to the cabin below deck.

A small bathroom and bedroom offered a good place for her to clean up after.

We lay on the bed, Brynn's head resting on my chest with the floral comforter that the boat came with covering up just over Brynn's hip bone. Each time she drags the blanket up her body a little further, I'd wait until she was distracted with a question I'd ask about her book, or growing up in Oklahoma that she wouldn't notice when I'd drag it back down to her hip bone again.

It's over ninety-five degrees today and the humidity feels like living in a hot armpit... there's no way she's cold. Her attempt at modesty is lost on me after her little strip tease earlier and the way she fucked me in the open air on my boat.

I don't want her covered up if I have a choice. And since she didn't grab her clothes off the deck before we came down to the cabin, and her naked body is plastered against the side of me with her leg draped over mine... I think she's comfortable enough being naked with me.

"So, you don't keep condoms on the boat at all?" she asks.

"I've never had a female on this boat who isn't related to me." I think for a second and then realize that my statement isn't completely accurate. "Well... except for Rita but she's told me time and time again that I'm not her type. I've stopped asking."

Brynn snorts out a booming laugh that crinkles at the side of her eyes.

We stay tangled together and lose track of time.

By the time I realize it, we emerge back to the top deck, both of us covered in towels, to find the sun is beginning to set.

"We should head back. It's getting late, and it's easier to park the boat before it gets dark."

She doesn't say anything, which prompts me to check in about what just happened between us.

"You're ok with what we just did, right?" I ask.

I've never asked this question after the fact with any other woman. Usually, the expectations of what we each got out of the deal is pretty obvious and I leave soon after, keeping the exchange as uncomplicated as possible. But with Brynn, everything's different because this isn't a one-night stand. We've spent almost two weeks together.

She nods but doesn't look directly at me. Instead, she looks out to the ocean with an unreadable look across her face. She doesn't look upset, but she also doesn't look blissfully happy... she looks impartial like coming back up from the cabin broke the bubble we were back to where we started when she came aboard.

Our "one last time" is very much over.

CHAPTER
TWENTY-TWO

Brynn

We ride back to the marina the same way we rode out to the fishing spot, with Seven at the helm inside the cockpit and me sitting out on the bench watching the sunset over the horizon.

The warm orange and pink painting of the sky has me reflecting on the fact that in less than seventy-two hours, I'll be headed back to Seattle to face my old life.

My old life... What an odd way to think of it, considering it's the only life I have. It's the life I've wanted for so long. A life with Daniel and a booming author career.

I glance back at the glass window where Seven is standing, only to find him staring straight ahead at the ocean as he drives us back to shore.

He asked me if I wanted one more time with him before I headed home, and I don't regret saying yes, but with the expiration date of this working vacation coming too quickly to an end, there's a part of me that doesn't want to leave.

I'll miss all of this.

I'll miss the warm sunny days that I won't get in Seattle, the long stretches of beautiful sandy beaches, the new friends I've made at Scallywag's, and even waking to the smell of the fryer permeating through the floorboards of the apartment when Miguel comes in to warm up the kitchen for the day. I don't get to take any of this home with me when I leave and that's starting to make me sad.

Cammy and Seven will be back in Seattle within a few days, but something tells me that the connection I have with both of them dies the moment I touch down on Washington soil.

I already know that carrying on a friendship with Seven would be inappropriate when Daniel and I get engaged. Having a relationship with Cammy would be nice but how would Seven feel about that? What if Seven finally starts to date someone? I'm not sure if I could handle Cammy keeping me apprised of Seven's romantic life.

Seven pulls into the boat slip and rushes out to toss the lines at the back of the boat to the marina attendant to secure them.

Once the boat is secured into place, Seven glances up at me from where he's standing down on the fishing deck.

"We're all set—let's go. I'll give you a lift back to Rita's apartment if you want."

He turns back and walks to the side of the boat, hoisting himself up over the side and landing on the dock.

"If it's not too much trouble..." I say, taking the steps down to the lower deck.

I walk up to the side of the boat and Seven steps towards me. This is the first time we've ever been eye to eye... with our clothes on.

"You're never any trouble and anyone who tells you differently doesn't deserve your time."

His piercing eyes meet mine, and I can guess who he's referring to.

"Tell that to the man who opened the door to the woman who showed up soaking wet on your doorstep."

His lips purse and the light in his eyes dim. He almost looks regretful. Now I feel bad for how I said it. It's not his fault I ended up uninvited at his beach house. It was a fraudulent online vacation rental website.

All things being considered, he did more for me than was required of him.

"I'm sorry for the way I treated you when you showed up. I wasn't expecting this."

"What? You weren't expecting some romance author to show up during a hurricane and seek refuge in your beach house? How unprepared of you. I suppose you'll need to add that to your hurricane checklist. Prepare for an unhinged woman to show up at your house and eat all of your groceries and befriend your next-door neighbor and your niece."

I was trying to make light of the situation, but he doesn't respond.

He reaches out his arms to help me out of the boat—his hands grip my hips while my palms drape over his shoulders to hold my balance.

He lifts me up with not even so much as a grunt from lifting my weight.

The second my feet touch the dock, he releases me and turns to head up the boat ramp.

I follow him as he leads us towards the parking lot where his jeep is located.

"We'll make a quick stop to get your necklace on the way to the apartment."

"Thank you for finding it. I can't believe I left it. I almost never take it off. Where did you find it?"

"Cammy found it," he says. "When she was folding the laundry. It was in my sheets."

"Oh God," I mutter to myself.

Cammy found my necklace in Seven's bedding.

No wonder she knew that Seven is the one who helped me check off my Mexico fling.

"Did she ask who it belonged to?"

Seven snickers at the question as if I just told a joke. He reaches out and opens the passenger door of the Jeep for me.

"You mean the same eighteen-year-old girl who tricked you into a fishing date with me and then sped off, leaving you stranded? No, she didn't ask who it belonged to. She already knew," he says,

Did he just say date?

"Wait. I'm sorry, did you just call this a date?" I ask. "I didn't know—"

"No," he says quickly. "I didn't think this was a date. I shouldn't have said it like that."

I nod and then turn from him to climb up in his lifted Jeep, trying not to let him see the disappointment on my face.

I take my seat and reach for the seatbelt.

"It's not a problem. I just would have worn something different if I had known it was a date."

I expect Seven to close the door, but he stalls after my comment and stares back at me.

"What would you have worn if this had been a date?" he asks.

I slide my palms over my denim shorts as I contemplate his question. I shouldn't be thinking about going on a date with Seven, but "Go on a first date" is an item on my list and as far as I can tell, Daniel hasn't had any problems going on dates, so why should I?

"If this had been a date, I would have worn one of my summer dresses over my bathing suit. Not exactly an ideal outfit for fishing. Why do you ask?"

"Because if this had been a real date, we'd still be laying on the cabin bed, fucking until the sun comes up tomorrow. And then I would have spent the entire morning trying to think of a way to convince you to go on a second date with me."

He shocked me into silence.

I stutter, trying to get a word or thought out in response to his comment, but I've gone mute.

"Watch your legs," Seven says once he's waited long enough for me to respond.

He closes the jeep's door next to me, then moves around the front of the vehicle and climbs into the driver's side.

He's already told me he doesn't do long-term, and I've already spent eight years being strung along in a relationship. I'm ready to be married and start a family. Seven isn't interested in any of that. Besides, he said one night and I agreed. I'm not going to ask for more even though I now know that Seven is capable of giving me several orgasms in a short amount of time.

"Did you have fun fishing today even though you didn't get to keep your catch?"

"It wasn't my catch. I'm pretty sure that, in hindsight, that fish caught me."

He chuckles from the driver-side seat as he drives us towards his house.

"That fish has good taste in women."

I smirk over at him. "I'm going to take that as a compliment."

"Good, I meant it as one."

Seven turns up the radio and then I belt out the lyrics to The Beatles song that comes on over the radio.

I glance over to find a soft smile across his lips as he keeps his eyes facing forward, driving us back to where all of this started.

We pull into the driveway, and the warm amber lighting of a beach firepit in the darkness of light illuminates the beach.

Seven jumps out of the Jeep and heads for the house to grab my necklace. I don't know how it could have come off during sex, but then again, the clasp has been a little finicky lately. It's getting old and I meant to buy a new chain for the pendent.

I hear the giggles of women's voices through the night sky, and before I know it, I see Cammy coming around between the two houses, a glass of wine in her hand.

With eighteen being the legal age here, she is within her right to drink.

"Hey! You two are back late. You must have gone fishing after I left?" she asks with a sly smile.

She's proud of her little trick, and since I caught a fish and got a couple of orgasms out of it, I can't be too upset with her. But she doesn't need to know that.

"That was a ballsy move considering who your uncle is. He wasn't thrilled with your little stunt. And what about me? What if he was mad enough that he had left me there with no ride home?"

"Seven? Leave you stranded at the marina with no way home? Not a chance. And besides, the bite marks he left all over your neck suggest the fishing went pretty well. You're welcome."

My jaw drops open and I quickly cover both sides of my neck with my hands.

I don't remember him biting hard enough to leave a mark but then again, I was too preoccupied with his very impressive cock to have been paying too much attention.

Cammy laughs at my reaction.

"I'm kidding. There aren't any bite marks on your neck. I just wanted to know if my assumptions about you two are correct. Thanks for the confirmation."

What a brat. But I have to hand it to her... she's clever.

"That's evil, Cammy," I say, though I can't wipe the blushing smile off my lips.

"Just fess up to it already. You and my uncle have it bad for each other," she says and then takes a drink of her wine.

If she feels comfortable enough with me to be so blunt, then she should be able to take a little of her own medicine.

"Why do you care so much about your uncle getting laid? It's a little strange if I'm being honest."

"Gross, I don't care if he gets laid. I just want to see him find someone to be happy with. He's lonely."

"He's not lonely, Cammy. He can have any woman in Seattle that he wants. My guess is that once the season is back in full swing, all of his female fans will be waiting in line to get their shot with him."

And since I know how good he is in bed, I don't blame them.

"He's not the player you think he is."

She's wrong in her assumption. I don't think he's a player. I know he has options, so why would he want to settle for the girl who can't sleep alone in a thunderstorm? And even if he is interested in me, he's already told me that he hasn't wanted to be in a serious relationship ever since his breakup with Josslin.

"Maybe not but at the end of the day, he and I want different things."

Cammy opens her mouth to respond when a voice calls out in the darkness.

"Got it!" I hear Seven coming around the side of the house.

Cammy and I watch as Seven finally emerges around the corner for the house, holding up my necklace.

Seeing the silver-plated necklace dangle in his hand brings me instant relief.

"Well, look who it is." Seven says, with one brow lowered.

"Hi, Uncle Seven."

Cammy doesn't look the least bit concerned with his tone.

"That was some dirty trick you pulled today."

"Huh... funny, because I'd wager a bet that it was the least dirty thing to happen all afternoon."

I burst out in a giggle and have to cover my mouth with my hand.

Seven shoots a look at me. I know he wants to ask if I told Cammy anything about what happened between us on the boat, but I avoid eye contact. I'm not getting in the middle of this friendly fire. I'm not equipped for battle like these two always seem to be.

These two know exactly how to push each other's buttons.

The Wrenley family should be studied for scientific proof that personalities are genetic.

He clears his throat and it seems like he's going to drop it. I guess he knows his niece can pull the information out of him, just as she did me. He's smart enough not to implicate himself.

"I saw that you girls are having a bonfire. Is Rita keeping your mom in line?" he asks.

"We're having a girls' night. We already painted our toes and did papaya face masks. And Rita has mom as straight as an arrow... for the moment, anyway. I was just coming by to see if Brynn wanted to join us for a glass of wine. Rita pulled out the good stuff," she says, looking over at me.

"Thanks, but Seven was just about to take me home. I don't want to put him out."

"One glass of wine, and then Seven will take you home. I'd drive you myself, but we've all had too much to drink," Cammy says.

"If you want to stay for a glass, I can wait."

"Are you sure?"

Before Seven can respond, Cammy pipes up.

"He's sure, come on," she says, opening my door. "This might be our last chance to get drunk around open flames before you leave us all."

She has a point.

I leave soon, and I would like to spend a little more time with Rita before I go. Who knows when or if I'll ever see her again?

I look over at Seven, but he doesn't say anything. He just stares back at me as if waiting for me to make a final decision.

"Ok, I'll stay."

Cammy grins wide. "Good. I knew you would come to your senses."

She steps back to let me slide out of the Jeep and then I step down carefully.

I follow Cammy through the corridor between the two houses—Seven directly behind me.

I see the bonfire even more clearly than before raging out in front of us with the moon midway up the sky and the sound of the waves thrashing onto the beach way out in front of us.

Two women sit in a couple of the Adirondack chairs where Seven and I sat the night that Rita tricked us into a bonfire with wine, just the one of us last week.

Rita holds up her wine and cheers when she sees us coming.

I watch the moment that Josslin looks over to find us all headed in their direction. Her eyes dim when she sees me, but then the moment she looks behind me, a smile stretches across her face when she sees Seven.

She pulls some of her blonde hair over her shoulder and plays with it, almost like a nervous tick.

"Cammy convinced you to stay, I see?" Rita says to me as Seven and I walk around the chairs and take a seat.

"She did. She reminded me that I only have a few more days left here and then I'm heading back home. This might be my last ocean-side firepit for the foreseeable future."

Seven clears his throat and when I look at him to my left, he's staring into the flames with great focus. I wish I knew what he was thinking about.

I watch Cammy fill up a glass of wine for me.

"Oh, I certainly hope that isn't true. You'll come back again, won't you? You're always welcome to stay with me. Or if you're coming to write, and need the place to yourself, the apartment is yours whenever you want it. In fact, stay as long as you can... you don't have to leave," Rita says.

I see in my peripheral that Seven seems to perk up a little at her offer and the firepit no longer holds his interest.

"I appreciate the offer but I actually do have to go home. I'm supposed to meet with the publisher in person when I turn in my manuscript in a few days. Otherwise, I would consider your offer. I've really enjoyed my time here, and I've never written so quickly. I might take you up on your offer when it's time to write book number two."

"I hope you do. I'll have the guest room ready for you," Rita says.

"When are you going to start book two?" Seven asks.

"I'm not sure yet. Maybe around Christmas. It might be a nice time to go somewhere warmer."

And Daniel usually has some time off during the Christmas break but I'm not going to tell Seven that part.

Cammy walks over and hands me my glass and I take a sip.

This is delicious, just like everything else I've tasted while at Rita's house. The woman has impeccable taste.

I change position in my chair for a moment and wince when I hit my hip against the wood chair. My bruise from smacking against the side of the boat when the marlin tried to pull me overboard must be starting to set in.

"Are you ok?" Cammy asks.

"Yeah, I just could use a long hot shower and then an ice pack. I'm a little bruised from that big fish I hooked today."

"You should have seen it. Brynn caught a marlin," Seven tells Cammy and Rita.

He doesn't spare even the slightest glance for Josslin.

Cammy chuckles.

"Is that right? You got all those bruises from the fish?" Cammy asks. "Any chance this fish was six foot five, two hundred and fifty pounds plus, and plays professional hockey?"

"Cammy Wrenley! That was inappropriate. Maybe you've had too much to drink," Josslin says.

"Not even close," Cammy says and then walks back over to the table with all the alcohol and snacks that they brought out here.

I walk as she grabs a handful of shot glasses and a bottle of something clear in her hand.

This can't be good.

Cammy places a shot glass in front of Rita and then one in front of Josslin and fills them up. Then she heads in our direction and fills a shot glass up for both of us.

"I don't need one. I have to drive Brynn back soon," Seven tells her, but she doesn't listen.

She walks back to the table and fills the last shot glass up for herself.

How did she know we would show up here and have the correct number of shot glasses?

"I want to make a toast," she says, lifting her shot glass. "To booking vacations on scam websites and making new friends along the way."

Rita and I both laugh and then take our shots, along with Cammy. I forgot how bad these shots burn going down. Josslin hesitates for a second but then takes the shot.

"Uncle Seven, you better take your shot or else I'm going to," Cammy says and then marches towards him.

"Like you need any more tonight. Besides, mixing isn't a great idea. You're going to regret that later," he tells her.

Cammy starts heading straight for him so Seven takes the shot quickly before she can reach for it.

"There, are you happy?"

"Yes... very. Though I don't think it's safe for you to drive now."

"It's not a big deal," I say, looking over at Seven and then Cammy. "I'll just call a rideshare. I'm so tired after today, I think I'll call now."

"That's a good idea. Sometimes it can take a while for them to get all the way out here. We wouldn't want you waiting all night," Josslin pipes up after being so quiet.

"Why even go home? Stay here. The three of us are having a girl's night, and I'm staying in one of Rita's guest bedrooms for a sleepover. There's plenty of room at Seven's. You can stay in my room," Cammy says.

Now I know what the shot was for. To ensure that Seven would agree not to drive after drinking.

"Or she can have my guest room at Rita's and I can stay at Seven's," Josslin offers.

"You're not setting foot in my house," Seven snarls.

Everyone around the firepit goes quiet at Seven's outburst towards her. It's not as if Josslin doesn't deserve it but it's obvious that his patience with her is wearing thin.

"I could just sleep on the couch in Rita's living room. It's not a big deal," I suggest.

"You stayed in my house for a week already. We made it work. We'll be fine for one more night, but these two are getting out of control," he says, shooting looks at Rita and Cammy. "Are you ready to go?" He asks me.

I take the last sip of my wine and then nod. "All set," I say.

"Just place the wine glass on the armrest; we'll take it in," Rita offers.

I do as she instructs, and then Seven walks over and offers his hand to help me out of the chair.

We haven't held hands since that night at the restaurant when he pulled me out because of the drunk bachelor party.

He doesn't need to help me up, I can get out of the chair just fine on my own but I won't turn him down because I like this attentive version of him.

I slide my hand into his, and he helps lift me to my feet. I wait for the moment when he drops my hand, but he doesn't, instead he fans out his fingers and slides them in-between mine.

"Good night," he says, giving a quick wave to the three-woman sitting around the fire, offering me no explanation for why we're still holding hands.

Rita and Cammy echo the sentiment, but Josslin remains quiet, her eyes locked on our joined hands.

I give a quick wave two and then Seven leads us away from the group and up towards his house.

"You might want to check your birth control and make sure no one tampered with it," he tells me, looking back over his shoulder with a smirk.

"A baby is a serious commitment. They wouldn't go that far. That would be insane."

"Exactly. It would be insane or desperate, two things I wouldn't put past them."

He inputs the code to the front door lock. As soon as it unlocks he opens the door wide for me to walk in behind him.

The moment I pass through the door, Seven releases my hand to close the door and turn the deadbolt.

Of course, he wouldn't hold my hand all the way down the hall. That would be strange, especially for him.

"Thanks for letting me stay," I say.

"Like I said, it's no trouble. And now I'll have someone to cook breakfast for tomorrow. Cammy doesn't like eggs."

I chuckle at the thought of Seven sulking in the mornings because Cammy won't eat his monster-sized portions of food.

"I will happily accept your egg breakfast in the morning."

"Good," he says simply.

I turn down towards the hall, and Seven follows behind me.

I reach for the guest bedroom door and twist the handle to open it.

"Hey, hold on. You might want this back."

I turn to find him pulling my necklace out of his boardshorts.

Oh right! I almost forgot about it because of the unexpected invite to the bonfire.

"Can you put it on me?" I ask.

"Yeah, turn around."

I pull my hair out of the way and give him my back. He takes a step closer, unclasping the necklace and lifting his hands over my head. I feel the coolness of the small pendant the moment it touches my collarbone.

He clasps the necklace together and gently lays the chain down against my neck. His fingers brush against my skin, and goosebumps rise along my arms and shoulders at his simple touch.

I reach for the pendant immediately, rubbing the tiny Seattle Space Needle between my thumb and pointer finger.

"Thank you again for finding it for me," I say."

"I'm not the one who found it, remember?"

How could I forget?

"Yeah, right..."

I still feel Seven at my back. He hasn't moved away yet, and the heat of his body is still radiating near me.

"Can I ask you a question?"

His voice is low and raspy.

"What is it?"

"Does Daniel give you goosebumps like this when he touches you?"

I cross my arms over my chest to pull them from his view, but it's too late, he's already seen them.

And asking a question like that isn't fair. It's normal for those butterflies and goosebumps to disappear after eight years, right? You can't expect those for a lifetime.

Seven takes a step even closer, his chest brushing against my back.

"Do you get as wet for him as you do for me?"

I shake my head. "No," I whisper.

His hands slide over my hips as the bulge in his boardshorts presses up against my ass when he steps closer.

I can't remember ever being as turned on as I am whenever I'm with Seven. He's unlike anyone I've ever been with before, and he and Daniel couldn't be any more different.

"I already know he doesn't make you come. But I do... don't I, Brynn?" He asks against the shell of my ear and then lays a kiss against my neck.

My head falls back against his shoulder as he continues a line of soft kisses down my throat, each one better than the last.

"Why are you saying all of this?" I ask.

"Because I changed my mind."

"About what?"

"When Rita locked us out of her house the first time and we sat around the firepit alone, you told me that your agent sent you here to finish your book and to find someone to have a fling with. I told you I wasn't interested in being that man."

"And now?"

"Now, I want your last days here. Do you want that, too?"

I spin around in his arms to face him.

"Yes, I do!" I say quickly.

I didn't intend to seem too eager, but it can't be helped. I'm not ready for whatever this is between us to be over. Soon enough I'll have to face reality and head back to Seattle. I can only hope that by the time I board the aircraft in a few days, I'll feel more ready for it.

Right now, I just want to live in this alternative universe, with all these incredible people in this gorgeous place, and forget I have a life waiting for me back in Seattle.

Seven dips down and scoops his arms under my ass, lifting me up and then turning with me in his arms, heading down the hall.

"Oh my God, Seven," I gasped, unprepared for him to pick me up and take off with me. "Where are we going?"

"I'm taking you to my room to see if we can break our personal best record. What was it again? Five?"

CHAPTER TWENTY-THREE

Brynn

I wake to the feeling of a warm hand sliding off my belly and the feeling of the bed moving as Seven flips over onto his back.

My eyes flicker open to find that I'm still in Seven's bed. The alarm clock on the side table next to me says it's just before six am and the sun is just barely up for the morning.

This is the first time that I've fallen asleep with him and woken up in the same place.

Why didn't he move me back into the guest bedroom last night?

"Good morning," I hear him say.

I turn towards the side of the bed where he's lying.

"How are you feeling this morning? Are you sore?" he asks.

Last night we barely got any sleep. Seven proved his impressive stamina yet again and made good on his promise to beat out our personal best.

"A little... yeah. But it's a good sore. It's nothing a long hot shower can't fix."

"Any chance you can wait on that shower for about an hour? Silas is headed this way to hit the gym down the street with me. I forgot that we had plans. If you wait for me, we can shower together, and I promise you that it will be worth the wait. Then I'll make you breakfast before I take you back to the apartment to write."

I can't stop myself from grinning. Morning sex and then breakfast sounds perfect. And with the last chapter, I need to write being the ending, the inspiration he gave me all night last night should help me to put the finishing touches on this manuscript.

"If you're offering morning sex and bribing me with breakfast, I don't see how I could turn it down."

"That's the spirit," he smirks.

He slides an arm around my back and pulls me close, leaning down to kiss me. I wrap my arms around his neck and bring him even closer, taking his kiss deeper—morning breath be damned.

Seven's phone rings and he reaches over to pull it off the charger.

"That's him. He's probably checking to make sure I'm still coming to meet him."

"Then you'd better go."

Seven leans over one more time for a quick kiss and then he flips his blankets off of him.

I watch as his perfectly sculpted glutes push out of bed and walk to his closest.

"Hey," he says, still inside his walk-in closet. Then, he appears in a pair of gym shorts, his perfect abs still on display. "I need to spend some time with Cammy today, but would you want to go on a date with me tomorrow?"

"A date?" I ask, my eyebrows stitched together. "When's the last time you went on a date?" I tease.

"It's been a while. A couple of decades, I guess. Admittedly, I might not be very good at it, but would you want to go on a first date with me anyway?"

First date?

How much did Cammy tell him?

"Oh my God, did Cammy tell you everything that was on my list?" I ask, and then cover my face at the thought of how juvenile some of them probably sounded to him.

"She might have given me a few items that I could help you check off your list."

"You want to help me? I thought you hated my bucket list items."

"I don't hate the list. I just don't like the person behind why you started it."

"Is the list the only reason why you're asking?"

"No, it's not. I want to take you on a first date... if you want to go, that is."

I bite down on my lower lip to keep myself from smiling ear to ear.

I would have never guessed that Seven can be this sweet but here he is, surprising me yet again.

"OK, what will we do on our date?"

"How do you feel about making sandwiches and then driving down to the beach to watch the turtles hatching? I can't guarantee we'll see any, but I've heard some researchers have been down there over the last couple of days waiting for the last few nests before the season is over."

"You want to take me for a picnic to watch baby turtles?"

My heart squeezes so hard I crutch the blanket to my chest and remind myself to breathe.

I couldn't plan a better date even if I tried.

"Is that stupid? Would you rather go out to dinner? Silas knows the manager at one of the most exclusive restaurants in Cancun. He can get us a table if you want."

"No!" I say quickly. "I'm sorry if I made you think I didn't want to go, I just wasn't expecting you to suggest that for a date. I can't think of anything I'd rather do. It's perfect... I can't wait."

He smiles and then disappears back into his closet for a minute and then reappears a second time in a gym shirt, covering up his body so I can't see all my favorite parts.

"Then it's a date," he says, bending down to pick up a pair of running shoes off the ground before heading for the door.

I nod, trying to not giggle like a schoolgirl with a crush.

"Stay naked and don't leave this bed until I get back. Got it?" he asks playfully, pointing his finger at me.

He opens the bedroom door and lifts an eyebrow at me as if he's waiting for the answer.

"I'll be here. As naked as you left me," I say.

"Good girl."

He dips out of the room, closing the bedroom door behind him as he goes.

I listen for the garage door to open and the Jeep to rev up to life. Seven doesn't take long to back the Jeep out and take off towards the gym.

I decide to keep my word and stay in bed. After all, who knows how he might reward me if I do what he says.

I pull up my phone to see if Sheridan has responded to the last chapters I sent her, but I haven't seen anything yet.

Instead, I see a text from my mom.

> **Mom:** How's the weather there? Are the beaches still intact?

> **Brynn:** It's a little worse in Cancun but it's fine here. The beaches are still in good shape.

> **Mom:** Do you think your father would like it there? He's so picky about vacations.

Would he like it here? It's hard to imagine anyone would hate it here.

> **Brynn:** Yeah, I bet he would.

I hear a knock on the front door, and though I told Seven that I wouldn't move, I doubt he meant in this situation. For all I know, it could be Cammy at the door and she got locked out and needs help to get back in.

I flip the sheets off and grab a shirt out of his closet, pulling the large shirt over my head.

I'm not exactly trying to prove to Cammy that we slept together last night, but she's the one showing up bright and early in the morning after she tricked us into sleeping under the same roof.

If it grosses her out to see me in her uncle's shirt, then maybe that's the hard truth of her actions that she needs to see.

I hear another knock at the door. This time, a more anxious knock.

"I'm coming!" I yell out to Cammy.

I flip the deadbolt and the lock on the handle and then swing the door wide open, but the person on the other side of the door isn't who I expected to see.

It's not Cammy at all.

"Josslin," I say in surprise.

She takes one long look at me in her ex's shirt and I can see her trying to hold back her grimace. She's not exactly going to win any Academy awards with her performance of the "not jealous" ex. It's becoming more obvious as time goes on. She beams whenever Seven is anywhere near and scowls at me when she thinks I'm not looking. It wouldn't take a detective to see what's happening here.

"Can I come in?" she asks, trying her best to smile.

"Seven isn't here. He just left," I say, hoping she'll quickly retract her request.

"I know. I saw his Jeep pull out of the garage. I want to talk to you, actually."

Damn it.

I glance behind her hoping that Cammy or Rita are behind her, coming over as a buffer, but she's alone.

"Ok... come in," I say, opening the door wider for her.

She walks in and I close the door behind her.

"Does Cammy know that you're here?"

"No, she thinks I went for a walk on the beach."

That doesn't sound promising.

"We can sit in the kitchen if you want?" I ask.

"That's as good as any."

She follows me through the kitchen, and we both take a seat at the kitchen table.

"Can I get you something to drink?" I ask.

"You certainly seem to have made yourself at home here. Offering me a drink as if you live here, wearing Seven's clothes."

Her tone isn't accusatory, it's more pained. Like she harbors regret that she's not in my position.

But her regret isn't my problem.

She could have had this life.

She could have had Seven.

That realization almost makes me sick to my stomach to think that if she had made one different choice in her life, I wouldn't have had these experiences with him. Why does that make my heart pound with anxiety. I don't know.

"Why are you here Josslin?"

"I came here to talk to you woman to woman and ask you for a favor."

A favor?

"That depends on what the favor is."

"Seven doesn't know yet, but I've come here to tell him."

"Tell him what?"

"That Cammy is his."

My heart just about leaps out of my throat, and I feel the blood drain from my face.

"Cammy's his? How could that be? He told me that the timeline doesn't work out and that you swore that Cammy was Eli's."

I blurt out.

How could she not have told him already?

He's going to be crushed.

No. More than that. He's going to be obliterated when he finds out that Josslin lied to him about Cammy.

Oh God. Poor Seven. He lost out on Cammy growing up.

My heart breaks instantly for him, and he doesn't even know yet.

"How could you do this to him? Haven't you seen the way he is with Cammy, and he only thinks he's her uncle? He's never going to forgive you for this." I say, knowing I'm saying more than is my business... but she came to me.

"Let me worry about Seven. He's not your concern."

"Not my concern? How would you know that?"

"I heard Cammy telling Rita about your boyfriend in Australia. I know that Seven is just your fuck toy until you head home."

Did she just say, "fuck toy"?

"Excuse me?"

Her eyes clamp shut, and she shakes her head.

"I'm getting off track. I didn't come here to argue or offend you; I came here to beg you to leave Seven alone and let our family mend. I'm going to tell him and I know he's going to be upset, but he'll come around. He always wanted a family... I can give him that."

"I can, too!" I almost blurt out, but I don't.

"A family? Cammy's eighteen years old, and they already have a relationship."

"I can give him another child. He's always wanted a big family."

I can't believe this is what she came here to tell me.

"Do you really think he's going to trust you after this?" I ask.

"I don't know but I have to find out. His brother is finally going to get the help he needs. He's going to a rehab facility for six months as part of my agreement to not cut him out of our family, but we're separated and I'm leaving him. Cammy needs a father right now and Seven is that person. We need him—his family needs him."

"What does that have to do with me?"

"He needs to focus on his brother and on his daughter. He doesn't need a distraction right now. Especially someone who's using him until she gets back together with her fiancé."

The moment she says the words, I know they're true.

Ever since I showed up here almost two weeks ago, I've been using Seven. I just didn't realize how much until she said it.

For his house.

For his protection.

For his breakfast cooking skills.

For his orgasm-inducing cock.

And what have I given him in return?

A splitting headache for being a colossal pain in his ass for the last week and a half?

"Besides, do you think it's any coincidence that he hasn't moved on with anyone since I broke off our engagement?"

I never thought about the possibility that Seven hasn't been in a relationship in all these years because he's still stuck on her. Could that be true?

"I just want him to be happy," I say.

"Me too. I've known him since we were little kids riding our bikes in our neighborhood. Seven, Eli and I grew up together. I've never met anyone who felt so strongly about the importance of family like Seven used to. I want to give him back his family, Brynn... and I can do that but I'm only here until tomorrow. I only have one chance before I leave. Do you care about him?" she asks.

Of course, I do, or this decision wouldn't be so hard.

"Yes, I care about him very much."

"Then help me give him back his heart... which is his family. He's been apart from it for too long."

If I care about him, I don't think I have much of a choice, so I stand up from my chair.

"I'm going to get dressed."

"Cammy is just about to leave for the restaurant. If you hurry, you could catch a ride back."

"Thanks," I mutter and head out of the kitchen.

I head down the hall and back into Seven's room to put on the clothes I had on last night.

He might be mad at me for leaving when I promised I'd stay, but if there's even a sliver of truth behind what she says about Seven being the way he is now because he lost his family, then I have to step aside.

Even in the best-case scenario, Seven and I only have another forty-eight hours together before I leave for Seattle and return to my life.

I can't sacrifice his potential happiness just because I selfishly want every last hour with him that he'll give me before I go.

After I get dressed and I walk back out of his room, I head for the front door.

Passing by the kitchen, I overhear Josslin on the phone.

"We're legally separated Eli, remember? I've begged you to get help for years and you refused. You've been a stranger living under the same roof as me and Cammy, and I have loved you through every moment, but it's not fair," I hear her tell him. "Please stop making me feel guilty about this. Loving you out of it didn't work. Now I have to move on with my life."

She doesn't hear me walk past, and maybe that's for the best.

What Josslin did to Seven wasn't right. I'll never give her a pass for what she did to him. And what she did to Cammy by withholding a father who would have moved heaven and earth for her wasn't right either. But there's this little piece of me that feels the pain she's going through as she loses her first love. The more time I spend here, the less clear my future with Daniel looks.

I've loved him for so many years that the idea of not being with him, scares me. And the pride my father shows at the match I've made with Daniel is the one thing I feel like I've done right in his eyes. I want to make him proud of me like he is of my older brother.

I open the front door and walk out, closing it behind me.

I hear a truck running and turn for Rita's to see if I might be lucky enough to catch a ride.

The driver's side door is open, and then I see Cammy leaving Rita's house.

"Hey," I say. "Are you headed to Scallywag's?" I ask.

"Yep. Want a ride?"

"That would be great, thanks."

Cammy jumps in and waits for me.

I head for the truck and then jump into the passenger side door.

"Oh... hey... is everything ok?" she asks.

She must see the sadness on my face that I have no more energy to hide.

I'd like to tell her the truth so I tell her what I'll keep telling myself until I'm back safely in Seattle, putting all of this behind me.

"No, but it will be."

CHAPTER TWENTY-FOUR

Seven

It's been almost an hour since I left Brynn, and I'm already counting down the minutes until I'll have her up against my shower wall, helping her create content for the next dirty scene in her book.

After some cardio and weight lifting, Silas and I move over to the squat rack to finish up for the day.

"I haven't heard from you about your hurricane intruder in a while. I have some openings at the hotel now if you need a room for her," Silas says, finishing his set on the squat rack.

"Thanks, but Rita ended up giving her the apartment to stay in, and she's only here for another couple of days."

Discussing Brynn's expiration date here and the inevitable conclusion that she's headed home to get back together with her ex, unsettles something in my stomach.

"What a weird situation, but I guess she couldn't have known that she had booked a scam vacation rental. You must be relieved that it's over."

"Not exactly," I say, finishing my last rep and dropping the bar and weights on the padded gym floor.

"What does that mean?"

"It means she stayed the night last night and she's still in my bed waiting for me to get back."

"Shit, that situation changed fast. So you kicked her out of your house but now you're sleeping with her?" he asks, one eyebrow lifted in question.

I don't blame him. I was hellbent on getting her out of my house the last time we talked and now I'm trying to think of ways to keep her in it until she leaves.

"That's the gist of it."

"How long has this been going on?" he asks.

"It's been on and off for a couple of weeks, I guess."

"Sounds complicated... especially for you," he says and then reaches for his water bottle to take a drink.

"What do you mean "especially for you"?"

"I just mean that I've known you for fifteen years now, and in that time, you've maintained a strict rule about never bringing a woman back to your place. I've never seen you date anyone seriously and I've only seen you with a small handful of women over the years.

"Ok, what's your point?" I grumble.

I know where this is going since I already get it from Cammy and Rita. Working out with Silas is supposed to be my escape from those two, but now I can see that I'm going to get flak from all sides.

"My point is that this woman shows up out of nowhere, and you change all your rules."

"I haven't changed any rules for her."

"You just admitted that she's still in your bed waiting for you to get back and looked fucking happy about it. I've known you for long enough to know this isn't like you. This one's different, and I think you already know that."

"She has a boyfriend," I admit.

"Whoa... what?" he asks, turning to me quickly.

I guess I could have worded that differently.

"They're not together right now, they broke up when he moved to Australia temporarily. But now he's coming back and they're getting back together."

"But they're not together right now, correct?"

"No, they're not. Not until he gets back in a couple of weeks."

He grabs his keys, towel and water bottle off the floor.

"What are you doing?" I ask.

"I'm headed back to the hotel. We got in a good workout, and you have somewhere to be."

"Oh yeah? Where's that?"

"At home, convincing this girl not to get back together with her ex."

He turns and starts to walk away with all the items he brought in with him.

"Silas, I don't want a relationship. I'm not cut out to give her what she needs," I call out after him.

He turns back around to face me.

"You're scared that you're going to fall in love with her, and then she'll leave you for someone else," he says.

I cross my arms over my chest, not liking his analysis of the situation. I never told him about Josslin but I suspect he's pieced together enough of it in order to come up with that conclusion.

This isn't the kind of conversation I want to have at the gym... or anywhere for that matter. The gym is supposed to be my escape. The place where I sweat out whatever is bothering me and then walk out those doors like nothing ever happened.

When I don't answer him back, he speaks up again.

"Or maybe it's too late. Maybe you're already in love with her, in which case, you don't have much of a choice now. Win her over or let her go—those are the options. Which one can't you live with?"

Then he turns and walks towards the exit, giving the receptionist a wave before he pushes through the glass doors.

His question hangs in the air and I don't have to dig very far to find the answer.

Unfortunately, there's more to this equation— an entire second half... her.

What does she want?

The lawyer with the normal life and the steady job, who's rising up the law firm's corporate ladder and who she's spent the last eight years of her life with?

Or a broke-down hockey player with only a couple of seasons left before his body can't handle anymore, who's out of town half the year playing in different cities and sees his future on a fishing boat in Mexico and his weekends doing little chores around Scallywag's to keep busy.

Picking up my water bottle, I drop it in my duffle bag before swinging it over my shoulder and heading for the exit.

The receptionist gives me a small wave and tells me to have a nice day, and I do the same. I push through the glass doors and head for my Jeep.

I guess there's only one way to find out if this thing between us is still just a fling, or if it's turning into more.

I'll have to ask her.

As soon as the Jeep is parked inside the garage, I whip open the driver-side door, jump out, and head straight for the house.

My conversation with Silas made me realize that if I let her leave without knowing if I ever had a shot, I'll always wonder, and he's right, there's only one of those options he listed that I can't live with. I can't live with her ending up with Daniel... not if I had a chance to change the outcome. But I need to know if I'm her first choice. I've already been the second choice and I can't be that again... not with her.

"I'm home," I say, taking long strides toward my bedroom, where she promised she would stay until I got back.

I push the door open to find that not only is the bed made and there isn't a beautiful brunette waiting for me in it, but Brynn's clothes aren't on the bedroom floor anymore.

"Brynn?" I call out. "Where are you?"

"She's not here." I hear a familiar voice call out from the kitchen.

My blood pressure rises at the sound of her voice.

Josslin

She knows she's not supposed to be in my house, and with Brynn no longer here, I can only guess she's responsible for that too.

"Where's Brynn?" I ask, walking through the hall and heading straight for the kitchen.

"She left so that we could talk."

I step into the kitchen and find Josslin sitting at the breakfast table.

Note to self: burn that kitchen table in Rita's firepit tonight, it's tainted now.

"Talk about what? Whatever it is, it could have been handled over text. You didn't need to come all the way out here."

"You never respond back to my text messages, so here I am," she says.

"Fine, if it gets you the hell out of my house, say what you need to say, and make it quick so that I can go find Brynn and fix whatever shit you did."

I plant my hands on my hips and stare back at Josslin. It's the first time I've ever seen her look slightly nervous.

"Your brother finally agreed to go to a rehab center in Arizona for vets with PTSD. They have a great program for addiction too. It seems the two can often go hand in hand. The center seems perfect and offers family counseling, too."

"That's great. I'm glad he's finally going to get the help he needs, but you didn't need to fly all the way out here for that. A simple text could have saved you a flight."

"That's not all. I need to tell you something else and I need you to promise to let me speak before you fly off the handle and bolt out the door."

"What an opening," I say, but leaving me for my brother who she moved into the house I bought her pretty much takes the cake. I doubt anything could be worse than that. "Ok, say it as quickly as you can. Preferable as you head for the front door, closing it on your way out."

"Seven..." she says, standing out of the chair she was sitting in. "I should have told you sooner but with Eli going to rehab, she needs you more than ever to step into that role for her."

"What are you talking about?"

"Cammy... she's yours."

My vision almost turns red and my hearing short circuits as if I'm hearing every word underwater.

"No... no, you told me that she's Eli's. You swore to me that you were only a couple weeks pregnant."

"I was six weeks pregnant. I got pregnant when I flew out to watch you play the San Diego Blue Devils in San Diego and you didn't have any condoms with you."

I can see her eyebrow turn up and worry coats her expression, but if I know her, she's only worried about herself... not the fact that she just dropped the bomb of a lifetime on me.

"You were on birth control. I saw you take them."

"Yes, I did but I had a stomach flu a few days before I came out to see you. I couldn't keep anything down for a couple of days. I hadn't thought about the fact that missing those days would affect it so dramatically."

I thought leaving me for my brother was bad enough, but never telling me that I fathered a child? That's unforgivable. It's worse than unforgivable and if it were my brother standing here instead of Josslin, I'd hit him so hard it would knock his teeth out and send him to the hospital... if I didn't kill him first.

"I want you the fuck out of my house and I never want to see you again," I tell her, pointing to my front door.

"Seven... please..."

"I have nothing to say to you. Leave or I'll call the authorities to remove you. You won't do well in a Mexican jail cell and I sure as hell won't be bailing you out."

She stalls for a second but she's staring back at me with some fear in her eyes. I probably look like a man about ready to go on a killing rampage.

She starts heading out of the kitchen and straight for the door.

I hear the door open but then she speaks again.

"I don't expect you to forgive me or for this to be a good enough excuse to right the wrong I did to you, Seven. And I can't imagine you've ever experienced that feeling of being looked over for so many years that when that one person sees you, your whole world comes to life. That's what happened to me the day that Eli came home from overseas. After loving your brother since I was six years old, he finally glanced over from the sofa in your parent's living room and actually saw me. I think it was the first time he had truly seen me as more than the little tomboy who lived down the street and chased you two around the neighborhood."

"While you were trying to get his attention, I was trying to get yours. When you agreed to marry me, I thought I'd won the lottery. We'd been dating for a year but I still couldn't believe you said yes. If only I knew that you'd be the biggest mistake I ever made."

"I had no idea that you felt that strongly about me."

Of course, that's her takeaway. Not the fact that I regret ever looking in her direction.

"That's because you're too self-absorbed to have seen anything outside of what you wanted for yourself. That's why you used my daughter to trap my brother. You didn't care that I wouldn't get to raise my own child and miss out on her first words—her first steps—everything. And you didn't care that my brother, who isn't in the mental state to care for a child, was forced to raise a child who wasn't his. Nor did you care that Cammy ended up being raised by an alcoholic father who would rather interact with random people playing video games online than attend a single one of her volleyball games, graduations, or birthday parties."

"He was so bad Seven. I thought finding out that he was about to be a father would pull him out of his darkness. I just wanted to give him something to look forward to."

I spin around to face her.

"Do you want to know what I actually think happened?"

She stands there waiting for my response.

"I think my brother came home, jealous about my NHL career and saw the one thing of mine that he knew he could have. He wanted to prove that he could have it if he wanted it. So he slept with you for a couple of weeks to make himself feel better and then when he was about to leave you, you trapped him with my kid."

I can see in her eyes that I just hit a nerve because tears well in her eyes.

"I didn't trap him. He could have left."

"My parents would have disowned him if he would have left after you told everyone that the baby was his."

There's a silence for a moment and I can see the gear working in Josslin's head to come up with a way around this.

"Eli and I are separated and I'm moving to Seattle to be close to Cammy. I'm not saying that it will happen right away but over time, I think you'll come to forgive me and we can be a family."

"Josslin, you have one second to turn around and close that door before you end up sleeping in a jail cell until your estranged husband decides to wire money for your release."

Her face crinkles together like she's upset that she couldn't spin this into some long-lost family reunion.

What the hell was she thinking?

She finally leaves and closes the door behind her.

Then another thought dawns on me... Cammy.

I turn and head back down the hall headed for my Jeep.

What the hell do I say to her once I see her?

"Funny story... your mom should be in a straitjacket and I'm actually your dad?"

I'll work on my delivery in the car.

CHAPTER TWENTY-FIVE

Seven

I take a seat up on one of the bar stools and it doesn't take long before Cammy joins me, sitting to my right.

"Aren't you on shift?" I ask.

"I'm on break."

I nod and look up at the football game streaming on the TV above the bar.

"She told you, didn't she?" Cammy asks.

I nod, trying to hide my surprise that Cammy already knows that I'm her dad.

"What will it be?" Rita asks, walking up behind the bar.

"Whatever Miguel feels like making today," I say.

"You got it," Rita jots it down and then heads back to the kitchen to put in my order.

There's a moment of silence, and then Cammy speaks up.

"I wanted to tell you when I found out but I was worried you would be too mad at mom to give me a chance to get to know you. By the time I knew you wouldn't hold it against me, I was moving to Seattle for school, and I was worried that now you would be mad at me for waiting so long to tell you."

I wouldn't have been mad at Cammy. It's not her fault that she was kept from me but how long has she actually known that Eli isn't her dad and I am?

"I'm not mad at you for any of it. It wasn't your responsibility to tell me that you existed. Your mom shouldn't have waited until you were eighteen to tell me. How did you find out?"

"Grandma put up my sophomore volleyball team picture next to one of you on your high school hockey team that's up on the mantel. If you gave me a buzz cut, you wouldn't be able to tell the difference between us," she chuckles. "I asked grandma why we looked so much alike and she told me about your history with my mom, then she told me to check my birth certificate. I wasn't premature like mom told everyone I was. What nine-pound baby is four weeks early?"

My mom knew too.

"Grandma knew this whole time and didn't say anything?"

"She only suspected. She couldn't prove it. And she was worried that if she asked my mom about me that mom wouldn't let Grandma see me anymore. Why do you think grandma was always trying to get you to come home? She thought that you'd take one look at me and know that I'm yours."

All those calls I didn't take from her. I'm starting to regret those now.

"Cammy, if I had known—"

"I know. But look at the bright side. At least Mom isn't a gold digger. Can you believe that she loved Dad that much to give up the lifestyle of being married to a multi-millionaire hockey player? And now that I'm old enough, she can't come after you for child support."

"Cam, I have more money than I'll ever spend. I would have paid her whatever she wanted so I could be in your life. Missing out on the first sixteen years with you wasn't worth any dollar amount," I say, wrapping my arm around her shoulders.

"Really?"

"Of course."

"Mom's trying to get you back."

"I know."

"Please don't cave. Especially not for me."

It's not as if I'd really considered it but why wouldn't she want Josslin and I together?

"Why not?"

"Because mom has never been alone a day in her life. It would be good for her to stand on her own two feet for once. She's been in a one-sided marriage for so long; I don't think she would know what a functional relationship is even if she were in one. And though she won't admit it right now, she's still in love with dad," Cammy darts a look up at me. "Does it hurt your feelings when I call him dad?"

I think about it for a second.

It's the name that she grew up calling him, and based on the information that she's told me about how absent he's been in her life over most of her childhood, I know that the name is just what she's used to calling him—not a term of endearment.

"No, it doesn't hurt my feelings. He was there when I wasn't."

Whether he earned the title or not is a different story.

"What should I call you now?"

I hadn't thought about it until she asked.

"Do I call you dad too?" she asks.

"No, not unless you want to. But Uncle doesn't seem right either. How about just Seven... for now until we figure it out? There's no rush."

She beams back at me. "Ok, Seven it is."

Rita brings out our food but it's so busy in the restaurant that she can't stay and chat. She takes off again to grab more orders.

"Are those the only reasons for why you don't want me and your mom together?"

"And because you don't love her anymore, you're in love with Brynn," I just about choke on a bite of my carnitas taco. "Mom doesn't get to ruin your life a second time. And you and I are fine just the way we are, aren't we?"

"Yeah, kiddo," I say, smiling down at her and then give her shoulder a bump with mine. "We're fine the way we are."

In my peripheral vision, a beautiful brunette catches my eye. Brynn.

"Excuse me, I have someone I need to talk to."

Cammy looks over in the direction I'm staring and then turns to me and smiles.

"Don't screw it up."

I shake my head. Now I know where Cammy gets it from.

I walk towards Brynn and I see the moment she sees me and then cuts eye contact, pretending she doesn't see me.

I reach out and touch her arm.

"Hey, can we talk?"

Brynn cuts her eye contact to a table that needs clearing.

"Um, I have a lot of work to do. Can it wait until after my shift?"

I see Cammy slide in front of us and quickly start to clear the table that Brynn seems to be worried about.

"I got it. Take your break," Cammy says over her shoulder.

Brynn looks back at me, realizing that she has no viable excuse now.

"Ok, sure I guess."

I lead Brynn by the small of her back out to the front of the restaurant.

It's too loud inside and there are too many distractions.

We push out through the doors into the sunny morning.

"Josslin said that she came to see you this morning."

"She did," Brynn says, folding her arms over her chest.

"She told you about Eli?"

"Yeah... you should probably go home and see him."

"And she told you about Cammy?"

She just nods and stares out at the cars.

"Did she tell you that she used Cammy to keep my brother?"

She nods but still doesn't look at me.

"But now you know. How does Cammy feel about it?"

"She seems fine with everything. She was worried about how I would take it."

"Your family needs you," she says, finally looking at me.

"Cammy's fine, Brynn."

"You're whole family needs you. There's so much broken that it seems only you can fix it."

That sounds exactly like what Josslin would tell her.

"They're not my priority except for Cammy."

"And you," I want to say.

"Maybe they should be."

"And what about us?" I ask.

"What about us?"

"Does this end in Mexico?"

Brynn stares up at me. Her eyes widening as if surprised by my question.

Has she not thought about me as a contender when we get back to Seattle?

She opens her mouth to speak when someone behinds us calls out her name.

"Brynn!"

The look on her face the moment her eyes connect with whoever is walking up behind us doesn't bode well for our conversation.

"Daniel? Mom.... dad?" I hear her say.

I look back to find three people headed directly for us, smiles on all their faces.

"Surprise!" I hear the woman say, who Brynn just referred to as her mother.

"What are you doing here?" Brynn says, shock still coated over her face.

The minute my eyes connect with the man I assume is Daniel, we both size up the other.

I know what he's doing here.

He walks up to her, wrapping his hands around her biceps, and pulls her in for a kiss. She's quick to move and his lips land on her cheek. When he pulls back, he attempts to cover up his irritation with her reaction but it gives me the smallest amount of hope that she's not jumping into his arms.

He takes a step back, releasing her and I'm glad he did because I feel my body tense the longer his hands are on her.

"Daniel turned in all his miles and got us two airline tickets to come out. We had a four-day weekend and thought it was time to come out and check on you," her mom says.

"You must be that hockey pro. Wrenley, right?" her dad reaches out to shake my hand. "I've heard you're the man to thank for taking my daughter in during the storm. I can't believe her agent booked her on a scam website."

"It wasn't her fault, Dad. That company is known for scamming vacationers. She couldn't have known," I heard Brynn say.

"Well, none the less, I'm grateful for your hospitality towards my daughter."

"Yes, very hospitable of you," I hear Daniel say condescendingly under his breath.

Her father doesn't hear it but Brynn flashes him a look.

"You three didn't have to come all the way out here. I have to be back in two days to turn in my manuscript. We could have met in Seattle," Brynn says.

"Your dad and I haven't been on a mini vacation in forever. And besides, Daniel and I have been discussing a destination wedding. You should see the resort we were able to get into. It's gorgeous, and they take care of everything. They book up quickly so we would need to get on their schedule," her mom beams.

My shoulder tense and my stomach turns hearing her mom discuss wedding plans for Daniel and Brynn.

Brynn senses my reaction, though I thought I hid it well and glances up at me quickly and then back to her mom.

"Daniel and I have a lot to discuss before we jump into wedding plans. We haven't seen each other in eight months," she says, her attention shifting to Daniel, whose jaw tightens at her response.

What was he expecting her reaction to be after he blindsided her.

After he told her that he fucked his way through Australia and now that he's sure that her lack of orgasms isn't his fault, he's ready to marry her.

Who wouldn't be overjoyed to see the prick?

"This is the restaurant that you've been working at? I'd love to meet Rita and thank her mother to mother for watching out for you while you've been here," Brynn's mother says.

"I'm actually still on shift right now and I'm only on break for another minute," Brynn says.

"Well, I'm starving. We just got in a couple hours ago and haven't eaten," her father adds.

"The food is great here," I chime in.

"Come eat with us," Brynn's mom says to me.

Daniel is just about to say something which I'm sure is some kind of rebuttal to her invite, but I beat him to it.

"Thank you, Mrs. Fischer, but I'm spending some time with my daughter today. Another time, maybe."

I look over at Brynn and I see a softness in her eyes. Probably at the fact that I called Cammy my daughter.

It's going to take a while to get used to but I'm looking forward to it.

I always felt a closeness to Cammy since the moment I met her for the first time, and now I know why.

"A single father, huh? You're not a deadbeat dad, are you?" Daniel says, glancing over at Brynn.

"Daniel..." both Brynn and her mom say in unison as if to warn him that he was out of line for what he said.

I shake it off.

If anything, the fact that he's concerned enough about me to try to make me look bad in front of Brynn, tells me that he's not sure of his place. The desperate attempt to fly here unannounced and bring her parents as reinforcement and trying to plan a destination wedding with Brynn's mom is another indicator that Daniel isn't confident that she's chosen him over me.

"You four have a good lunch. I'm sure I'll see you around," I say, and then I head for my Jeep.

Cammy and I are supposed to go fishing this afternoon and I'm looking forward to getting off land for a little while.

Brynn

Marie seats us after I introduce her to my parents and Daniel. Finally, Rita shows up to take their order.

"Rita, these are my parents, Dale and Gabby Fischer," I tell her. "And this is Daniel."

"Her fiancé, nice to meet you," Daniel says, reaching out a hand to shake hers.

Since Cammy already gave Rita the low-down, based on what Josslin told me, Rita doesn't look the least bit shocked.

I'd like to correct his title as ex-fiancé but since my parents still don't know that Daniel and I broke up during his work trip, I'm stuck with the fiancé title floating around.

Rita and her usual southern hospitality reached out and shakes his hand.

"Well, isn't it a pleasure to have you all here today. What a surprise," she says, glancing over at me.

"Yes, it was a surprise. A big surprise," I tell her, trying to hint that I had no idea and that I'm as shocked as she is.

"What can I get you all for lunch? The rush should be starting up soon, so I'll get your order in first."

"I have to get back to work but will you take care of them for me?" I ask Rita.

"You really have to work? We all came a long way to see you," Daniel complains.

Rita is just about to say something to let me off for the day but I give her a quick look before answering.

"I'm on the schedule and you didn't give me any warning. I'll see if I can get off tomorrow, ok?" I say and then slip out of the booth.

Although I'd like to visit with all of them, I need a second to adjust to my real world combining into my vacation/fantasy world.

I head off to go find my black tray that Cammy took to clean off my last table.

An hour later, my parents, Daniel and I are standing outside of the restaurant.

"Come back to the hotel with us. Our room is beautiful, and you can sit around the pool instead of bus tables for a restaurant. You make too much money to be working for your room and board," Daniel says.

I hear my father clear his voice and then I look over.

"If you've committed to something, you should finish it. I'm proud of you," he says.

"OK, fine but come stay with me at night. Or I could stay here with you," Daniel says.

Panic hits.

I'm not ready to kiss him on the lips, evident by the way I dodged him earlier. The last thing I'm ready for is to sleep with him.

"I still have a few more chapters to finish and I could use the peace and quiet."

"Then meet us at the hotel for breakfast tomorrow." my mom begs.

I can't blow them completely off after they came all this way to see me, so I agree and I hug them goodbye.

Daniel tries to kiss me again but I'm able to block it off a second time without making it seem too weird in front of my parents but I see the annoyance on Daniel's face.

"See you tomorrow," my mom waves and Daniel backs out of the parking space and then waves before pulling onto the street and heading the hour back to Cancun where they're staying.

How could my life be any bigger of a mess?

CHAPTER TWENTY-SIX

Brynn

Rita offered to let me take her truck into Cancun for breakfast.

Walking into the where we agreed to meet, I see Daniel wave from across the room.

I head straight for them.

It's a breakfast buffet so we don't have to wait to order or for our food to arrive. This is for the best since I wasn't able to finish my chapters last night. All I could think about was Seven meeting Daniel... and Cammy being Seven's daughter... and Josslin wanting Seven back... and Daniel showing up unannounced, expecting us to start wedding planning before we even got back to Seattle.

It's not as if there won't be any wedding planning in the future, but Daniel and I just spent months apart and we've been with other people. There's so much we need to unpack first, both literally and figuratively.

"You look beautiful," Daniel says as he stands up, kissing my cheek this time instead of going for the lips like he tried twice yesterday.

He must have figured my parents would catch on if I kept darting away from his kiss.

"You really do Brynn. Mexico must really agree with you. Your skin is practically glowing," my mother says.

I want to tell her that it's probably from all the orgasms I'm having, but that would be inappropriate at the breakfast table.

"Thank you. This vacation was a much-needed trip. I think all the vitamin D has been helpful."

She doesn't need to know that by vitamin D, I actually mean Seven's dick.

"How's your book coming along?" my father asks.

"I'm so close to finishing but I do have to go back and finish another chapter that I didn't get written last night."

They all make an audible groan of disappointment.

"You'll need to delay getting back for one hour. I have a surprise for you. Daniel and I booked a wedding venue walk-thru for after breakfast," my mom beams.

Oh God...

"Hold on... what?" I ask, trying to hide the unwelcome surprise.

"I had to slip the guy a little cash to make it happen since you're flying home tomorrow. Unless you can move your flight?" Daniel asks.

"Unfortunately, I can't change my flight. I have to fly home tomorrow morning as originally planned; my publisher is waiting, and I have an in-house meeting with the editor the following day. I have to get home."

"I'm proud of you for pushing through on this one. I know it was a tough one but you got it done," my dad says.

His praise always means the most to me. Maybe because he doesn't give it freely most of the time.

"Thanks, Dad," I smile at him, and he smiles back.

Over the next two hours, I sit with them, eating food and discussing Daniel's Australia trip and the timeline of my trip that started out as the worst vacation of my life, and then turned into the best.

We walk through the venue but I excuse myself at the end, leaving Daniel and my mom to continue their questions to the event planner.

As I drive down the road, I see a sign for the beach that Seven had mentioned the turtles would be at today for our first date. A date that would no longer happen.

I pull into one of the parking spaces and get out.

I find a spot high on the beach where I have a clear view all the way down to the ocean.

I watch as researchers take notes and prepare cameras—essentially busy work as they wait.

"Is this spot taken?" I hear a deep, raspy voice say beside me.

I look over to find Seven towering over me.

My belly flips at the sight of him.

"No, it's open," I say. "How did you know I'd be here?"

"What do you mean? I came here for the turtles," he says, taking a seat next to me in the sand.

"Oh..."

I feel stupid for assuming he stalked me here.

I sort of liked the idea that he might have followed me to get a moment alone together.

"I'm kidding. I saw Rita's truck and she told me that you were driving it this morning to get breakfast with your family. When I saw it parked here, I figured I'd stop. I'm surprised to see Daniel let you out of his sight. You didn't stay at the hotel with him last night?"

I glance over at him and give him a raised brow as if to ask if he's seriously asking me if I slept with Daniel last night. I took Rita's truck so he already knows the answer.

"Sorry, it's none of my business what you do with your fiancé."

"He's not my fiancé... not yet anyway. We have a lot to work out."

"What does it mean that you have a lot to work out?"

"It means that we need to get home and think through everything. We've been apart for eight months and..."

"And he doesn't do it for you. What more do you need to know?"

"I put eight years into this relationship. I can't just walk away from it. I need to know if it's still viable. I can't do that here.

Once we get home, he and I can discuss everything and figure it out."

"Why can't you do that here? What's holding you back?" he asks, but we both know what it is.

"Being here is too big of a distraction."

"Does it have anything to do with me?"

"Of course it does, but that doesn't matter. You have a family that needs you."

"Brynn, Josslin and I aren't getting back together if that's what she told you is going to happen. I could never trust her again, and even if I could, too many years have passed and she deliberately kept my daughter from me to hold onto my brother."

"Even still, you already admitted that you're not interested in a relationship and that you haven't had one in almost twenty years. I already put eight years into a relationship Seven, I can't do that again. I need someone who wants the same things as I do."

"I can give you that. I can give you a relationship if that's what it takes."

"You're only saying that because it's what I want, not because it's what you want."

"I just want to make you happy. Whatever that means."

"Exactly. You don't want this. And someday one of us will have to give in and then that person will resent the other. I'll resent you because I won't want to force you into getting married and having kids, or you'll resent me for pushing you into a life you never wanted. We can't both have what we want."

"It seems as though you've made up your mind," he says.

I look down at my hands.

I wish things were different.

If I could believe that Seven wanted the same things that I do, and if I wasn't so hellbent on making my dad proud, this decision would be so much harder.

At the end of the day Seven needs to fix his family and I need to find out if my eight-year relationship has finally run its course.

"I'm sorry," I say softly, tears welling in my eyes, but I don't let a single one drop.

I grip at my necklace, rubbing the pendant space needle between my fingers.

"Don't apologize, Brynn. I had you for a time and I'm grateful for every minute. I wouldn't take any of it back."

He leans in, pressing a soft kiss to my temple and then stands.

He doesn't say anything else as he heads for her Jeep.

I listen for his Jeep until I hear it rev to life and pull out of the parking area.

He's gone.

And now I have to pick myself back up out of the sand and live with the decision I've made.

Just as I stand, I see little speckles of black emerge from the sand.

Baby turtles are finally hatching in one of the nests as researchers go crazy, keeping a safe distance but getting all the pictures and data that they need.

I watch for a little bit and then realize that though seeing the baby turtles pop out from the sand and head for the sea is a cool experience, the real excitement I had for this date, was getting to spend it with Seven.

Without him... something's missing.

My phone chimes with an incoming text and rip the phone from my pocket, desperately hoping that it's Seven but then I see the name.

> Fiancé: I got my flights switched over to tomorrow morning. I couldn't get seats together but I'll check when we get there in the morning. I'm leaving the rental car for your parents. Do you think someone can give us a ride to the airport tomorrow?

I should be overjoyed to be flying back with Daniel but for some reason, I was looking for the last bit of alone time before Daniel came home from Mexico. This is what I wanted for the last eight months and now here he is, making grand gestures left and right. Showing up here to see me, bringing my parents, changing his flights.

But those grand gestures also feel... I don't know, off a little. Maybe a little pushy? Or controlling. Maybe I'm reading too much into it.

I send a text to Rita and she agrees to drive me in and pick up Daniel on our way to the airport.

Then, I decide to make a change to my contact list.

> Brynn: Rita and I will be there to pick you up bright and early. See you tomorrow.

> Daniel: Ok, see you soon. I love you.

He's the one I chose, so why does it feel so wrong when I write out the words? I've said them to him a thousand times before. This should be no different... but then again, everything's different. Or maybe it's only me that's no longer the same.

> Brynn: Love you too.

Walking into Scallywag's, I make my rounds to say goodbye to everyone.

Rita makes me promise to come back again when I'm ready to write book two, Marie and I exchange social media handles so that we can keep up with each other, and Cammy plans a coffee meet-up at a cafe that I've never been to called Serendipity's Coffee Shop for a few weeks after we both return to Seattle to give me time to get through my book one edits and for her to get familiar with the new fall semester.

I'm relieved to be leaving with a connection to this place and these people. The idea of returning to work on book two already has me anxious to make plans with Rita, but with book one not even launched and Daniel and I needing to make some major decisions about our relationship, it will probably be months before I'm back.

I say goodbye to everyone and then head up to finish my last few chapters and pack the rest of my things.

The only person I didn't see downstairs was Seven. but I guess we already said our goodbyes.

What more is there to say?

CHAPTER TWENTY-SEVEN

Seven

I wake to the sound of my phone ringing.

Rita

Reads over the screen.

"Hello?" I say, my voice groggy with sleep.

"Morning, did I wake you?" she asks in her chipper voice.

"I'm up now, what's up?" I ask, looking over at the clock that reads just after five in the morning.

I'd usually be up around now if I were going to a morning run but with what happened yesterday, I gave myself today off. Besides, in less than a week, I'll be back in Seattle and my workout regimen with the guys to resume its usual scheduling.

"I need a favor," she asks.

"I figured since you're calling so early."

I sit up in bed and sling my comforter off my bed. Whatever it is, I'll likely have to be dressed for it.

"I told Brynn that I would take her to the airport this morning but there's an emergency at the restaurant and I need to go down and check it out with Miguel."

Take Brynn to the airport?

That doesn't seem like the best idea after our conversation yesterday.

"What's the emergency? Maybe it would be better that I stay and take care of that and you can take Brynn to the airport."

"It's a supplier issue and the owner only likes to deal with me. I have a softer touch than Miguel. And if I sent you, it would take you less than two minutes with the owner before he would shut down our accounts."

She's right. I'm not always an asshole and I can be charming when I want to be but since this is connected to the livelihood of the restaurant, I don't want to risk it.

"Yeah, sure, I'll take her," I say, standing up and heading to my closet.

Seeing her again before she leaves probably isn't good for my mental health.

Leaving her in the sand yesterday took everything I had not to beg and plead with her to reconsider taking a chance on me. But I swore after Josslin that I'd never let myself be someone's second choice again.

If her belief in my indifference toward having a serious and committed relationship is the only thing keeping me out of the top spot, I'd do anything that's asked of me to prove that I can commit to her. I'd give her anything and everything she wants.

Marriage.

Kids.

A house with a white picket fence.

A minivan with a stick figure family on the back.

She'd get it all, and then some.

"I knew I could count on you. You're the best," she says. "And don't forget to pick up Daniel on your way through as well, Ok? Bye."

She quickly hangs up and now I know that I've just been had... again.

The last thing I want to do is drive Daniel to the airport, but I agreed to it and now I'm stuck.

After dressing and knocking on Cammy's door to let her know where I'm headed, I'm in the Jeep and headed to Scally-wag's first to pick up Brynn.

When I pull up, Brynn is standing outside Scallywag's with her baggage already packed. I jump out and start loading her luggage into my Jeep and then we head off for Cancun.

We keep our conversations around her second book in the series that she'll have to start writing next and the hockey schedule for home and away games that will be coming up for me.

When Daniel sees us pull up, he stares back at me, a little surprised to see me. He must not have gotten the memo that I was driving instead of Rita.

He tosses his luggage into the back of the jeep and then gets into the back seat of the Jeep, not hiding the fact that he doesn't like that Brynn is upfront with me.

The airport isn't far and we make it there with just enough time for them to get checked in.

Daniel jumps out of the Jeep and yells over his shoulder at us.

"I'm going to run in and get our seats moved so that we can sit together. Seven can load our bags for you on a cart."

Then he's gone behind the sliding glass doors of the terminal.

I find a cart and walk over to it, pulling it back to the Jeep. Then, I load all of the items onto it for her.

"You're all set," I say, looking over to find her double-checking to make sure that she has her ID and everything she needs to make it through security.

She finishes and then glances over at the cart with all of her and Daniel's luggage on it.

"This is it then," she says back.

"I guess it is."

"Thank you for the ride to the airport," she says. "And for everything else. I don't know what would have happened if you hadn't opened your home to me that night."

"Brynn," I say, stepping closer and tucking a few loose strands of hair behind her ear. Goosebumps spread across her shoulders and down her arms from my touch to her ear. "This is probably the last time I'll ever get to ask, and I need to know. Was I ever in the running?"

Her eyes cast down to the cement sidewalk of the terminal and she swallows.

"No," she says, softly.

My heart drops the second she says it, but then I realize that she didn't make eye contact with me when she said it.

"Brynn, look at me and say it again."

Her eyes shift off the cement floor but they still don't connect with mine. She shakes her head, refusing to make eye contact. It's the last bit of hope I have to hold onto.

"Brynn!" I hear Daniel's voice from the automatic glass doors. "I got us seats together. Let's go... hurry. We still have to get through TSA to make our flight on time."

"I have to go," she says and then grips the cart, pulling it behind her.

I watch as she walks away.

I don't move until she disappears behind the airport's glass door and further into the airport.

She's gone.

I lost her.

Brynn

Just as we reach altitude, Daniel turns to me.

"Are you happy to finally be getting out of there? I know I am. Australia was great, too, while it lasted, but I'm ready to be back in my own bed," he says, laying his head against the headrest and closing his eyes.

"Right...yeah," I say, barely listening to a word he says.

All I can think about is the look on Seven's face when I lied to him outside of the airport.

I wasn't prepared for his question, and he hit me with it at the worst timing possible.

In front of an airport terminal with Daniel inside trying to get our seats assigned.

The real answer was yes.

Yes, he's been in the running, but up until yesterday, I had no idea that he wanted to be. Why couldn't he have told me sooner?

I hated lying to him but whether or not Seven sees it, his family needs him right now, and I think Josslin could be right. I think I could be the distraction that Seven could do without.

"The first thing I want to do when we get home is take a hot shower with my gorgeous fiancé."

"Stop," I say finally. "Stop calling me your fiancé. It's driving me crazy, and it feels like you're forcing the issue. We're not engaged, nor are we technically in a relationship."

Hearing him call me his fiancé for those last two days when we haven't even discussed our relationship status and then blindsiding me with a wedding venue tour when I show up for breakfast feels like he's trying to push me into a marriage that only eight months ago he didn't want. Instead, he wanted his freedom.

"What are you talking about? We agreed that we'd get back together when I got home."

"Yes, I know we did, but a lot has happened since then and you're not supposed to be back for another couple of weeks. I thought I had more time to reflect on us and what our relationship would look like moving forward."

"The project finished early, and they let us go sooner, so I booked a flight to see you because I missed you. I thought you'd be happy that I came."

If he thought I'd be happy, why didn't he tell me ahead of time what he was planning?

"You missed me? Really? Because until you found out about Seven, your texts were once every other week, and your calls were even less frequent. Showing up here to surprise me feels more like you showed up unannounced to check up on me while using my parents as camouflage to your true intentions."

It's a stretch to assume all of that, and I have no real evidence, but there's something about his impromptu visit that makes it feel self-motivated in some way.

"Whoa... where is this coming from? I thought you'd be happy to see me."

"I am it's not that—"

"Does this have anything to do with Seven? Are you disappointed because I ruined your plans to be another one of his nameless puck bunnies on his roster for a couple more days?"

I can't believe he's being like this. He's the one who had a woman in his bed before I ever slept with Seven, and I have no idea how many more besides her that he had.

"That was uncalled for and harsh. And seeing other people was your idea, remember?"

"No, of course, you're right," he says, pulling his eyes away from me and staring over the seats in front of us. "I'm sorry... I guess I'll call first next time to make sure he's done with you before I show back up with your parents for a little vacation that they never get to take."

He's guilt-tripping me, something he's been doing more and more frequently, and I can't handle it. I need space from him to figure this out. This isn't like him, but I've never seen him jealous before because I've never given him a reason to be.

"I think you should stay in the guest bedroom until you can find an apartment of your own. We need some time to think about whether this relationship is still one that we both want."

That gets his attention, and his eyes bolt to me. He gently grips my hand across the armrest.

"Hey, hold on... Brynn, I'm sorry if I offended you, Ok? I didn't mean it. Maybe I got a little jealous and wanted to see what was going on between you, too. I'll admit to that. And I promise I'll ease off."

"I'm not ready to jump back into a full-fledged relationship with you. You hurt me when you broke it off and until I went to Mexico, I thought I deserved it. That I needed to fix myself to be worthy of our love, but I don't believe that anymore. There's so much that's changed over our eight years together. We're not those college kids anymore, and the last eight months since you've been gone have seemed like it created the biggest gap between us."

"Let me guess. Seven told you this?" he asks, his eyes narrowed.

"No... it was more of a team effort from all the people there who care about me."

I think over Rita, Cammy, Marie, and Seven. They all helped me to see that I don't need a fix-me list.

"Can you slow down for a second? Before I left, you were practically in tears watching me pack my bags for Australia; now you're kicking me out of the apartment."

"I'm not kicking you out. You can stay until you find something, but I want to take our relationship slow and casual and that will be easier if we don't live together."

He stops me. "No, it's fine, I don't need the guest bedroom. I want to make this work, so if space is the quickest way to get us back on track, then I'll find a couch to sleep on. I know a couple of guys in the law firm who would put me up for a month or two. I'm serious about us, Brynn. I'll be better from here on out, I promise. I love you," he says, pulling my hand up to his mouth and kisses it.

I appreciate that he's willing to stay somewhere else while we work on things and that he agreed to slow things down and date for a little while, as if we're starting over fresh.

"Does casual mean that you're going to date Seven, too?" he asks.

"No," I say simply.

He looks over at me, but I don't meet his eyes. Because the truth is, after this conversation and the last two days with Daniel, if I have to pick between Daniel or Seven...

...Daniel doesn't stand a chance.

CHAPTER TWENTY-EIGHT

Seven

Three weeks later...

"You ready for our first home game tomorrow night?" Lake Powers says, starting the treadmill next to me and jumps on.

He messes with the speed until he falls in perfect rhythm with me, matching my stride step-for-step. His eyes reach up to the large screen TV that has the sports channel on.

"The team looks tight out there. It won't be an easy win tomorrow, but as long as we play like the team practices, we'll put up a win."

I'm glad to be back to work. I need the distraction to keep me from thinking about the one thing that continues to play on repeat in my head—Brynn's answer to my last question.

If we hadn't been standing at the airport with her flight about ready to take off and Daniel lurking around, I would have pressed her harder on it, though I don't want to force her answer. I want her to give it to me freely.

"Tessa talked to ticket sales, and we're sold out for every game this weekend. We'd better give them a good show," he says, his breathing starting to labor just slightly.

"Don't we always?" I smirk.

I've played for the Hawkeyes for longer than anyone else on this team and there hasn't been an opening weekend that we haven't sold every single ticket. Still, it's reassuring to see that the fans still want to come. Without them, none of us have a job.

The program on the TV takes a break and the weather report comes on.

"Rain expected tonight with possible thundershowers later in the evening," the meteorologist says.

Immediately, I think of Brynn.

I haven't talked to her since she left for Seattle with Daniel, but I know that Cammy has been in touch.

I'm tempted to text Cammy and ask her to reach out to make sure that Daniel is in town tonight but the shit I already get from Cammy about how I didn't fight harder for Brynn will only earn me more backlash. If I so much as bring up Brynn's name in the presence of my daughter, she'll start her rants all over again.

After hitting the showers and then heading out of the locker room, I check my phone for the weather to see if anything has changed in the last thirty minutes. Obviously, it hasn't in that short of a time.

I'm angry with myself for keeping the blinds to my apartment shut since the day I got home. The last thing I want to witness is Brynn in her apartment with Daniel, moving on like nothing between her and I ever happened, but now I have no idea if he's there to comfort her tonight.

The memory of Brynn on my guest bedroom floor, cradling her legs in her arms and shivering from a panic attack, has me about ready to swallow my pride and text Brynn myself to at least warn her about tonight.

It's a short walk back to my apartment building and I can't stop myself from taking long strides to my apartment balcony, opening up the window shades. I search every window for Brynn's apartment, but I don't spot her in any of the windows directly across from me. Some windows have the lights turned out or their shades pulled down... I might have to wait and check back later if she's not home.

I check the windows below and the windows above. Maybe I had it wrong that she was on the exact floor as me but still no luck on either of the floors either.

I give up and decided to check back later when I realized that I'll be late to meet Briggs if I don't leave now. I agreed to sign Hawkeyes merch for a charity auction at a local children's cancer hospital today.

I pull my window shade back down and head for the front door of my apartment.

Unfortunately, stalking Brynn like a creep will have to wait until later. Maybe by then, I'll have come to my senses.

But I'm not holding out hope.

Brynn

Breathing a sigh of relief, I step into the dry comfort of my apartment, completely soaked from head to toe.

I knew that rain was forecasted for this evening, but I didn't anticipate the torrential downpour that Sheridan and I got caught in after dinner and celebratory drinks following the meeting earlier this evening with the publisher.

There's not a single dry spot left on my body, but the publishing house loves the first book in the series and is hoping to move up the deadline for book two. With only a few notes back from the editor, I'll have this book wrapped up and then I can focus my efforts on the next book.

A text comes through from Cammy.

> Cammy: That's great news! When are you headed back to Rita's to write book two? Please tell me it's over the Christmas break. I'll go with you!

Although I love the idea of spending Christmas with Cammy and Rita, I can't imagine that Cammy would leave Seven behind, and I don't think spending the holidays together is the best idea. Not to mention, what would I tell Daniel?

Though we're still taking things slow, I don't think he would take it well to know that I'm going on a Christmas vacation with the man I slept with during our break.

Brynn: Let's discuss it over coffee tomorrow.

Cammy: Looking forward to it.

I can barely keep my eyes open as I kick off my shoes at the entrance of my apartment and set my keys on the key hook hung on the wall next to the door.

I look out my window to watch the rain continue to pour when a flash of light comes streaming through the sky, and then the thunder rolls right after.

My entire body jumps at the loud crackle that echoes through the sky. Goosebumps cover my body and I can already feel my hands begin to shake.

My phone had given me an advisory warning on the rideshare back to the apartment that lightning and thunder were expected this evening, but I had hoped that my phone's weather app was exaggerating.

I make a fist, balling up my hands to resist the signs of a panic attack. After everything I've learned in Mexico and all the things I've overcome, I know this is a test. A test I need to pass.

I consider grabbing my phone out of my pocket and asking Daniel to come to the apartment tonight, but I know that he has an early morning tomorrow with a deposition and he won't want to risk not getting enough sleep tonight to accommodate me. It might also blur the lines on the casual dating situation that we currently have in place.

Stepping closer to the window, I reach for the shades to pull them down, but just as I'm about to reach for them, my phone pings with an income text.

I look down at my phone that's still in my hand to see the incoming text.

Seven.

My heart gallops the moment I see it, and I can't open the text fast enough.

> **Seven: Where's Daniel?**

What? That's what he sends me?

Seven and I haven't talked in three weeks, and the first text he sends is about Daniel.

> **Brynn: I'm not sure. He's living with a friend right now. I don't know about his whereabouts at the moment.**

Another text comes through.

> **Seven: He won't be with you tonight for this storm?**

> Brynn: No, he has a big court case to-morrow. It's better if I don't keep him up.

> Seven: Did you call to ask him?

> Brynn: I already know he'll say no. How did you know that Daniel isn't with me?

> Seven: Look out your window.

I look directly across the dimly lit night with the rain clouding my visibility, but there's no missing the large man standing on his balcony practically right in front of me in a tight-fitting gym shirt and a pair of grey sweats. God, he's gorgeous.

It's crazy to think he's been right there all these years. Close enough that if I would have just looked out my window, I would have seen him.

> Brynn: Are you spying on me?

I watch as he pulls his phone up to read my text. The blue light of his phone light up his face.

I can't see his facial expression, but I can see his fingers moving quickly over the phone to respond.

> Seven: Just checking in on you. I don't like that you're alone tonight.

That makes two of us.

Another streak of lightning and a clap of thunder has me jumping out of my skin a second time. There's no way I'll sleep tonight.

I look down at my phone and start to type up a response but mid-way through, I look up and Seven's gone. No longer standing on his balcony and he turned off all the lights to his apartment.

Did he go to bed?

Without saying goodbye or goodnight?

Getting to talk to him again after three weeks apart is the most exciting thing to happen to me since I left. That and the meeting with my publisher.

I debate sending my text but change my mind.

He obviously was ready for this conversation to be over and after I told him that he never was in the running, I don't blame him.

I head for my bedroom and pull off the rest of my wet clothes. I pull on a t-shirt and a pair of pajama bottoms, and then head for the bathroom to wash my face and brush my teeth, when I hear a knock on my front door.

It's after ten o'clock at night and I can't think of who would be knocking on my door this late, though my neighbor locks herself out regularly and now leaves a key at my place for emergencies.

Looking through the peephole, my heart leaps the second I see Seven standing in my hallway in a pair of sweats and a t-shirt.

I bite down on my lower lip to keep from smiling from ear to ear but it doesn't stop the smile from spreading in the least. I turn to the mirror hanging next to the wall to make sure I don't have mascara under my eyes or that any of my hair is sticking up.

I check back again through the peephole to make sure I'm not imagining it.

"Are you going to keep staring at me or are you going to let me in?" he says.

I flip the deadbolt and the handle lock and swing the door open.

"What are you doing here?" I ask.

"There are thundershowers tonight and you need someone to sleep with," he says, giving no more explanation.

He walks past me and into my apartment.

I can't believe Seven walked across to my building, found someone to let him in and figure out which apartment is mine.

But I shouldn't be surprised. I've never met someone as resourceful as him. He always seems to find a way to get done whatever needs to be done, and he's always prepared.

"Wait... don't you have a game tomorrow."

I ask, closing the apartment door and locking it.

It's a force of habit but if he needs to leave, we can unlock it just as easily.

"Yeah, I do," he says, looking down the hallway. "Come on. Let's get you to bed."

He walks down the hall toward my bedroom, and I quickly follow suit, catching up behind him.

Is he really here to sleep with me through the storm tonight?

It's not lost of me that Seven showed up tonight and Daniel wouldn't have even if I begged.

He pulls the comforter up and then motions for me to get in.

I crawl in as instructed, and then he walks over, turns off the bedroom lights, and scoots in behind me, laying an arm over my middle as I face away from him, his chest at my back.

"Once you're asleep, I'll move to the couch. I won't leave until the storm is over, though, OK?"

I don't want him to sleep on the couch, so I grip his forearm.

"Please don't sleep on the couch. Stay with me."

He nods against my hair, and I savor the feeling of having him this close again.

Silence falls between us.

The sound of the rain and Seven's breathing are the only sounds that fill the air around us.

"Seven?"

"Yeah?" he says, the sound of sleep in his throat.

I don't know what spurs me on to say it, but I do.

"I haven't slept with Daniel since before he left for Australia."

"Why are you telling me this?"

"I just thought you should know."

"Do you think that makes it any easier on me? It barely helps to settle the twisting in my gut when I think about how this inevitably ends. With you married to him."

I attempt to twist around to face him but his hand grips my hip to stop me.

"Don't turn around Brynn, or I'll leave," he says, his voice demanding.

He's serious.

"Why not? I want to see you."

"Because if you turn around, I won't be able to stop myself from kisses you. And if I kiss you, I won't be able to stop myself from touching you. And if I touch you, it won't be long before you're under me, coming with my cock buried inside of you."

I let out a shaking breath, wanting nothing more than what he just told me he's barely stopping himself from doing.

"He and I aren't together. We're seeing if we have anything in common anymore or if the only thing holding us together was our mutual experience during the tornado. We're not exclusive."

"I'm not going to fuck you tonight, Brynn, because every time I do, I lose a little more will to walk away. And as long as Daniel is in the picture, you don't belong to me, and that makes me the second choice."

I wish he didn't see himself that way... as anyone's second choice.

"I don't belong to him either and you're not the second choice."

"But I'm not the first either."

We don't say anything for a while after that, and even though the thunderstorm is louder tonight than I anticipated. I end up sleeping through it all.

I wake up early the next morning, hoping that Seven and I can talk, but when I wake, I turn to find Seven isn't in bed anymore.

I get up and head for my living room to check the couch.

My heart sinks when I walk out, only to find that Seven isn't there either and he didn't leave a note on the kitchen counter like he used to in Mexico.

I go to the window to see if I can see him in his apartment, but his window covering is down, and I can't see him.

CHAPTER TWENTY-NINE

Brynn

Walking into Serendipity's Coffee Shop, my mouth waters as a barista walks past me with a warm cinnamon roll for a table off to my right.

I've lived in this city for years and I've never seen this quaint coffee shop before.

I love finding new places around Seattle and I can see how this one might be my new favorite stop. I'm already itching to bring my laptop down here and find a corner somewhere to write in the ambiance of this coffee house.

My eye catches on someone waving in another corner of the building.

Cammy.

The minute our eyes meet, Cammy's smile stretches wide, and she stands out of her chair. As soon as I get to the table, we embrace in a warm hug and then take a seat.

"I ordered you tea. I saw the kind you had at the beach house and they make a really good blend here that's similar," she says. "Did you find the place ok? It's kind of tucked in here between these huge buildings."

"I did. The red door was a dead giveaway, and my navigation app brought me right here. I can't believe I've never seen this place before since it's only a few blocks from my apartment."

"Penelope says that it's the city's best-kept secret, but it's not much of a secret. This place is usually booming. It's close to the stadium so whenever I'm interning at the stadium, I walk down with some of the other girls in the office to get coffee or lunch."

I look around to find that most tables are taken.

"It gets busier than this? It's hard to imagine any more people would fit in here. And who's Penelope?" I ask.

"Oh, this is nothing. It's standing room only in the mornings and at lunch," she says, taking a sip of her latte. A little bit of foam covers her top lip, and she licks it off. "Penelope is the Administrative Assistant for the General Manager of the Hawkeyes'. Or actually, I guess her new title is Assistant General Manager but she's juggling both jobs to keep her old position open for me once I graduate. She'll be at the game tonight. You should come with me and meet everyone!"

"Come with you to the game tonight? Isn't it sold out?" I ask.

I've seen the banners around town about the Hawkeyes' opening weekend.

"Yeah, but I always have my dad's tickets."

My heart leaps the second she calls Seven dad, bringing Seven to the forefront of my mind again. Something I've been trying not to think about when I woke up this morning to find him gone, no note left behind... only the faint smell of Arctic Blue Glacier three-in-one shampoo, conditioner and body wash wafting through the air of my apartment.

"How are you two handling everything? Did he ever call home to check on Eli? What's going on with all of that?"

Cammy pulls her mug up to her lips and hides the devilish smile behind it.

"If you're so interested in how my dad's doing, why don't you just come with me tonight and ask him yourself?"

Even if I wanted to, I already have plans with Daniel to meet up at the bar across from his office after he gets off work tonight. We're supposed to discuss our relationship, and honestly, after last night with Seven, I'm more confused than ever.

I've only seen Daniel a handful of times since we got home. Between my meetings with the publisher, editor, and PR team and his busy schedule trying to catch up with the firm's backlog of work from having half their team gone for the last eight months, our schedules haven't matched up.

"I can't. I have plans with Daniel tonight. Can I get a raincheck?" I ask, just to be polite.

The last thing I should be doing is putting myself in a position to see Seven in his element, decked out in hockey gear.

Why is that so damn sexy?

"Ok...I'm just going to say it," she says, putting her mug back down on the solid wood table. "Dump the idiot and date my dad."

She leans over the table and stares back at me.

"Cammy, I—"

"Don't give me some lame excuse. You already know that you two should be together—we all do."

"Cammy, he doesn't do relationships. Twenty years is a long time and is evidence enough of that. I'm not going to ask him for something that he'd only be doing for me."

Her eyebrows stitch together, and a deep frown forms, replacing the smile that's been there since I showed up.

"Doing it for you? Are you kidding? The man is crazy about you, don't you see that? He's nurtured plenty of relationships over the last twenty years without any issues. Look at his relationships with Rita, Silas, and me... and the twenty-three men on the team's roster who he's been friends with for years."

"Yes, but those aren't romantic relationships. He hasn't had one of those since your mom, and he hasn't wanted one since. What happens when he makes concessions for me, and then, over the years, he resents me for it? I couldn't live with that."

She chews on the inside of her lip for a moment as she thinks. She's trying to come up with a rebuttal, and as pathetic as it is, I hope she comes up with one strong enough that I can believe in, too.

"Do you think my dad does anything he doesn't want to?"

I think back on all the things that Seven has done for me and for others that he didn't want to do but did anyway. He tries to act like he could care less about the people around him, but that's not who he is. He'll do the right thing even if it doesn't serve him.

"Yes," I say simply.

Cammy laughs. "Ok, yeah, he probably does, but not in this case. He wouldn't enter into a relationship he didn't want to be in just because you asked him to. Otherwise, he'd be back with my mom right now."

Josslin— the reason he puts on that rough exterior is to protect himself from being taken advantage of again. I understand that more now than I ever have before.

What I wouldn't give to see him shed that armor for me.

Maybe last night he did.

My head is reeling with what I'm going to say tonight to Daniel. I can't agree to moving forward with him when I have feelings for Seven, can I? Is that fair to Daniel, or Seven... or myself?

Cammy's phone alarm goes off on the table.

"Shoot, I have to get back to the stadium. I'm helping Shawny and Juliet decorate the lobby before tonight."

"Who are they?" I ask.

"Come tonight, and you can meet all the player's girlfriends. You might as well make friends with them now; I have a feeling you're the next add-on to the group," she stands before I can refute the possibility.

I shake my head, but the idea of being Seven's girlfriend and coming to all of his home games has excitement bubbling in my belly until I remember that I can't because I need to meet Daniel. The bubbles all dissipate into instant dread and my stomach turns at the thought of having to make a decision that

will end a relationship, whether that's with Daniel or Seven...
I'm still not sure.

"I'll leave a ticket for you at will-call... just in case," she winks.
"Coffee next week? Same time, same place?" she asks.

I nod but stare back at the wall in front of me.

What am I going to do?

Then I hear her head for the door, calling out a goodbye to
the baristas as she leaves.

My phone begins to ring as I consider getting up to leave but
then I see the name on my phone and I stay in my seat.

Dad.

It reads.

"Hey, Dad."

"Hi, honey. Your mom told me all about the good news that
the publisher loved your book. That's great news—another start
to a successful series. I know this one was hard for you to write,
but I'm proud of you for sticking it out. Putting the final period
on things is important in life."

I know that my dad means to say that finishing what you
start is important; he's told me that all my life, but the way he
worded it this time hits differently. It's as if he's telling me that
sometimes it's important to end things. Like the period at the
end of a book.

"Yeah, I think you're right. It feels good to have this book
done but now I have to move on to the next."

"Moving on is important too," he says.

Lord. Could he be more cryptic?

My father has an analytical mind and never speaks in riddles...
until apparently today, of all days. He lives in black-and-white

factual knowledge, which is why he and my brother get along so well, nerding out over science and mathematical equations. They're the same, whereas my father and I have never quite seen eye to eye. It's why his stamp of approval on Daniel has always meant so much to me.

"How is everything else going?" he asks.

"It's fine. I'm going to meet Daniel for drinks later tonight after he gets off work."

"That sounds nice. How's the wedding planning going?"

I pull my cup to my lips, take a sip, and then swallow, buying myself some time to get my thoughts together. But it turns out that no amount of stalling is going to help me find a way to sidestep this conversation.

"Umm, it's..."

I let the unspoken words linger there for too long.

"Brynn...is everything ok? You seemed tense when we walked around the wedding venue while in Mexico."

My dad and I rarely discuss feelings, so the fact that he's bringing this up prompts me to ask a question.

"When did you know mom was the one?" I ask.

I never ask my dad sappy questions of emotion usually, but I need to know from his point of view.

I hear him chuckle on the other line as if he's remembering the moment exactly.

"The moment I knew your mom was the one was when I took her out on our third date. I was a poor college student with not much money and I decided to save the little I had to take her to dinner instead of putting fuel in my car," he says. "Needless to say, we ran out of gas, but instead of hitchhiking to the nearest gas station, your mom pulled out a pack of crackers that she had in her purse, and we sat on the side of the road for hours, snacking on crackers and talking about... well, I don't even remember now."

"I've never heard this story," I tell him.

"Yeah, well it might not have stuck out to her. But at that moment, I knew that if sitting in a broken-down car on the side of the road with a pack of crackers was the highlight of my year, that marrying your mother would be the highlight of my life."

"What if I don't have that moment with Daniel?"

I think quickly through our history to determine if Daniel and I ever had *that* moment. The moment when you realize that it's not the experiences in life that make life worth living, but the person you get to experience them with.

"Then you need to think about whether or not he's the one."

"I don't want to let you down," I say.

"Let me down? How? By not marrying Daniel? That's absurd. I don't even like the kid that much."

Wait... what?

"What are you talking about? You're always saying how at least if I marry him, he'll take care of me if my author career implodes. You don't like that I decided to be an author, and you've always wanted me to marry him because he has a stable career," I say, trying to keep my voice down.

"That's what you thought I meant? Why would I send you flowers for each book release if I wasn't proud of your career and your accomplishments?" he asks.

"I don't know... I—"

I hear him sigh on the other end.

"I'm sorry if I ever let you believe that, Brynn but that's never what I meant. I've always been proud of you. And I have only ever said those things about Daniel having a stable career because it's his only positive attribute. I think the kid is a pompous, arrogant asshole, but I've tried to be supportive and believe that at least he'd take care of you if something happened to your career. Maybe I harped on that point too much, but it was only because I had nothing else good to say about him."

Relief floods through me and I start laughing.

So much of the reason I wanted to make things work with Daniel was because I thought that marrying Daniel was the only way to make my father proud of me. Now that I know that he doesn't even like Daniel, I feel like a weight has been lifted off my shoulders.

It's not the only reason I've been holding onto Daniel but it's certainly one of them.

"Really? You wouldn't care if I didn't marry him?"

"Honey... I'd be relieved."

Oh my God... I want to break out in tears.

"Do you think I'm a terrible person for breaking up with him after he followed me to Seattle? He gave up a spot at his father's firm to move to the west coast for me."

"No, Brynn, you're not a terrible person. When he got the job at the law firm out west, he was bragging to me that he was happy he wouldn't have to work at the mom-and-pop law firm where his father is a partner. He said that his talents were made for bigger things. He was trying to impress me. He knows I don't like him all that much."

"Thanks for the call, Dad. You just helped me make a really big decision."

"Hey, if I make a trip out to Seattle, any chance you can get me tickets to watch your new boyfriend play?"

My ears heat at the words new boyfriend.

"How did you—"

"I saw the way Wrenley looked at you when we surprised you at Scallywag's. He looks at you the way that I look at your mom," he says. "I don't know all the details of what was going on between you and Daniel at the time, but for how hard he was pushing your mom to convince you to book a wedding date at the hotel, I suspected Daniel was on his way out and he was desperate to hold on."

"Thanks for calling dad," I say.

"I'm glad I did. We should talk more. And while I have you on the phone, roses or orchids this time? My florist is asking."

"Surprise me," I say.

"You got it, kiddo," he says, and then we hang up.

It's then, when he calls me the same thing that Seven calls Cammy, that I realize that Seven and my dad are so much alike. They both have a hard time showing their feelings, but at the end of the day, they both show love in the only way they know how.

My dad sends me flowers and Seven shows it with acts of service.

I didn't see it before, but I do now.

I get out of my rideshare a couple blocks away since traffic is a nightmare tonight.

Getting a little fresh air to think through how I'm going to start this conversation with Daniel isn't the worst idea.

Walking up to the bar hours after getting off the phone with my dad, my heart is racing, and my palms are sweaty.

After all, giving up eight years with Daniel requires that I do this in a way that we can still be friendly towards one another.

The conversation with my father makes this breakup so much easier, though. I've given Daniel loyalty because of the things in our past, but I've always let those moments cover up all the things in our relationship that weren't right.

A text comes through as I round the last block from the bar.

> **Sheridan:** Have you decided what you're going to do tonight?

> **Brynn:** I'm going to end it.

> **Sheridan:** Thank God! She's come to her senses.

> **Sheridan:** Call me tomorrow. Let me know how it went. You're doing the right thing... just in case you're wondering.

> **Brynn:** I should have listened to you sooner.

> **Sheridan:** I know

I giggle at her last text and then push my phone back into my purse.

I take the last turn on the sidewalk, and I can see the bar's sign illuminated.

A few steps more and I begin to hear the sounds of a lover's squabble and realize that here in a few minutes, that could be me and Daniel too, only, the closer I get, the more that the backside of the man looks a lot like Daniel.

With every step I take, the man's voice becomes clearer, and his backside becomes more detailed.

My eyes turn to the woman to find that it's someone I've met once and twice at Daniel's office. She's one of the younger female partners at the firm.

I'm directly across the street when I finally see the face of the man, and my stomach drops when I confirm that it is, in fact, Daniel arguing with his co-worker.

His beautiful co-worker.

What was her name?

Courtney, I think.

Their voices carry all the way over to where I'm standing.

"So, you just used me in Australia to get a junior partner vote from me... is that it?" She hisses.

"That's not what happened. We were just having a little fun."

His explanation makes me a little sick. I know that I'm about to break up with him, but as of this morning, I was still debating us getting back together.

"A little fun? You call fucking me for eight months just a little fun?"

"You knew that Brynn and I were going to get back together. This was just supposed to be a short-term thing for us. Before we left Seattle, you agreed that we would use this time to get "us" out of our system before I married Brynn."

I feel the vomit rise in my throat.

"She's a grown woman who can't sleep by herself in a thunderstorm. You're practically dating a toddler. You only keep her around still because she's a big earner. Well, so am I. I have just as nice of an apartment as she does that you haven't minded staying in for the last three weeks while you date her on the side."

He's been staying with her all this time. We haven't been exclusive, but now the reason why he's been too busy to see me more than once a week makes a little more sense. And why he offered to stay at a "co-worker's" apartment while we work on things.

"That's not it. We've been together for too long to break up now."

"You were broken up, you idiot! You dumped her so you could spend eight months screwing me, and now I'm pregnant."

A gasp breaks through my lungs at her news and then they both turn to find me still across the street.

"Brynn!" Daniel yells and then starts running across the asphalt, but a van drives by and almost hits him.

I start walking quicker "Whatever you heard, I can explain," he says when he finally makes it across the street and runs up behind me.

"I think I heard it all firsthand. I don't need you to explain anything."

"Brynn, please stop. I don't love her... I love you, and we were broken up when she and I were together. You can't hold that against me."

My feet increase in speed. In heels, I'll never outpace him, but I can try.

"How about when you two were working out your little Australia vacation? Were we together when you hatched your plan to break up with me so that you could sleep with her?"

He doesn't answer right away and now I know the truth.

He may or may not have physically cheated on me while we were together... I'd prefer not to know at this point anyway, but he was unfaithful by making plans with another woman while we were still together. The woman who was in his bed when he called and was whispering in the bathroom, was her. The time I heard her show up to her apartment to "work" was all a lie.

"Brynn, we can fix this. I don't love her."

I see a taxi that has its vacant sign on, and I wave it down.

It pulls quickly to the curb, and I open the door.

"That's inconvenient for you since it sounds like you have a baby on the way. Good luck with your life. I'll have a moving company deliver your things to your office. Goodbye, Daniel," I say, and then I slip into the cab, pulling the door behind me.

"Brynn!" I hear him call out, but the cab is already back on route and headed for the destination I give the driver.

"The Hawkeyes stadium, please."

CHAPTER THIRTY

Brynn

Staring down at the stadium below me with my ticket clenched in my hand, my eyes immediately shoot over to the goalie on the home team.

The game is already well into the first period, and the score is tied one to one.

From this distance, I can't make out any of Seven's features except for the layers of padding covering every inch of his six-foot-five body.

I watch as the players all skate full force toward him, an opposing player makes a shot, but Seven blocks it, and the stadium erupts in cheers with a few boos from the away team fans.

Now the home team has the puck and starts skating as hard as they can in the opposite direction.

I start to ease my way down the stadium stairs, looking for Cammy.

I check the ticket for the row and find it says Row 1.

We must be close to the plexiglass.

Right before I get to the Row, I see Cammy sitting in her seat with an open one next to her, wearing a Wrenley jersey. This is the first time in my life that I've ever wanted to wear someone's jersey. To wear someone's name on my back as if he owns me and I own him.

Cammy jumps out of her seat, cheering, and high-fives all the fans sitting around her when the Hawkeyes get one past the opposing team's goalie.

She must feel my eyes on her because just as she's about to sit down, she looks up and her eyes connect with mine.

She squeals with excitement seeing me coming down the stairs, but I can barely hear it over the roaring of the crowd as everyone besides us is watching the game.

"You came," I see her mouth more than I hear the words.

I shrug as I make it to the last step.

"Excuse us, can you let her in?" Cammy asks of the people standing in our row, not seeing me walk up.

They all smile and step back towards their seats.

"You're here. You made it," she says as we embrace.

"I ended up having free time."

"Wait... how did it go with Daniel?" she asks.

"It's over. It's actually been over for a long time... I just didn't know it."

"Oh my God, are you serious?" she beams.

"You could pretend to feel sad for me," I chuckle.

"But you don't look sad in the least. Are you?"

I just had a major relationship end, and I couldn't be more relieved. It's weird.

"No," I say, my smile widening.

"Are you here to tell my dad?"

I nod, and she reaches over and squeezes my hand.

"Did I miss anything good?" I ask.

"Not yet. Powers has been in the penalty box once already, but no surprise there. No good fights yet, but it's still early. You have to give them a little time to get good and angry before fists start flying."

"What about your dad? Do people ever mess with him?" I ask.

I've watched a few games, but I've never seen him in a fight except to help another player.

"Oh no... that's a cardinal sin. There's an unspoken rule that you don't screw with each other's goalies. That's how you get an entire roster of players jumping over the wall to beat the shit out of you."

"That sounds a little terrifying."

"Oh yeah, if anyone fucks with my dad or Reeve Aisa, you'll see twenty-two players put the beat down on one guy. That's how you get whole teams in a brawl... it's not pretty, but it makes for good TV to watch the refs try to break up forty pissed-off hockey players."

"Oh..." I say.

The thought of Seven stuck in the middle of that isn't entertaining to me at all.

We're still standing when the first period ends, and the players are skating towards the tunnel to head for the locker rooms.

As Seven walks by, his eyes catch on Cammy and he gives her a smile and a nod. Then as if in slow motion, his eyes reach over to mine.

I can see the moment that recognition of who I am hits him.

His eyes flare, and then he shoots a look at Cammy and points at me as if to say, "What is she doing here?"

He doesn't look happy to see me.

Could something have happened between last night and now?

"She broke it off with Daniel," Cammy screams from across the distance.

Seven's eyes flash back to me, and he stops in his tracks until a player behind him runs into him trying to get off the ice.

His jaw drops and his eyebrows furrow, the most facial expression I've seen from him in a while.

I turn to Cammy once Seven disappears behind the stadium walls.

"I shouldn't have come. This was a mistake to have shown up like this. I should have called ahead or something."

If me being here affects his playing, then being here was a mistake.

I turn to leave but Cammy grips my arm.

"Why are you leaving? The game just started."

"Seven doesn't want me here. You saw the look on his face."

"You just surprised him, that's all. Don't leave."

Cammy releases me and I start moving past the next person seated in the row.

I'm almost out to the staircase when I hear the crowd cheering. Everyone is going wild.

I glance behind me at the jumbotron and see a Hawkeyes player running down the staircase on the screen.

But not just any player... the goalie with all of his gear on except his helmet.

It's Seven.

I have no idea where he is in the stadium or why he's in the stands.

I turn back around and start heading back up the stairs when I see someone barreling down towards me.

My belly fills with butterflies the moment I realize it's him, a jersey clenched in one of his hands.

I stand still, unsure what to do or where to go, until he takes the last step near me. His already six five stature is hovering over me. Add the blades and the extra stair step higher and the man is a mountain.

"You broke up with Daniel?" he asks, his hair wet and messy from sweating through a tough first period, but he's just as sexy as ever.

I nod. "I should have done it a long time ago."

"Why are you here?" he asks, his eyes searching mine.

"I didn't mean to distract you. Aren't you going to get in trouble for leaving the locker room?" I ask.

"Maybe... if you keep me for much longer, but the worst they'd do is fine me, and I don't care about the money. I'd rather hear why you came to my game. And stop hiding behind what you think I don't want."

"I'm not doing that."

"Aren't you?" he says, lifting an eyebrow. "You've accused me of not wanting a relationship with you, and now, saying that you're a distraction. But I'm not really the reason we're not together."

"Brynn!" I hear Cammy yell.

I look back to find her pointing at the jumbotron screen.

The kiss cam is on us. I almost don't want to turn to face him but I don't have much of a choice.

When I look back at Seven, his eyes are on the screen too. He's watching us up on the kiss cam for all to see.

His eyes lower back to mine.

"So? What's your reason?"

"You told me once that you didn't want to be anyone's second choice, but the truth is, you're the only choice I can't live without."

His eyes soften, and then he bends down and reaches both arms around my back, lifting me up until I'm face to face with him, my arms wrapped around his neck.

"Can you see yourself spending the off-season in Mexico with me? We don't have to stay during the hurricane—we'll leave. I'll take you somewhere safe."

"I don't mind the storms as long as you're there beside me. And I kind of like being boarded up in a house with you," I say, tightening my arms around him. He smiles at me. "It turns out I do my best writing with no electricity and a hot man in my bed."

He laughs.

"I fucked up Brynn. I fucked up the second I opened my front door, didn't I?"

"We both made mistakes. I held onto the idea of Daniel, and it held me back from realizing that I wanted to be with you. I shouldn't have left with him. I should have stayed with you. But does any of that matter now?"

"No, it doesn't as long as you're mine now."

"I am."

"Will you wait for me after the game? I still owe you a first date."

"A first date? What are we going to do?"

"I don't care what we do... as long as I'm with you."

"Me too."

He looks back up to the jumbotron behind me for a second and then looks back down.

"The entire stadium is watching. Can I kiss you now?"

I wet my lip in anticipation for his kiss. "Yes, and do it quick. You were such a tease last night."

He smiles and then bends down, pressing his lips against mine. The entire stadium erupts in applause and catcalls.

I giggle into his kiss at the ridiculousness of thousands of fans cheering during our kiss.

"Do they always get this excited over a kiss cam?" I ask when Seven finally pulls away.

He looks around the stadium for a second, a wide smile across his face and then he looks back down at me. "Everybody like a good underdog story."

"Underdog? Is that what you are?"

"I wasn't favored to win this one, if you recall."

I shake my head. "Don't remind me."

"Can I come home with you tonight?" he asks.

"As long as you promise to leave a note before you leave this time."

"I don't plan on ever leaving... not this time."

THE END

Want More? Sign up for Kenna King's newsletter to get the Lucky Score – FOUR YEARS LATER bonus chapter HERE!

Cammy's story, Lucky Goal now on PRE-ORDER Here!

To be in the KNOW about all the NEWS, subscribe to Kenna King's newsletter so you don't miss a thing click HERE

Thank you for reading and supporting my writing habit ;). If you missed any of the other books in the series, you can find the series in Author Central.

Feel free to reach out via email (kenna@kennaking.com) or Instagram (@kennakingbooks)! I love hearing from you.

Thank you for reading Lucky Score!

To read the next book, Tough Score, you can find it on Amazon or on my website.

Keep up with Kenna by following here:

Made in the USA
Columbia, SC
16 February 2025

53900702R00226